Visions

Knights of Salucia – Book 1

C. D. Espeseth

Cover art by Melanie Moor on Dreamstime

Contents

This would not have been possible without the support and encouragement of my family and my loving wife, Claire.

You inspire and strengthen me beyond measure.

This book is dedicated to them.

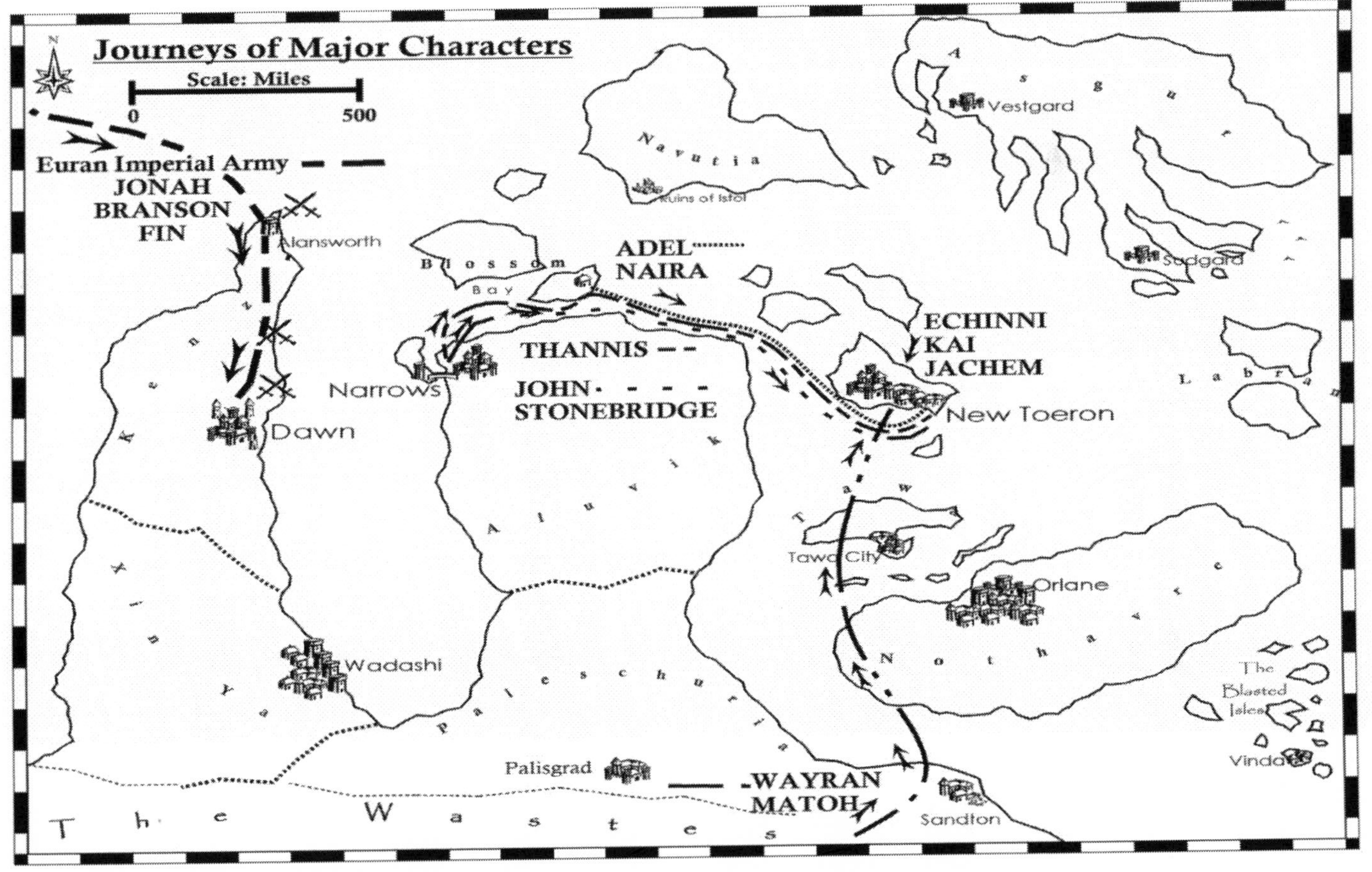
Journeys of Major Characters
N
Scale: Miles
0
500
Euran Imperial Army
JONAH
BRANSON
FIN
Alansworth
Dawn
Kenz
Narrows
Blossom Bay
ADEL
NAIRA
THANNIS
JOHN
STONEBRIDGE
Navutia
Ruins of Isfol
Asgur
Vestgard
Sodgard
Labran
ECHINNI
KAI
JACHEM
New Toeron
Aluvik
Taw
Tawa City
Orlane
Nothavre
The Blasted Isles
Xinya
Wadashi
Paleschuria
Palisgrad
WAYRAN
MATOH
Sandton
The Wastes

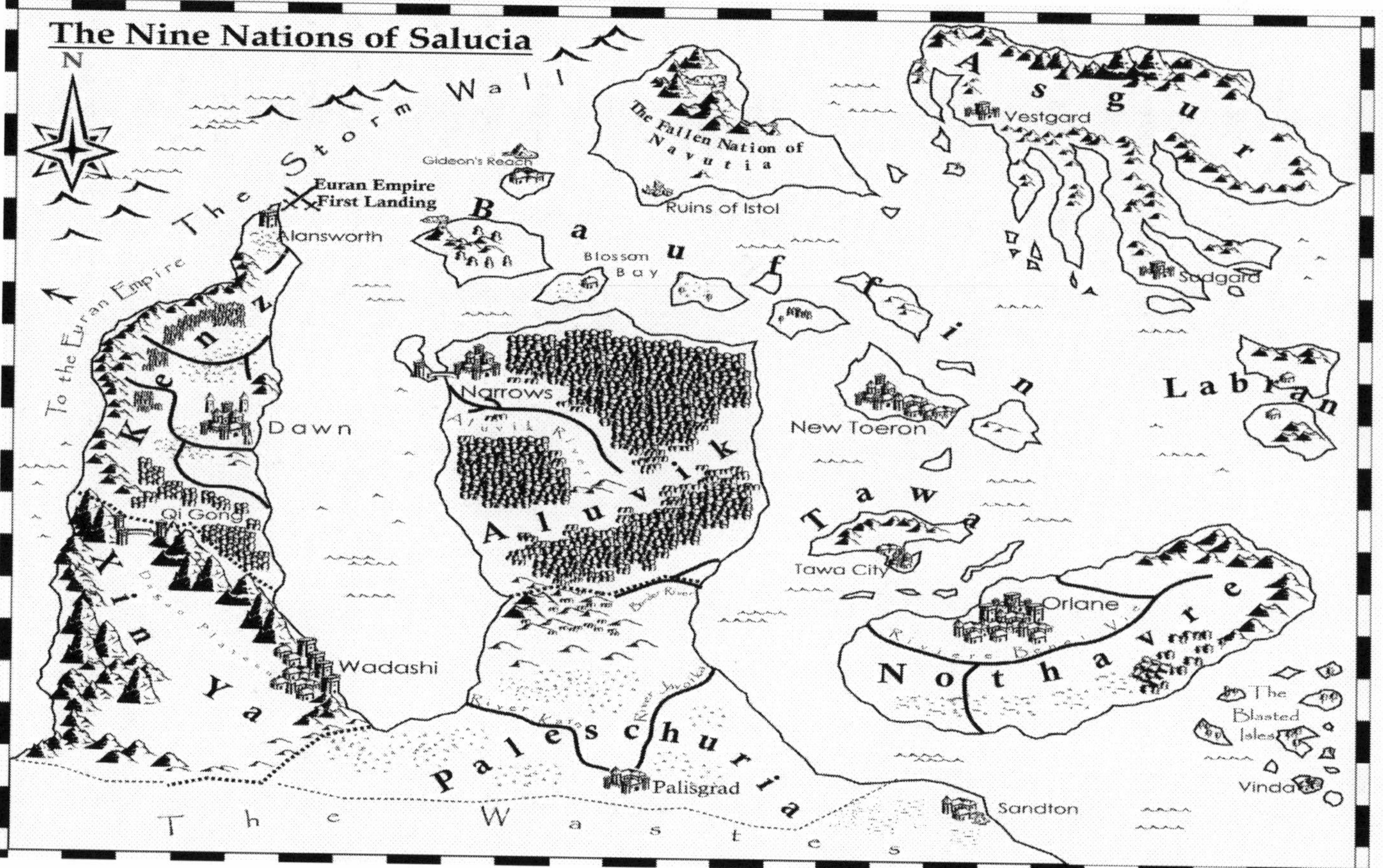
The Nine Nations of Salucia
N
The Storm Wall
Euran Empire
First Landing
Alansworth
Gideon's Reach
Baufin
Blossom Bay
To the Euran Empire
Kenz
Dawn
Qi Gong
Xin Ya
Wadashi
Narrows
Aluvik
New Toeran
Tawa
Tawa City
The Fallen Nation of Navutia
Ruins of Istol
Asgur
Vestgard
Sodgard
Labran
Orlane
Nothavre
The Blasted Isles
Vinda
Paleschuria
Palisgrad
Sandton
The Wastes

1 - Storm Chasing

My name is Robert Mannford, and I saved the world by killing it.

Now, I sit here, watching everything die around me, knowing I had to do it, knowing I am the monster who caused this.

If there is a heaven, I will not be in it for I am a murderer, an exterminator, but I may also be our world's saviour.

There is not but the hope of the future left to me, and that is what I must build.

First, however, I have to watch what I have wrought. I have to witness their end.

I owe them that at least.

And then, when the last fires go out, I will hope and rebuild.

- Journal of Robert Mannford, Day 000 Year 00

Wayran

The Wastes

Wayran stood atop the dune, across from a hulking warrior, as sand rasped across the wavy crest between them. In his hand Wayran held a spear, a silver one like his mother's. It seemed to glow a brilliant white as he held it.

The warrior across from him, however, had much more than a spear. His opponent was covered from head to toe in black chitin-like armour and carried a massive two-handed sword.

"Give me the key, Wayran," the monstrous warrior demanded.

The very air shook with its voice, and Wayran saw red eyes glaring at him from within the slits of its nightmarish helmet.

"You are going to destroy everything," the armoured monster said.

"You've been chasing a lie."

"You're wrong," Wayran replied. The words made him sad, and he wondered how things had come to this. Where had it all gone wrong? The wind picked up and began to howl. Sand bit at his skin and Wayran tried to shield his eyes. "It's not a lie, I have to do this. No, *we* have to do this. It's the only way!" Wayran knew his words were a desperate attempt to sway the monster before him; he was almost assured to fail, but he had to try.

"Stop being so blind!" the armoured monster roared. "This is your last chance, Wayran. GIVE ME THE KEY!"

The very sky erupted around them in a show of power. Lightning flashed within the raging sandstorm, illuminating a giant tower atop the next dune to his right. He had to get to that tower and the door at its base. He had to use the keys. Wayran knew there was nothing else he could say. He looked into the red eyes of the steel monster and saw hatred and rage there. Wayran had lost. He couldn't save this monster, but he could still use the keys. He threw his silver spear at the monster and ran towards the tower and the door.

The steel-clad warrior rushed forward, knocking the spear aside as if it were a toy. Its giant sword cleaved the air where Wayran had stood, and Wayran felt the sizzle of power against his skin as the strike missed.

Wayran rushed down the dune slope and glanced behind him. To his horror, the armoured monster began to change shape as it chased him. The black steel undulated and merged together into shining black skin from which glowing pustules of light burst forth. The giant blade the monster had held merged into dozens of golden teeth within a circular maw. The terrible worm-like creature hissed and shot down the sand dune after him. Dark clouds billowed out of smoke-stacks on either side of its head, and dozens of huge, steel insectoid legs tore into the sand as it shot towards him.

The wind picked up, and Wayran lost sight of the monster behind him as the sand whipped around him. He stumbled through the storm and pushed through the onslaught of wind and sand. Finally, he crashed into something solid.

It was the door.

Two metal rods shot up into the sky on either side of the tower, rising into the very centre of the storm. Lightning crackled and danced back and forth between the two metal rods and then ran down their lengths into the sand around him. The lightning trace odd spider-like symbols in the sand at his feet. He felt as if he should be able to understand them, but their meaning floated just out of reach.

The metal worm-monster hissed, steam soaked and scorched Wayran's back, as he turned then ducked just in time to see the razor-sharp teeth slashing towards him through the sandstorm.

He dived to his left and the monster crashed into one of the metal rods. Lightning snapped down into the creature and its glassy pustules grew brighter, yet it remained still, it's metal gears and organs puffing and whirring as it started to morph again into something else.

Wayran fumbled in his pocket and found the key. It was shining white with a rainbow sheen atop it like the inside of a clam shell. He found the keyhole in the door, framed by the same material, pushed his key inside and turned it. He threw his weight against the door. Nothing happened. Too late he realised the storm had also ceased around him, and the world was deadly silent.

Wayran turned and saw the worm change shape into a tall, well-groomed man. The man wore an expensive suit adorned with golden trim. His long hands slid along a thin golden chain and retrieved one of the new marvels of their time, a pocket-watch. The man smiled with golden teeth as if at a joke as he looked down at the gears ticking away beneath the glass surface. He carefully put the pocket-watch back and then unsheathed two heavy-bladed knives.

"You should have stopped when you had the chance, you're out of time now," the tall man said with a shrug, then laughed. He looked at Wayran, tilted his head in curiosity, and exploded forward.

Wayran screamed as the air left his lungs, and he stared down at the two knives buried to the pomel in his chest. The man smiled, laughing as he did, opened his mouth to and sank row upon row of needle like teeth into Wayran's neck.

* * *

"Wayran!" A voice called.

He felt hands holding his shoulders. Someone was shaking him.

Wayran shot upright and sucked in a giant mouthful of air. His heart pounded, and he saw a tall, strong young man holding his shoulders and looking concerned.

"I'm here, it's alright," the young man said. "Which one was it this time?"

Wayran had to breathe in and out twice more before he recognised that the young man holding him was Matoh, his brother.

"The monster and the tower," Wayran said as he began to recognise his surroundings. He was in their shared bedroom aboard their uncle's airship. Wayran heard the soft hum of the floating hull and the occasional creak of rope. The circular window to his right peered out onto a landscape just lighting up with the first rays of morning.

"Did you get inside this time?" Matoh asked.

"No," Wayran said as he shook his head to try and clear the fuzziness he felt. Things were slowly coming back to him.

"Too bad," Matoh sighed. "All these years of the same dream, and you never get inside that stupid tower. Where were you this time?"

"In the Wastes somewhere," Wayran answered. His heart had finally begun to slow. His hand slipped under his shirt and felt his chest where the knives had pierced him, but he found no wound. It had been so real.

"Well, that figures," Matoh chuckled as he cocked his head towards the window. "You'd think you would have had enough sand during the day. Dreaming about it now too? You're completely obsessed aren't you?"

"Yes." Wayran tried to laugh. "I guess I am." He paused as he remembered something odd about the dream. "There was something different this time," he said as he stood and walked to the window. He looked out onto the vista of sweeping dunes rolling beneath the airship. "Two metal rods were attached to the tower. They were huge and stretched up into the sky. What do you think that means?"

Matoh grinned evilly. "It's quite obviously repressed sexual desire."

"What!" Wayran turned and punched his brother's muscular arm.

Matoh just laughed and lay back in his hammock. "Come on, the signs are all there."

"Oh, shut it." Wayran rolled his eyes, and then rubbed his arms against the slight chill in the air. "You never take things seriously. Recurring dreams are worrying."

"Honestly, the dreams could mean anything," Matoh snorted. "The tall man could be someone you're scared of; the weird worm monster could have been something you saw yesterday. The armoured man, I don't know, me going to the Academy, perhaps? We wear armour there. Or some skewed vision of Mum? They're just dreams. Tell you what, though, I certainly haven't missed being woken up like that. Ever since you left home to come out to the Wastes, I've slept better than the dead." Matoh laughed. "I'm seriously regretting my decision to come visit you."

"Thank you – for snapping me out of it, I mean," Wayran said. "And for coming to visit me. It must have been a long trip."

"Yes, yes. Don't get all sentimental on me," Matoh said with a smile, but then looked thoughtful. "Why would there be two giant metal rods sticking up out the sand in the middle of the desert?"

"I don't know. Why would there be a door I can't open, or a shape-shifting monster chasing me?" Wayran asked.

"Good point. I forgot to ask about the monster." Matoh lay with his arms crossed behind his head. "What was it this time?"

"A knight, then a worm, and then the tall man."

"Hmmm." Matoh rubbed his chin in thought. "The tall guy's handsome, right? You've said that before."

"Yes, so what?"

"So a tall, handsome man, a worm, and two long metal spikes?" Matoh's eyebrow rose. "*Suggestive* just isn't a strong enough word. You've got issues, brother."

Wayran rolled his eyes and flopped back into his hammock. "Oh, shut up. It was a nightmare. Why do I tell you anything?"

Matoh laughed, "You feel better, though, right?"

Wayran sighed. "Yes. I suppose there's that."

"So, we win, and nightmares lose," Matoh said with a note of finality. "Come on, we might as well get up. The sun's rising, and it's your big day today."

Wayran didn't need reminding. He shook his head once more to clear any lingering elements of the nightmare, and then took a deep breath. "Alright. I won't get back to sleep anyways."

They dressed quickly and crept through the small corridor into the kitchen. Wayran made sure he walked beside the hot water pipe running along the length of the small hallway. The nights were somehow still so cold in the Wastes, but the lovely warmth running through the metal arteries of the airship from it's boiler-heart always made him feel at home.

Aunt Sandra, who was also the ship's cook, was up and preparing breakfast for everyone.

"You two are up early," Aunt Sandra said as she sliced through a pineapple. "Nervous are we, Wayran?"

"Yes, though I don't know how I couldn't be." Wayran picked up a honey-glazed bun, an apple and a slice of ham before pouring himself some hot water from the big kettle on the stove for a cup of tea.

"I'm sure you'll do just fine. You haven't had any trouble on the smaller runs," Aunt Sandra said with a quick, reassuring smile.

"So, Uncle Aaron is pretty sure that today we'll find a big one?" Wayran asked. "How can he be so sure?"

"Well, when you've been out in the Wastes for as long as we've been out here, you get to know the rhythms of it all. Yesterday was very hot, and today is going to be a scorcher as well, you can already feel it in the air. Plus, your uncle's charted a lot of barometric pressure readings with that gizmo Chronicler Rutherford made for him. Aaron say's the pressure's been getting lower each day, and since we're headed towards the coast, we should run into a dry cold front."

Wayran bobbed his head, putting together the pieces. It sounded like Uncle Aaron was right, which shouldn't really surprise him.

"You understood all that?" Matoh asked, raising an eyebrow at Wayran.

"Yes, you see the lower pressure indicates –"

"Stop." Matoh held up a hand. "I don't want to know. There is only so much room for understanding in a person's mind, and I don't want that nonsense pushing out anything useful."

"I'm pretty sure that's not how it works." Wayran squinted his eyes at his brother and knew Matoh was only pretending to be thick. Matoh could understand anything he set his mind to, he just wasn't the slightest bit interested in science.

Matoh winked at him as if knowing what Wayran was thinking.

Wayran rolled his eyes and turned back to Aunt Sandra. "So it's probably going to be a big one today?"

“Most likely.” Aunt Sandra pushed all the pineapple pieces into a large bowl. “Go on, get your plates full and then get up top. I’m sure there are a dozen things you need to check before you’re ready, and I’ve got meals to prepare.”

Wayran grabbed another honey-glazed bun and some of the pineapple while Matoh filled another plate completely before they made their way up to the top deck.

A hint of sunrise still coloured the horizon as they climbed the narrow ladder up to the main deck. Wayran once again found himself marvelling at the incredible vista. He didn’t know if he’d ever get used to seeing things from so high up in the air.

He followed Matoh across the main deck to the edge of the bespoke landing platform. Most sailing ships never entertained the idea of a glider landing platform, but then again, most ships were built to stay on the sea and never entertained the idea of being hoisted up hundreds of feet into the air by a floating Jendar hull.

Wayran looked up in wonder at the ancient and otherworldly Jendar hull above them. It looked like a giant grey egg, yet if you looked closer at the skin, you could see sparkling pebble-like bumps all the way around it. But the real marvels were inside this giant floating egg. Purple gaseous light danced within the hull, with lines of ghostly blue filaments floating through it.

No one really understood how it worked, but Uncle Aaron had figured out enough of the ancient Jendar controls to make the floating hull go where he wanted it to. Thus, *Deliverance*, the only known airship in the entire world, came to be, after Uncle Aaron had tied his old caravel to the bottom of the floating hull.

Wonders like the hull overhead were the real reason Wayran had been working so hard to get a place on his Uncle’s crew. No one could get as far into the Wastes as his uncle with this airship, and deep within the

Wastes was where Wayran was going to find out what really happened to the Jendar. How had the ancient and vastly technologically superior civilisation simply ceased to exist? They had disappeared almost overnight leaving nothing but ruins and relics of their glorious past. So much had been lost, but all of that forgotten knowledge was waiting for him to find somewhere beneath the sands.

Wayran popped another piece of pineapple into his mouth hoping the sweet juice would help wake him up. He walked across the main deck to peer out at the horizon, seeking a glimpse of sunlight off glass somewhere in the distance. He had seen the flashes before. They were the tell-tale signs of Jendar ruins and their soaring glass towers.

He stared out past the horizontal masts of the airship, which extended like massive fingers into the sky beside them. Wide triangular sails billowed from the masts both above and below the landing deck. The sails on the bottom flowed out sideways like inverted bat-wings, while the sails above soared to the top of the bulging Jendar hull looming overhead like a giant wingless bee. Rigging crisscrossed between the sails in every direction, tying Uncle Aaron's very standard wooden caravel to the amazing floating hull in an intricate web of which even the most fastidious spider would be proud.

"I can see why you like this," Matoh said as he stared out towards the horizon. "Pretty spectacular, I have to admit. I'm glad I caught you all in Sandton. This is probably the last time we'll get to spend together for a long while."

Wayran was surprised at the sentiment, but Matoh was right. Once Wayran passed his test, he would be travelling through the Wastes for most of the year with only the occasional trip back to any form of civilisation. Whereas Matoh would almost immediately start training at the Royal Military Academy once this run in the Wastes was completed.

"Yes," Wayran agreed. "Sad, when you put it that way."

They sat sipping their tea in contented silence, just watching the world wake up. Finally, Wayran shook himself out of his reverie and looked over at Matoh. "Try not to do anything stupid today if you have to fill in again, alright?"

"We were having a moment," Matoh scoffed, but saw Wayran was serious. "Fine, I won't do anything stupid, as long as you try not to be so patronising." Matoh's all too familiar crooked grin lit his face.

"I'm serious, Matoh. Just follow the plan," Wayran said.

"I do follow the plan!" Matoh protested. "Well, the spirit of the plan anyways. There is always room for improvement once you get into the field."

"That's not your call. You're just filling in because James broke his arm a few weeks ago. Uncle Aaron doesn't need you messing things up just because you want to show off," Wayran said. He knew his words were doing nothing but antagonising Matoh, yet he couldn't stop himself. His nerves were already making him edgy.

"Wayran, stop freaking out," Matoh said with more calm understanding than Wayran would have given him credit for. "Things will be fine. If Uncle Aaron needs me again today, I'll go and do my job. You just focus on what you need to do."

Wayran took a deep breath. Matoh was right, things would be fine. He'd complete this run and then Wayran would have a permanent place on the crew.

"Alright. I'm going to go check on my glider." Wayran nodded to Matoh and set off to give his glider another inspection. He needed to do something to take his mind off the impending run, and he could practically feel the electric charge in the air.

Uncle Aaron had predicted accurately. Today they were going to see a big one.

* * *

Wayran felt the wind rushing past him as he let his bodyweight shift in the glider harness. The right wing tipped up, and Wayran turned to fly straight into the edge of the approaching sandstorm.

He smiled as lightning jumped through the massive cloud of churning sand particles, and just then he couldn't think of anywhere else he'd rather be.

"Wow! This is great!" Matoh said a few dozen feet to his left. "Uncle Aaron was right, it's huge!"

Wayran sighed inwardly. Matoh being this excited usually presaged them getting into some sort of misadventure. "Just stick to the plan, alright?!" Wayran called over to his brother.

Out of the corner of his eye, he saw Matoh give a sarcastic shake of his head. Wayran ground his teeth but said nothing. He didn't have time to worry about his brother's lack of commitment right now. Matoh already had a plan at the end of the summer, and it had nothing to do with flying gliders out over the Wastes.

Just before the sun was completely blocked out by the wall of oncoming dust and sand, Wayran saw something flash in the dunes below. He traced it and saw the buried edge of an enormous building, and felt a quick thrill.

The building was undoubtedly Jendar.

His mind wandered for a moment, wondering what treasures, or better yet, what answers might be hidden inside the enormous structure; but then all light faded as they flew under the edge of the storm and wind-whipped sand began biting into his face.

"Here we go!" Wayran yelled over at Matoh.

Matoh waved back at Wayran, signalling he was ready.

Please don't let him be an idiot. Wayran prayed to any god which might be listening as he secured his mask, adjusted his specially made goggles, and then attacked the storm.

Thunder boomed from somewhere within the dust cloud and jolted his mind into focus. He checked his position and could just make out Matoh's shadow on his left and the flight lead in front of him, as another blast of wind hit their group of gliders.

Don't fight it, Wayran reminded himself, feeling the force of the air and how it wanted to move the glider. *Use it instead.*

He shifted his weight and angled the wide triangular wing above him to catch part of the gust. It jerked the glider back and upwards, and Wayran gasped slightly at the sudden change in altitude, but he regained control quickly and steadied himself.

His skin tingled on his left, which told him which part of the cloud to head towards. He could just make out the shadowy outline of the lead glider, and saw their flight lead's hand drop low, which told the rest of the team to prepare themselves.

Wayran let himself smile. This next part was great.

The flight lead's hand rose and dropped twice in quick succession. They were in position; it was the signal to start harnessing the energy around them.

Wayran closed his eyes, concentrated, and began to siphon.

Siphoning was why he had been allowed to even entertain the idea of flying with his Uncle's crew. Few people could siphon in the latent energy of the environment around them, but both Wayran and Matoh had been born with the ability, inherited from their parents.

Chaotic energy in the air around Wayran's body began to order itself as he focused on pulling it into his skin. He felt the air temperature drop as all the energy immediately around him was pulled into his body. He blocked out all other thoughts, as holding the energy for too long inside of him was dangerous. He focused on moving the numbing, tingling sensation into a cohesive ball in his chest. The tingling sensation built almost to the point of pain.

Wayran felt the thin metal wires woven into the bodysuit he wore, called a *trisk,* begin to warm. His *trisk* was specifically rigged for this job and had several large copper conduit discs sewn into the fabric down the length of his back.

Finally, he couldn't pull any more energy into himself, and the tingling pain intensified suddenly as a lightning strike flashed in a distant cloud.

Now! The energy numbed Wayran for the briefest of moments as he snapped it through the lines of his *trisk* and into the conduit points on his back. He felt the copper discs warm against his skin, telling him the push had been successful.

He sucked in a breath as his body recovered from the first round of siphoning.

He could see the faint glow of *santsi* globes atop each of the gliders flying in the storm around him. They looked like giant fireflies floating within a hazy sky.

The globes were a wonder of this age. Able to hold siphoned energy for long periods of time, santsi globes had become the most sought-after commodity in the Salucian Union. Out here in the Wastes, Uncle Aaron's crew were able to fill the biggest and best globes to full capacity.

Wayran grinned and swung forward in his harness, making its nose drop. He felt his stomach fill with butterflies as he experienced the moment of weightlessness and dived back into position behind the flight lead. Wayran opened himself up to the potent energy within the sandstorm and began collecting energy for his next push.

Each time he pushed more energy into the santsi globe, it would become increasingly difficult to push again. More and more energy was used up trying to force the next bit in, a bit like trying to pack more and more things into a rucksack. Each new item in the sack impeded the next item you tried to stuff in. All this meant Wayran had to save a lot of his strength for those final siphoning pushes into the globes: the santsi globes on top of his glider were the biggest and best money could buy. He had to pace himself.

This was what it meant to be a Storm Chaser. Pushing yourself to your siphoning limit while literally chasing storms to collect the awesome amount of latent energy within those storms, and it was all to fill up the biggest santsi globes available to then sell the storm charged globes to the highest bidder.

It was possibly one of the stupidest ways to make money ever conceived, but what a rush!

Lightning lit the sky just in front of them, and Wayran saw the flight lead waving for them to swing left and get back to the edge of the storm. They were getting pulled too far in and were way too close to that last lightning strike.

As crazy as the Storm Chasers were, they still weren't stupid enough to try and take on the full power of a sandstorm. They had to stay right on the edge of the storm, or they risked being sucked in and killed. They exited the spitting sand cloud once again, and lightning struck once more as if trying to snap at their heels.

Wayran's head whipped to the side. In the sudden light of the flash he saw two enormous metal rods sticking out of the sand like the antennae of some great insect.

No way! They were just like the ones he had seen in his dream.

Heavier sand began to hit him and he lost sight of the metal rods, chastising himself for not paying attention to the storm. You always had to respect the storm. As soon as you lost that respect, the storm would kill you.

He circled his glider back and got behind two other gliders to ensure he was far enough out. He kept looking towards where the metal rods had been, but he couldn't see any hint they had been there.

Had he imagined them?

The flight lead signalled for them to wrap it up quickly. Wayran shook himself and focused on preparing to siphon again.

Wayran opened up to the energy once more and gasped as the magnitude of the force slammed into him like a fist. His entire body felt like it had been rung like a giant bell. Immediately the tingling pain set in and he forced the torrent of energy through the conduit point on his back. His body throbbed from the attack.

"Wow," he managed to choke out as his body stopped buzzing. This storm was a big one! He had heard some of the other glider pilots talking about the big ones, but nothing could have prepared him for this.

"Lady take me!" Wayran heard Matoh's curse from beside him. "You alright Wayran? That was something else!"

Matoh looked concerned but he wore a smile and Wayran could see the wild look in his brother's eyes even behind the goggles. He was enjoying this even more than Wayran was.

Wayran gave Matoh a thumbs-up to show he was alright. "That was big! Won't take long to fill our globes with a storm like this!" he called, although he didn't know if Matoh could hear him.

Lightning flashed again, and Wayran felt the charge of its proximity slash through him, making his body freeze solid for a moment. Thank the gods he hadn't been siphoning when that blast ripped through the air. He felt his heart pounding in his chest, and he was more than a little glad when he saw the flight lead's signal to pull back another two hundred yards. The wind increased yet again.

"Did you see that?!" Matoh called over to him, pointing to something below them.

Wayran looked down and saw the two metal rods again.

"The metal rods!" Matoh yelled over the noise of the howling wind, "Just like you said! Look! The lightning keeps hitting them. They're absorbing the lightning!"

Wayran saw the flight lead turn sharply to the left and saw the lead's outstretched arm rotating in a wide arc. It was the signal to get into a climbing circle formation: they were to finish filling their globes as they rode the thermal up, and then get the hells out of there.

"It's too dangerous!" Wayran yelled at Matoh, "We have to go!" Wayran's body tensed as his glider's wing bounced with a gust of wind. He moved into position and repeated the flight lead's arm signal for those behind him.

The metal rods would have to wait; the storm was growing too large. They had to get back to their grounded airship so they could ride out the rest of the storm as it blew over.

As his glider arced away from the storm, Wayran thankfully felt a slight drop in the energy field around him. There had been so much energy in the storm, it had been like having your entire body covered with pins and needles.

In his peripheral vision, he saw other gliders fly in behind him, mirroring his slow climb up and away from the storm.

Then someone veered out of position and flew away from the group.

Wayran's heart sank in dread; he knew who it was.

"I'm going to check it out!" Matoh yelled.

No! Wayran's eyes widened, and he screamed, "Matoh, get back here!"

Thunder boomed and drowned out any chance of Matoh hearing him.

Wayran lurched in his harness as he tried to look over his shoulder to where he had last seen Matoh.

Sand belted his face mask as a gust of wind slammed into the glider's wing and threw Wayran's craft about as if an angry god had decided to slap him. He tried to compensate and found himself rising sharply in the middle of the thermal. He tilted the glider's wings and arced back around so he could see where Matoh had gone.

He turned just in time to see Matoh's glider sailing straight back into the churning cloud of sand and lightning.

Two bolts of lightning flashed directly in front of his brother's position, and Wayran saw the shadows of the giant metal rods in the lightning's afterimage.

"Damn it, Matoh," Wayran cursed. The other Storm Chasers hadn't seen Matoh veer off. It was up to Wayran to bail out his stupid brother.

"Get back here, Matoh!" Wayran yelled, and tipped the nose of his glider down, swooping towards the disappearing shadow of his brother and gaining speed. *He's going to get himself killed.*

Another bolt of lightning struck. In the flash, he saw Matoh's tiny glider silhouetted against the giant bolt.

Then Matoh was gone. Hidden behind a wall of billowing sand.

Wayran's heart pounded in his chest as he tipped his body up and dived forward, trying to catch up with Matoh.

A gust of wind smashed into him, and heavy sand pounded against his bodysuit. They delivered such force that even through the suit it felt like thousands of biting ants.

Another gust and Wayran lost his grip on the steering bar. He grabbed for it in panic as his glider's nose pitched upwards and he was thrown back. He fought for control and grabbed the bar just as the top of a dune came rushing towards him from out of the blowing sand.

He strained with everything he had to push the glider back up into the air. His feet clipped the top of the dune, and as the glider's wing cleared the other side, hot air shot him back up into the sky. His stomach lurched as the ropes on his harness groaned in protest.

A metal rod appeared in front of him, he veered to avoid it, and saw Matoh circling around the rod above him.

Lightning struck, hitting one of the metal rods, and the bolt of plasma jumped from one rod back to the other, rippling down into the sand between them.

Thunder ripped through the air and knocked the breath from Wayran's lungs.

He rode the up thrust of warm air so he could get above Matoh. He couldn't ignore how spooked he was about seeing the metal rods from his dream, but he had no time to dwell on it as they were about to be vaporised at any moment. Wayran pushed the nose of his glider up as he felt the thermal push up against the glider's wing. He had to get Matoh out of here.

Their impending doom was apparently lost on his thrill-seeking brother as Wayran heard the words that had always made his heart jump.

"Watch this!" Matoh yelled.

It was then Wayran saw the three dark globes atop his brother's glider and Wayran knew what was going to happen.

"Don't!" He stretched his hand out.

An enormous lightning bolt split the sky as it slammed into Matoh's glider and the world went white.

Wayran was blind, and all he heard was a sharp whining in his ears.

After three long heartbeats, his vision cleared. Where Matoh had once been, now spun a smoking glider. Matoh's body hung limp in the harness, and Wayran watched in terror as his brother plummeted towards the dunes far below.

Wayran's guts twisted into knots and the blood in his veins seemed to freeze. Time slowed as he watched Matoh falling to his death.

It was then Wayran felt himself siphoning, almost unconsciously. The energy felt different and all at once events began to unfold before his eyes. A ghost image of Matoh hitting the dune made his mind snap back to reality. *I have to save him.*

Dozens of possibilities and choices began to play out in his mind. He saw himself try to intercept and grab Matoh's glider wing, saw himself jump out of his harness and try to gain control of the caterwauling glider.

Then Wayran saw the possible future he wanted. He grabbed hold of that vision and executed what he had seen in his mind's eye.

Wind rushed up to meet his craft as he pointed his glider's nose straight down. He put all of his weight onto the palms of his hands and held himself straight up in the harness as if he were doing a handstand on the steering bar. The air began to hiss off the fabric of his glider's wings, but he kept his mind focused on what he had to do, on what he had seen happen.

Momentum was the issue, and the glider's frame would only take so much strain, especially from a sharp impact. The faster he went, the more stress on the frame when he needed to bank out of the speed and change direction. Yet Wayran had seen the solution.

Like an arrow fired straight down, he watched as he flew past Matoh's prone form spinning in the drunkenly listing glider. He was below Matoh's position now. He had to follow the dune and had to time this just right.

Now.

He pushed himself back in the harness, and his arms shook with the effort to stay in control.

The glider's wings flexed, and then Wayran felt it begin to turn.

The turn couldn't be too sharp, or else the wood of the frame would snap. Not enough and – well, he couldn't think about that.

The weight of his body pushed against the harness as he felt the wings begin to flex under his weight. The edge of the dune swept beneath him, and Wayran dived down just above its slope, his stomach brushing the sand. He clenched his body tight and pushed back to lift the nose ever so slightly.

His speed was incredible. Sand lifted from the air in his wake, hissing behind him.

Wayran inched the nose of the glider up again, and the wings groaned but held.

It had to be now. He forced the nose back up towards the sky. Ropes creaked, wood flexed, and Wayran felt the full momentum of his speed pulling him into the face of the dune.

His feet touched the sand, and then the glider snapped back skywards. He saw Matoh as Wayran's glider shot straight up at him from below.

Wood splintered around him as finally the wings had taken too much. In a flash of clarity, his mind's eye blurred through various scenarios and he found the one to latch onto.

He siphoned with everything he had, but not from the air. He pulled everything he could from the charged santsi globes still connected to the conduit point on his back. Wayran had never been trained to siphon in this way, but somehow, he had seen what to do. He pushed everything he had into the silver lines running through his *trisk*.

Flame flashed around him, and suddenly he was free of the broken glider. Pain crisscrossed his skin, but the harness burned away, freeing him to fly upwards with the speed of a falcon.

Wayran braced and slammed into the wing of Matoh's glider. Together they spun, but sideways, not down. Santsi atop Matoh's glider were flung away, exploding with the stored energy as they smashed against the sand around them.

The brothers skipped across a dune's crest, were airborne once again, and then slammed into the second dune in a tangle of bodies and broken glider wings.

Wayran tasted blood as the air left his body from the impact.

He tried to suck air in, but it wouldn't come to him. He lay gasping in the strange silence atop the dune. Thunder boomed in the distance, and finally he pulled in a breath.

Don't be dead, don't be dead. Wayran rolled and fought through the fabric that was covering his brother, which had once been a glider wing. *Don't be dead.*

He sank to his knees beside his brother. Matoh wasn't moving; his whole body looked limp. Wayran dared not breathe as he tried to detect any sign at all that Matoh still lived.

In the stillness, he heard a sound like something slowly cracking. All around him, the sound repeated. It sounded like glass about to pop.

Above them, atop the crest of the dune, he saw the metal rods beginning to sink into the sand.

It was then Wayran felt a vibration in the sand beneath him, and a sound like giant cogs whirring together.

The cracking sound grew louder.

Wayran thought he heard a hissing, and he looked back to a spot of charred sand where a santsi globe had exploded. The blackened sand began to disappear as its centre was pulled down into a vortex, just like it did within an hourglass.

Another crack sounded, this time closer, and more sand began to slide towards the growing vortex.

"Matoh get up!" Wayran yelled. He grabbed his brother by the shoulders and tried to pull him up and away from the sliding sand. Yet Matoh was unconscious and his body a dead weight.

There was a great popping sound as all of the sudden the ground around Wayran gave way beneath him. He held onto Matoh as they fell into the giant vortex of sand and were sucked down below the dunes.

2 - Beneath the Sands

How omnipotent the sands feel. The last remnants of grasslands have been overtaken, and now there is only sand. Sand and dust. Dust and Sand. In this isolation, I have nothing better to do than track the long protracted movements of the dunes, like giant cream waves upon a time-slowed ocean.

Always encroaching, always hissing in the wind, skittering across the surfaces of its brethren. Always moving. And it gets everywhere. Into every crack and crevice. Into every device and mechanism. Clogging things up, disrupting my contraptions with an unfathomably high order of entropy. Eventually, everything submits to its encroachment and is in turn claimed by the sand. Against its never tiring onslaught there is no victory, only delay. And the sands have limitless patience. They know I cannot last forever. And in the end, they will take me and this place, like they do everything else.

In the end, there is just sand.

Always, in the end, there is just sand.

- *Journal of Robert Mannford, Day 075 Year 68*

Matoh

The Wastes

Something was pushing him forward. Like a massive hand, impossible to resist, gently thrusting him forward.

Matoh turned his head to see what it was, but there was nothing. He turned back, still moving forward, towards some sort of threshold. It looked like a barrier of some sort, and suddenly his chest met resistance.

Yet the invisible hand kept pushing. It was crushing him, slowly, yet unflinchingly.

Matoh put his hands up, trying to feel the barrier; his hands moved but were slow, dragging as if he were weighed down.

And the pressure kept increasing, forcing him into this resistive shield, which flexed but began to smother him as he ran out of space. He couldn't breathe. Matoh pushed against the invisible hand, trying to dig his heels into something, anything.

And still the pressure increased. He tried to scream, but more air left his lungs.

He had no options ... No! There was one. Forward.

He braced against the invisible hand and surged forward into the smothering barrier with everything he had left. His body shook with the effort; he was going to black out.

And suddenly there was light.

Bright sunlight shone down on his shoulders; he could feel its warmth. He stood in a golden field. Grass as tall as his waist waved in the wind and he could smell flowers.

He had a sword in his hand.

Matoh looked down at the weapon in his hand, puzzled. *How did that get there?*

The sword was impossibly large, nearly four feet long and half a foot wide, but it felt light as a feather. A blade of burnt gold ... but then it changed: first into a wicked black longsword, then into a brilliant white dagger, then back into the great golden two-hander. The weapons flickered back and forth. Yet they all felt the same somehow.

Matoh tightened his grip on the hilt and he felt strong, stronger than he ever had before. The weapon knew him, recognised him. He had the strange sensation it had been waiting for him.

He looked up across the waving grass to see a man standing in front of him, silent and motionless. He wore an odd hat, wide and conical. It was made of woven grass, like one a farmer might wear. The wind rippled across the field and Matoh felt its chill, but the strange man was not touched by the wind, he waited, watching him. Somehow Matoh knew this man as well. This whole scene was ... familiar.

He's here to kill me. Matoh didn't know how he knew, but he did.

Another sword, this one long and slender, appeared in the strange man's hand as if it had been summoned. Its form changed as well; it seemed to be settling on the black longsword, where his own weapon seemed to be flickering more often to the golden blade.

The light itself shied away from the jet-black blade in the man's hand, as though there was a pool of darkness there which the sun couldn't touch. Matoh felt hunger from the black sword, and then he remembered his own golden blade. His sword began to glow, drinking in the sunlight, and blue runes emerged from the central fuller. This too was familiar.

The man tilted his head as if in curiosity, and the sun crept in under the wide hat. A face of polished silver surrounded a set of glowing red eyes. The man was impossibly thin, more like a skeleton, yet Matoh could see armour running the entire length of his body like a second skin.

And now Matoh wore his own armour. A full set of Syklan Knight's armour. He had huge santsi globes atop his pauldrons. This too felt right. He was meant to be a Syklan. Matoh had always known this. He was a greater warrior than even his mother, the Silver Lady, Natasha Spierling.

I must win. Matoh knew this battle was what would define him. It was everything. The fate of the Union rested on his shoulders. He had to win.

They stared at each other across the grassy field for an eternity. The metal man seemed to hesitate, waiting for him. *A mistake,* Matoh thought. '*Hesitation kills as surely as a blade*': they were his father's words.

"You are here to kill me," Matoh stated. His voice was powerful, surprisingly so, and was somehow not quite his own, as if he was hearing someone else speak with his lips.

"Yes." The word was spoken softly, almost sadly. The silver face had no mouth with which to speak, but Matoh heard the word as if it had been whispered in his ear.

Again Matoh felt he should know this man. But that didn't matter; what he did know was that the man was his enemy and he had to beat him. He had to win to save them all.

Matoh surged forward, and the heavens roared with him. He lifted his sword and blue fire blazed along its edge. A hum, like a swarm of giant bees, rushed through him as he swung the great blade. Nothing could stand in his way. He wielded the power of the gods. The metal man's black sword rose up to meet his, and the world shifted.

He was on a street.

Moonlight shone down upon the lifeless eyes of a hundred corpses in front of him. A tall man, dressed in rich black silks, laughed with delight as he licked the blood from his long hunting knife. A manic hunger lit the man's eyes as he turned to Matoh; then he smiled showing a mouth full of fangs and blood dripped down his chin.

Matoh tried to run, but couldn't.

The man laughed at his weakness. "I was hoping you'd find me." The dark man smiled and launched forward, diving straight into Matoh's chest. He felt a hole in his body. The monster was inside him.

The world shifted.

Matoh's heart pounded. Had he just died? What was happening?

Something touched his arm, making him jump. It was a young woman. As Matoh stared at her, her hair colour shifted from dark to light.

"Time to go," the woman said holding out her hand. Matoh reached for it, but when he looked up it was no longer the young woman, but his mother.

Matoh was a child again, on the cliffs across from the Red Tower. It was the last place he had seen his mother.

"Don't leave me," he said, but his mother only smiled down at him, now dressed in her shining Syklan armour. She patted his head sadly.

A wave crashed below, and a fine mist rose up from the rocks below surrounding the clifftop. Matoh could smell the ocean.

"Be strong, my young prince," his mother said to him.

"Don't leave me!" Matoh wailed, trying to run, but his legs were so small.

"Goodbye, Matoh." His mother waved and stepped into the mist.

He was alone.

* * *

Matoh sat up. Cold sweat covered him. Sweat and something else ... sand?

He put a hand to his chest as he felt a tightness there. *In the place where the evil figure had dived into his body.* The memory of it made him shiver.

He lifted a hand to shield his eyes from a strange pale blue light above, but the motion made his head swim. "Where am ... ?"

"Matoh!" Wayran yelled – far too loudly for Matoh's taste.

"Shhhh." Matoh put a finger up, closing his eyes against the ringing pain between his ears. "Not so loud."

"I thought you were dead!" Wayran's voice had an edge of panic to it.

"I may have been," Matoh groaned as he tried to stand up. He seemed to be half buried in the sand. "Do the dead have really weird dreams and feel terrible?"

"I doubt it," Wayran said, and slid in under his arm, trying to steady him. "The dead don't really feel much from what I gather. Do you have pain anywhere else?"

"You mean other than everywhere?" Matoh squinted some more, and finally the room came into focus.

He saw Wayran's concerned face. "No, really, Wayran. I'm fine. A little woozy and my chest hurts a bit, but it's nothing really. Weren't we meant to be flying?"

"Are you serious?" Wayran said in disbelief. "You pulled lightning, you idiot!"

"What?" Matoh scoffed. The memory of something flashing just before he blacked out did seem familiar, but that couldn't have been what happened. "Come on," he said, "that's not possible."

"What were you thinking?!" Wayran threw his hands up as he stepped back from Matoh. "Do you have some sort of death wish or something? That was the stupidest thing I've ever seen you do. Flying straight towards where lightning keeps striking! Yes, that's a great idea. What could possibly happen?!"

Matoh ignored his brother's comments as he began to see where they were standing. "Where are we, Wayran?"

"I can't believe you're not hurt." Wayran shook his head, pacing back and forth and staring at him.

"Sorry to disappoint." Matoh put his hands on Wayran's shoulders to stop his pacing.

"We need to get you to Quirin. She'll be the one to decide if you're alright." Wayran pointed his finger at him. "As soon as we get out, straight to a healer."

"Ok, fine." Matoh turned from Wayran slowly to look back at the wall across from them. "But first tell me where in the nine hells are we?"

Across from them stood a wall of interlocking metal panels and black glass, but the oddest part was above them. Light came from a rod in the ceiling which glowed with a pale white-blue light. The room was like nothing Matoh had ever seen before.

"It's a Jendar building of some sort, as far as I can tell," Wayran growled.

Matoh could see, however, that his brother's concern was lessening with the mention of the Jendar.

"I had to wreck my glider to save you, and the practice one Uncle Aaron gave you is completely destroyed," Wayran said as he shook his head in disgust, "not to mention the fortune of santsi globes we lost."

Matoh grimaced at that. "Sorry," he said, and he genuinely was. "I know how long you spent saving for that glider. I'll help you get another one. But Wayran, how did we get here? I remember circling those strange pin-like spikes sticking up out of the sand. I wanted to see them catch a lightning bolt."

Wayran quirked an eyebrow at him but then shook his head. "Well, if this place is Jendar, it could be possible, but flying towards them was still stupid."

"Fine, I'll admit that." It was then Matoh remembered falling. "Wait, did you smash into me in mid-air?"

"Yes," his brother said, and now it was Wayran who looked distant, as if he too were trying to piece together what exactly had happened.

"How are we both not dead? Alright, say I believe you about the lightning." Matoh remembered the feeling of a massive amount of energy as he siphoned it. "But then I fell. How – what ..." He didn't know where to start. "Just tell me what happened!"

"I don't ..." Wayran looked at a loss for words. "I don't quite understand it myself; but I saw you pull the lightning." Wayran looked up at him. "And then you were falling and I just, sort of, saw how to save you. It was as if everything had slowed down, and I felt" – Wayran scratched his head – "I don't know, it was something massive, something so big I can't explain it." Wayran shook his head in frustration.

"So how does this turn into you smashing into me in midair?" Matoh quirked an eyebrow and flicked the small braid on his left side behind his ear.

"Well, I couldn't stop you from hitting the ground, so I tried to stop you hitting it with so much momentum. I dived below and then flew up to hit you. I guess it was enough to make a difference."

"Have I ever told you, you read too many books?" Matoh shook his head and brushed a hand through the stripe of hair on his head, dislodging some sand. The leather skullcap he had been wearing must have been lost, as were a large number of the crow's feathers he had woven into his hair for luck.

Bad luck that, he thought to himself, *losing crow feathers*. The thought was a bit of an understatement, and he laughed aloud. He turned away from the metal wall with another chuckle and looked at the pile of sand sloping sharply up to what remained of a thick glass roof. "So we fell, but how did we get in here?"

"The santsi," Wayran said, as if that explained everything.

"The santsi?" Matoh spread his hands, waiting for Wayran to continue. He had got used to this lack of explaining from his older and more scholarly brother. Discussions sometimes felt like pulling teeth.

"The santsi you had filled during the lightning strike flew off when I hit your glider. They must have been super-charged from the lightning and detonated on contact with the sand. It would have sent a shockwave through the sand, thus cracking the glass dome. We were sucked down as the sand poured into the open cavity beneath. Luckily there was enough room in here for most of the sand above, or else we'd be buried alive." Wayran pointed up at the remnants of what must have been a rather magnificent glass dome. "Sad really. That dome would have been standing for nearly three thousand years."

"Yes, poor dome." Matoh rolled his eyes. "Can we climb back out?" But he thought he already knew the answer, looking at the mountain of sand behind him.

"No," Wayran said. "The collapse of the dome would have caused the dunes above to shift as well. There must be at least another hundred feet of sand above the glass."

"What about up those spikes, any chance with those?" Matoh pointed at the giant pin-like spikes they had seen from above.

"No, thought of that. Looks like these spikes are pushed up through the holes in the roof and through the dunes. We'd just get stuck in the sand, or fried by lightning." Wayran pointed at one of the spikes. "They've been hit twice since we fell in. You could feel the heat and crackle of energy coming off them after a strike. We're stuck down here, unless you want to try and take the energy of another lightning bolt?"

"Once is enough for me." Matoh stretched, looking around once again. "So ... we need to find a different way out."

Wayran nodded.

"A part of you loves this, doesn't it?" Matoh said. This was pretty much what his older brother had been dreaming about doing ever since they had visited the Chronicler Archives as kids.

"You mean apart from the fact that we are probably going to die a slow and agonising death down here?" Wayran asked, still studying the room around them.

"Yes, besides that." Matoh twisted and felt a satisfying pop as the pressure in his neck released. He flexed his muscles and knew he would have several ugly bruises – if they ever got out of here.

Wayran finally began to smile as he looked around the room. "I know I should be scared to death, but ... I'm not. I mean, yes, I'm scared and worried, and I think we are probably going to starve before we suffocate. Marcus probably doesn't have a chance of finding us down here, and –"

Matoh put up a hand. "Stop talking. You're beginning to make me think we're in trouble." He smiled as he too studied the room around them. “I have to admit. This *is* pretty amazing, other than the impending doom part of course.”

Wayran looked at him seriously. “Are you sure you’re alright?”

“Ask me that again and I’ll show you just how ‘alright’ I am,” Matoh growled. “Come on, there has to be a door somewhere.”

They set off to look around the room.

* * *

“The Jendar did actually use doors, didn’t they?” Matoh asked after they had spent what must have been hours searching for an exit. They had circled the room over a dozen times and found nothing that even resembled a door. “You know, an opening, usually framed, with a moving barrier in it, something which connects one room to another.”

“I know what a damned door is, Matoh,” Wayran cursed; they were both getting tired. Wayran looked to be favouring one leg more than the other, suggesting that he was hurt more than he let on. “Maybe we’re missing something, but I’m tired of walking in circles,” he said as he sat down.

“Would it be underneath the huge pile of sand?” Matoh grimaced, hoping Wayran would say no.

“I don’t think so; some Chroniclers talk about amazing lifts or moving stairways in other ruins, but there were lots of references to doors as well. Doesn’t seem to fit that the entrance would be directly in the centre of this huge room.” Wayran lay back against the pile of sand. “And even if it were, we’d never be able to dig to it. More sand will just fill in whatever we move. I wish I could have found out what actually happened to the Jendar. To see some of the wondrous things the Chroniclers talk about in those archives.” Wayran waved at the room around them. “To find something that would explain why the people who made all of this just suddenly disappeared.” He took a deep breath in an attempt to calm himself. “But we’re trapped, and probably going to die down here."

"Hey, don't talk like that. We'll get out of this, you'll see." Matoh sat down beside his brother and patted his shoulder. "We're just getting tired. Let's sit and think for a minute."

"Bah!" Wayran stood up, angry now. He looked down at a large chunk of glass lying on the floor and picked it up. He positioned it on his finger and thumb like a skipping stone and hurled the glass shard across the room. Then he sighed. "I wish I could have at least seen more of this ruin." The glass caught the eerie blue light, glistening as it spun off into a dark corner of the room.

The glass hit the far wall with a sharp *ting*.

"Nice throw." Matoh nodded. "Useless gesture, but it was a nice throw."

Just then, the ground beneath them began to shake, and the entire room rumbled.

Sand began to fall from the dome above.

"Move!" Matoh yelled, and Wayran darted back just as more glass started falling.

"Get back to the edge of the room!" Wayran yelled, sprinting forward to get beyond the collapsing dome.

"What's happening?!" Matoh yelled over the rumbling noise.

"The spikes! Look!" Wayran pointed.

The giant metal spikes were descending into the floor, shaking the entire room.

Matoh felt his back hit the wall. Wayran's did the same, and they watched sand pouring down from above. The strange overhead lights flickered but stayed on, fully illuminating the sand pile creeping closer and closer to them.

"I thought you said we weren't going to get buried!" Matoh yelled.

"I said we were lucky not to have been!" his brother answered.

"Looks like we might have used up our luck." Matoh began to sweat. Buried alive was not a good way to go. The sand was nearly up to his knees, and he could feel the cool metal wall behind his back. He closed his eyes.

And the rumbling stopped.

He opened his eyes and saw the sand's descent slowing to a halt in the faint light from the glowing rods in the ceiling. The pin-like ends of the spikes could just be seen poking out of the sand pile, which now dominated the room.

"Ha!" Wayran exclaimed, "Still a bit of luck left, it seems!"

A strange buzzing noise came alive within the wall at their backs, and suddenly the light from overhead brightened to a brilliant white as if someone had just turned on the sun. Lights began to flicker in the tiny gaps between the metal wall panels.

Matoh pulled himself out of the sand and scrambled up the slope, pulling Wayran with him. "Get back, we don't know what other surprises there are."

The entire wall now had lines of tiny lights running along it, as if the wall itself was waking up.

The buzzing in the wall stopped, replaced by a whooshing sound off to their right. The sand began to move from that direction.

"It's a door!" Wayran yelled, and scrambled towards the source of the noise.

"Where in Halom's name did that come from?" Matoh shook his head. He knew they had passed that spot nearly a dozen times and had inspected the wall thoroughly.

"Who cares, let's get out of here!" Wayran said as he shuffled through the sand towards the exit.

Matoh was right on his heels.

His brother was through the door already, and Matoh moved to follow, when something caught his eye. It was a piece of glass, and it looked almost identical to the one Wayran had thrown. In fact, he was sure it *was* the same piece of glass.

There was a sharp crack and then a ping from above. Matoh looked up to see the snaking line in the remaining glass overhead grow longer.

"Come on, Matoh!" Wayran beckoned from the other side of the doorway.

"Just a second." Matoh fought his way through the sand and grabbed the shard of glass Wayran had thrown.

Another crack boomed through the room. Sand began to fall like rain onto his shoulders. "What are you doing! Get in here *now*!" Wayran yelled.

Matoh ran for it, but his feet kept getting trapped by the falling sand. "Not yet, Lady Death," he growled. "You can't have me yet!" He pushed with everything he had, more swimming through the sand now than walking.

A deafening pop sounded from above as the rest of the glass dome gave way and the enormous dune above crashed into the room. Matoh dived forward with every ounce of strength he had but felt the weight of a mountain smash down around him.

Then there was silence. He couldn't move, he couldn't breathe.

Everything was dark.

Then something scratched his fingers, and then he felt his brother grab his hand.

"You stupid idiot," Wayran growled as he alternated between pulling and digging Matoh out of the sand. "What could have been so important that it made you go back in there?"

Matoh spat the sand from his mouth as Wayran gave a final heave to pull him free.

"This." Matoh opened his hand to show Wayran the shard of glass. It had cut his hand, but it was still intact.

"What?" Wayran frowned, looking exasperated.

Matoh stood up and brushed himself off. He held up the shard to see it better. "This is the piece of glass you threw."

"So?!" Wayran held out his hands flabbergasted.

"Well, you made a wish, and it opened a door for us." Matoh shrugged his shoulders. "I figured it might still be useful."

Wayran rubbed his eyes in frustration and sighed, "Let's just go." He walked down the hall, not waiting for Matoh.

"What?" Matoh asked, shrugging his shoulders as he pocketed the shard. "It makes sense to me." He took a few quick steps before catching up with his brother, and together they walked deeper into the Jendar ruin.

3 - Paradise Found

Lost Wandering
Looking at the walls,
Wondering if this is home.

Blurred memories of storied pasts,
Tugging at heartstrings with pain and pleasure.
Glistening in the back of the mind,
Calling like a harpy's song.

Blurred arrows of raining misery,
Tugging at back, sinew and bone.
Glistening metal tips light the way,
Beckoning like the fabled Lady's call.

Looking at the walls,
Knowing home is forever gone.

- *Jonah of Clan Shi*

Jonah

Alansworth, Kenz

Mist swirled gently through the underbrush as pairs of tiny feet sprang from cover onto the lush green grasses. Long ears poked up out of the low-lying fog as the very air waited with bated breath and watched as they silently bounced through the white haze.

Jonah Shi crouched in the wet leaves beneath the great oak spreading its gnarled limbs above him. Autumn's kiss had only begun to touch the thin green leaves, and in the twilight the vibrant colours bursting forth in the canopy above were dimmed in the silver moonlight. His hand found the coarse bark of the trunk and he let his fingers play across it for a moment as he watched the serene meadow with fascination. The enormous trees were everywhere in this land, great hulking things spread like stalwart forest guardians populating the rolling hills. He breathed in the night air and could not help the smile which spread upon his lips. *There is life here,* he told himself, *and it is all around us.*

"What are they?" a quiet voice whispered. The speaker seemed nervous that even his soft whisper might be enough to break the spell which encased the meadow.

Jonah wiped a hand through his course black hair before his hand went to rest on his longbow. The touch was enough to tell him he was not dreaming. *Ilene would have loved it here.* The familiar sadness made the breath catch in his chest. *One day, my love, I will show this to you.*

"Are they some sort of forest spirits, do you think?" Fin asked. His whispered voice was growing in volume and excitement, which made Jonah smile. Innocence must be what kept Fin so young at heart. He looked over at his big companion and envied him. Jonah had lost his innocence a long time ago.

Fin's question needed to be answered, however, or Fin would continue generating stories, each one wilder than its predecessor.

Jonah could see Branson rolling his eyes. A leather hood hid most of Branson's rugged features, but Jonah knew the veteran foot-bowman was fuming inside. Jonah didn't have to see the expression on his old friend's face to know he was scowling. Branson had told Fin several times he'd have to be quiet.

"I think, my superstitious friend, that these are in fact called *rabbits,*" Jonah whispered, making sure not to startle the creatures. *I am the wind in the leaves, my little friends,* he thought to the rabbits, *nothing to worry about.* He kept his eyes glued to the dozens of pairs of ears bobbing through the mist, hoping he would not see any of them bolt.

Fin looked as if he was mulling over Jonah's answer. "Rabbits? Never heard of 'em. You sure they're not spirits, Jonah? There could be all sorts in a forest like this. Little furry spirits, I bet."

Branson shot Jonah a look that could have melted glass. The whites of his eyes shone with anger, making him look almost demonic. The moonlight brought out the contrast of Branson's white hair and beard against his midnight skin and dark leather cloak, which made the old man's anger all the more intimidating.

Jonah signalled for Branson to be patient, which only elicited a disgusted look in return. Jonah grimaced; he would have to appease the old badger with some of his good tobacco, no doubt.

"Well, I'm willing to risk it for a chance to have some meat," Jonah told Fin. "Quiet now and I might be able to show you what a rabbit is." Jonah kept his gaze on the small shapes grazing the meadow. *Branson must be ready to kill the both of us by now.*

The fog was thickening; soon the small creatures would disappear altogether beneath the thick white blanket. It was now or never.

Jonah drew an arrow from his quiver slowly and fitted it to his bowstring. He kept his eyes on the bouncing pairs of ears in the meadow while his finger played across the soft feathers of his fletching. He felt the thick but loose shield shape of the goose feather and knew it was one of his hunting arrows. The weight had confirmed its type, but he had checked the fletching just to make sure. The thick feathers and lighter weight were needed to compensate for the power of his war bow, which he had made himself. The Shi Clan were good at building, and he had modified his bow with some very unique counterweights and sights, which gave him what he considered a truer shot. Jonah's hand reflexively checked the fletching one more time as a horrific image of what an enormous black arrow would do to a rabbit flitted through his mind.

He lifted his hand to Branson, signalling he was ready. He raised the bow and pulled the bowstring back with his three leather-clad fingers; thousands of hours of training had made the motion so fluid it felt as natural as walking. In Jonah's mind, he held nothing but the target. It was this moment he loved: the clarity, the absolute perfection of that instant when everything was in alignment. His body would know when it was time, his muscles going through their familiar dance as they flexed and compensated for the almost imperceptible sway of his body. Jonah let his mind drift into an emptiness devoid of all emotion, of past wrongs, of pain, and, most importantly, devoid of memories.

The target was everything, consuming every part of Jonah's mind, until the moment when all the swaying converged into that perfect union and the target floated into position.

Now.

His fingers slipped off the bowstring.

The yellow dyed fletching spun through the mist and a pair of ears dropped.

His heart beat and he saw another pair of ears. *Notch, Draw, Release.* Another moment of nothing but a target. Peace. Clarity.

Notch, Draw, Release. And it was over.

Three spots of yellow stuck up in the mist. Jonah knew they had found their targets, but he felt a flash of regret. He would have to wait for another excuse to fire his bow, before he could once again float in the void of emptiness. *Tomorrow morning I'll get a chance.* He sighed as he watched dozens of ears disappear into the mist.

"Come on." Jonah stood up. "We need to be back soon."

"That was incredible, Jonah!" Fin crashed through the bush to clap him on the back. The big man had an enormous grin on his face. "Where in the blazes did you learn to shoot like that?"

Every Shi knows how to do that, he thought. “The Clan master taught me,” he said. “Lots of rock lizards near Tin City.” He caught Branson’s chastising look and could almost hear his old friend’s condescending voice: ‘*For every lie you tell, you must invent a dozen more to make it true.’* Jonah didn’t like lying to Fin, but he had some secrets which needed to stay hidden.

Branson knew most of those secrets, but the old badger would take them to his grave with him. Whatever his other faults, Branson was loyal through and through.

Too many secrets, Jonah thought as he stepped from the bush to recover his arrows; *so many in fact there are some I have forgotten*. He thought that should be funny, but he found it troubling instead.

Always his mind came back to this. The feeling that something were missing. There was something he should remember, it seemed important, but the thoughts wouldn’t solidify. It felt like trying to focus on something out of the corner of your eye. He would catch phantom slivers of memory, and as soon as he noticed it, the memories would fade away, like smoke on the wind.

He clenched his jaw as a familiar headache began to throb behind his eyes. *I’ve been down this path before.* Jonah remembered the pain; it came every time he thought he was about to remember.

Branson was glaring at him, and shaking his head slightly. *He’ll tell me to stop pushing it. To leave it.* And Branson was most likely right, but Jonah couldn’t leave it. He should, though, it didn’t really matter. All that mattered now was his duty as a bowman, his duty to the Empire, and finding a way to make Ilene happy again.

The Prince had led them across the Barrier Sea, something which hadn’t been done for millennia. They had found a magical land hidden by the great storms, and Jonah knew he wasn’t the only one in the army who had suddenly begun dreaming again. This land held answers for more than just himself.

Dozens of his fellow soldiers had begun talking about what they might do if they settled down on this side of the sea. Opportunities were presenting themselves, and that hope was reinvigorating souls who had all but given up.

Jonah let his hand touch the grass as he started making his way to the rabbits. The mist felt good against his skin, and the sensation began to tickle memories once again. *We made love on a night like this,* he remembered. It was the grass, it reminded him of the gardens in Eura City, where he had his first night with Ilene. He remembered her shy smile when she slipped out of her white silken gown. Even now, the memory made his heart flutter. *She said the mist felt good.* She had laughed and danced naked through the grass. Ilene had been happy then. For a brief instant she had been happy, and on that night Jonah had known no other woman would ever compare. It was the night which changed his life in Court. Jonah had started neglecting his duties in the Fertility Circles and had found reasons to keep his Clan functions close to those of Ilene's. Their secret hadn't stayed a secret for long, and they had been labelled "rebellious", as if monogamy were some great sin. Some of the tribal clans in the far desert still practiced marriage vows, and Jonah and Ilene had found the idea inspirationally romantic. Romance, however, had no place in the Euran Empire, at least no place within the Fecund Blood. No, if you were fertile in their desolate empire, your duty was to further your line, expand your Clan, and ensure humanity's survival.

Yet this place beyond the storms, it was holy. Jonah could feel it all around him. Life teemed everywhere, and its discovery would change everything.

Fin's long stride carried him to the rabbits first and he stood over the little creatures with his hands on his hips. His face was a picture. It looked like he didn't know whether to be sad at the demise of the wondrous little things or happy at the prospect of fresh meat after the long months at sea. "Well, would you look at that." He peered down at the still form lying in the grass, making no attempt to hide his rapt fascination. "Craziest thing I ever did see! Look at the ears ... wow." His eyes still looked a bit sad, despite the big man's excitement.

"Don't worry, Fin. We'll say a prayer for the little souls and give thanks for their sacrifice." Jonah patted him on the shoulder to try and alleviate his sadness. "Plus, you'll be much happier when you smell them cooking. Fresh game beats salt pork or herring any day." Jonah was thoroughly sick of herring. *Every day for the last month.*

Fin seemed happy at the mention of food. His close-cropped blond hair and slight baby-face made him look much younger and simpler than he actually was. It was a stark contrast to Jonah's own dark and rugged image and Branson's grizzled features.

Despite his often foppish appearance, Fin was an excellent warrior. He was a good foot-bowmen, and in fact carried the biggest foot-bow in all the Black Rain; but what set him apart was the giant claymore sword he also took with him into battle. Jonah had seen Fin single-handedly defend a retreat by chopping down two charging horsemen with that long slender blade. When Fin drew that giant weapon, all sense of innocence evaporated from him and the northern barbarian heritage, so visible in his features, came out in full.

Jonah watched Fin reach down to check if the rabbits were dead, but he knew his shots had hit their mark. The rabbits hadn't suffered: two through the heart and the third in the head.

"It sort of looks like a big rat. But with no long tail ... and a shorter nose ... and longer ears. Oh, and the fur, Jonah! It's so soft!" Fin had hold of the rabbit's legs and held it suspended in the air while he gently stroked the velvety fur. Jonah's yellow-fletched arrow was still in the creature's side.

"So not really like a rat then," Jonah said quirking his eyebrow at Fin. "Here, let me see." He took the rabbit from Fin and studied the plump creature. It was twice the size of the chickens back home – *incredible.* These creatures were just another confirmation that the desolation that plagued the Empire was not everywhere. The rabbits were healthy, robust even. The only things which survived in the wild in Eura were desperate and deadly beyond comparison.

Jonah said a quiet prayer to the Empress and the Fates for bringing him to this land. He looked at the meadow again and imagined what it would be like to live in a place so full of life. *I'd build us a farm.* He nodded to himself. *A farm with chickens, and pigs.* There would be enough grass even for cows here. Then he and Ilene could indeed live out their romantic dream of being man and wife like they had heard in the stories of old.

Jonah pulled his arrow free from the rabbit and examined the spade-shaped arrowhead for any damage. Seeing none he wiped off the blood with the cloth hanging from his belt and slipped the weapon back into his quiver. These arrows had rounded sides and pulled free easily, unlike his war arrows with their wicked barbs which punctured armour and ripped flesh. Jonah liked these arrows so much more than his war ones.

Jonah held the rabbit up. "I sure hope it tastes better than rat."

"Course it will, Jonah. Look at how healthy it is." Fin smiled sadly at the rabbit. "Thank you for your sacrifice, little rabbit."

Fin tied the rabbits together with a leather cord, slung them to the end of his bow, and hoisted them over his shoulder. "Now let's get back to camp before we get into trouble. Can't spend all night sightseeing can we?" Fin waded back to the brambles on the edge of the meadow. "We are required to attend a siege in the morning!"

Branson hadn't waited for them and was already through the

brambles with his rabbit. *Branson will laugh about it later, once he has some meat in his old guts,* Jonah thought.

Jonah stopped to look around one last time. The mists were beginning to thicken and soon the rabbits would venture back out, as even the bowmen's sharp eyes would not be able to pick them out hopping through the long grass.

He took a deep breath and stared back towards the army campfires in the distance. *The fires of war,* he thought, *it's eerily beautiful.* Thousands upon thousands of lights twinkled like stars upon the beach as rows of trebuchets, ballista and catapults launched burning projectiles at the walls of a castle atop the giant crag overlooking the sea.

It was only a matter of time now before the local lord capitulated.

The Eurans had lost only three ships to the storms, which was a drop in the ocean given the hundreds which had left Eura. The thousands of men and women who had landed from those ships were just as eager as Jonah to explore and discover the wonders this land held for them.

"Looks like they started without us," Fin said from beside Jonah. "That's just downright rude."

"Yes, appears they did." Jonah laughed quietly, watching the fiery objects arc through the night to crash into the castle. He drew his gaze away and looked out into the blackness behind the Euran ships, across the Barrier Sea and towards Eura.

They had sailed for months and months into what they thought was certain death, yet the Prince's faith had never wavered. The Barrier Sea had been deathly quiet during those months, as if the very world was holding its breath. So many had thought the storms would return and drag them down into the icy depths of the aptly named sea. No one in the last millennium had dared try to cross its length and lived to tell the tale. Yet the ever raging seas had remained calm and allowed them to pass like favoured sons and daughters in some holy scripture. The Empress's

Blessing had proven true, and they had done what no one had done since the founding of the Empire.

Jonah shook himself out of his reverie. He was here now and he had a job to do. The Prince had known his soldiers needed a release after months of believing themselves doomed. The war machines had been offloaded first and been cranked into action before even the whole fleet had landed.

Commander Naseen had assured them that the Black Rain wouldn't be needed until first light, but Jonah wondered if those walls would last even that long.

"Come on, Jonah." Fin clapped his big hand on his shoulder.

Yes, I will have plenty of time to gawk at burning castles now that we're here, Jonah thought.

He waded out of the tall grass, his leather breeches thoroughly soaked with the evening dew. They raced back towards their tents to start cooking what had only a day ago existed in fairy tales. Soon, after a fresh meal and a good sleep on the solid ground, it would be time to start building an empire on this side of the sea.

* * *

The Black Rain had shot from dawn till dusk: thousands of huge black arrows flying over the castle walls. The walls had indeed held until morning, and the occupants of the besieged castle had even mounted a counter-attack which had spooked many of the commanders for some reason. He hadn't seen it, but apparently there were some very different warriors on this side of the Barrier Sea.

Jonah let the rumour slip from his mind as his aching muscles demanded his full attention. His entire body ached with the memory of a long day placing his feet against the thick yew foot-bow and using his full weight to haul back the bowstring. He would hold until an order to fire was bellowed by Commander Naseen, and then he'd let the giant war arrow fire up into the sky between his feet at a precisely ordered angle. *Nock, draw, hold, release.* Hour upon hour of the same motion had left him with few thoughts he could hold on to other than: get food, get a drink, then find somewhere to sit and pass out.

Nearly a full day had passed in blissful release from the ghostly fragments of memories floating through his mind, almost a whole day where the only thing had been the target. He had floated within that emptiness, within the stillness of his mind. No emotion, no pain, just the image of where he needed to send his arrow. He had lost track of how many arrows he had fired, but he didn't care. The runners had kept placing arrows beside him, and so he shot, keeping pace with the drum. *Notch, draw, hold ... BOOM, release,* over and over again until the flag went up signalling for the Black Rain to stop. They had encountered no enemy fire, which wasn't entirely surprising. Even from the defenders' elevated position, the Euran foot-bowmen were still forty or fifty paces out of range of the enemy's arrows.

Individually, the giant foot-bows were cumbersome, yet if allowed to set up from a defensible position, the weapon became an advantage. Thousands of men would lie down to put the force of their entire body into the great bows and fire the massive spear-like arrows well over two hundred yards, while being shielded from cavalry charge by lines of pikemen around them. The strategy had served the Euran army for hundreds of years and appeared to be just as effective in these lush green lands, as the besieged town and fort had offered up little effective resistance.

Commander Naseen had come to the Black Rain after the siege to praise them for their efforts. "Find the red flag along the battlements. Prince El'Amin has deemed you worthy of a reward. A dozen kegs of ale!" A roar met her announcement, and a procession of bone-tired archers shuffled through the castle gates trying to find the red flag along the battlements. That was where Jonah was headed now. *Fin and Branson are probably already there, drinking my share.*

As he made his way through the streets, he saw the damage wrought by the trebuchets, catapults, arrows and sappers. The lower town was a smoking ruin covered in thousands of the massive black arrow shafts. They littered every surface, some even lodged into stone, like enormous cactus needles. The sappers had opened up a hole where the front gates had been, and the infantry had crept in behind the falling wall of black arrows to deal with any who survived the onslaught.

Jonah tried not to look at the dead. Carts loaded with corpses were being taken out of the castle in a steady stream. He knew what his arrows did, but it didn't mean he had to like it. He considered himself cowardly for actively ignoring how his moments of calm also resulted in the death of others. Firing the arrows felt good. Yet as he saw the wagon loads of dead, that very same thought made him sick.

The Empire always wins, he thought, *the sooner that lesson is learned, the better.*

He followed the carts with his gaze until they passed through a gate. It was then he saw the burst of white, as dozens of Logistics Officers scurried in and out of buildings, already conversing with the survivors of the siege and organising them into queues.

How long would it have taken the white-suited bureaucrats to break down the local language? Hours? Minutes? Jonah often wondered how it was possible for them to dissect the essence of a language so quickly and precisely.

Just as the Imperial Army honed the skills of its soldiers into specialised and elite troops, so too did the Office of Logistics with its personnel. The white-suited officials could remember hundreds of laws, speak dozens of languages, perform amazingly complex mental mathematics on the spot and sort out logistical nightmares in minutes.

Yet the most important function of a Logistics Officer was the ability to sense who in the population carried the holy seed or cradle of fertility within them, with but a touch of their hand. Their order was a blend of cleric and clerk, and yet, as they so fondly reminded others, they were also the very bones upon which the empire survived, hence the white uniforms.

The Logistics Officers, in those clean uniforms, stood out like white roses amongst the brambles of the dirty, battle-worn people around them. And as Jonah watched the group, he could see the words of the officials cut through the fear and animosity of the conquered crowds just as surely as if they had been wielding swords. A group of local people dressed in very rich clothes were herded together and seated at a table across from a white-suited officer. The Logistics Officer wore the badge of a magistrate, and was no doubt flushing out secrets, local politics, and an assortment of data of every kind.

Another Officer sat at a table outside a building now infested with white-suited officials. An orderly queue of people waited in line, looking sad and dejected. Each waited their turn to come to the table. It was most likely a census table. Jonah had seen this before.

The Logistics Officers would create records of the names, family trees, trade skills, current dwelling, sum of their holdings, and anecdotal notes on every person left in the town, for these people were now Eurans and expected to be productive citizens. The Empire's records and bureaucrats were as ruthlessly efficient as any of its armies.

Jonah walked by another group and caught a snippet of the conversation. Something about how to properly honour the dead. Made sense: these Logistics Officers were encountering a new culture for the first time in centuries. It almost seemed odd that the Officers hadn't already known the traditional burial rites as they would have for any town in the Empire. Part of the resilience of the empire, however, was how it incorporated so many local customs and tried to keep the status quo. As long as taxes, labour, and loyalty flowed the right way, which was always towards Eura city, the Empress would be happy. Some Imperial rules trumped local ones, but as long as those rules were adhered to, people could go about their business almost as if the Empire had never arrived.

Jonah's fingers felt raw, despite the leather gloves he had worn, but it was worth it. The castle had finally surrendered. If they had been in Eura, the castle would have opened their gates as soon as they had landed. The Imperial standards floating above the army would have been enough. Hard lessons had been taught to those who resisted the Empire, and it looked like those lessons would have to be repeated to those who lived in these green lands.

Jonah's legs wobbled and he steadied himself against the wall of a quaint little house. *Thatch and plaster.* He looked up at the white walls and followed the dark lines of the thick oak beams. He smiled. Some of the mountain villagers in Northern Sandahar province built houses like this ... and with this thought a memory tried to work its way to the surface. There had been some big gathering of his clan, the Shi. He and Ilene had gone together. She had been angry with him for some reason. *What had we been fighting about?*

A headache blasted into him, and Jonah fell into the muck and mud of the street. It was all he could do to keep his head out of it. He closed his eyes and could do nothing but hold himself in this position until the wave of pain, vertigo and nausea subsided. When it did, he was left shaking.

"Over here, Jonah!" Fin waved down to him, but then his voice caught. "What are you doing down in the muck there?"

"I – uh ..." Jonah tried to answer, but it was all he could do to breathe steadily. A few moments more on his knees and he'd be alright.

"Here," Fin said. He had come down the stairs and pulled Jonah to his feet as if he were a child. "Looks like you might literally need a helping hand, friend." Fin was smiling, but there was concern in his eyes.

"I'm alright, Fin." Jonah breathed easier as his vertigo and headache began to subside. However, the headache had sapped every last speck of energy from him. "Though I wouldn't mind some help up those stairs."

Fin practically had to carry him up the last few steps as his legs began to wobble again. Thankfully the keg of ale was not far along the battlements, and before Jonah knew it he had a mug of dark ale in his hand and a spot at which to lean against the wall. Unsurprisingly, Branson was slouched beside him, also mug in hand.

"Another headache?" Branson whispered quietly to him.

"Yes, I don't know what brought it –" Jonah began.

"Best not to think about it." Branson cut him off. "I'll brew you the tea when we're finished up here."

"You're good to me, Branson," Jonah said.

"Probably too good," Branson huffed back, but there was no anger in it. Jonah's old friend hid his concern better than Fin, but Jonah could see it all the same.

They sat sipping their ale while they watched the Imperial messengers and arrow collectors running back and forth below. They moved with such speed it made Jonah exhausted just looking at them. Before his very eyes the buildings, which had just a moment before looked like pincushions, were being revealed in all their humble glory.

"Do you think they ever get mad at us?" he asked, pointing his mug down at some of the arrow collectors. "They bring us those tidy bundles of arrows, we fire them off into the air, and then they have to go and fetch them and bundle them back up, over and over again." He took another sip of the dark ale. He didn't know if he had ever tasted anything so good in his life. "That would get on my nerves I think, if I had to do their job."

“Each piece of the great machine does its part,” Branson answered, his words already beginning to slur. “Discipline is the backbone of the Imperial Army.”

“Thanks, drill sergeant.” Jonah rolled his eyes. “I’d keep a bundle for myself so I would know that at least one bundle would stay tied.”

“You wouldn’t. That’s stealing from the Empire, technically. You’d get the skin flayed off your back for a measly bundle of foot-arrows.” Branson finished the last of his ale and let the wooden mug slap against the stone floor. “Them collectors, they have their own pride. They do a good job and do it fast, there’s satisfaction in that.”

“I suppose.” Jonah finished his own ale and looked sadly at the wooden bottom of his mug. But before he even thought of the poor ale’s demise, his mug was snatched out of his hand and replaced with a full one. He grinned, already feeling the effects of his first mug.

Fin grinned over at him and Branson. “You couple of old farts will be snoring on each other’s shoulders in another five minutes I reckon.”

“Not all of us are built like bloody oxen,” Branson growled at Fin; but his heart wasn’t in it as he smiled when his own ale was replenished.

“Built like gnarled roots by the looks of you.” Fin winked down at them. “Good thing too, from some of the maps I’ve seen the Logistics officers recover it looks like we found a type of empire on this side of the sea. Salucia is what the locals call it. We landed in but one of nine nation states. The Prince’s gamble might end up making him Emperor.”

“How big did it look?” Branson asked.

“It’s at least half the size of the Euran Empire,” Fin replied.

“Empress save me; my feet won’t make it half that far.” Branson cringed as he rubbed a foot.

“Oh!” Fin stood up and pointed. “Here, stand up for a second, you’ve got to see this.”

Jonah clasped Fin’s outstretched hand and the big man hauled him and Branson to their feet. “What are we looking at?”

“Just there.” Fin pointed to an archway on the other side of the courtyard below them.

Jonah followed the line of Fin’s finger and saw a warrior walking with head held high down the street. She was clad from head to toe in metal and being escorted by no less than seven of the Eternal Hand.

“Their word for her is ‘*Syklan*’,” Fin said, “and I pray to the Empress I never meet one of them on the battlefield.”

The Syklan’s armour wrapped around her body like a dark grey second skin. The heads of snarling sea beasts were carved into her pauldrons, each one housing a strange globe in its maw. Jagged spikes lined her vambraces and adorned the knuckles of each gauntleted hand. The helm itself was almost skeletal.

Jonah felt the hairs rise on his skin as a shiver went down his spine. She looked like a demon from children’s fairy stories. Even under all that metal she walked with a deadly fluid grace, bespeaking her skill. Despite being all the way up on the battlements, Jonah didn’t feel he was safe. It was like watching a leopard calmly walk amongst them. She made the Eternal Hand seem more like her honour guard than her captors.

“Seven of the Eternal Hand? That seems excessive.” Jonah could see the seventh member of the elite royal guard trailing the other six. He was holding an engraved war hammer with a wicked spike on its back. Thin lines of gold ran along the hammer and converged in small circles of gold near the handle, head, and spike. The gold seemed too decorative to be utilitarian. Why put soft metal into a bludgeoning weapon? It didn’t make much sense.

“Seven might not be enough.” Fin said.

The calm in his voice unsettled Jonah somewhat. He heard the admiration in Fin’s words.

Branson spat at the sight of her. “She’s human, same as what we got up here. Put an arrow through a gap in that armour, she'll bleed and die just the same."

"I don't know," Fin said. "They say when that hammer of hers struck, lightning cracked out of its end. Men went flying as if they were toys. Those orbs on her shoulders glowed like magic."

"Hmm, that might explain the gold," Jonah said. "All the precious metals conduct energy, and gold is the best of them. Interesting. But how could she generate such a large charge in the first place? The armour must act as an enormous capacitor of some sort." Jonah was so enthralled by the woman and her story that he had postulated out loud without a second thought. The sudden silence around him, however, stopped his train of thought dead in its track. He turned and saw Fin and several of the other Black Rain staring at him. Branson's eyes were wide with panic.

The ale had loosened his tongue. Not many in Eura were as well schooled as the Fecund Blood, especially in the sciences. No commoner who trained as an archer their whole life would know such things. Jonah had just blundered terribly. He had to think of something quick.

"Oh!" Branson snapped his fingers as if remembering something, and then guffawed in laughter. "That's from *The Wizard and the Metal Man.*" Branson rolled his eyes and then looked at his fellow bowmen. "You know the play? By Hindelion?!" Branson stepped up to Jonah and ruffled his hair. "Quick, this one is. It was a line by the Wizard, we saw the play a couple nights before we set sail from Port Barrier."

A few feigned nods of recognition – most likely they didn't want to appear thick. The lie spread just enough confusion to distract them.

"Sorry," Jonah said, "I like Hindelion's plays and thought that would be funny. Guess it only works for those of us who like the theatre." He tried to look suitably embarrassed but wasn't sure how many would buy their story.

“Strange sense of humour,” Fin said, shrugging it off, and looked back at the Syklan woman as she passed below them. “She killed five of the Hand before they got a hold of her.” Fin shook his head. “Dark magic I say.”

“Five of the Hand is it?” Branson laughed. “And who’d you hear that from? Come on, even you know better than to listen to them rumours. Next we’ll hear they can change into animals or sprout wings from their backs and fly. Give it a rest, Fin.” Branson went back to his place against the wall to nurse the last of his ale.

“Both of those things are also in Hindelion plays,” Jonah quipped, this time getting a few chuckles and head shakes from the bowmen around him. He hoped it was enough.

“You look at the Hand.” Fin pointed down. “They’re giving her a lot of space, as if they’re still wary of her. I ain’t never seen one of the Hand worried about anyone.”

Jonah saw what Fin was alluding to. Each of the Hand held twin-bladed staves in guard position and looked ready for an attack at any moment. He thought there was a sliver of truth in Fin’s idea, and wondered if this woman was the reason the Commanders had been spooked earlier this morning. He wouldn’t blame them. A warrior clad all in metal wielding a flaming and sparking hammer would unsettle anyone.

Head to toe in dark grey steel, Jonah thought to himself. A person wouldn’t last an hour in armour like that upon the Dissorian sands. They’d cook inside that steel like just as surely as a stew did in a pot above a fire.

The Syklan left the courtyard and was escorted to the church, which now flew the Prince’s flag.

“Can you get any closer to ‘*letting a sand lion into your tent*’ without having an actual lion?” Jonah said as he watched the woman disappear into the church. He doubted he would have let that woman within a hundred yards of him if he were the Prince.

His thoughts had somehow led back to the beginnings of a headache, so he switched to more pleasant things. “Any more of that ale?” he asked, breaking the stunned silence which had settled over the tired archers around him.

“Another sip for all, I’d guess,” the man pouring from the cask said.

“I’ll have mine now then,” Jonah said handing over his cup.

The archers sat down to rest their bodies and watched as the town returned to some semblance of order below them. They rested, for they knew tomorrow would mean marching to the next town.

A town which Jonah hoped was devoid of Syklans.

4 - Hunting in the Night

The plan was executed perfectly; it was truly a work of collective genius. But now my mind has gone a bit numb from watching the devastation on my monitors. The raw power of nature is truly awesome to behold, and my colleagues would be amazed to know Kali is even more effective than anticipated.

Their loss was regrettable. They were loyal and committed members of our cause.

But there can be only one monster left alive to see this through, and I am he. The rest would not have made it to the end if I had not the force of will to lead them. In that, they were as guilty as everyone else, and therefore had to die.

I've reset civilisation so we can try again. I've given us a chance for redemption, a chance to prove we should be allowed to continue as a species, and it only cost the lives of a few billion unworthy parasitic souls.

The world would tell you it was an easy price to pay, akin to cutting off a gangrenous limb to save the body.

Eventually, I know I will mourn, the shock of this will wear off, and I'll have to live with our decision; but for now I cheer as I watch Mother Nature wipe opulent city after opulent city right off the map.

I'll cry bitter tears later, but right now, I cry out in victory.

- *Journal of Robert Mannford, Day 000 Year 00, 2nd Entry*

Thannis

Narrows, Aluvik

Tonight all Thannis's planning came to fruition. His most complicated trap would culminate in his sweetest kill. It would work. It had to.

Thannis had waited so long. Nearly two months of hiding, of playing a role, of instituting the right rumours and half-truths – but tonight's reward would be unique. *It will all be worth it.* The thought made Thannis's body quiver with anticipatory pleasure.

He caught himself daydreaming, and his sharp mind reprimanded his slip in character. He could give no outward sign of his real intentions. The guards would be looking for things out of place. *Only a few hours more of this charade,* he told himself. Everything was in place; the only thing left was to play his role to perfection. Any slip and it would all unravel, for his prey tonight was intelligent, wary, guarded and armoured against the very act Thannis was about to attempt.

Thannis smiled reservedly to the high-ranking nobles who had stepped ahead of him in the queue leading into the Aluvikan Grand Hall. He was to appear to be a very proper, dark, and brooding gentleman tonight. His alias was on the list and expected to attend, though was also of low enough rank to warrant very little notice. In reality, however, Thannis was in fact the Crown Prince of Nothavre, and there were dozens of people in attendance who knew him, would jump to appease him, and would ruin his trap and shatter the illusion he was weaving. Thus, he wore a disguise, which he was confident in, but still ... there was always that chance.

The risk only added to his pleasure.

Thannis climbed the stairs with perfectly measured steps, waiting his turn to be let in. He was nearly at the top and could now see through the arching doorways and into the Grand Hall. He felt a flutter of excitement at the entrance, but not from the splendour of the high vaulted white ceilings soaring overhead, the gold leaves and intricately painted vines on the carved marble columns, or tapestries hanging like silken ribbons. No, Thannis had grown up with riches and splendour. The excitement was instead because she was down there, walking through the throng of nobility just as a magnet moved through iron filings.

Though outwardly Thannis's face showed the appropriate level of impression from the lavishness of the ball, his persona of a young brooding noble showed a flicker of spirit. Not enough to displace the stoic handsomeness he wanted to portray, but just enough for the doorman to notice it – and dismiss it as a typical reaction.

"Name, sir?" The man's Aluvikan accent was thick upon his words but Thannis had no problem understanding. Emulating accents was one of his greater accomplishments.

"Lord Michael de La Quan." Thannis gave the name while continuing to display the proper level of boredom with this ritual. He knew his alias was on the list. He had seen to that detail weeks ago, even ensuring a small amount of drama about whether Lord Michael would go or not. In truth, this was an easy alias as there really was a Lord Michael, one who looked remarkably similar to him and had been planning to attend. The man would wake up a few nights from now in his bed, wondering just what had happened in the past few days. It would have been easy to kill Lord Michael, but a real life doppelganger was not something you discarded so easily.

Thannis smiled politely and waited as the doorman checked the list for his name. *Hurry up, you imbecile.* He squashed his impatience down. His cravings had reached an almost unbearable limit, and he could feel himself becoming edgy. He imagined his hunting knife ripping open the man's throat. The thought gave him some respite from his urges.

"Of course, my Lord, go right in if you please." The doorman bowed, and Thannis was surprised to catch a hint of a downturned lip at the sound of his fake Nothavran name. *Even Michael de La Quan should have been shown more deference than that.* Could it be that the High King's imposed peace was already beginning to chafe? Typically, Thannis would revel in the chance to stir up the old hatreds between Aluvik and Nothavre, but tonight his other mischiefs took precedence.

He scanned the room as he entered, making himself see it slowly. He re-checked his exits, noting that a large display of flowers had been moved since yesterday and was now in front of what looked like a locked door. Thannis subtracted that exit from his plan and continued cataloguing the relevant details of the room: the positioning of the guards, any rotations, where they were scanning. He checked for blind spots should he need to use them, and quickly noted the best objects to use as distraction or weaponry. It was a routine Thannis had drummed into himself which helped him to remain focused and sharp. There would be time for glorifying excess and abandoning control later.

His height allowed him to see over most of the crowd, apart from the occasional spindle of long, vibrant feathers woven into several intricate hairstyles. He smiled appropriately at the pair of women whispering to themselves as he passed by. He gave them just enough to stroke their egos, but not enough for them to think about pursuing anything further. Tonight, Thannis wanted to float through this crowd like a ghost, and then trap the attention of the most exotic prize here.

He was confident his looks and ability to flirt could entice one of these local belles into his trap instead, if things went wrong tonight; but it would be a hollow consolation.

All thoughts of a back-up plan vanished as the crowd broke in front of him, and then there she was, the beauty Thannis had been searching for.

Elise Syun, daughter of the Xinnish Queen, was a princess of exquisite beauty with no equal. Her long silky black hair hung down over bare shoulders. Soft pale skin ran down her plunging neckline, hinting at perfectly shaped breasts. Her dark red dress with silver embroidery hugged her exquisite figure. She drew the gaze of every man in the room

– but seduction was not his game tonight. She would see through such an obvious trap. Elise Syun had probably been through dozens of kidnapping scenarios and would recognise one when it appeared, so there was danger in his plan yet. She still might not take the bait. The uncertainty made his heart beat hard in his chest; he would have to play this just right.

Thannis noted the two fully armoured guards by her side. One was wearing santsi globes in his pauldrons and looked to be Asgurdian was Captain Ole Sigurn, a fully knighted Syklan, noted for being absolutely devastating with shield and sword. To Princess Elise's other side was the Hafaza, Henriette Gelding, noted for her almost artistic violence with the long-bladed spear she held and her devastating blasts of Presence. Thannis forced himself to keep his breathing even and his heart rate down.

Ole Sigurn or Henriette Gelding would each have been worthy and extremely challenging targets themselves, yet he was after an even greater prize than them. The extra danger they posed made tonight all the more tantalising.

Thannis would have all three before the night was done if things went to plan.

He stalked the trio through the throng of tailored suits and elegant dresses as a tiger might a deer through tall grass. He found a spot along the line of those hoping to greet the princess, and waited for his turn. When Princess Elise let her hand be kissed by the person three places down from him, he subtly reached into his pocket and let the tiny glued ball of explosive powder roll onto the floor. From the corner of his eye, he saw it roll a few rows behind him. The slender line of incendiary thread was still attached to the copper thimble in his pocket. He placed his finger in the thimble and let his other fingers touch the small, expensive santsi globe in his other pocket. The stored energy within the globe flowed into his hand and he began to feel the energy within the globe.

Siphoning was a skill few could master, and fewer still could become strong and subtle enough to make it useful, yet Thannis had found he was abnormally gifted in this somewhat magical skill. He had found from a young age that he was sensitive to the energy fields around him and could siphon off huge amounts of the energy from the world around him. He would channel and direct that flow of energy into objects for spectacular effect. The santsi globe he held in his pocket, made from specialised sands and glass, was akin to a type of capacitor, one which the person siphoning could draw stored energy. Pushing the energy out of the body usually required a conductive metal of some sort for the best transference. Thus, as Thannis concentrated on pulling the energy into him and felt the familiar icy-hot tingle, he made sure to place his index finger into the copper thimble he would use to direct that energy back out. Soon he began to feel the copper heat to the point where it began to hurt.

The damned person beside him was taking longer than he had guessed. He held onto the pain, letting the tingle grow in his hand until his fingers began to numb. It was going to be close.

Princess Elise nodded to the person beside him, politely indicating that the conversation was over. Thannis forced himself to keep his relief hidden. He cleared his throat to cover up the slight hiss, and he pushed the remaining energy into the copper thimble. He felt the slight release of pressure as the incendiary string lit. No one noticed the tiny flick of flame leave his pocket, as his throat-clearing was as much of a social faux pas as spitting when meeting a princess. The crowd around him would be looking at the response of Princess Elise to such a crude man.

"Your Highness," Thannis said, and bowed. He forced himself to keep from cheering as she extended her hand mechanically.

A loud snap exploded three rows behind him as the explosive ball went up. The crowd jumped, women and men gasped in surprise. Thannis took his opportunity and put the note into the princess's outstretched hand. Their eyes met, and he deftly squeezed the note into her grip as he kissed the top of her hand. "A pleasure, Your Highness. Lord Michael De Le Quan at your service." He motioned with his eyes to her guards. Ole and Henriette had weapons ready and were scanning the crowd, who were all in turn quite bewildered, as any trace of what had made the noise had disappeared.

Princess Elise caught his look. Thannis shook his head almost imperceptibly and then politely stepped back into line, averting his eyes in an obvious move to draw no further attention to himself.

"Someone must have stepped on a glass ball perhaps," Henriette said, her Hafaza robes shifted to display her scaled armour beneath.

Ole simply grunted, sounding much like the bear he resembled.

Princess Elise stared at Thannis for a heartbeat longer. Thannis flexed his jaw to show tension and a bit of anxiety.

"Princess?" Ole asked, and his hand drifted closer to his sword as he took a step towards Thannis.

Thannis held his ground, keeping in character, eyes down but displaying a slightly heightened measure of anxiety, as if he were about to be revealed. He let his eyes dart nervously up to Princess Syun. He let his crossed hands relax, and his fingers tapped out the hidden code he had saved for just this moment. Each finger of his right hand tapped his thumb and then reversed the procession.

Princess Elise's eyes widened for the briefest of moments. "Ole," her voice snapped, "I'm sure Henriette is right, nothing of consequence." Princess Elise flicked her hand dismissively. "Let's move on."

The elation Thannis felt nearly rocked him, but he held his character: letting everyone see he was appropriately chastised and nervous from his encounter. Nothing out of the ordinary, just someone who had slightly embarrassed themselves. No need to pay attention.

He waited for another minute until it was polite to leave the line. He melted back into the crowd and found a spot where he could watch unobserved.

Princess Elise almost rushed through the rest of those who waited to introduce themselves, and her hands opened the note almost immediately after her last obligatory greeting.

RJ is alive. He waits for you. Thannis mouthed the words he knew Elise Syun was reading. He gave her credit, for Elise did not pop her head up right away to frantically scan the crowd for him. Instead, she folded the note carefully and placed it in the small handbag she carried. She composed herself and began walking towards another group before she began to search for him.

Yet Thannis remained hidden in his chosen blind spot. It was not yet time for the second part of the trap. He needed the Princess's mind to dwell on the message for a time yet. He needed her to work herself up into enough of a frenzy to do something stupid.

She had been so close to him that his anticipation had nearly overwhelmed him. His heart was pounding, but things were going well. This was what he lived for.

The next half hour was spent carefully navigating the crowd so Princess Elise did not catch even the remotest glimpse of him. He would turn his head at the right moment, or begin talking to someone in the right position to block the Princess's view of him. His height made the task more difficult, but his actions would add to the mystery surrounding his cryptic message.

Finally, the band began to play, and the nobility started to take their positions for part of the night's entertainment and the first dance of the evening. It was time to begin stage two of his plan.

* * *

Thannis took a deep breath and filled his lungs with the intoxicating night air. Things were going very well so far.

He had waited until after the first dance so as to surprise Princess Elise when he appeared next to the dance floor with an air of urgency she could not ignore. She had taken the bait and sought him out. Thannis had made sure to make gestures to indicate that they were being watched and it was possible their words were being overheard. For who could be certain how many people here were in the employ of her nefariously untrusting mother, Queen Marin Syun? He propositioned the Princess for a dance, indicating that it was the only way to talk more intimately. Captain Ole Sigurn had looked as if he wanted to snap Thannis in half right there, but he had truly hooked Princess Elise. She had seen the utmost seriousness in the look Thannis had given her.

***

During the dance, Thannis had relayed details of how Princess Elise's secret love, Robert Jameson, had gone missing. He told his prepared story about Robert going into hiding because suspicions were getting too close to the truth concerning their affair.

"Robert told me to use the hand signal," Thannis had whispered in her ear. "What does it mean?"

"Nothing of consequence," Princess Elise had said. Yet Thannis knew it was anything but inconsequential. He knew the little rhythm of finger tapping was a nervous habit of Robert's, one which he only exhibited in the private company of Princess Elise. It seemed to indicate Robert's excitement when the two talked about their forbidden future, for Elise Syun was publicly known to be promised to Maric Uuliath, Prince of Asgur. The scandal of falling in love with Robert, a minor noble from Kenz, would unravel the political marriage and aggravate tensions between Xin Ya and the Salucian Union.

It was all very political, passionate, and best of all, secret. Thannis had exploited these facts, and it had led to Princess Elise coming to meet him tonight in the Forest Gardens, where he had assured her it was safe to relay the rest of the message from Robert.

Of course, Thannis had to allow her to be accompanied by her fearsome bodyguards. Otherwise the Princess would have been too suspicious of a trap. But he was still confident he had sufficient information to separate her far enough from the two guards to make his plan work.

Thannis forced himself to take another deep breath. He closed his eyes and calmed himself once more as a moment of doubt washed over him. *She might not come. Was it enough? Does she still suspect a trap?* Then he quieted the questions in his head. Princess Elise was not yet very late, and the hunter did not give away his position because the deer was being cautious.

So he would wait. Things were not over yet, he had planted his bait well, and in his estimation Princess Elise had gobbled it up. It would still work. His nerves were on fire, jittery with excitement. The ending would be so sweet, so rich.

To calm himself, he went over the important details he had tortured out of Robert Jameson. The man had been particularly sensitive about losing fingers, and Thannis had revelled in the sweet energy that fear had released. After the first two fingers, Robert had given him everything Thannis needed, such as key phrases and peculiar habits. Robert had talked about their plans for the future as well, and with that information Thannis had drawn Elise that much closer. Everything he used were things which only she and Robert would know.

He growled inwardly thinking about how his father would actually approve of the removal of Robert Jameson, and even the death of Elise Syun. Anything to keep Kenz and Xin Ya at each other's throats and churning out opportunities for exploitation. It galled him to further any agenda of his father's, but this time he couldn't avoid it.

It was then Thannis heard the crunch of stones on the garden path. He listened – yes, three sets of feet. They were here.

His hands shook with excitement as he re-checked his knives.

This was it.

The forest was thick with night mist. Moonlight trickled through the bows of the giant cedar trees above him in the small clearing. Now he stepped out of the shadows into that moonlight so they could see him.

He said nothing and did not move as they approached, waiting for Princess Elise to set the scene. It would allow her to feel some control over the situation. Which must, of course, be screaming at her as suspicious. Best to keep her guessing.

"How do you know Robert?" Princess Elise demanded; all pretence of propriety had disappeared. He could see her heartsick worry.

Love is such weakness – disgusting really, Thannis thought with a grimace, and he focused instead on the imminent kill and found himself almost trembling, this close to the end. Yet his face portrayed nothing but the gravity of the situation.

"Robert is a friend of mine. We met at court in Nothavre. As you know, Robert's family has many ties to the canvas industry as well as several trade contracts within the Nothavran shipbuilding guild," Thannis began. Every part of this story was true, in so far as the real Michael De Le Quan had known and dealt with Robert Jameson. "I owe Robert my life. I was on the *Heraldry* with him when it floundered off the coast of Tawa. Robert was the one who dragged me and several of my travelling companions from the water," Thannis explained. All of it, amazingly, still true. "Robert knew he could trust me to get the message to you."

He stopped talking and allowed Princess Elise to digest this new twist and connect his story to those she knew of Robert. The next part was the crux, the fulcrum upon which his night balanced.

"The message?" Princess Elise demanded with bated breath.

Thannis was about to speak when he stopped, noticing Henriette shift her stance to lean slightly closer, just as he had hoped – indeed known – she would. He let his eyes dart back and forth so only Princess Elise could see, and then he whispered, "Princess ... how well do you know and trust your bodyguards?" Then he let his eyes flick towards Henriette.

Recognition blossomed a split second later. Princess Elise had just had her suspicions confirmed about her Hafaza bodyguard's loyalty. Henriette Gelding was selling information about Princess Elise to many outside the line of Syun while also relaying every move to Queen Marin Syun to keep herself ingratiated with the Royal Family.

Princess Elise turned quickly and caught Henriette's heightened attention to their conversation. Ole was also now leaning in to hear what was happening. "You two will stay positioned there. Lord De Le Quan and I shall move to the bench over there."

Princess Elise pointed to the only furniture within the clearing. The guards would still see them, but the bench was definitely out of earshot, and it was that bench which was precisely the reason Thannis had chosen this part of the garden.

Ole grunted again, and Henriette looked slightly embarrassed and angry, but they both nodded curtly as they could easily see the bench.

Together they walked over, and Thannis's heart began to pound. This was it.

He offered his hand to Princess Elise as he indicated her to sit first. She put her hand on his wrist and he guided her to the right side of the bench.

"Ouch," Princess Elise quipped as she jerked slightly, as if she had just sat on something sharp, for indeed she had. Her hand went down to the side and touched the grey painted thorn which had blended in with the bench. “Odd,” she said as she turned back to look at Thannis.

“Not really so odd, as I placed the thorn there,” Thannis said with a quick smile. “No doubt your lips are beginning to feel numb. Most fascinating plant: it is a type of belladonna bramble which grows deep in the Vinda jungles. It has a very high level of atropine in the berries, but the interesting property of this particular strand is its ability to leave the unfortunate victim very conscious instead of incapacitating them.”

Princess Elise tried to scream for help, judging by the look of desperation in her eyes and the way she tried to open her mouth. But the scream never came as her body inevitably started to go numb and rigid.

“Don’t worry, it won’t last very long, but you’ll have an excellent seat for the show.” Thannis’s heart was pounding, and he couldn’t help gloating, though he knew he shouldn’t yet, as things were about to become chaotic.

“Help!” Thannis cried stepping back from Princess Elise, waving his arms in frantic apprehension. “Something happened to her! Help!”

Both bodyguards sprang forward, Captain Ole Sigurd pulled free his thick sword and grabbed hold of his huge shield at full tilt. Henriette Gelding followed him ten steps, stopped to plant her bladed spear in the ground and pulled the bow from her back with practised fluidity. She turned to cover Ole’s back as both, no doubt, suspected an ambush. She had an arrow notched and ready, looking for any sign of movement behind them as Ole barrelled into Thannis, slamming him aside to reach Princess Elise.

“Princess! What has been done?!” Ole reached the Princess’s side and quickly surveyed the scene. Thannis counted ten heartbeats before Ole found the thorn beneath Elise’s bottom.

“What have you –” Ole rounded but Thannis had recovered quickly from the bodyguard’s shove. He rolled out of the push and bounded to his feet after retrieving the throwing daggers he had hidden beneath the leaves. Ole was just in time to see Thannis finish the throw and watch the dagger whip through the air to embed itself up to the hilt in the side of Henriette's neck.

Ole bellowed like a giant bear and rose to his full height. Thannis had the fleeting thought that the man might actually be bigger than a bear. The thick sword carved the air with such force Thannis thought it could have cut right through a tree trunk.

He fell backwards, bending fluidly at the hips as he felt the wind from the heavy blade. Ole continued to charge as Thannis knew he would, for he had studied the man's practice sessions for weeks under another alias. Thannis would have but one chance at this. He somersaulted backwards forcing Ole to continue; then he let three of his throwing knives fly at Ole's face, holding one back. The giant shield went up, already humming with electric shock energy from the glowing santsi on Ole's pauldrons. Ole meant to deflect the blows and smash Thannis like a bug against the giant cedar behind him.

But Thannis knew this particular cedar, had rolled to it for a reason.

The shield lifted to protect Ole's face as Thannis let the last knife fly. It was the move Thannis had needed.

He stopped backtracking and shot forward onto his stomach and rolled to the side. His hands found the hilts of his long hunting knives beneath yet another hiding spot. He swiped out from his position as he rolled to his feet beside Ole. He felt the knife dig deep through leather and skin as he found the gap in the armour around Ole's ankle. The great man's leg buckled and, instead of crushing Thannis, the huge man's helmeted skull crashed into the tree.

A stroke of luck, and Thannis capitalised on it. He ran over and started plunging his knives into the tiny gaps in the huge man's armour. Two, three times through the gaps near the shoulders. The joints were the key: anywhere that needed movement revealed small openings, and as Ole thrashed to get Thannis off of him, more gaps presented themselves.

Eventually his strikes were enough to stop the huge man's limbs from responding, and at last Ole Sigurd lay trapped in a metal case beneath him. Thannis kicked open the face guard of the helmet.

"You'll rot in –" Ole started, but Thannis didn't let him finish as he drove his hunting knife down into the Syklan's exposed face.

It was then he heard whimpering from the bench. Ah – the atropine was wearing off. A bit early, but it would do.

"I was worried about this one." Thannis breathed a sigh of relief as he pointed his retrieved knife from Ole. "Big brutes just need to catch you once and it's all over. Good thing I've killed a dozen like him before. Father always did want me to train with the best."

Princess Elise started making scared noises as he walked over to her.

"You're going to run for me," Thannis said as he walked over and let his finger slide along her full lips. He could see the terror in her eyes and felt his body quiver. "The atropine will wear off shortly, but this will help."

He plunged another hollow thorn with a small bottle on its end into Elise Syun's arm. It contained a lovely surprise for her. He watched as her eyes widened in shock. "Adrenalin," he said with a smile, "should give you a bit of a head start."

He turned and threw thorn and empty bottle into the ferns and walked into the trees, finding shadows to cover his tracks.

Now all he had to do was wait, like a wolf stalking a deer.

* * *

A quail squawked in anger as it flew from its resting place off to Thannis's right. He had waited a full count of sixty before beginning his hunt, but the frightened bird was the sign he needed to set himself moving. He glided through the soft ferns and beneath the giant cedar trees like a wraith.

The absolute terror Elise Syun must now be feeling would intensify his experience. This would be the pinnacle of all his kills. So far it had been a glorious night.

He could hear Elise's footsteps, whereas his steps were light, deliberate, and perfectly balanced as he ran. He avoided fallen twigs and dry leaves on instinct. The night air was rich and sweet, it pumped through him, and he thought he could run forever on a night like this. He was able to loosen his tight control and live in the moment.

It was perfect.

Yet it was time to finish this, as Elise was getting too close to finding a way out.

Ferns parted, and he saw the red dress flash into the trees ahead of him. The moonlight shone off her long silky black hair; her pale skin glowed radiantly.

Five strides, lightning quick and silent, before he was in the air. Elise sensed him and turned, opening her mouth to scream.

Silver flashed in the moonlight.

The scream died on her lips with the kiss of Thannis's blade.

The dark brown pools of her eyes were wide with shock.

He felt her warm blood pumping through his fingers to the rhythm of his own pounding heart. Thannis wiped his blade on her dress and this time he did not try to calm himself. He stared into her eyes as he lowered her to the forest floor.

Her lips moved, but he had severed her windpipe. He smiled and stopped them moving with his finger.

"Don't try to speak, you will understand soon, my dear," he whispered into her ear.

He knelt and placed his hands on the sides of her head so he could better feel the life slowly ebbing away beneath him. He closed his eyes and began to siphon, pulling at the energy trying to escape the dying shell.

The enormous flow took shape and slammed into him. Elise's eyes shot open in horror.

Her energy surged through him and his skin was on fire, but inside was a pure icy rapture. Ecstasy overcame him, and his back convulsed under the torrent.

His world had become sweet euphoria, alive with the succulent blend of life and horror within the dying woman. Each time Thannis had done this, it was different; a revelation unmatched by anything else he had ever known.

There was nothing more worth living for than moments like these. Everything else paled in comparison.

Just as suddenly as it had begun, the energy began to ebb away, and his body shook with the effort of maintaining the siphoning link, but he wanted more. *Not yet. Not yet.*

But it was no use, the energy was gone. She was dead.

He looked down at the twisted features between his hands. It was as if Elise Syun now wore a grotesque mask of pain, revulsion and horror. It was not her. He had felt who she had truly been.

Thannis stopped siphoning and pushed the empty shell away in disgust. That was not how she had felt. She had been beautiful, delicious, wild. Like a caged lioness.

Each experience had its own flavour, just as each person lived a unique set of circumstances. Each act within their life altered the taste of the energy somehow, as if events were recorded uniquely upon the very soul.

Thannis wiped the blood from his hands and fell to the mossy floor. His body twitched with the remembered ecstasy, the intoxicating blend of pain and bliss which merged into one experience at their extremes.

The world now seemed to be less. The feel of a woman, the thrill of a proper duel, the delight of a plot coming to fruition were nothing to him now. Not compared to touching the very essence of what a person was, to have it course through him as an overwhelming rhapsody.

Only the incubi and succubi of old legends had been able to do such things. They called this power evil, called it an abomination.

They were all fools.

Thannis knew that what he could do was glorious, that nothing so overwhelmingly beautiful could be wrong. But now it was over, and far too soon, to his mind. He had planned and executed the perfect murder, had got to someone considered untouchable. He'd bested a renowned Syklan and an impressive Hafaza guard. It was time to take this to the next level, to operate in a hunting ground large enough to experiment hundreds of times over. One in which he could find people from all walks of life. For Thannis now knew he could get to anyone, and there was only one place he knew of in the world that fit his new criteria.

He left the already forgotten body where it was. Whatever allure it had once held had disappeared with Elise Syun's life. He didn't bother hiding the corpses; he knew it would take time for any pursuers to find out where Princess Elise had disappeared to. By then, he would be long gone.

Without a look back, Thannis disappeared from Aluvik like a whisper on the wind.

* * *

The forest remained still long after Thannis had left and as the sun began to rise. The wrongness of what had happened had left its imprint upon the very air. The stillness tensed further as the giant cedars watched a shadow slither towards the scene, detaching itself from the trees to stand softly beside the dead woman.

A sigh of annoyance slithered from its purple and black stained lips. The King of Nothavre would be happy with this result, but more needed to be added to the scene to delay those who were far closer to Thannis than the young prince presumed. The shadow was named Esmerak, who was a witch in the employ of Thannis's father.

Esmerak moved to grab the delicate porcelain body. Left like this, the body would prompt too many questions from the Senior Prefect, who was far too close to discovering the truth about these murders.

A hound's deep bark tore through the choking silence and Esmerak hissed in anger. She could hear the sounds of people crashing through the brush calling the dead woman's name.

She would have no time to fix this! The Senior Prefect must have already been in the Narrows. He must have been watching the royal gala. She slipped back into the darkness between the trees and watched as the constables in their long brown cloaks began to surround the body of Elise Syun.

Esmerak watched the constables gasp in horror as they rolled Princess Elise over and saw her vacant dark brown eyes screaming silently up to the heavens. Everyone seemed shocked, except for one, the Senior Prefect; he already had his pen out and was taking notes.

Esmerak would have to think of something else to distract this Senior Prefect. Her Prince had left too much of a mess this time.

5- Detritus

Orcanus, great servant of the deep
Harbinger to souls of the endless sleep

Great Grandmother, into your eye I peer.
The end of my wandering path has drawn near.

You must escort me down beneath the sea,
Lest my soul quiver and I try to flee.

Your black fins guide towards another plane.
Great Spirit, keep me safe, it's grown cold and my heart has begun to wane.

- *Poem originating somewhere in the Northern Shards – Chronicler Henrietta Martin in* A Study of Salucian Mythology

John Stonebridge

Narrows, Aluvik

John saw a single knife slash across the young girl's neck. Her skin was ghostly pale; the dark red stains on the detritus of the forest floor showed exactly where her colour had gone. The information around him told John Stonebridge that Elise Syun was quite obviously dead, but the patterns he saw also indicated exactly who had murdered this poor young girl.

A Xinnish girl. Another dead Xinnish girl lying at his feet. The spectres of John's past threatened to overwhelm his calm exterior, but he said a silent prayer to Halom and asked for forgiveness. Eventually, his memories faded and he forced his mind to focus on just *this* girl instead of the ghosts in his mind.

She was not just any girl either; she was a gods damned princess. The Xinnish Princess. Her nationality and race shouldn't matter in these modern times, but they did to a fossil like him. He knew that to be sinful, so John made a mental note to ask the local chaplain for absolution later. Now he forced himself to truly see the little girl he hadn't been able to protect.

Lady take him, he had seen too many dead Xinnish eyes, and John had nightmares aplenty without any more being added; yet these dead Xinnish eyes were different. Those eyes...they were *his* calling cards. They were the signature of the killer John had been chasing for months. It was always the eyes, looking strangely alive, as if frozen in a scream.

A bit like Keisha's after we found her. John's mind drifted to the old aching pain buried deep within his memories. His younger sister's eyes had screamed at him then as well, yet that had been different. That was nearly fifty years ago, a simpler and more violent time. But John still saw her face as clearly as if it had been yesterday. They had found Keisha face up in an alleyway, her tiny neck snapped as if it were a twig. Jefferson Akevan, a brutal bull of a psychopath, had been the one doing the snapping. That bloody animal had left Keisha lying there in the street like another piece of trash to be swept away in the gutters. *I shouldn't have left her. I should have been home.*

The decision he had made that night had haunted him for the past forty-eight years, and John knew it would follow him to his grave. *If I had been home, she would never have run away, she would have been safe.* He ground his teeth in an attempt to force his memories away once more. *I killed Akevan though*; at least he had given Keisha that. Not that the constabulary knew about it. He wouldn't be wearing the constabulary's long brown coat if they did.

John touched the dead leaves and soft soil beside the body. It was still sticky, as not all of the blood had soaked down through the forest floor yet. In another few hours the blood would be hidden, spirited away into the earth beneath his feet. The long fronds of the ferns, lying like a lime green carpet below the silent cedar pillars, would have drunk it in like a sour cocktail.

Even the ground has a taste for blood, he thought darkly. The forest took care to sweep its past away. Death was only another part of the cycle here.

A bird chirped high above in the canopy as a few rays of light slipped between the full cedar bows. *It would have been better for Keisha to die in a place like this. More peaceful.*

John stood up and motioned the waiting constabulary over to the body.

This was going to be bad, really bad. The Xinnish Princess murdered on Aluvikan soil. What a gods damned mess. This was going to go all the way up to the High King, it had to. If this monster could get to Elise Syun, heir to the Xinnish throne, then ... the thought didn't bear finishing.

Gods, this was bad.

A crow tried to land next to the body, no doubt after the eyes, and John waved it away angrily. "Mangy scrounger," he growled, "go find something else to pick at." The bird croaked a protest and flew back up to a branch just above the body. John eyed the crow silently as the brown-jacketed constabulary officers wrapped up Elise Syun's body. She was to be taken back to Narrows and her family, to be entombed with all the other Syun monarchs.

I take it back, he thought, *Keisha wouldn't have been better off here.*

"So what do you make of this then, Johnny? You don't mind if I call you Johnny do you?" Miranda Holvstad, his new junior partner, chirped beside him.

He fixed her with as hard a look as he could conjure. "Yes, I mind." He let the word hangs and his gaze linger until Miranda dropped her eyes. No one but Keisha had ever called him that, and John was going to keep it that way.

He looked over at the lithe Junior Prefect whom the constabulary had deemed it necessary to work with him. She was pale, hard, wiry, and had a crop of short dark hair, but what drew John's attention most was the bone ring punched through her eyebrow. That only meant one thing in this part of the Salucia: Xinnish.

She had to be bloody Xinnish. A dead Xinnish Princess and a Halom's damned fresh Xinnish recruit. He was surrounded by them. The bloody world was making it hard for him to forget things. Sure, Kenz and Xin Ya were allies now, but he still had vivid memories of scale-armoured Xinnish warriors butchering men and women he had fought shoulder to shoulder with during the Border Wars.

Yet that was thirty years ago, and everyone was expected to play nice now under the High King's Salucian Union.

"It's our guy," he grumbled, after letting her squirm under his angry gaze for long enough.

"You don't say. Details maybe?" Miranda said, quirking her eyebrow at him in obvious irritation.

He had hoped to cow whatever enthusiasm this Miranda Holvstad had, but his first attempt was shrugged off like water off a duck's back. John sighed to himself. *She's going to be hard work.*

"He can't be far off, right? Princess Syun went missing last night – so he's, what? less than a day ahead of us?" She seemed to be expecting a response.

"Astute of you," John replied coldly. He knew she didn't deserve his anger. She was supposed to be a good prefect by all reports: young, strong, determined and very sharp from what he had heard, but he found it difficult to forget the past. She idly touched the jagged bone ring on her brow and he shivered. *I remember when that meant they were going to kill you; now it's nothing more than a tic.* The world had moved on, he had to remember that.

John removed the wide-brimmed Akubra hat from atop his head. He always played with it when he was thinking. It was a good hat. His fingers played across its course texture, found the centre dent, shuffled down to the brim and back again; a familiar dance for his old fingers. "He hunted her," he began. "This was premeditated and carefully executed. Look at how well it was planned. That thorn we found has an extremely rare toxin on it, and there is a small mark on the Princess's right buttock suggesting she sat on it. That was no accident." John gestured back to the clearing where they had found the two other corpses, of Henriette Gelding and Ole Sigurn. "A single throw took the Hafaza down, straight through the neck from a dozen paces, and this same man somehow bested a fully armoured Syklan, a Captain no less. These bodyguards would never have let an armed man this close to the Princess, meaning the weapons used were already hidden in this spot."

John pointed back to the dead princess. "He let her run, even though he had her dead to rights with that toxin. He must enjoy these hunts, like it's some sort of game." John stood, "You will find no defensive wounds on the body, which indicates how incredibly fast and accurate our killer was. These are the same sort of precise cuts we've seen before."

John leaned back and pushed his fists into the small of his back and heard a satisfying pop. "We need to get a ship. He's got nearly four days on us judging by the body." He tried to regain a somewhat professional demeanour: the eyes of the corpse had unsettled him more than he wanted to admit.

"A ship?" She looked over to him.

"Yes, a bloody ship. Are you going to question everything?!" he growled, fighting the urge to yell at her and that ridiculous clipped accent of hers. "Just go get us booked on the fastest naval ship you can find, you bloody slant-eyed bone-worshipper."

There was a collective gasp from the officers around him, and John cursed himself for his misstep. *Stupid,* he cursed himself again, hating how, try as he might, he couldn't keep his bloody mouth shut. *I'm such a racist prick.* He eyed the white and navy shield shaped patch sewn onto the shoulder of her uniform jacket, the same as his. Two crossed sai pointed down, to symbolize defence, with the scales of the court behind them, and the rope of a meteor hammer encircling all of it. That crest, the practical dark brown uniform of the constabulary, and the odd Akubra hat had become symbols of safety to the new Salucian Union. That included safety from racism as well.

"Wait!" he growled before Miranda could run off. He was meant to be teaching her, not berating her or insulting her. For all his faults, John did believe in the constabulary and what they tried to do. He had to be better, he had to swallow half a lifetime of being racist and move on. He took a breath and forced himself to speak. He knew he should really be apologising, yet he couldn't make himself say the words. The best he could do was explain. "He's gone. This was a major assassination and I've ordered the constabulary to have the Narrows locked down. Our perpetrator is already in the wind." He pulled his hat back down on his head hard. "This killing was on another level. If he can get to Elise Syun..."

"He can get to anybody," Miranda finished, not giving any hint of being insulted. Rather, she was all ears, listening to what he had to say. She pulled a long, ornately carved calumet pipe from a coat pocket and packed a thumbnail-sized portion of tobacco into it. Small pictures of wasteland cats were carved into the flat sides of the bowl and stem. Miranda's hand-held flint-striker dropped sparks into the bowl.

John waited for her to take a few puffs. "Smoking gives you the wet cough you know," he said, smelling the full fruity smoke.

"Health tips? That's rich, coming from an old *Guilan* who drinks like a fish," Miranda said. Her use of racial slur was equally offensive as John's own, yet there was a playful sparkle in her eye when she delivered it.

John barked a laugh. "I haven't heard that one in years." *Guilan* was Xinnish and translated to something like 'white-skinned book fornicator'. At the time, it had enraged the Kenzians like nothing else, and was usually heard just before the Xinnish charged their lines. Gods, this kid had balls saying that to him. It made him smile.

He watched Miranda as she carefully fanned the smoke over herself and then towards the body of the young princess. It was a mark of respect for the dead. He had seen the ritual several times.

"So where would he go?" John asked. *If I'm meant to teach, I'll teach.* "Analyse the pattern." He reached into his pocket and pulled out his notepad. He had been taught to write and made sure he made good use of that skill. He recorded every detail of every crime scene he had ever been to on his notepads. You never knew when something which seemed insignificant at the time would turn out to be useful. He cleared his throat and began summarising his notes. "First some farming villages in Nothavre, then the same in Labran. Then the brother and sister in Tawa; the Singer and her guard in Wadashi; and the Princess and her guards now makes five in and around Narrows." John flipped closed his notepad. "What does that tell you?"

Miranda thought for a moment before pointing the butt of her pipe at him as if it were a conductor's baton. "The centres are getting larger each time. Narrows was the biggest so far. He's growing more confident and is escalating. He's either going to go after a harder target or try a much more complicated hunt."

John nodded, slightly surprised. "Right, so he's headed to ..."

"New Toeron would be my guess." Miranda spoke with confidence. "Palisgrad is too dangerous. The Paleshurians would tear the city apart looking for him and not care about collateral damage. Dawn would most likely be too uptight and boring for him, given the pattern of stalking beforehand. New Toeron, however, is so big he could hide for months and months on end before anyone even knew he was there, and it has an extensive selection of nightlife, and high-profile visitors. We need to find the ferries headed to the Shards."

John looked at his young Xinnish partner appreciatively. *Not bad, kid,* he thought. "Guess where a ferry is meant to leave for just this morning?" He grinned. "He's probably sitting on that boat right now waiting to leave the port. We need to get there first, but if I can't stop it from leaving, I want you to get us a naval ship, something fast and nasty. I'll meet you at the docks."

"Where are you going?" She stopped, and gave him a rather obstinate glare.

"You my mother now?" he snapped. "To question that fella they got locked up. Where d'you think? Now shut it and go get us a ship."

Miranda rolled her eyes but did as she was told.

"You there, big fella!" John waved over at one of the local constables. "Take me to the prisoner."

A bloody Xinnish partner. John shook his head. At least she's got spirit.

* * *

"What do you mean the travel request has been denied?" John asked the woman sitting behind the long wooden desk in the Narrows Constabulary office.

"I, uh, I have the paperwork right here," the mousy-looking woman squeaked back at him with an apologetic face. The woman gingerly handed him a written note with the Narrows Chief's seal stamped in red ink and a clearly lettered 'Denied' at the bottom of the request.

John looked behind the desk to the office. The High Constable was watching him through his office door.

Bloody Gary Hornwright, it had to be him, that little snake. John smiled politely and held up the request for the High Constable to see. "What sort of bureaucratic tripe is this?" he said, loud enough for the whole office to hear.

"I'm sorry, Prefect, the Chief is busy at the moment," the mousy clerk piped at him.

"Is he now?" John smiled down at the woman. "You won't mind if I check?"

John calmly unlocked the knee-high divider and pushed it aside. He caught the clerk's hand in his own as she tried to stop him. "You have lovely hands, my dear. Best use them for their intended purpose." He planted a kiss on the top of the one he held. She jerked it back in surprise.

"I won't be a moment. See that we're not disturbed," John said calmly.

A large young constable stepped in front of him with his brown coat hanging across his broad shoulders. He held up a hand, apparently meaning to stop him.

Poor, stupid kid.

John pretended to stumble, and the big Constable caught his arm reflexively, trying to help. "Careful, old-timer, don't want to get yourself hurt."

"It's Prefect, actually." John stood and snapped the butt end of the sai he had drawn against the young Constable's inner thigh. The young man went down in a heap as his leg buckled. "And I was about to suggest the same thing to you, son." John smiled and tipped his hat politely as he walked by. "Now, if you'll excuse me."

"Oh, Gary?!" John tapped the pommel of his sai on the door, "I just need a quick word with you is all." He tried the handle, but it was locked. He sighed and slid the request under the door. "Gary, come on now. I need you to explain this paperwork. Gary?" He reached into his pocket and found the leather-bound set of lock-picking tools.

The commotion in the office behind him was growing as the remaining constables sorted out who was next in line to challenge John.

"It is an unnecessary use of funds, you hooligan!" Gary sputtered from behind his door.

"No need to get personal," John said as he glanced over his shoulder. Two rather determined constables looked as if they had decided they needed to do something. John had to hurry.

"Screw it," John cursed, and slammed his sai into the door, took a step back and push-kicked with everything he had. The heel of his boot smashed into the butt end of his sai and blasted the blunted weapon right into the simple locking mechanism. The door flew open and John had the satisfaction of seeing Gary Hornwright practically piss himself.

"Did you know your door was locked, Gary?" John asked, and then slammed it shut and wedged a chair under the now broken handle and sat down upon it to barricade the two of them in.

"Gods damn it, John!" Gary seethed from a cowering position behind his desk.

John stooped down to pick up the denied request form on the floor. "So what I would really like to know, is why, in your infinite wisdom, you would believe it is not necessary to pursue a mass murderer who just killed the gods damned Xinnish Princess!?"

Gary visibly made an attempt to collect himself and puff out his chest. "Because we've already caught him."

"How's that?" John asked. He didn't believe it possible; even so, Gary Hornwright must actually be getting dumber with experience.

"The culprit is down in the holding cells as we speak." Gary held his chin out proudly.

"I see." John nodded, holding back the dozens of names he wanted to blast Gary with. He continued in as measured a tone as he could muster, "I'm sure you won't mind if I ask him a few questions then?"

"Be my guest, Senior Prefect," Gary said, "he's already confessed it all. We'd cornered him in an alley outside the palace grounds and he told us everything down to the last detail. He even told us about a few of his other murders. It's cut and dried, John."

"I'm sure." John shook his head. This was hopeless. "And I suppose you haven't locked down the port like I asked?"

Gary held his hands out in a placating gesture. "Hardly seems necessary when our man is already down in the cells."

It took everything John could muster to walk out of the room without impaling Gary Hornwright to the back wall with the flagpole sitting beside that trumped up toad's desk, but he managed it. John took his sai back from the big young constable on the way out, whose leg looked to be able to support his weight again. The kid would have a nasty bruise but no lasting damage.

"Come with me, Constable, I need to see this prisoner of yours," John said. The big lad looked surprised but jumped to obey.

John already had his pen out. There was something strange going on here, something other than the fact Gary Hornwright had managed to stay chief for so long.

It was time to start taking details. He looked up at the young constable, who was eager to help in a prefect's murder investigation. "Now where did they find this man who confessed to everything?"

John's pen began to fly across the page.

* * *

The cells were surprisingly adequate considering how the Narrows Constabulary had inherited a decrepit old tower for their offices. John could see the fresh-cut stone and new mortar framing sturdy iron-bar doors all along the corridors. The cells even had fresh straw beds. At least Gary could do this right.

As John walked along the corridor, he saw that most of the cells were empty. “The inmates out working today?” John asked the young constable, whose name he had gleaned was Ned.

“They’re up at the granite quarry today, up near Scatter’s Pike,” Ned replied. “High King has requested great stone obelisks along each of the major roadways to serve as landmarks.” Ned looked to John with a bit of a smile. “Prisoners have been so tired and sore for the past month they haven’t had a chance to think about escape.”

At that John nodded: similar systems of punishment were being incorporated all over the Union. If they had to feed prisoners and keep them healthy, they were damn sure going to make them work for it.

Ned took the keyring from his belt and pointed to a cell. “Here he is. Last door on the left.”

John looked at the wretched creature huddled in the corner of the cell and knew immediately that this was *not* the man he had been chasing for eight months.

“One of our constables cornered this one, says his name is Jerun Smitsen. Didn’t put up much of a struggle. Confessed to all the murders, talked about how he lured the Princess away to the woods,” Ned said.

“And Gary just swallowed the whole load. Halom take me,” John said as he flipped back a few pages in his notebook and cleared his throat to read. “Tell me, Ned, does this Jerun Smitsen look like ‘a tall, wide-shouldered, athletic, well-groomed, and attractive young man’?”

“No, not really. I mean, he could be young, although you’d have to clean and shave him to tell that." Ned lifted an eyebrow. "Why do you ask?"

John wiped his brow in frustration, "Because that's how Michael de La Quan was described by the doorman and two others who remember seeing the relatively low-ranking noble dancing with Princess Syun!"

Ned clamped his mouth shut and tried to look somewhere else before muttering, "I was just told to lock him up. I –"

"I know," John hissed, "just – shut up."

Ned nodded.

"So, Ned, what point would there be in having a desperate man, who quite obviously doesn't fit the description of our killer, confess to all of those murders?" John began writing a side note to make a formal complaint of incompetence against Gary Hornwright the next time he got back to a Prefect's Office.

"So this one is like a decoy?" Ned stated more than asked. "Which means this fella is here to delay the investigation, in my estimation."

John turned on his heel in amazement to look at Ned. "Halom be praised. Someone working here does have half a brain. And the point in delaying would be ... ?"

Ned squinted his eyes. "So the real killer could get away?"

"That's it," John exclaimed. "I'm going to recommend you for promotion, Ned."

Ned puffed out his chest a bit at that, but then worry seemed to strike him. "Shouldn't we get back out there then? The real killer is on the loose!"

"Calm down." John held up a hand. "You put a few things together and figure you're running the show. I've got a good idea where he's headed. Though if there hasn't been any delay or lock down at the ports I doubt we'll catch him before he makes landfall, regardless of the ship Miranda gets us."

"So why are you here?" Ned said, squinting once again in thought.

"To find out why someone would volunteer for a death sentence of course." John walked up to the cell, indicating for Ned to unlock the door. "So, Jerun, is it?" John said to the man still huddled in the corner.

The man twitched in response. "That's me." Jerun got to his feet slowly.

"And you killed Princess Elise Syun?" John asked, taking in the man's build before flipping to an entry about the murders in Wadachi. He read it silently to himself: "*The victim was roughly six and half feet tall, and nearly eighteen stone of hard-working muscle. Footprints suggest the victim attempted to struggle but the attacker quickly overwhelmed the resistance with precise cuts to the hamstring, wrist, knee, and shoulder. The victim was then cut upon repeatedly before death."* John stopped reading and looked back at Jerun's shaking hands. Two of his fingers had obviously been broken sometime in the past and healed into knobbly lumps. Definitely not hands which could slice tendons with pinpoint accuracy while a giant musclebound pit-fighter was trying to rip your arms out of their sockets.

"So why did you do it?" John asked.

Jerun stared straight ahead as if he were looking past him. "She acted like she wanted it, but then wouldn't give it up." The forlorn man looked back at John, straight into his eyes. "No one denies me and lives."

John stopped himself from laughing at the absurdity of it, for there was something not quite right about this man. He focused on writing down Jerun's words verbatim.

"And Halik Wu in Wadashi?" John asked, "The big pit-fighter? Why him?"

Jerun eyes went distant once again, and his passionless voice regurgitated the tripe John now knew he was meant to say. "He was arrogant, showing off his muscles to all those women. Pride is a sin, Mr.

Stonebridge."

Now that was interesting. John hadn't given his name, but the other details were close enough. He made a show of flipping calmly through his notebook. "Tell me about the eyes. Why do you place coins on them?"

Jerun looked past him again, but this time there was a twitch. Sweat began to break out on his brow, and his body started to shake, and his eyes darted back and forth frantically. "The coins ..." he started, and looked almost ill. "It's a Tawan tradition, an offering to Orcanus for the dead who are returned to the sea."

This answer had been different: Jerun had looked down at the floor this time, and the body language had changed. *He's afraid,* John thought. *He's been conditioned to answer somehow.* This was getting stranger and stranger.

"It's not him," John said, still watching Jerun. "Ned, put him back in his cell. The murder charges are to be dropped. However, this man is deliberately hampering an investigation of the His Majesty's Constabulary – a crime which carries its own sentence if I'm not mistaken. Have the paperwork drawn up."

Ned nodded and grabbed Jerun by the arm.

"No!" Jerun struggled against Ned's strength. "That's not true. I killed them people. It was me. I told you everything."

"There are no coins, Jerun," John said quietly. "That was a lie, but you didn't know."

"No. I killed them people. It was me. I lured the Princess into the woods, we played a game, and I killed her, slit her throat. It was me. It was me. It was me ..." The prisoner's eyes glossed over as Ned put him back in the cell. Jerun began to rock back and forth in the corner, repeating those same words over and over.

John watched him for a moment. There was something familiar about this. A memory from his past fought its way to the surface. *We were in Whales Head ... there was a woman ... from the Blasted Isles.* A chill went down his spine. He had seen this once before. A herb-gatherer had bewitched a man who had stolen from her. The thief had begun rocking just like this. Eyes rolling and blinking at the same time. "It's gods damned Vinda magic," John hissed.

"What?" Ned looked at him after locking the door.

John grabbed Ned by the lapels of his uniform. "I need you to get me a witch."

"A witch?"

"A Vinda, from the Blasted Isles. Right now, Ned! Go!" John pushed the big constable towards the stairs.

Ned scrambled to obey, and John watched him run down the corridor and up the stairs.

This was troubling: the Vinda Sisterhood did not get involved in things like this, and John knew the murderer was a young man. Unless it was a team of murderers? But that didn't fit either. The way the bodies were killed suggested the same tall, lithe, athletic man as described by so many people. Why was there a witch involved?

It was not long before Ned crashed back down the stairs, interrupting his thoughts.

"That was quick," John said.

Ned gestured to the squat woman following him carefully down the stairs. "My ma goes to Sister Tantos here for all her readings. She lives just down the street."

"Good job, son." John nodded, impressed by the young lad.

"You be havin' a spell to take care of, I do hear?" Sister Tantos waved her arm at Ned, shooing the big constable away. John grimaced at the witch's thick Islander accent. He'd always had trouble understanding the rolling speech of the Blasted Isles, and those from Vinda were the worst.

"I think that man is under a spell. I would be grateful for any help you can offer, Sister." John pointed to Jerun.

"I do be the judge of who be under spells, Mr. Prefect," Sister Tantos muttered as she waddled past John. The witch didn't look convinced as she went into the cell to have a look at Jerun, who was still rocking in the corner, repeating, "It was me," over and over.

Sister Tantos knelt slowly and grasped Jerun's head between her hands. "Let me have a look at him now." Her wrinkles and dark make-up nearly swallowed any sign of her eyes as she concentrated.

"Hmmm," the witch murmured. She reached into her long cloak and rummaged around until she brought out a thick purple crystal and placed it against Jerun's forehead. Then she began to chant.

The memories of the herb lady in the marketplace flashed through John's head once more and a shiver went down his spine at the haunting and alien sound of the witch's voice.

Bloody witches and spells. It just wasn't natural.

"Jerun, you be far away, but you return to us now," the witch intoned, while somehow the chanting did not stop. "Follow my voice back, Jerun. When I do clap, you be wakin' and rememberin' all. All that has happened, be rememberin'."

She clapped and took the crystal from Jerun's head. Jerun's body began to spasm.

"What's happening?" John demanded. "What did you do?"

"Not but what needed doing," Sister Tantos hissed at him.

Jerun's eyes widened as he looked at John, and then he threw himself to the floor and began convulsing.

"No!" the man shrieked, and grabbed his head. Blood began to run from his eyes.

"There was a woman ..." Jerun spit as he rolled to the ground. "A demon's face! A dem – AHHH!" He screamed and clawed at the sides of his head, drawing deep gouges in his skin.

“Stop him! Ned!” John yelled, but Ned was frozen in horror, just as he and the witch were.

John finally broke out of his paralysis and flung himself on Jerun. White foam spewed from the man’s mouth, covering the front of John’s jacket.

“Stop this!” John yelled at the witch.

“It were only a hypnosis,” the Sister whispered, “it should have worked.”

John fought to keep Jerun’s hands away from his face. A horrible gurgling sound rasped its way out of Jerun’s throat. “She’s in my head! Get her out! Get her out! Get her –” His back snapped taut with a crack, and John felt the man stop struggling beneath him.

The man was dead.

Sister Tantos was crying, grasping Ned in terror, whose own eyes were wide. It was then John made out what the Vinda witch was muttering. “Esmerak, it be Esmerak. Gods, Esmerak.”

John didn’t know the name, but the horror in the old witch’s eyes made his skin crawl.

“Who in the nine hells is Esmerak?” John stepped towards Sister Tantos and grasped the old woman by the shoulders.

“Esmerak. It was Esmerak.” Tears slid down between the wrinkles of her face.

“Who is Esmerak?” John repeated, and shook the witch hard to try and snap her out of whatever trance she was in; but it was Ned who answered.

“It’s one of the painted cards they use,” Ned said as he stared down at Jerun’s bloody face. “Esmerak is the dreamer, the Queen of Nightmares, the mind diver, the soul twister, the mother of dark illusions. She is like a demon in the Blasted Isles.”

“You’re telling me a Vinda demon decided to kill Jerun?” John growled.

"She once was a Sister, the greatest. But she do be dead," the witch whispered, looking with a tear in her eye at dead Jerun. "None but Esmerak could have done that to this man's mind."

"Could this be a man? Could a man know this?" John asked.

"No." There was certainty in the old witch's voice. "A man cannot learn the Vinda. A man has no *resan*, and this is of the deep *resan*. No, child, this knowledge is known by a woman, a woman with a dark heart and more powerful than any I be knowin'."

"There's two of them," John said aloud. "Why didn't I catch this before?"

"Maybe this evil Vinda witch wasn't needed before." Ned shrugged.

John snapped his head back towards the big constable. "What did you say?"

"I said, maybe this witch wasn't needed before." Ned looked like a cornered rabbit. "Maybe you were too close this time?"

The kid was right. That's what had been different about this one – which meant the witch had been around for a while now, monitoring things. "You're right," John said. This had been the first time they had been in the city when the murder had happened.

"Yes." John clapped Ned on the shoulder. "Good job, constable. Someone decided to clean up after our boy this time. How do you like the title of Chief, Ned?"

"Uh ..." Ned said, holding up an eyebrow.

"Don't worry about it." John patted him on the shoulder. "You'll grow into it. I need you to get a carrier pigeon away. I want the constabulary ready in New Toeron when I arrive." John stepped out of the cell and saw Miranda.

"A ferry left early this morning and guess where its port of call is?" Miranda said.

"New Toeron."

Miranda nodded.

"You find us a boat?"

"Yep, a quick little warship, two sails, twenty oars. Still don't think we'll catch them," she answered, but Miranda was looking past him at what remained of Jerun. "Son of an Onai! What happened to him?"

"I'll tell you on the way." John was already marching from the cell, pulling Ned with him. "Ned, escort Sister Tantos out, and then sign that transport requisition form on Gary's desk, which is now your desk, *Chief* Ned. I am exercising my right of recommissioning in the name of our High King, Ronaston Mihane." John pulled a writ out of his coat pocket with the golden seal of the High King on it.

Ned's eyes bulged as he saw the seal, and then the big constable laughed. "You're bloody serious?"

"Gary has been stealing a wage for years now, son. The Narrows deserves somebody with a head on their shoulders, and the High King's Royal Constabulary has entrusted me the authority to adjust things if I deem it necessary. Congratulations." John clapped Ned on the shoulders.

He left the Narrows Constabulary behind with a smiling, new, and hopefully much more competent chief constable. It was all John could do not to kick Gary down the stairs as he left, but already his mind was back on the case.

Their killer was important enough to have an extremely powerful Vinda witch making sure the Constabulary didn't get too close. However that was arranged, it would have taken some doing, and that didn't bode well. Everything had just become much more complicated, and John's gut told him big players were involved in this.

The whole bloody investigation had just become a hundred times more dangerous.

6 - Echoes of the Past

Why do I write all of this down? Is there any point other than to stroke my ego, or is it more to formalise my thoughts in a desperate attempt to keep myself sane?

I spent a small nation's fortune constructing this book so it would last well into the ages, and what have I filled it with? Nothing but the ramblings of a madman. For that is what I am now, here at the end, in all senses of the word: truly mad.

I'm old now, so old. Damn you, Time. Damn you.

Bah. Pointless. Yet still I write, filling these pages with my useless words.

- Journal of Robert Mannford, Day 288 Year 065

Wayran

The Wastes

They had been wandering for hour upon hour. The strange glowing blue and white lights followed Wayran and Matoh as they made their way through the enormous Jendar building, which was beginning to feel like some maniacal labyrinth.

The white-blue lights were always blinking. On, when they walked forward. Off, when they moved away from a spot, almost as if the lights were mocking them, letting them see what was there but then never letting them look far ahead or behind. Wayran felt as if they floated within the lonely pale light, moving from darkness into darkness, and always with the noiseless lights following them.

Yet Wayran also thought he was beginning to understand this place, and what he had seen only made him want to find more. They had found rooms filled with instruments and devices whose use Wayran could not even guess at. Yet each of these relics was a wonder unto itself. The intricacy and complexity of some of the devices boggled the mind. Wayran, having grown up with a father who worked closely with professors at the Academy in New Toeron, had been privileged with access to some of the top minds in the world at the time. Yet, for all of their combined knowledge, they would have been like small children to the minds of people who created the marvels around him.

"What about this one?" Matoh asked, holding up another of the black glass squares on what appeared to be yet another abandoned desk. It was if the people three thousand years ago had left suddenly, for signs of hurried departure were everywhere. "This could probably fit into a pocket easily, not too hard to carry," Matoh said.

Wayran watched as Matoh touched the centre of the black glass with his finger. The surface lit up, and within its light the brothers could see yet another of the rotating symbols upon a geometric field. "It's really clear, this one, very impressive," Matoh commented.

"What happens when you touch the symbol?" Wayran asked.

Matoh slid his finger across the face of the now shining glass square. "Same. Comes up with a box with some writing behind it. Can you read it?" Matoh handed the relic to Wayran.

Wayran looked down at the shining face to try and decipher the archaic writing. "A word here or there, but it's just as Chronicler Talbot says, most of what is written here is incredibly specific and bogged down with jargon. I wouldn't really have a clue where to start."

"So how do we choose?" Matoh asked, taking the glass relic back from Wayran.

"I don't know, Matoh," Wayran sighed, "we should just try to find our way out." They had blundered upon probably the greatest cache of Jendar relics to date, yet they had no way to choose what was important, or what the Chroniclers could use.

"I thought that's what we were doing." Matoh smirked and tossed his thin braid back over his ear. "But we shouldn't leave empty-handed. We've got to take something back. Otherwise, who's going to believe us?"

Wayran shrugged. Matoh was probably right. But what did they take?

"So what do you make of all this then?" Matoh asked glancing around the room once more. "You figure out what this place was used for yet?"

"If I was to guess ... I think it was a research building," Wayran answered somewhat absently. How he knew, he couldn't say. It just felt right somehow. He tried to justify his feeling. "Each room so far has been very similar, we've found hundreds of those glass squares, and the writing in each has been slightly different, but from what I could make out was very technical. Lots of words I've never seen before. Perhaps Chronicler Rutherford might be able to figure them out, although even he has a set of specific interests. This place reminds me of the Research Wing of the Academy."

"Huh," Matoh grunted. "That's what I was going to guess. It feels like that time we got to visit the santsi laboratories."

"Santsi are a more recent invention." Wayran looked around the room once more.

"Yes, I know." Matoh scoffed. "You take things too literally at times. I was trying to agree with you."

"Agreement accepted then. Shall we go?"

Matoh nodded.

Wayran turned to leave and froze in his tracks.

A man stood in the doorway.

A man with glowing red eyes.

Wayran started and put his hands up reflexively.

"What is it?" Matoh sprung forward to join him.

Wayran began to point, but when he looked back at the doorway, the man was gone. It wasn't possible. Wayran had barely shifted his gaze, but where there had once been a man, there was now no one. "Aaah ..." was all he could muster.

"Did you see something?" Matoh said, and before Wayran could stop him, Matoh sprinted to the doorway. One of the large metal canisters beside each of the doors was already in his hand as a makeshift club. Outside the lights sprang to life as Matoh moved into the hallway.

"Nothing here," he said, turning back to Wayran with a quirked eyebrow.

The lights hadn't switched on until Matoh moved outside. There couldn't have been anything there.

Wayran looked at the bench just behind him and picked up an empty cup and something which looked like a calliper. He walked up to stand next to Matoh in the hallway and put his forearm to Matoh's chest to stop his brother from walking forward.

"Wait a moment," he said. Matoh looked at him strangely again but complied, no doubt noting his odd tone.

Wayran threw the cup as hard as he could down the hallway. The lights followed the cup as it sailed through the air and then shattered against the floor. Immediately, he spun and threw the metal callipers down the corridor in the opposite direction, watching as the lights again followed the object down the hallway. All the while the light above them stayed on. The callipers eventually scraped to a halt. Now there were three lights in the hallway, one above them, and two others highlighting the now still objects he had thrown.

"While that does look like fun ..." Matoh quirked an eyebrow at him and smirked as he turned to look at Wayran "... care to explain brother?"

Wayran's heart was still pounding. "Just ... just testing a theory," he said, not quite sure anymore if he had actually seen something.

“Which was that cups break when you throw them and metal tools don’t?” Matoh grinned.

“No – the lights,” Wayran scoffed. “They don’t just follow *us*. They follow movement.”

“The lights have been following us moving this entire time. You just figured that out?” Matoh shook his head and patted him on the shoulder. “And I thought you were supposed to be the smart one.”

“Oh shut up.” Wayran grimaced. “Cups and metal tools are different from people; I now know the lights track everything, not just people.”

“Sure.” Matoh rolled his eyes. “It was still pretty random. We were going, weren't we?”

“Yes,” Wayran answered and started down the hallway. But he couldn’t help feeling now as if they were not alone down here. “Yes, let’s go.”

* * *

“This place is absolutely massive.” Matoh groaned as they reached yet another landing on yet another stairwell. “Surely behind this door ...” He moved forward and the door flicked open.

Wayran hoped his brother was right. His legs were so tired they felt as if they were about to buckle beneath him.

The lights blinked on outside the door, but they did not reveal another stretching hallway; instead there was a small chamber, with a large metal door barring their way. This door looked different, larger and more solid than what they had encountered so far.

“That’s new,” Wayran said, and they stepped into the chamber together.

“This one’s not opening.” Matoh stepped forward and bumped his chest against the solid metal door.

Wayran studied the enormous door. It seemed like one seamless piece of metal. He put his hand on the door and began to siphon, trying to pull in the small amount of energy in the air around him and push it into the metal.

The energy left his hand as if falling into an abyss, meaning the wall was very substantial. "It's incredibly thick. Steel, I think."

"Looks like it's time to find out what's down on the next floor." Matoh turned to go down the staircase.

"Wait. What's this?" Wayran had been feeling around the edge of the door jamb when one of the panels beside his hand suddenly flickered with light and began to glow. A voice cracked a command, making both brothers jump.

"Did the wall just talk to you?" Matoh asked.

Wayran nodded, his hand hovering over the faint blue panel.

"And what did the wall say?" Matoh prompted.

"It said to put my hand on the square." Those Jendar words had been clear enough, basic and precise.

"Well, who are we to argue with a wall," Matoh said, and pushed Wayran's hand onto the blue panel.

"Don't!" He tried to jerk away. "What if –"

Something within the wall hummed and the giant steel door slid up into the wall.

"See." Matoh shrugged. "It worked. Good job translating."

"What if it had been a trap? What if my hand hadn't worked?" Wayran gasped, pulling his hand off the panel.

"But it did." Matoh stepped forwards. "Are you coming or what?"

"Unbelievable," Wayran muttered to himself. "What if we can't get back out? Ever think of that?"

"There's another one of those panels on this side. It's fine, come on, you're gonna want to see this." Matoh waved him forward.

Wayran grumbled and stepped into the room, and suddenly any hesitation he had shown vanished.

The room was enormous, and all around them panels in the wall began to switch on, except this time they didn't glow blue, or show the odd boxes with writing on them. As each panel came to life they showed windows out onto the world, but they showed more than what was outside of the building. Wayran recognised some of the places. He saw one panel showing a street in New Toeron, bustling with people going about their daily business. Another showed a jungle scene; another must have been outside the city of Dawn, as he recognised the fabled skyline of the holy city with its dozens of temple spires and domes. One after another, the room was lit with the glow of scenes from all around the world, many of them places Wayran had never been.

"Have you ever read about anything like this?" Matoh whispered, the wonder obvious on his face.

"No," Wayran managed to say as he tried to take in the majestic sight. He stepped forward to get a closer look.

"Are they showing us what's happening now?" Matoh asked.

"I don't know," Wayran began, but then watched one particular panel more closely. "Yes, they must be, look." He pointed to a panel showing a desert scene. Within the glowing rectangle floated *Deliverance*, his uncle's airship. It was moored near the unique rock hill they had set out from this morning. It was meant to be their rendezvous point.

"Wow." Matoh stepped closer to a panel showing New Toeron. "Huh, look! That's just outside our house! It's Mrs. Peterson and her flower cart." Matoh's grin was so wide it threatened to split his head. "This is just amazing." He turned to walk into the centre of the room, still gawking at the glowing panels all around him.

"Wait, Matoh." Wayran jumped down to grab his brother's shoulder. "Look." He pointed to what looked like a chair dominating the centre of the room, and a hunched form sitting upon it.

Matoh froze mid-step, and both brothers studied what was obviously the form of a person. “Hello?” Matoh said, and began sidestepping, trying to get a better look at whoever was sitting in the chair.

There was no response, so they crept together to the front of the chair. The largest of the glowing panels was directly in front of this chair, and this central panel kept switching from scene to scene almost as if it were turning pages of a great book.

“Hello?” Matoh said again, but as they found themselves directly in front of the figure, they understood the reason for the lack of response.

Vacant sockets stared back at them from the mummified corpse sitting in the chair. An open mouth screamed in silence as the screen behind them once again changed scenes. The brothers said nothing as they imagined how this person must have died. They had encountered no other bodies within the massive complex. Whoever this person had been, they had died quietly and alone.

“Creepy,” Matoh said, shaking himself.

“This room was like those old crypts the Navutians liked to use for their dead,” Wayran said somewhat absently as he continued to stare at the corpse. It had been a man, if Wayran were to guess by the size of his shoulders and what remained of the clothing.

“Who was he?” he asked himself. He stepped forward for a closer look. It was then he saw a book resting beside one of the mummified hands. It was covered in dust but looked to be in excellent condition. He reached to grab it but halted as he leant over the corpse.

Eyes which hadn’t been there a moment ago stared up at him from the mummified skull.

“Woah!” Wayran sprung back.

Matoh yelled, “Holy Halom! It’s alive! Lady take me!”

Wayran scrambled back several steps, his heart pounding in his chest. “Who are you?” he demanded. His fright made his words sound harsh.

It was then he noticed three bright lights shining from pinpoint sources around the room and which appeared to coalesce into the ghostly form.

The glowing man stood up, but as it stood, the mummified corpse was once again revealed, and yet the lights seemed to move to follow the ghostly figure. Something clicked within the chair, and a powerful voice boomed through the room.

The glowing man was speaking to Wayran, but as he moved the glowing eyes did not track him. Was this somehow like the images on the glass squares? It had the same feel, like this too was a predetermined sequence of images set in motion when Wayran had tried to grab the book.

"Is it a ghost?" Matoh asked, still with his hands curled into fists waiting for the luminous and transparent man now standing in front of the corpse to make a move. "Do you understand what it's saying?"

"Not a ghost," Wayran said, staring at the apparition. Wayran couldn't translate what was being said, but he recognised enough to know it was Jendar. These were the dead man's last words, a man who had waited here while everyone else had abandoned this giant facility. "I need a quill – something to write with!"

"A quill?" Matoh asked dumbfounded. "Where am I going to find a –"

"Just get me something to bloody write with!" Wayran waved Matoh on, yet was transfixed with what the man was trying to tell him. He was saying something about a river? Time to get to the river? Changing my destination? Wayran couldn't make sense of it. Here was someone actually speaking in the long dead dialect of the Jendar, and he couldn't understand any of it! The apparition was talking too fast.

"Here, use this!" Matoh handed him something which looked a bit like a pencil. "I don't know if it's their equivalent to a quill, but it made a blue line on my hand."

Wayran didn't hesitate. He let the strange quill roll over his arm, trying to get down what was being said in phonetic form. Maybe a Chronicler back in New Toeron could make sense of it if he could write down something close.

The glowing blue man finished and abruptly disappeared. The points of light that had connected to the man blinked off. The brighter lights from overhead switched back on and the room was once again dominated by the flashing images of the panels all around them.

"Okay," Matoh said, "that was odd."

"It was important," Wayran whispered, more to himself than Matoh. "I couldn't understand, and I needed to. I bet it was important."

They heard something rumbling and then the floor began to shake around them. A horrible screech of metal grinding against metal ripped through the building. A panel fell off the wall and crashed to the floor with a pop and shower of sparks.

"Look!" Matoh pointed to one of the glowing panels still on the wall. "It shows another storm. That looks like it could be just outside. There!"

Wayran watched as the panel showed a long metal spike shaking as it poked its way out of a sand dune.

Another horrible screech echoed through the complex. A giant bang shook the room and this time dozens of panels fell.

"We need to get out of here!" Matoh yelled over the noise. "There's got to be another door!"

As if commanded by Matoh's voice a large part of the wall began to slide sideways. They could see light flooding into the room from behind it.

Light from outside. Wayran could see sand dunes.

"That's our way out! Let's move." Matoh was already running.

But Wayran couldn't just leave. He needed to take something back with him, something to show he had been here. To prove that this wasn't all just a dream.

He looked back at the chair and its skeletal occupant. *The book.*

Wayran dashed forward as more of the glowing panels flickered to black and crashed off the walls around him.

Another horrible screech of metal on metal, then the floor lurched up, knocking him to his knees. The spire was going to rip this place apart.

His hand closed on the book, and from the corner of his eye he thought he saw a person. He turned and saw the red-eyed man staring at him.

Something grabbed Wayran's wrist.

"Damn it, Wayran! Come on!" Matoh had returned to get him. "Let's get the hells out of here!"

Wayran looked back to where he had seen the man, but again there was nothing.

"The door is sliding back closed!" Matoh yelled as he pulled Wayran away from the chair. "Move it!"

Wayran didn't argue this time. He held tight to the book and ran for the now disappearing daylight.

A section of roof fell to the floor from above. Wayran threw himself to the side, but a piece of metal bar smacked into his head. He felt warm liquid trickle down his face, and suddenly he was on the floor of the corridor outside the giant room.

"Wayran!" Matoh yelled, and a strong hand pulled him up and dragged him forward into the corridor leading outside. The wall slipped closed behind them in a cloud of dust. There was no going back it seemed.

Suddenly all was quiet. The floor had stopped shaking; the screeching of metal gears had disappeared. The only sound was the quiet bass of thunder as the storm rolled away.

It was eerie, but Wayran's head was throbbing, and they didn't have time to stop. They needed help fast.

"That doesn't look good," Matoh said, looking up at his head with more worry on his face than he had shown the whole time they had been trapped inside the building.

Wayran had his arm around his brother's shoulder for support. He didn't know if he could stand without him. He felt so dizzy.

"Can you walk?" Matoh said. "We need to get out onto the sands. The Storm Chasers might still be in the area."

"I'll try," Wayran said, holding his free hand up to his head. He still held the book with the other. His fingers came back slick with blood.

"Here." Matoh untied the sash on his waist.

Wayran held up a hand. "No, that's from the general." The red sash had finely stitched yellow lines of flowing Paleshurian script on it. It had been a gift from General Kiprosov in remembrance of their mother, whom he had fought alongside during the Union wars.

"Can't be helped," Matoh said and pushed his hand aside.

Wayran winced as the soft silk sash touched his forehead.

Matoh finished tying off the makeshift dressing, with only a slight grimace of remorse. "Come on. Let's get moving before this place starts trying to shake itself apart again."

The brothers took a few tentative steps down the hallway towards the open archway at the end. It almost looked like this had once been some kind of balcony. They were encased in a long corridor of curved glass which held back the dunes around them, yet at the end of the odd balcony there was an opening, and they could see daylight.

Matoh pulled Wayran along towards the daylight. Something gigantic and white flashed across the opening. Its huge shadow whipped by, blocking the outside light almost completely for that instant.

"What was –" Matoh started to say but was cut off by a piercing screech, although this time it hadn't been gears grinding. This sound was much more *alive*.

Wayran let go of him, and the pair stood frozen in place.

Matoh finally edged forward, his eyes scanned the opening.

A giant feathered head burst through the exit and let loose a terrible screech.

Wayran and Matoh jumped back.

It was a Roc, a giant raptor-like bird.

Wayran had no time to wonder how, or indeed why, the giant cliff-dwelling seabird was somehow in the middle of the desert. Its great white wings flapped once and allowed the Roc's huge taloned feet to touch down inside the archway.

The immense bird stood blocking the exit. Its luminous yellow eyes watched them, sizing them up, and waiting for them to spring.

"Wayran ... do you also see a giant white bird standing there?" Matoh backed up another step as the yellow eyes tracked him.

The Roc screeched again in defiance and Wayran wondered if his eardrums would burst. "Yes. I see it," he whispered, not daring to take his eyes from the terrifying bird.

The Roc stepped forward, its talons clicked on the metal floor, and the brothers tensed.

"You're going to have to run," Matoh whispered.

Wayran watched in horror as Matoh seemed to be slowly reaching for something in his pocket.

"Matoh, don't!" he hissed.

"Now!" Matoh cried.

Wayran watched in horror as Matoh launched forward, charging the giant bird.

His mind was in shock, but somehow his legs were moving.

The Roc shot forward meeting Matoh's charge, and a wing slapped out to try and block Wayran, but the Roc was too big, and Wayran ducked under a partially opened wing.

"Go!" he heard Matoh shout behind him. A pained screech ripped through the air. He looked back. Matoh was holding the piece of glass he had picked up from the room they had crashed into. His brother had stabbed the bird just above its eye and now waited to strike again with the bloody piece of glass.

The Roc thrashed about in pain. Matoh tried to run past, but the bird's giant head slammed into him and Matoh hit the side of the hallway hard. His head bounced off the glass wall.

Wayran felt his heart lurch. The bird was going to rip into his brother with those talons. Matoh was going to die.

The panic let something free inside of him, and once again he saw possibilities open up before his eyes. If he ran, he wouldn't get there in time. Shouting wouldn't distract the enraged bird. No, no, no! Choice after choice rolled through his mind, and each one showed Matoh dying. He saw it again and again.

His mind lurched as it brushed up against an idea. He was watching it happen ... but so was something else; another consciousness was following his thoughts somehow. In the slowed time of his mind's eye, he saw a figure standing back in the darkness behind Matoh and the Roc, waiting and watching him with red swirling eyes.

The book. The thought snapped into his mind. Possibilities and choices blurred before his eyes. He had to take it out of his pocket.

Wayran threw his hand into his pocket and whipped out the book. Red eyes hiding in the shadows seemed to widen. And miraculously the Roc stopped moving.

"Back!" Wayran yelled, moving towards the Roc, brandishing the book as if it were a torch. "Get away from him!"

Best be careful with that, the thought came into his mind, almost as if it were not his own. Somehow he knew it had been the red-eyed man.

A chill went up his spine. "Leave him alone or I'll ..." Wayran didn't know what he'd do. What could he do? It was a book, after all. That the Roc had stopped didn't make any sense, but he stepped closer and the Roc backed a step away.

Matoh groaned and Wayran gasped in relief. He was alive.

"Matoh!" he yelled. He had almost reached him. "Matoh, get up! We've got to move."

And where will you go? How can you escape? The strange voice echoed in his head. *You cannot outrun this Roc. You have angered the bird.*

Wayran shook his head, trying to rid himself of the voice. "Shut up!" he yelled at where the red-eyed man had been standing; but once again the shadowy figure had disappeared.

Matoh was finally up on his feet. His brother held his head and groaned, but somehow Matoh was standing. Wayran grabbed his hand, pulling his brother away from the Roc, which watched them with only one of its yellow eyes. The other was shut against the blood dripping down into it.

"It's still there," Matoh said, his speech a bit slurred as his eyes blinked open. "I had hoped it would fly away."

"Not yet," Wayran said through gritted teeth. They had inched backwards to the opening and Wayran cursed under his breath. They were at the end of the balcony, but only now did he realise that it stuck out of the sand dune. Behind them was a twenty-foot drop to the sand.

Give me the book! The voice yelled in his head, and a metal hand shot out from the shadows to try and grab him.

Wayran lurched back away from the hand, sending Matoh and himself falling towards the sand below.

Wayran hit with a thud and the air was driven out of his lungs as he rolled backwards down the dune. He stopped as his head slammed back into the sand, and lay dazed, looking up at the balcony they had fallen from.

Great white wings opened up above him and the Roc took flight overhead.

Wayran tried to move but for a moment couldn't, as the movement had made his stomach lurch and his vision spin; but then Matoh stood over him, pulling him up out of the sand.

"Here." Matoh shoved the ancient book back into his hand. "You dropped this. Whatever magic you were using back there; we might need it again. I think that damn bird is coming back."

"I don't know what I did," Wayran gasped, as his breath came back to him.

"It doesn't matter, move!" Matoh pushed him forward down the dune as they both saw the Roc bank sharply in the air above to shoot down straight towards them.

Wayran tried to run, but his feet kept getting caught in the falling sand they dislodged.

"Down!" Matoh dived, knocking him off his feet, as a screech split the air above them.

He heard Matoh yell in pain.

Wayran turned to get up and saw with horror the Roc standing on top of Matoh. Its hind talon had punctured his brother's leg.

"Matoh!" He scrambled to his feet and brandished the book at the Roc.

Its yellow eye found him and a wing snapped out from its body, slamming into his head.

The book fell from his hand and his vision swam. He tried to get up, but all he could do was watch as the Roc opened its razor-sharp beak to rip into his brother.

Matoh was gritting his teeth in pain and anger up at the Roc, and

Wayran somehow heard his brother's words clearly through the grogginess in his mind.

"I've had enough!!" Matoh roared in defiance, and Wayran saw something flash in Matoh's hand. The glass shard: somehow, in all the craziness, Matoh had held onto it. He plunged the glass into the Roc's foot.

Then the impossible happened.

The sand around them seemed to crackle, and then lightning shot straight up into a nearly cloudless sky, bursting forth from Matoh's hand. The Roc screamed in pain as it was blown backwards. The lightning streaked up and a thunderclap slammed through the air around them.

The force of the thunderclap sent a shockwave through the air and slammed Wayran back down to the sand.

It was one too many hits, and Wayran's world went black.

7 - Patients with Patience

The Jendar even had the power to alter the fundamental principles of human biology. Technologies they called "gene splicing" and "nanoengineering" allowed them to give living organisms new abilities, such as "electromagnetic sensitivity and manipulation". However, so great has the loss of knowledge been since those glorious days of enlightenment that deciphering the meaning of such terms is an almost insurmountable task.

Chronicler Rutherford believes the latter deals with what we now call Siphoning, but even he admits that there is almost no method which we could surmise to validate this claim.

Yet as Chroniclers, it is our hope, as always, to one day recover even more of the vast cornucopia of knowledge lost in the Ciwix, so that one day we might understand what happened.

- Chronicler Jason Hicks after the 487th Chronicler Symposium of 2766 A.T.C (After the Ciwix)

Matoh

The Wastes

"No!" Matoh sprang up and rolled. Something had been standing on him.

He fell and landed hard on a wooden floor.

It stunned him and he had to blink several times before he registered what he was lying on. He turned onto his back and squinted against daylight streaming through a round window. The room was familiar. The walls were lined with labelled white cupboards. Glass jars and bottles filled with an array of tinctures, herbs, and salves set into polished wooden holders lined several of the surfaces around him.

The medical bay. Matoh tried to clear his head, squinting against the pain that the bright daylight was causing him. *And ... I'm not dead.*

He breathed out slowly and found the movement a bit difficult. His chest hurt. Why? *The Roc!*

"Wayran!" Matoh sprang to his feet; his head spun and he had to grab the bed he had only recently fallen out of.

"Alright, that's quite enough, big fella," a familiar voice said from behind him.

Matoh turned, once again squinting against the light in search of the speaker. It was Ariel, one of the Storm Chasers.

"Where's Wayran?" Matoh demanded. "Tell me you found him." He stepped towards Ariel.

"Sit." Ariel's hand pushed him down onto the bed. "Your brother is resting, we got to both of you just in time."

"So, he's okay?"

Ariel nodded.

"What happened to the Roc?" Matoh asked, putting a hand to his chest and then to his leg. He found the bandages wrapped tightly and securely over his thigh, as he remembered the giant bird towering above him.

"I don't know about any rock." Ariel raised an eyebrow.

"No, the bird, you know, looks like a giant white falcon. A Roc!" Matoh threw his hands wide, demonstrating a giant wing span. It was then he noticed the bandages covering his hand. "What happened here?"

"You had a piece of glass embedded in your hand. Fairly ugly cut. Took fifteen stitches," Ariel said. "As far as giant birds go, we didn't see any; but that would explain your leg I suppose." She winked at him in a playful manner. "And, of course, there was enormous white feather you were clutching when we picked you up."

"You sound very calm, considering the two of us nearly died," Matoh snapped.

"And who in the hells' fault is that?" Ariel crossed her arms over her chest with a "don't you take that tone with me" look. "I seem to recall hearing about the Spierling brothers flying way out of position just as the storm was rolling in. Sounds to me like the two of you did most of that on your own." Ariel looked questioningly at him. "You're sure it was a Roc? You do know we are hundreds of miles from any sea or coastline?"

"I got rather a good look at it as it was stabbing me in the leg and preparing to rip my guts out with it's razor-sharp beak. It was a giant white Roc." Matoh shook his head.

"What was it doing way out here?" Ariel asked, arms still crossed.

"How should I know?" Matoh shrugged, exasperated, but his head had cleared and other than the cut on his hand and stiffness in his leg he felt pretty good, all things considered. "If I were to guess, I would say the Roc was guarding that Jendar building we came out of."

"Alright," Ariel said, and stood up. "I think you better lie back down and wait a few more hours for that head of yours to clear. You've obviously suffered quite a bit of trauma to the head as well."

"What? No, I'm fine. Let me see Wayran." He went to push Ariel's hand away.

"Ah, ah. Enough of that." Ariel wagged a finger at him. "You're obviously still fuzzy from what happened. There was no building anywhere near where we picked you up."

"What?"

"You hard of hearing now too? I said there was no building." Ariel pushed him back down onto the bed with more tenderness than her voice alluded to.

"But we fell out of a balcony. A giant glass balcony. It would have been right next to us, jutting out from a sand dune," Matoh said, now more than a little confused.

"Well, it wasn't there when we showed up. We saw that lightning blast as if the old storm goddess Esan was showing us the way to you two herself. Marcus found you both lying on the sands out cold," Ariel said as she gently pried the lids of his eye open, inspecting it and then the other.

The lightning. He remembered the Roc standing on him and then ... lightning? Wayran had said that was how he crashed, but that was impossible. Wasn't it?

"Do you still have the shard of glass?" Matoh endured Ariel's inspection patiently. "And Wayran had a book. That proves we were there."

"Well, maybe it does," Ariel said, her suspicious tone relenting slightly. "Hmm, you don't look like you have concussion." She placed her hand on his forehead. "And no fever." The Storm Chaser shrugged. "All I know is Marcus didn't mention any building, and from what you describe, it doesn't sound like something he'd miss."

"No ..." Matoh thought, frowning, "... he wouldn't have."

"Here." Ariel held out the shard of glass to him. "Try not to cut yourself anymore. I've had enough of stitching the two of you up for one day."

He took the glass shard from Ariel. She stood up and turned to leave. "Get some rest," she said. "The Captain wants to talk to you. I'll tell him you will be ready to see him after supper, which is in an hour."

Matoh nodded. The idea of trying to explain to his uncle why he and Wayran had lost two gliders and several fortunes worth of santsi globes was not one he relished. "Can I see Wayran?" he asked as Ariel was leaving.

She nodded. "Don't wake him though. That cut on his head was bad." She waited to make sure she was fully understood.

"I understand, I just want to see him is all." Matoh shrugged.

"He's just around the corner in the other bed." Ariel gave him one last stern look and then took her leave.

Matoh saw a set of crutches resting against the foot of his bed. He took them and slowly made his way over to Wayran.

He could hear the slightly shallow sound of Wayran's even breathing. There was a bandage wrapped around his head. The strange book they had found was on his chest, and even in sleep Wayran clutched it as if it were about to be taken from him. Out of all the wondrous things they had seen, Wayran decided to take a dusty old book.

That was just like him though, and the thought made Matoh smile.

He found a chair and pulled it over beside Wayran's bed. He sat down and, gently as he could, propped his injured leg on the foot of the bed, grunting slightly against a stab of pain.

Uncle Aaron can wait, he thought, and clenched his jaw against the image of how angry that decision would make their uncle. Just then, however, he pushed the thought away, as it was their father's words that resonated in his mind: *"Brothers are there for each other."* His father's soft words had more power than his uncle's anger ever could.

So Matoh let his head droop to his chest as he held the lucky shard of glass, and he waited, firm and resolute as a stone, for Wayran to return to him.

8 - Bad Dream

Tales spoke of how the Dread Queen led an army of Soulless against the young nations of the north. Most today believe "the Soulless" were so named because of their grisly accoutrements: armour made from the bones and skin of vanquished enemies. This theory has gained significant weight as digs in southern Nothavre have uncovered some of these horrific adornments.

The Soulless swept through the North with little resistance until they clashed with the Navutians and their culture of ruthless, efficient and brutal warfare.

The Northern nations united under the great Navutian warlord Rykavin Stonesplitter, and this unification turned the tide of battle against the Soulless and the Dread Queen.

Rykavin has been immortalised in dozens of poems, ballads, and myths in which he led the charge against the Soulless, wielding his mystic sword, Hunsa. In the myths, Rykavin personally cuts down hundreds of the enemy and almost single-handedly wins several battles. To this day every school child knows of how the Navutian Lord bested the Dread Queen to win the battle of Bransburg, now modern-day Palisgrad. Though the Navutians returned to their raiding and pillaging ways, the nations of the North owe them our freedom.

- *Chronicler Simon Rathelson in A Common History: 1851–2850 ATC, 45th Edition, 2850*

Wayran

The Wastes

It felt like he was swimming. No, not quite swimming – sailing, perhaps?

He couldn't quite place it. Whatever he was doing, there was a current of some sort pushing him forward, a great current, and it was all he could do to steer haphazardly from right to left, and yet always he had to move forward.

Wayran didn't question the direction, as it seemed as natural as the earth or the sun. Yet around him he could feel swirls of energy, eddies within the current, and within those eddies he dived into one of those eddies and the world changed.

A tall man, dressed in rich black silks, laughed with delight at the end of a city street. Wayran watched in horror as he licked blood off the long blade of his hunting knife. He was staring at him, and he could see the manic hunger in the eyes tracking him. The man smiled showing a mouth full of needle-like teeth.

"This will change the world. Don't you see! This changes everything!" the tall man in black cackled at Wayran, just before he charged straight for him with the hunting knives gleaming in the pale light.

An eddy opened around him, and Wayran let himself be sucked into it.

The world shifted.

The black-robed man stood in front of him again. Yet this time his back was to him. Confused, Wayran stepped forward. The man was crying.

Some impulse made Wayran want to help the black-robed man this time. He put his hand on the man's shoulder, who then spun to look at him.

Matoh stared back at him.

"Why, Wayran? Why?" Matoh pleaded, tears in his eyes.

Wayran didn't understand and shook his head in confusion.

It was then he saw that Matoh held something in his hands.

Wayran looked down.

Wayran held the pommel of a golden sword, which morphed into a black sword and then a white dagger. The weapon had been plunged into Matoh's chest.

"How could you betray me?" Matoh asked as tears slid down his cheeks. His brother coughed up blood and grasped at his arm.

"Matoh, I didn't – I ..." Wayran couldn't breathe.

"HOW COULD YOU!!" Matoh screamed, and the world exploded in lightning and fire.

***

Wayran opened his eyes.

"Which one was it this time?" Matoh said as he stared straight at him.

"Matoh!" Wayran jerked and tried to sit up.

"Woah." Matoh put up his hands. They were not covered in blood. Though one was wrapped in bandages. "Easy. You were dreaming."

Wayran took a deep breath and tried to make his heart slow as it pounded in his chest. He looked at Matoh and felt sick as he remembered the end of his dream. *It wasn't real, Matoh's fine. I was just worried about him.*

"Nightmare again?" Matoh asked.

"Yes ..." Wayran trailed off, remembering the horror he had felt. He took another shuddering breath and could feel his heart begin to settle. "Yes, well, this one was different."

Matoh nodded and handed him a wooden cup. "Not surprising really, considering how we both nearly died. Here, have some water."

Wayran moved to take the drink and realised he was holding something.

The book. He still had it, and scrawled across his arm were his attempts at the words the strange ghost had spoken. He would have to copy the words down on something more permanent before the ink from that strange quill washed off or disappeared.

He carefully placed the book on his lap and took the drink from Matoh. As he drank, he couldn't quite believe he had a book which was thousands of years old. It certainly didn't look that old, yet it had to be. The ghost had been speaking Jendar, Wayran had recognised a few of the basic words.

"How did we get here?" he asked. "The last thing I remember was the Roc standing on top of you."

"Yeah," Matoh said, "that's about where I blacked out too."

Wayran looked at his brother and saw the world exploding in lightning and fire, the image from his dream. A shiver shot down his spine, and he forced the image away. Yet there *had* been an explosion.

"Lightning," he said as he remembered. "You did it again." He looked up at Matoh, trying to remember. "You stabbed it in the foot, and then ... lightning." Wayran tried to make sense of his memory. "The lightning – it struck upwards, away from you. As if it ripped itself out of you. How is that possible?"

Matoh's eyes went wide. "I remember things going white, but – are you sure? I mean, I feel fine. Wouldn't that have killed me? It must have just been a close strike again, like the one that knocked me out of the sky."

Wayran tried to remember. There had been lightning, and Matoh had caused it. He was sure of it. "The first one shouldn't have been possible either," he said, eyeing his brother. "What did you do exactly?"

"I honestly don't know," Matoh said. "I was just reacting. Trying to save our skins is all."

"Just reacting? That can't be it, I ..." but then Wayran began to feel dizzy and he put a hand to his head. Instantly a spike of pain sliced through him, forcing him to close his eyes and reach for the bedpost. His cup clattered to the floor, forgotten, as he tried to fight through vertigo.

"You alright?" Matoh was standing beside him with a steadying hand on his arm. "You took a really nasty hit in the head as we ran out of that big room with all the glowing panels."

"I'm fine." Wayran held up his hand. "I think."

"You better lie back down. What was that place anyways? Jendar obviously, but have you ever heard of anyone finding a place like that before?"

"No," Wayran admitted, taking Matoh's advice and lying back down.

"And why was there only that one skeleton? Was he the only person in that huge building? A king of some kind? But where were all his subjects?"

Wayran laughed. "I don't know, Matoh. Those are the sorts of things I wanted to find out, but right now thinking about it is making my head hurt."

Matoh chuckled then. "Oh, that kind of makes sense. Well, maybe if you take that book to the Chroniclers some of the answers will be in there."

"Maybe," Wayran agreed. Matoh was trying to cheer him up. It was admirable, but he knew this routine: Matoh was also stalling, which meant they were in serious trouble. "How angry is Uncle Aaron?"

His brother's cheerful demeanour vanished. "Ha, I was hoping to avoid that topic as long as possible. He kind of asked to see me after supper." Matoh grimaced. "That was two hours ago."

Wayran closed his eyes and sighed. "Really angry then, as we've lost a fortune's worth of santsi globes and the glider he loaned you – plus you've kept him waiting for another two hours. Why keep him waiting exactly? Just to rub salt in the wounds?"

"No." Matoh looked hurt. "I wanted to make sure you were alright."

Wayran sighed. He couldn't very well be mad at Matoh for that, which was all the more frustrating. "Okay. Well, let's not keep him waiting any longer then."

"No chance of food first?" Matoh asked.

"I think any food I ate would just come right back up," Wayran sighed.

"Oh, I almost forgot. Apparently there was no building around when they found us," Matoh said. "What do you make of that?"

"What do you mean 'there was no building'?"

"Well, Ariel said no one mentioned it, and she didn't see it when she helped us onboard." Matoh shrugged. "But you've got that book, and I still have my piece of lucky glass, so we must have been somewhere."

Wayran squinted, trying to make sense of it. "I don't know what that means."

"Could it have sunk back into the sand like those metal spires did?" Matoh asked.

"Possibly." Wayran pondered on it for a bit longer, but the concentration was making his headache worse. "I don't know, perhaps Uncle Aaron can shed some light on it as he rips our heads off. Let's just get this over with. Give me a hand would you?" It was then he noticed Matoh's leg and the crutches he was using.

"One of the Roc's talons. It stabbed almost all the way through," Matoh explained with a shrug. "It's pretty disgusting."

Wayran tried to give Matoh a reassuring smile, but it felt weak. They were both lucky to be alive, but at that moment Wayran felt anything but lucky. The two of them hobbled out of the infirmary to go and have a talk with their uncle, and part of him thought he would be less scared if he were going to face the giant Roc again.

9 - Course Correction

The wind hasn't abated now for fifty-three days. It feels like it's drilling through the hatch down into my mind. The world is screaming at what I've done.

Most days I cry.

Cry for the thousands of innocents, and when I'm done, I feel better.

Then I chastise myself for being weak.

For in truth, no one was innocent. No one stood up to say stop, no one did what was right when they knew our greed, apathy, and traditions were destroying it all.

No one stood up, except me. So, they had to die, and that is why I am damned.

- Journal of Robert Mannford, Day 073 Year 01

Wayran

- New Toeron, Bauffin

Wayran was no longer a Storm Chaser.

He had left to go into the wastes with a well-made glider, promises of discovering unsolved mysteries, and a chance to get rich doing it.

He was returning with an old book he couldn't read, no glider, no money, dashed dreams, a constant headache, a scar which had left him with a line of white hair upon his head, and the memories of a giant Jendar complex beneath the sands, a talking ghost and a weird dream. It had all left him in such a state of stunned bewilderment, he had been in a daze during the entire trip home. Hells, he was still in a daze.

Wayran had spent nearly all of the trip back home up on the top deck of *Deliverance*. He had watched the rolling dunes, the rock fields and the Jendar ruins of glistening glass for what was probably the last time. He had watched the bustling activity of the Storm Chasers, watched how each person had a role to fill and how they filled it with an eagerness and efficiency.

All of it was gone.

It had been Uncle Aaron's almost detached coldness as he explained to him and Matoh his accounting of what had happened. Their uncle had sat behind his big polished redwood desk. Uncle Aaron had meticulously and deliberately cut two pages out of the back of his ledger book. Quietly Uncle Aaron shifted through a set of other papers he had and began to jot down what looked like figures and notes from these papers onto the ledger paper.

Neither Wayran nor Matoh had dared breathe during this display. The ominous quiet in the room communicated everything which needed to be said.

Uncle Aaron had handed each of them one of the pieces of ledger paper.

"What you have in front of you is an accounting of just how much your little stunt has cost my operation. See, what you failed to understand is that I run this ship as a business. Let me repeat, a *business*. And it is a very specific business at that. It's not a sightseeing tour, nor a month-long escape for rich thrill-seekers, as your actions suggest."

It was with that opening volley that Wayran had seen his dreams disappear, and he remembered the rest of the tirade word for word, with painful clarity.

"Those santsi were part of a chain, you see. Merchants, craftspeople, artisans, even kings entrust to me their highly priced santsi globes. It is my job to come all the way out here to fill those same globes to capacity.

The process of said filling, as I thought you knew, as you promised me you understood, is quite a dangerous process. The globes return to those merchants, craftspeople, artisans, and kings with a level of energy no one else in all of Salucia has been able to match. It is our techniques and the storms we find all the way out here which allow us to gain this marginal advantage over the competition. And it is the margins which matter in a business."

Wayran remembered that Matoh had opened his mouth at this point. As if about to say something. Uncle Aaron had stopped in mid-flow and the halting of his words made the silence which followed crack with ominous repercussions.

Matoh's mouth had closed then. Their uncle continued in complete control, as a judge delivering a verdict to the condemned.

"Those very finely crafted, very expensive globes, which very wealthy people entrust to me will have to be replaced, because our reputation with those very wealthy people is everything. A reputation of repeatedly delivering excellence within such a risky enterprise draws investors like sharks to chum. It draws potential glider pilots like flies to a dung heap, and all of those people have mouths. Mouths that like to talk and carry rumour like wildfire on the plains. Continue to be successful and all are happy. Everyone wants to join the feeding frenzy." Their uncle's tone changed then, turning icy. "Just imagine, though, if those same people heard about some of my glider pilots disobeying orders, heard about them flying off to go sightseeing with other people's expensive santsi globes strapped to their backs. Now, that could be the sort of rumour that would make a captain mistrust his pilots, or even worse, the kind of rumour which could lose a business its reputation." Their uncle had let those last words hang between them for a moment.

Wayran had understood then, and he hung his head in shame.

"Yes. You see now, don't you, nephew? You know what I have to do."

Uncle Aaron's words had a tiny measure of sympathy in them, but that sympathy evaporated like a drop of water on a hot skillet. Wayran had felt tears on his cheeks then. He hadn't wanted them to come, but it had all been too much. He cried in stunned silence, waiting for his sentence.

"Listen to these words above all else ... *nephews*. You never crashed. You never flew gliders with santsi attached to them. You never found a Jendar complex, a complex which doesn't exist, because if it did, you would have to explain how you got out there. Understood?"

Marcus's secrecy about what he had found when he rescued them had clicked for Wayran then. He had to tell Matoh later about why there was a cover-up, but it made sense. This meant they really had found an ancient Jendar complex, but their story was being buried so thoroughly that no one would ever believe them if they told it, not even most of the crew aboard *Deliverence*. Which meant no one would talk about the disaster.

Their uncle had continued, "I allowed you to take a few gliding lessons as a favour to your father, and you both returned happy and satisfied. Your father will know the truth of the situation, and my investors will have to be satisfied with whatever we've collected so far. I will return you both home, where you will begin a repayment plan to pay back the damages in full. Once home, however, you will never set foot on this ship again. You will not tell the story about what happened out here. Understood?"

Wayran sat on his bed now, still and numb, looking out of his window at the street below. Watching the humdrum everyday existence he had seen out that same window his whole life as he dreamed of something more, of something important. He still heard part of his uncle's last words to him on that trip reverberating through his mind: "never set foot on this ship again". The words were like nails in the coffin of his dreams, and he had no idea what to do.

Yes, he understood. Hells, he even understood his uncle had been lenient with them given the possible damage it might do to his business. Yet that knowledge didn't help. He was indebted to his uncle and had no way to pay him back quickly as everything he had saved had gone towards his glider and getting on the crew in the first place. He had no other recourse but to pick up some menial job to pay off the enormous sum, because despite his uncle being family, Uncle Aaron was still a Koslov, and they never let debts slide.

He might be able to get a scribe position with the Chroniclers. Heck, they took anyone who was willing to believe in what they were doing. He'd be able to study Jendar relics, and might eventually work his way up to a full Chronicler and get to spend most of his time in a chosen field of research. He might even be able to go out with a Romak caravan heading into the wastes every now and then.

Wayran sighed at the idea. Chroniclers were notoriously poor. They devoted everything they had to their research and relied on the meagre earnings from selling Jendar trinkets. He winced thinking how long it would take to pay back all those smashed santsi, working with the Chroniclers.

He watched the people in the busy market below as they bartered and sold goods. Most of them seemed happy, content with their lot in life as they tried to eke out a decent living, thankful for the peace and stability that High King Ronaston's reign had brought.

Why can't I be like that? Wayran thought, yet deep down he knew he wasn't like them. He had always been a dreamer, looking to the future, longing for some just and noble cause to be part of. His father had always said he was like his mother in that sense. She had believed in Ronastan Mihane before he had become the High King, believed in what he was creating, and saw how it could be great. Wayran had never thought this to be a fallacy until now.

He turned from the window and flopped down onto his bed. He stared up at the thick wood beams crossing the ceiling of his room. Today they reminded him of the bars of a cage; a cage which grew smaller and more suffocating with each passing hour.

Finally, he had had enough of his moping and slapped his hands down on the bed. “Enough,” he told himself, and stood up. There was another option open to him, albeit one that he had never wanted to take.

He could apprentice under his father, making *trisk* for the military and anyone else who had enough money to commission one of the metal and fabric woven suits. But it was a path Wayran had always resisted because to him it felt like standing still, and the easy option.

He looked at himself in the mirror and saw the new stripe of white hair running across his head. The skin had scarred from where the piece of the roof had struck him, and the shock of the blow had turned the hair above it white.

I'll always be reminded of my failure, he thought. That bloody white stripe would always be there, taunting him with what could have been. *If only Matoh hadn't* ... But Wayran stopped that train of thought. It was he who had followed Matoh out to those spires; he could have let the other Storm Chasers retrieve his brother, but he had decided it was his responsibility to chastise him. It had been stupid, and now he had to pay for that stupidity.

He sighed and pulled on a set of work clothes and headed downstairs to begin swaging metal wire to be woven into *trisk*. If he was going to sulk, he might as well do something useful while he did.

***

Wayran pushed down the long handle of the crimping pliers to secure the swage, which was used to bend the metal, onto a length of copper wire. With the swage set, he rotated the threaded end into the drawing crank, and then clamped the die into place over the copper wire. He double checked that everything was secure, and then began to turn the handle.

His shoulders burned from the effort but the pain felt good. Over and over he turned the crank handle, each click of the gears pulled the copper wire a bit further, forced the wire to thin as it came through the die. This wire he was drawing would need to go through another three dies before it was thin enough to be woven into a *trisk,* but it was all part of the process.

Sweat dripped from his brow and he wiped it away without a thought. He was in a rhythm now and the beat of it absorbed his mind. The crank of the handle spun and his body pushed it forward and back, forward and back, forward and back, until the length of thicker wire being pulled through the die popped through or the spindle was full of thin copper wire.

He felt the release of pressure coming and slowed his cranking to let the end of the thick copper wire pull through the die. He cut off the last bit of the wire he had pulled through, as it wasn't as uniform as the rest of the wire. He picked up the small piece of waste copper and put it in a pot with the other clipped ends.

Wayran popped the locks on the crank and pulled out the now heavy spindle of thin copper wire. His biceps ached as he hefted the wire out of the crank and turned to go and put it on the shelf with the others he had swaged.

"That's probably enough wire, son," a deep, gravelly voice said beside him, making him start in surprise.

It was his father.

"Sorry, didn't see you there, Dad," Wayran huffed between breaths as he grunted to heft the spindle onto the shelf. His father stepped over and grabbed one end of the spindle, helping him shift it into position.

"I believe this shelf was empty this morning," Harold Spierling said with a nod. “Appreciated.”

“It’s grunt work,” Wayran said, only now noticing how heavily he was breathing. “Helps clear the mind.”

Harold Spierling nodded again, his thick grey and black moustache jutting out in thought. “I thought the doctor told you to rest until those headaches of yours went away.”

Wayran hung his head slightly; his father had his arms crossed in the no-nonsense manner Wayran and Matoh had grown to recognise so well. “I know,” he said. “It’s just sitting around all day is driving me insane.” He looked up to meet his father’s eyes. “I don’t know what to do with myself, and the exercise feels good.”

His father’s moustache hitched up on one side in a sort of half-grin. “You’re like me in that sense, son. I never could sit still for too long either.” His father looked at him for a moment, narrowing his eyes as if deciding something. “Come with me. I’ve got something you can do that won’t countermand the doctor’s orders too much.”

They walked through the large open-plan workshop on the bottom floor of their house. It was another new design, with rivetted steel I-beams replacing load bearing walls. Harold Spierling had continued buying up properties beside his original terraced house as his *trisk* business continued to grow. The neighbours were given double what the properties were worth and slowly mortar and brick replaced old wooden timber, and now steel and glass was beginning to replace some of the brick. Today, the workshop had spread to encompass the ground floor of the entire terrace and took up a small city block.

Dozens of apprentices, smiths, steel-workes, smelters, and even *santsi* specialists milled around the workshop. Furnaces glowed red, new steam-powered riveting guns hissed as they popped against sheets of steel. They even had one of the new flying-shuttle looms which Marian McGee had rediscovered from some old Jendar relic she had unlocked.

The could now make their own bespoke bolts of cloth without the need for hand-weaving it.

The new loom however had required a quick learning curve as the bits of fluff flying off the machine had immediately become a enormous fire hazard. They had used it once, and had then spent the next hour swearing to all the gods they knew and running around the shop putting out fires as the floating remnants of the cotton slowly drifted throughout the great space. The loom-room was now positioned as far away from the forge and furnaces as possible.

Wayran quickly found the spot for his tools, hung up his swage and replaced the die in its holder beside the workbench before following his father into his smaller private workshop. More than a few of Harold Spierling's apprentices on the shop floor watched them enter the room with both reverence and envy, yet to Wayran this private workshop had been part of his life for as long as he could remember. After long days of working, the three of them would quite often have their meals in this room; they would sit on chairs eating a thick pasty from Mrs. Gilchrest down the road, and would watch as their father put the finishing touches to whatever project he was working on. To Wayran and Matoh, their father's office and workshop sometimes felt more like home than the rest of the house sitting above them did.

He entered and noticed for what must have been the thousandth time how amazingly stuffed full of tools it was, yet at the same time wasn't cluttered. Everything had a place, and Harold Spierling knew exactly where that place was, often without even looking. His father's often quoted words came to him then: "When you need to lay hands on a tool, you want to know where it is, and that it's there." It was good advice for any potential layman, and it was a quality he respected in his father.

It was then Wayran noticed the black outline of a suit as it stood on a wooden dummy in the centre of the workshop. "What is that?" he asked in wonder.

"It's a new design the High King commissioned," his father said with arms crossed over his chest as he studied his creation. "It's taken me most of a year to make, and I haven't let any of those dough-heads out there see it yet." Harold Spierling hooked a thumb back towards the door indicating the room full of his apprentices.

Wayran rolled his eyes at the comment. He knew full well the apprentices outside were anything but dough-heads: most of them were excellent craftspeople, they had to be, to get an apprenticeship in his father's shop. But he also knew his father was the one who had invented the *trisk,* so when it came to *trisk*-smithing, Harold Spierling had no equal.

Wayran stepped up beside his father to study the creation. It was incredible and looked almost flawless. Patches woven into the suit flashed with a purple and blue sheen that he thought he recognised. "Is that ... covellite?" He leaned in closer to study a nearly translucent glassy line running along the middle of the suit's chest.

"It is," his father said with that half-grin on his face.

A spiderweb of gold, silver and copper wire radiated from the centre line out into the rest of the suit. Two more lines were stitched into the forearms and another, wider line of the shimmering material ran along the spine. It was a work of art. "It's amazing," Wayran said shaking his head. "How did you get covellite that thin? Won't it shatter?"

Covellite crystals were used primarily in the production of santsi globes. Wayran had never seen it applied this way before.

"It's a new process they developed up at the Academy; Professor Attridge figured out how to coat the covellite in a resin which allows smaller covellite crystal structures to stay intact while also being somewhat flexible and pliable. Soon as I heard about it, an idea hit me like a thunderbolt. I started working on a design and went straight to the

High King with it. He commissioned a suit on the spot. Which was lucky, as the High King is probably one of the only people in all of Salucia who could afford a suit like this."

And you probably know the High King will fund anything you put in front of him because of what happened to Mother. The thought snapped across Wayran's mind, and he felt immediately guilty and would never voice it. His father's relationship with the High King was ... complicated. There was history there that neither would ever talk about, but both Wayran and Matoh knew it had something to do with their mother.

"No kidding," Wayran whistled as he banished his gloomy thoughts and focused once again on the marvellous *trisk*. Covellite deposits were exceedingly rare. A fistful of it would make any copper miner rich for the rest of his life. "So ... what will this *trisk* be able to do?"

His father's smile widened. "I don't quite know yet." It was then Wayran noticed him looking at him expectantly. His father continued, "That's what I was hoping you could help me with ... if you're feeling up to it?"

Wayran's jaw dropped. "You want me to wear the High King's *trisk*?"

"I'm sure the High King could find someone to test it, but with something like this, well, a craftsman wants to know his creation works before he gives it to a king." His father shrugged. "I'd test it myself but I don't have the strength or control of siphoning that it needs. The High King is a bull of a man, and he can pull in more power than I've ever seen. Matoh probably has enough siphoning strength to give it a good run, but you have the control, and I trust your judgement."

Wayran didn't know what to say. So he just said, "Yes," and had his shirt off in a heartbeat. His father let out a throaty laugh.

"Don't be too eager!" His father clapped him gently on the shoulder. "If the High King hears about this he'll tan both our hides."

Before long Wayran had the High King's *trisk* on and a charged santsi globe strapped into a holster on his back. The *trisk* was far too large for him, but they had compensated by carefully cinching the covellite patches closer to his skin with a series of belts and ropes.

"Now don't get crazy with it. That much raw covellite could do some wild things. Don't draw too fast on that santsi, and make sure you are pushing with everything you've got into your conduit here." His father tapped the practice hammer with the lengths of copper running through it. "As a matter of fact, just put that hammer straight onto the copper contact point there on the dummy's chest. And for Halom's sake, take it slow."

Wayran could see the concern on his father's face. "I'll be careful. Don't worry, I'm in no rush to destroy another fortune's worth of equipment."

His father grimaced slightly, then took a step back, nodding for him to begin.

Wayran took a deep breath. *Alright ... here goes.*

He focused his mind and started to siphon.

His entire body seemed to buzz. The dummy exploded away from him as a giant blue spark erupted from the hammer's blunt end.

Wayran stood shocked. The dummy, now burning as it flew through the air, slammed itself off a workbench and crashed to the floor.

"I said take it slow!" Harold Spierling jumped forward, a blanket somehow already in his hand, which he tossed over the dummy snuffing out the flames.

"I did! That *was* slow!" Wayran protested.

"Lady take me," his father cursed under his breath as he pulled the blanket off the singed wooden dummy. "Are you alright?"

"Yes." Wayran shook himself, finally lowering the hammer. "Yes, I'm fine."

His father turned to look at him; they met each other's eyes and looked back down at the dummy his father was now straddling with a slightly burnt blanket.

"Well," his father said, "that was unexpected."

They both burst into laughter.

"Wow," Wayran said after they had stopped laughing, "I think you might just be the High King's new best friend. He's going to love this." He looked down at the covellite strip on his chest in wonder.

***

After three more equally explosive tests, they decided the rest was up to the High King. Wayran had taken off the *trisk* and replaced it on the wood dummy. He and his father stood looking at it, somewhat awed at what it could do.

"You don't have to stay and work with me at the shop you know. You have other options," Harold Spierling said.

Wayran turned to see a sympathetic smile on his father's face. "What do you mean?"

His father clapped a hand down on his shoulder. "I know this thing in the wastes is a significant setback for you, and that the thought of staying here in the shop rankles like nothing else, despite the fact we both know you'd be an excellent *trisk* maker. I remember what it was like to be young. You need an adventure more than money sometimes." His father smiled as his eyes went distant, no doubt recalling some of the tales he had told his two boys.

"It's not the work, Dad, it's just –" Wayran struggled to explain.

"Don't worry, son, I understand." His father gave him another reassuring clap on the shoulder. "Now listen, your uncle can be as stubborn and ornery as an old mule, but that old mule is run by his pocketbook above all things. If you pay him back, that ultimatum of his might just soften a touch."

"It's a lot of money, Dad." Wayran looked down at his hands. He didn't like admitting failure to his father. He always wanted to make him proud, and this complete bungling of his chance made him feel small in his father's eyes.

"Well ... I just might have a solution to that." His father hesitated. "Though you will probably not like the sound of it."

Wayran was curious now. "What is it?"

"You can go to the Academy, train as an officer, try to be a Syklan, like Matoh," his father said; his hands were up almost defensively.

The statement almost made Wayran retch. He didn't know what to say, it was like his father had chosen the worst idea in the world to taunt him with. "You can't be serious." He shook his head and could feel anger and frustration building within.

"Now, I know it's the last thing you want to do." The look of sympathy returned to his father's face. "You've always said the military wasn't for you. We've talked about it before, and I'm not going to bring up old arguments, so I'm going to lay it out for you logically, just like in some of those science books you like to read."

Wayran started to object, but his father held up a finger. "Just listen, Wayran, and if you can think of a better plan, then we'll discuss it."

"Alright fine." Wayran crossed his arms. "Let's hear it."

"First of all, you can always come back to work at the shop later; there is always a place for you here, you know that. However, you probably already know as much about *trisk* making as any of my apprentices so you wouldn't be learning that much, and right now the last thing you want to do is spend your young adult years tending shop with your father." His father smiled.

Wayran grinned reluctantly. They were accurate observations, and he had to admit his father the point, so he nodded.

"Second, even if you did work with me, I wouldn't be able to pay you much, as most of my apprentices, I'm only slightly ashamed to say, work for a pittance. They all want the chance to work for the High King's *trisk* maker, which is a fact I use ruthlessly against them." His father winked at him. "Keeps my operating costs down. Plus they know when they finally get out from under my thumb and start making *trisk* for themselves they'll make back ten times over what I've withheld during their apprenticeship. If I paid you more than them, and it would be quite a bit more to repay your uncle in a short amount of time, resentment would grow within the shop. Also, I'm fairly sure, as you're my son, that you would rather eat glass than have your father step in and pay back his brother-in-law for you." His father paused, watching him, seeming to know that he had struck true again.

Wayran rolled his eyes and nodded. The thought of his father paying off the debt made him cringe. Uncle Aaron would never respect him again for as long as he lived if that was how he chose to pay off the debt.

"All of which means of course that working here in the shop is not the right option." His father paused, letting him mull his words over.

"So that leaves us with a few goals when deciding what to do: make money quickly, and find a job which might teach you something useful, while still having a chance to provide you with some sort of adventure. Yes?"

Wayran shook his head as a sudden anger began to rise within him. The arguments were good but he just couldn't get over how he felt about it. "It's logical but I just can't go to the Academy."

His father held up his hands. "Peace, son. I know we've talked about it before, but it would meet those goals. And the Chroniclers are right there in the Academy; you would have access to all the Jendar gizmos you could get your hands on when you were off duty. Maybe even meet a girl?"

"Dad," Wayran groaned, "I'm in New Toeron, one of the biggest cities in Salucia, I don't think I have to go to the Academy to meet women." He had barely had any time for women. He had of course fantasised about one-day meeting someone who would take his breath away. He had even daydreamed that he and Ariel might eventually share a moment while on *Deliverence,* after he had become a full Storm Chaser of course. He would come back all dusty from a big storm, and then she'd be there... waiting for him.

Wayran shook himself from his dreaming. That was all gone now. "A relationship is the last thing on my mind right now."

"Maybe not," his father said with a smile, "and I didn't say anything about a relationship, but you'll meet a lot of strong, smart women there. The best young minds and bodies come from all over the nine nations to train there. You'll meet people who dream big like you do, people who can challenge you."

"Sure, you're probably right." Wayran was growing exasperated. "But that's Matoh's dream, and I ..." He thought of his mother. She had fought for this, and the Academy was one of her dreams, which she helped to create; but part of him, deep down, blamed the military for taking his mother away from them. Yet he couldn't bring himself to say it, so instead he said, "Well, what if we have to go to war? I don't want to kill anyone."

His father nodded at this, turning back to the *trisk* on the dummy. His fingers tugged at the suit slightly, making some minor adjustment. "I can understand that." His father had to think about those words, and Wayran knew he had found a good point. "It is not an easy thing to kill, and it is something I wish my sons will never have to do. Yet sometimes it is justified." Harold Spierling looked up from his idle work. His eyes grew distant and sad.

His father never spoke of the battles he had fought in during the Unification Wars. There was pain associated with those memories, and

Wayran could see that pain now behind his father's eyes.

"To defend, to protect those who cannot protect themselves from the violence imposed upon them. Those are reasons to kill," his father said as he turned to him, "but it is my hope that you would not have to, in your time with the military. We are at peace. The Nine Realms have never known such stability. Most of a Syklan's role is to keep the peace, to stop people from inciting violence. To uphold the High King's laws, to serve and protect. That is not so bad. And I can think of no other place that will pay you to do so, while also giving you the kind of training and education many young men and women around the Nine Nations dream of."

Wayran was running out of arguments. His father had him, he knew it, but every part of him wanted to resist. He could only imagine Matoh's reaction. It would not be favourable to say the least.

Yet the more he thought about it, the more it began to make sense. It was a logical solution to many of his problems, which only fuelled his irritation.

His father must have seen some of his resistance dissolve, for he went to the door and opened it. "Think about it, son. Just promise me you'll consider it. I really do think it is a good fit for you right now."

"Isn't it too late? This year's initiates have already been chosen." One final protest, though he knew it was weak.

His father shrugged. "I've already asked – your mother's name was all I had to say. They'd take you in a heartbeat, plus it's not like you wouldn't be qualified. You have the skillset they are looking for anyways. There is a place there for you, if you will take it."

Wayran shook his head, feeling outmanoeuvred and defeated. Nothing would top the pay he would get as an officer in training. He would have his living costs paid for and be earning a salary. He ran some quick numbers in his head; he could probably have his debt to Uncle Aaron paid off in the first three years of service; the next two years he would be making money. Easy enough to buy a new glider ... and he could probably find time to continue his research on the Jendar. *Maybe even enough of the old language to translate the book?*

His father had always told him and Matoh that their mother had wanted them both going to the Academy. Back when she had said it, the Academy had only been a dream. Yet it had never been Wayran's desire, a fact which made him feel guilty, made him feel like he didn't deserve this potential place as an initiate. His motives weren't pure, not like his mother's dream had been, not like Matoh's desire was.

He paused beside his father. "It just doesn't feel right. I –"

"She'd be fine with it," his father said. "Above all, your mother loved you very much. She would be happy to have created the opportunity for you. That's what she truly fought for. To give you both the hope of a better future, Wayran. Trust me, you would have her blessing in this."

Sometimes it felt like his father could see right through him. A lump in his throat grew as his anger vanished. He bowed his head, trying to hide his emotion. "Alright," he whispered, "I'll go."

His father patted him on the shoulder as he left the inner workshop.

Wayran plodded through the larger workshop, past the apprentices, and reached the door leading to the stairs up to their house above. He grabbed the handle but something caught his eye out on the street.

A man was watching him. A large conical hat sheltered the man from the rain that was only now beginning to fall, and kept his face in shadow. As soon as he knew that he had been spotted, the man in the street turned to leave, but not before Wayran had caught a glimpse of something beneath the shadow of that hat.

Red swirling eyes had glared at him from that darkness.

He ran to the open side of the workshop.

But the man was gone, and Wayran could see no sign of him on the street.

Was he really there? But the thought provoked another headache, and he had to retreat and go back up to his room to take another dose of his medicine.

It *couldn't* have been the man from the wastes. The headaches and stress were causing him to see things. He was just on edge was all.

10 - Leaving Familiarity

The first successful attempts at integrating our specialised electric generating organs into new nervous systems were considered highly controversial to many in our society. I still laugh at this, for if they knew what else we did in the bowels of our glass towers, their common, uncomprehending minds would have been truly terrified.

They would have condemned us for playing God.

I look at my monitors now and want to tell them, we weren't playing.

\- *Journal of Robert Mannford, Year 000 Day 002*

Adel

Blossom Bay, Bauffin

Adel's foot snapped up above her head. She sent her siphoned charge coursing through the thin disc of copper atop her foot sewn into her *trisk*. There was the familiar crackling sizzle of electric shock as her foot made contact, but it had been too slow.

The metal staff in her father's hand blocked it, and Adel felt the blast of icy air as her father siphoned in, pulling the energy from her attack into his weapon.

Adel pushed the reserve of energy she held back into her next attack. It coursed through her other leg painfully, and the copper atop her foot grew hot, but the feint had worked. Her father had still been siphoning in and was caught off guard by the extra energy.

She continued her onslaught: a flurry of lightning kicks followed up the shock she had given her father. A foot arced overhead, her heel slammed into the top of her father's staff, it came free of his hands and she flicked the weapon away.

Adel siphoned in hard and the tiny line of santsi globes running along the spine of her *trisk* sparkled bright blue. She landed the spinning kick, planted herself, and thrust forward with a twin palm strike.

This time, the energy snapped in the air from the contact points on her palms.

Her father toppled backwards. Another angry grunt escaped.

But her victory was short lived.

Her father tucked and rolled backwards up into his defensive stance. His eyes flashed dangerously. "Good." He said the word almost as a growl. He had rolled and recovered the staff, which now began to whirl before her eyes. The santsi in his *trisk* lit with energy.

That small bit of praise was everything to Adel at that moment; it lifted her spirits like nothing else could.

The first staff strike came and she took it on her left armguard, siphoning in the energy her father was pushing into the attack. This dance of pushing, pulling, stealing and countering siphoned energy had now become as natural as breathing for Adel.

Her right armguard blocked the second strike. Adel had seen the shimmer of heat from the end of the staff and stopped siphoning, to prevent the overload. *Shock, fire, or ice? Which will he use next?*

She pivoted a step back, lifting her leg out of the way of another strike, and dropped to her knee and crossed her armguards overhead to catch the staff. She guessed wrong.

He used shock again, and her muscles froze for a split second.

Yet, that was all he had needed.

The thrust kick slammed into her chest. Adel felt the air leave her lungs as the strike threw her backwards, but she didn't have any room to roll. The barn wall hit her back hard, and she heard the pop of some of the santsi in her *trisk* shattering.

It was all she could do to drop down as her father's fist snapped into the wood where her head had been. She heard boards crack and thanked Halom it was the wood above her rather than her skull making that noise.

She thrust out with a leg from her sitting position and kicked the front of his knee, buckling his leg backwards. Yet instead of retracting the kick for another strike, she kept her foot on his knee and siphoned in hard through the copper pad on the bottom of her booted foot. Energy burned inside her body now instead of in the santsi as she had pulled too much, but Adel had pushed past this forbidden boundary before, and knew she could make her body use that extra energy.

As she kept siphoning in the energy from her father's leg, his muscles stiffened as if he had been sitting in the snow for hours, stiffened enough to prevent a counter, and it gave Adel the split second she needed to sweep forward with her other leg as she pushed hard away from the wall.

Her father fell. She heard another crunch as some of his santsi popped, and she jumped onto his hips before he could set up a leg guard.

An elbow smashed up against the side of her head, her world spun, but Adel held her position and slammed her forehead down onto her father's chest before the next attack came. Her open palm snapped into his ribs and forced all the energy she held through into a shock strike.

Her father's body went rigid and she took advantage of the opening to rise up and slam down with both hands onto his exposed face.

It stunned him, blood ran from his nose, but Adel could already feel him try to twist beneath her, to buck out of her mounted position. A knee slammed into her back, knocking her forward.

She ducked her head down as again an elbow strike snaked up from the ground, but it missed as she was too close to his body.

She couldn't take much more of this. He was too strong.

Her knife flicked out of its sheath on her hip. Its blade rested against his exposed neck. Adel siphoned all of the energy she had left into the blade, making it burn hot.

Her father stopped twisting.

"You should have had the knife out as soon as you mounted." Leonard Corbin's hard, icy eyes looked up at Adel. The burning blade on his throat did nothing to affect the stony gaze. She could have been holding a feather to his throat for all the surrender he showed.

"Yes, father." She stopped siphoning, feeling drained, feeling like she was ready to drop, but she knew she couldn't. The lesson was not yet finished.

"Why did you hesitate?" her father questioned.

"I don't know, sir." Adel shook her head, ashamed. She could already see the red burn mark in the shape of her knife blade on the skin of his neck. He would have an ugly scar from that, and it made her almost sick to think of it. But he would have been disappointed if she had done anything else.

"Will your enemy hesitate?" His eyes bore into her. She could tell no lie under that gaze.

"No, sir." She gulped. The pain in her face from the elbow strike was warm. Whether it bruised or welted mattered not. She had been hit several times this lesson. Each one was a failure. She had to do better.

"You were distracted." The almost unperceivable nod of his head signalled the lesson's end. She rolled off him, and her father got to his feet.

Adel said nothing in response to his observation. She knew it was true.

"A lot of energy was needed to freeze my knee like that." Her father's statement insinuated and accused all at once.

Adel knew there was no point hiding the truth. He would know the lie before it left her lips. "I didn't use the *trisk,*" she admitted.

Even now she could feel the residual energy tingling through her body.

Her father clenched his jaw and looked down at the wooden floor of his barn, a barn which housed no animals except the one horse and a goat, both in the far stable. He seemed to be considering something.

"How many times now?" He went to grab a cloth from the rail. He wiped the blood from his face and held the cloth to his nose calmly. This was nowhere near the first time they had needed to stop blood from flowing during a lesson.

"Twelve," Adel answered.

"You will need to find Fellow Callahan at the Academy." Her father shook his head and continued, "He is an expert in the unnatural."

Leonard Corbin looked sad, and Adel had never seen him sad before. It scared her. "Yes, I will, sir. I'm sorry, I don't understand. You mean this year? Leave for the Academy this year?"

"Tomorrow, with Naira. I already have arrangements in place. You have a place waiting for you. Halom has chosen to make you his servant ..." Her father trailed off and went to the far wall of the barn to bend down to the floor. He poked a finger into a wooden knot in the board and Adel straightened in shock as she heard a click as the floorboard sank into the ground and rolled away. She heard the whirring of metal gears for a moment and then, there, beneath the floorboard, was a long metal safe concreted into the foundation of the barn.

Her father reached under his shirt and pulled out his necklace with the somewhat eccentric metallic Singer symbol of a man with two hands held skyward. The odd bit was that this symbol also had a crown over the man's head, whereas all other icons she had seen were missing the crown.

To her surprise, her father undid the leather thong holding the symbol, turned the metal object upside down and slid it neatly into a small hole on the safe.

It was a key. He had been wearing a key around his neck all these years.

"Father, what is all this? How long has that been here? What's inside?" Adel asked with wonder and trepidation.

Instead of answering, her father pulled a long cloth-wrapped object from the safe. He pulled the cloth and Adel saw the long black enamelled shape as it fell away.

A sword; and one which had a presence. It felt as if a demon had just been conjured into the room and was staring at her with lidless eyes.

Her father touched the sword's pommel to his head and closed his eyes. Adel caught the hint of a prayer on his lips, and then he pulled the sword blade half free of the scabbard. Only then did she notice that the sword was also completely black, a black so dark that the light itself looked as if it faltered around it. "Halom has chosen to make you his servant, just as he chose me so many years ago."

The words sounded like a ritual to her. Her father looked her in the eye and then ran a thumb along the edge of the blade, drawing blood.

"You can do what I do?" Adel asked, confused.

"No, my gifts were different, but I know enough to recognise His touch when I see it." Her father watched the droplet of his blood touch the sword with such intensity, it was as if his life depended on it. In a trick of the light, it looked almost as if the sword drank in his blood. Her father grimaced and dropped down to both knees and closed his eyes.

"Father, you're scaring me ..." Adel could feel the tears in her eyes now, and she couldn't stop them. She hadn't meant to use this horrible form of siphoning. It had just started happening to her.

"It's alright, my child." Her father snapped the blade back into its scabbard. He bowed and presented the sword to her with open palms. "This is Halom's instrument, and with it, you will judge the wicked. Adel, this blade is your birthright, but not only that, it will help you with this new power you struggle with. Take it."

Adel knew her father was bestowing a great honour on her, but she hesitated. She could feel the power of the blade he held, and it scared her.

"Adel ..." There was urgency in her father's voice now; he kept his head bowed, but she saw his cut hand falter as if it wanted to grab the pommel once more. "Adel, I ..."

She grabbed the proffered sword and immediately felt her body cool. Only then did she realise she had still been siphoning. Her heart pounded, to think how close she must have been to burning herself out.

Her father released the blade and his arms slumped to the floor as if drained of their strength.

"The sword adds another measure of control to some people's abilities," he said in a breathless voice, "and it can hold more than any santsi globe; ten times more. It will help keep you safe." He looked at the sword with a strange sadness, as if he were saying goodbye to an old friend. The gash across his thumb was forgotten.

Leonard Corbin got to his feet and put his hand on his daughter's shoulders. "That blade is more than a sword. For me, it helped clarify my path. It was as if, while holding the sword, all the wicked magics of the world melted away and I would suddenly know what needed to be done." His eyes went distant then, as if he remembered past glories. "You will have more training at the Academy than just that of a Syklan in the High King's army. You are Halom's chosen warrior. Fellow Callahan will help you unlock your true potential. He is an ally and a true believer."

All of these words echoed through her like a ritual. Then he looked at her and his mind returned from whatever memories had come with the catechism. "I'm sorry, Adel, Halom has plans for you, my daughter, just as he had plans for me."

The father, who had trained her to be tough, trained her to be unyielding, trained her to be stronger than all the others, the father who had forever been strict, and hard, and distant, stepped forward and hugged her.

It was everything Adel had ever hoped for, and with this unexpected act of kindness, the dam holding back the torrent of emotion within her let go. Her anxiety about leaving the only home she had ever known, her fear of the wide world beyond her farm, and the little girl she had never been allowed to be, caused her tears to flow unchecked, and her father held her.

"You walk Halom's path now, my daughter." His voice boomed within his chest. "May it be a better path than mine." He rested his hands on her shoulders, and Adel looked up to see the tears in his eyes too. She had never seen him cry. "Now go get your things. We have to get to Blossom Bay by first bell and catch that ferry. Naira will be waiting."

11 - A Fresh Start

The Corsairs were originally a mercenary group, headed by Captain Sarah Granger, which could be hired to protect and escort merchant vessels on the Broken Sea. Effective protection from Navutian Raiders was in short supply and the Corsairs quickly found themselves in high demand.

Captain Granger found herself exceedingly rich, which allowed her to expand her fleet so they were able to provide protection even beyond the Broken Sea. The Corsairs became the most formidable naval fleet in all of Salucia. Their discipline and tactical dominance soon began to match the overwhelming numbers of Navutian Raiders.

The conflicts between Navutia and the privately financed Corsair fleet continued to escalate in ferocity and brutality from generation to generation until the open seas were in an all-out war. Many believe this laid the foundation for the Unification Wars, during which Ronaston Mihane of Asgur rose to power, rebelled against his Navutian overlords, and convinced the then Corsair Protection Guild to become the Salucian Naval Fleet. However, all members of the Salucian Navy still refer to themselves as Corsairs despite the fact they are now nationally funded.

- Chronicler Simon Rathelson in A Common History: 1851– 2850 ATC, 5th Edition, 2850

Naira

Blossom Bay, Bauffin

Mother was home.

The demons which that particular thought dredged up within Naira O'Bannon had been haunting her for her entire seventeen years of existence.

She stared at the all too familiar tar-stained door in front of her, trying to steel herself to push it open for what would most likely be the last time. She had been avoiding this for as long as she could, but she could wait no longer. Naira took a deep breath and pushed the weather-beaten piece of wood aside and entered the dank hovel she had had to call home for as long as she could remember.

The horrible smell of fish-soaked leather and woodsmoke assaulted her as soon as the door had moved, but she had long ago grown used to it. It was the smell of mother, of anger, of vulnerability, of hurt, and of pain. It was the smell of home, and today was the day she was going to leave that behind. Already she could feel the lump in her throat forming. A large driftwood chair faced the fire, and Naira knew the interwoven lengths of gnarled bone white wood hide the hunched form of her mother.

"Thought you could sneak away without seeing me, did you?" The accusation held only a small portion of the usual venom, yet it still hurt as it always did. Every word from her mother was like another lash on her back.

"You know that's not true." Naira measured her words carefully, keeping a tight control on the flood of emotions threatening to overwhelm her. "Adel and Mr Corbin are meeting me at the port, you could come too if ... " She couldn't finish. Naira knew her mother would through the invite back in her face. She wanted to say so much more, but couldn't. "I need to change, and to collect my things."

"Humph," her mother grunted. "Things my money paid for. Ungrateful is what you are. Ungrateful for everything you've been given. Go on then, run away to your other family. I know that's what you want."

Her mother leant over the thick wood of the chair's arm to glare at her, challenging her to say different. Naira knew there was no point in correcting her mother. Naira had bought or made her own clothes ever since she was old enough to get her own shifts on the docks. Everything she had in her corner of the tiny shack she had bought and paid for herself, but her mother would never admit that. *The only thing your money has paid for is the dozens of bottles of that swill Gregor sells,* Naira wanted to say, but she held her tongue. Her mother however had sensed the concealed insult.

“Go on, say it, you ungrateful little harlot, say what you mean. You won’t get away with swinging your hips and showing your tits in here.” Her mother’s eyes were half crazed.

“This again?” It was another of her mother’s common insults. Her other job was waiting tables at Johnny Blin’s betting house, something which her mother was no doubt jealous of. It was true she wore a somewhat revealing uniform, but men could think what they liked so long as they didn’t try it on with her. “That’s rich coming from you; you’re the one who taught me. Not that it would do you any good anymore,” Naira spat back at her. Too late: she had tried to restrain herself but failed. She knew her insult would cut deep, and knew it was petty, but it had slipped out, and a part of her was glad she hadn’t held back. The other parts wanted to cry.

Her mother had been pretty once, but years of drinking and the fists of drunk men had changed that forever. Her mother had never been kind, but she had shown Naira how to survive. "I'm sorry, I shouldn't have said that," Naira made herself say. She closed her eyes and forced herself to stay calm. *She wants a fight; she’s trying to manipulate me, just like she always does.* Yet Naira also knew it was the only way they talked anymore.

"Oh, don't apologise, I only gave up my whole life to raise a daughter I didn't want. Go on, take your cheap shots. Kick a defenceless old woman the world has beaten down. Leavin' me on my own to die in the damp and cold. Ungrateful. Ungrateful ..." Her mother grimaced and trailed off as she reached for the greasy jug of what Gregor called wine. Naira knew that what was in that jug was so potent it would leave most grown men reeling, but her mother drank it down as if it were water. *Don't feel sorry for her,* she chided herself, remembering the black eye she had received the last time she had shown her mother sympathy.

She turned her back on her mother, ducked behind the filthy curtain separating her tiny corner from the rest of the room, and pulled it closed behind her. If truth be told there was really almost nothing to gather up, for she had learned not to keep anything valuable in the house lest mother decide that Gregor's finest was more important than food, clothes or Naira's privacy. Most of what she needed was at Johnny Blin's, and his betting house was really the only place she had needed to visit. She had clothes there too, but she had told herself to come here anyways. *I have to say goodbye,* Naira told herself. *Whatever else she's done, she deserves a goodbye.*

She changed out of her apron and work clothes in silence, trying not to give her mother the opportunity to comment. Naira had scraped the thick leather apron as clean as was possible; her mother could still get a few years' use out of it, and the clothes might fetch a few coins, though she doubted it. She would leave them anyways, just in case there was a use for them. She slipped on her tight breeches, blouse, vest and jacket, somewhat surprised that they were still lying on her hammock where she had left them this morning. She undid the tight bun of her hair and shook out her long dark locks before looking around for a final time at her little corner. *I won't miss it,* she admitted to herself. Naira had thought there might be some feeling of nostalgia, but as she anticipated leaving it behind all she felt was excitement. She took a deep breath and pushed the curtain open and left it there.

Stepping to the door, she hesitated. It had to be now. "Mother." Naira turned to look at the driftwood chair. “I’m leaving now ...” It fought against all the years of hurt and anguish she had suffered under this woman’s roof, but she made herself say it. “I love you.”

Silence followed those three little words, a silence filled only by the crackling wood in the fireplace and the pounding of her heart. Naira had never felt so vulnerable as she felt just then. She had dug through the tough and calloused walls protecting her heart to say those words, and now she waited, feeling so much like the scared little girl she had always been in this house.

Finally, the driftwood chair creaked as her mother shifted. "Naira ...” her mother started, still not able to look at her standing by the door “... when some bastard puts a baby in your belly, make sure you drink that blue tea.” Her mother finally turned and her flinty eyes met hers. “I wish I had. Kids ruin your life.”

It was the final dagger. Naira had expected it, yet somehow she had hoped it wouldn’t come. The words cut right down to her core. She knew then that she would never see her mother again, but as much as she had expected that final parting shot to devastate her, she felt pity instead. Her mother would spend the rest of her life rotting in this shack like a cancerous growth upon the docks. It was sad, but Naira knew she had to leave it behind lest her mother’s darkness suck her down with it.

She found the steel in her soul once again, just as she had for so many years, the steel that gave her strength and made her strong. She stared back into those hateful eyes and made them submit, stared at them until her mother knew she would never come back. "Goodbye, mother." Naira opened the battered old door and walked out of her past and into the rest of her life.

The door closed behind her, and it was then that she felt the tears roll down her cheeks. She cried quietly there, with her back against the wooden door, shaking with the pain of the moment. It was done, she had said the things she had wanted to say, and had restrained herself from fighting as best she could. *I tried,* she told herself. *I tried.*

A pair of fishwives walked by and gave her a pair of sympathetic smiles. “Cheer up, love, the sun is up and Halom is smiling on us. You’ll see, mark my words, by the end of the night, a pretty young filly like you will have some handsome brute trying to sit you on his lap,” one of them said.

“Thanks.” Naira wiped her tears away and returned what she hoped looked like a genuine smile. They waved at her as they left. *See,* she told herself, *not everyone is horrible.* They were trying to be nice (although the last thing Naira wanted was to be sitting on *some handsome brute’s* lap by the end of the night). But they meant well, so she waved back, and with that Naira set her shoulders and strode down the docks towards Johnny Blin's.

The trip was only a short one and with each step away from her old house her excitement began to rise. She still felt raw from the encounter with her mother, but it felt like sailing out of a storm: you were battered, bruised, and exhausted, but the relief was so strong you felt almost giddy.

Naira turned the corner and saw the big painted sign with the white dice and playing cards emblazoned upon a field of red, with ‘Johnny Blin's’ written in scripted gold letters. On the boundary between the high town and the docks, Johnny Blin's was the perfect spot for the lowborn of the docks to gamble away their sorrows hoping to get rich, while also being equally equipped for the well-to-do of Blossom Bay's high town for nights of drunken debauchery. It was a taste of high-class accessible to the docks, and also safe, dirty fun for the rich, who didn’t have to worry about getting knifed in an alley. Naira was so glad to see the sign that she was smiling by the time she pushed open the door.

"Naira!" Johnny Blin bellowed at her, "Come to work one more shift before you go, my sweet?" The big balding owner wore his usual ridiculous outfit of matching red and gold jacket and pantaloons. Johnny's grin was so large it looked as if his extraordinarily waxed moustaches would touch the ceiling.

"Sorry, Johnny, not tonight, gotta catch a ferry." She couldn't help but smile at the extravagant man. He was as crude as you like, but she had grown to respect him.

"Such a sad day, I'm losing one of my best table wenches!" He held his hands up to the high ceiling as if he were lost without her. "Now come here and give your Uncle Johnny a hug."

You won't be calling me that anymore after tonight," Naira said as she shook a finger at him. "What's the fine for insulting an officer of the royal navy?"

"Lucky for me then you have to actually be at the Academy for that to take effect." Johnny said, smiling as he still had his arms outstretched.

Naira let herself be squashed by the big man's arms. The kind gesture felt good, even if in the back of her mind she knew the hug was only half an excuse for 'Uncle' Johnny to have one last feel. He always made sure to push her chest up against him a bit too much. She sighed to herself, *At least it's a better reception than I had earlier.* She had learned that all men wanted her, but Johnny at least paid her on time, kept her things safe, and was true to his word. She could surrender to awkward hugs for that.

After a bit too long he released her and put his hand on her shoulder. "I'm expecting you'll want your things." He motioned for her to step behind the bar, but then, like a bird of prey, he spotted something on the gambling floor.

"Cletus!" he shouted to the giant, boulder-shouldered brute meandering among the tables of gamblers. "Keep an eye on that table. Don't like the look of those kings." He pointed to the playing cards on a green baize table top. The four men at the table all froze wide-eyed as

Cletus trudged over to them drawing the thick cudgel from his belt.

Johnny smiled over to the four card players. “I’m sure you won’t mind exchanging that deck with Cletus on the next hand, gentlemen?” He waited for any objections, and there were none as Cletus loomed dangerously beside their table. “No? Then carry on, my good fellows.”

Satisfied, Johnny moved behind the bar, through the kitchen and into his small office at the back. Naira watched as he ceremoniously pulled a long silver chain from under his shirt to reveal a set of keys set against a leather pad. That was another good thing about Johnny Blin, he didn’t trust anyone either, and he had ingrained that wariness into her during the last few years she had worked for him.

“I take it you want everything?” Johnny asked as he selected a small key and unlocked a large drawer on his desk and pulled out a leather bag.

“I want my letter from the Academy, my clothes, my rucksack, my knives ... but only half the money.” Naira hesitated, seeing the questioning look on Johnny’s face. She would need to explain. “Sell whatever stuff I have left, and use that with the rest of my money to pay somebody to drop a pack of food around for my mother once a week. Nothing extravagant, the food needs to stretch as long as it can.”

Johnny's face softened a bit. "Very touching, my dear. I will see to it myself. Though in my opinion she doesn't deserve it."

Naira took a step towards him. As much as her mother warranted the remark, she still didn’t like others putting her down.

"Sorry, I know I'm not supposed to talk about the mother." He held his hands up in apology, though she doubted he was really sorry. Johnny's greasy smile returned as soon as Naira stepped back. "What will I do without you, my beauty? My regulars will cry in their cups at your departure."

“Not my problem anymore, Johnny.” She smiled and winked at him. “I’m sure you’ll figure something out, but it won’t be with me. I’m off to bigger and better things.”

“Don’t get too shiny now,” Johnny chastised. “Knights and Corsairs have to protect us slime right alongside them snooty nobles, as well you know.”

“No one said anything about protecting slime! That’s it, I take my application back.” She feigned shock. “Besides, I thought Corsairs were meant to arrest pirates, not protect them.” She winked at him flirtatiously. “You wouldn’t happen to know any pirates, would you, Johnny?”

“Me?” Johnny over-exaggerated his innocence, once he had Naira’s things on his desk. “I don’t even know what a pirate is.”

“You see.” Naira played along. “Nothing to worry about. I knew you were the good kind of slime.” She collected everything up into the rucksack he had retrieved for her.

“Oh stop flirting.” Johnny rolled his eyes. “Your charms have no effect on me, young O’Bannon.”

Naira just smiled. She knew that for the lie it was, but she let it go. It was not good to remind a man of what he couldn't have unless you wanted even more attention. "Well ..." She held out her hands. She had to get going, the ferry must have arrived by now and would be waiting in the port for only a few hours before casting off again. Time to say another goodbye, and this one was much different. "Thank you, Johnny Blin, for giving this smelly fish-gutter a chance.” She smiled. “You were good to me and I won’t forget that.”

"I would have been stupid not to employ you. Tips went up considerably the day you started wiggling through those tables." Johnny winked at her and moved from behind the desk to give her one last, overly familiar hug.

Naira sighed to herself, *Men never change*. Finally, she was released from Johnny's crushing embrace. "Right, I'm off. Remember not to be a pirate," she said, pointing a finger at him with a squint as she left the room with everything she was taking from her old life contained within the small rucksack on her back. The lack of weight felt incredible.

As she left, she stopped beside the card table that Cletus was watching, and jumped up and planted a kiss on his cheek. "Thanks, Cletus!"

The four card players looked envious as they gawked up at the slow sentinel. She had never seen Cletus smile before, but he was beaming at her like a child. *He deserved one,* she told herself. Cletus had always protected her from grabby aggressive customers and had never abused his position.

She was almost to the door, but as it opened, the last person she had wanted to see today stepped through: Barry Stenson, son of the Lord Mayor of Blossom Bay, along with his group of lackeys. Naira groaned inwardly, there was no way to get by them.

“Naira! I’m so glad you’re here.” Barry spread his arms wide like the over-expressive jerk he was. “Fetch me a drink, wench!”

Barry's weasel-like smile, along with his cronies giggling behind him, made her stomach try to empty itself. She would like nothing more than to wipe that cocky smile right off his face – but she didn't need that now. All she had to do was get to the docks.

“Sorry, Barry, I’m not working today, I was just leaving actually.” She moved to let them go by, but Barry stood there looking at her.

"Is that so? Well, I say you *are* working today." He stepped forward, reached around and smacked her bottom, before grabbing it in front of everyone. "Now be a good wench and fetch that drink." His breath already smelled of wine, no doubt today was another day on which he and his rich friends were slumming it and making trouble for everyone.

She heard a table move, and Cletus growl. “Cletus. No.” Naira held up her hand to the big man. “I’ll handle this.” She had had a lifetime of these situations. Retaliating, in any way, always turned out bad for a girl from the docks and anyone who helped her, especially when it was the Lord Mayor's son doing the provoking. She knew she should just get the drink and slip out later when they were preoccupied. No repercussions, no trouble for anyone – but today was different.

Today she was a somebody. Today she was leaving this little hovel of a town to become a Corsair, and a Corsair wouldn't have to take this from a backwater mayor's son. Maybe it was her frayed emotions from her confrontation with her mother, maybe it was too many awkward hugs and men assuming they could get away with it, but whatever it was, today she just couldn't take it anymore. *Sorry, Johnny.*

"Wench?" Naira reached down and grabbed Barry's wrist, jabbing her fingers hard into the pressure points she knew were there. He tried to snatch his hand back in surprise, but she wasn't finished with him. Her fingers dug in and wrenched the hand which had touched her bottom up behind his back.

Barry squealed like a frightened child, eliciting a laugh from the room full of watchful patrons. She watched his eyes bulge in pain and confusion as she bent his wrist back on itself. The leverage on his elbow must have been excruciating. Part of her wanted to push just a bit further until she heard bones snap. "You don't get to call me that anymore, Barry. You will call me sir, or ma'am, as my rank will dictate."

One of his lackeys moved towards her. She swivelled and smashed the heel of her boot into big man's dumb face. She heard the crunch of nose cartilage breaking and Barry squealed again at the sight his henchman crumpling to his knees.

Naira eyed the second one. "By all means, step forward and see what happens." She kept her voice calm despite her pounding heart and fixed the second goon with as evil a grin as she could muster. She twisted Barry's wrist a fraction more and this time he whimpered. "Stay back, you idiot! She's going to break my arm!" Barry cried.

The second henchman put his hands up and backed away.

"Good." Naira moved herself to the door and leant to whisper in Barry's ear. "This arm, Barry," she gave his arm a slight shake, "is now my property, and if I come back to this gods-forsaken hole of a town and hear you've been molesting Johnny's girls ..." she leant in closer, "I will take this arm, Barry, and I'll nail it to the mast of my ship so my crew can laugh at the man who disobeyed Naira O'Bannon!" She threw her weight into his back, let the wrist go, and slammed his head against the wall. Barry dropped to the floor with a bloody nose.

She left Johnny Blin's to uproarious applause and walked out into the late morning light to pump her fist with joy. "Oh, that felt good!" she shouted, and for the first time in a long time Naira smiled simply because she was happy. She adjusted her rucksack – the few things she would keep from this place – and ran down the street with the smile still on her face, for she ran towards a boat, and it was taking her far away from here.

12 - Entangling

The Arbiter was reputed to be only a man, but accounts regarding his actual appearance seem confused. Descriptions vary from demon-like, with fangs and talons, to huge a reptile with glistening black skin. Some even say he doesn't have a body at all and instead floats across the battlefield as a shade. The only consistent features are that he wields some sort of otherworldly dark blade and that it is death to face him. The Arbiter is meant to be the Hand of Halom and enforcer of the Singer faith; however, from our collected descriptions, the Arbiter seems more likely to be a disciple of the Dark Lady, Mishakiel.

Note: Further research required. Chronicler Simon Rathelson has submitted to have this entry moved into his upcoming edition of A Common History by historical significance.

- Chronicler Henrietta Martin in A Study of Salucian Mythology

Naira

Blossom Bay, Bauffin

Naira's feet pounded down the wooden planks of the pier as she ran towards the queue of people already beginning to board. She had made it, but just barely. Naira scanned the crowd for Adel and saw Mr Corbin's severe figure waiting with his daughter in a small space within the crowd. Those who knew Mr Corbin in Blossom Bay respected him, but still tried to give him a wide berth, as though he were a wolf walking amongst dogs.

The two appeared so different from each other: Mr Corbin was tall and angular, with an intelligent raptor-like face, dark hair, and cold icy-blue eyes, whereas Adel had long golden hair, a short, muscular physique, and innocent emerald-green eyes. Naira assumed Adel looked like her mother, though she had never met the woman. Adel's mother had died in childbirth and Mr Corbin had had the difficult job of raising a daughter on his own while still trying to run a small farm by himself.

Naira watched them a moment longer. A pigeon spooked a few people in the crowd near them, but both father and daughter reacted as predators would, with a calm detached cataloguing of the action. Naira was one of the few people who knew that the pair's differences were only on the surface: both father and daughter walked with an air of expected action and implied consequences. They both exuded a physical confidence and capability that was far beyond that of anyone else.

Yet despite his severity, Mr Corbin had always been kind to Naira, and if truth be told he was the closest thing she had to a father figure in her life; and yet his presence still unnerved her.

Mr Corbin never spoke about what he did before he settled near Blossom Bay, only that he had fought in the wars, but Naira knew he was more than just a soldier. She had met soldiers before, served them at Johnny Blin's, and they didn't have what Mr Corbin had. It felt like being in the presence of a shark. No, that wasn't quite right: sharks were primal; but he had that same promise of instant, horrible violence if needed. Naira had seen some of Adel's training sessions with him at their farm. It was like watching a pair of tornados fight.

Mr Corbin saw her then and waved her over. "I was worried we might have to go looking for you," he said with genuine concern. She saw a lifting around the corner of his eyes, which was as close to a smile as she had seen from the man.

"No need, sir. I was just wrapping up a few things in town. Took longer than I thought. Apologies." She nodded formally to him.

"We weren't waiting long." Adel smiled and grabbed her hand, giving it a squeeze. "I have to tell you-"

Mr. Corbin cut her off, “Naira, Adel will be accompanying you to the Academy. It’s a bit of a surprise, but I’m sure you agree Adel is ready. Apologies for not informing you of this sooner. We decided it was better to go with someone she knew rather than wait a year and go it alone.”

Naira couldn’t believe it. “That’s great news!” Naira jumped excitedly. They had always talked about going together, but Adel said Mr. Corbin wasn’t going to let her go yet. Naira had never really understood why. Adel had probably been Academy ready for years already.

“I’m glad you’re alright with it.” Adel said with a relieved smile.

“Are you kidding? Now I already know someone there. It’ll be great!” Naira was smiling, but she had noticed something shaky about Adel’s voice. As if she had been crying not long ago. Naira reached over and gave her a hug. “No need to worry, Pix,” she said with a wink, watching as Adel rolled her eyes at the private nickname.

Naira had said once when they were young that Adel looked like a pixie, and the name had stuck. Granted, Naira also thought it was quite funny to watch Adel roll her eyes like that, but the name also worked because a girl nicknamed “Pix” was not expected to kick the living daylights out of you.

“I won’t leave you on your own,” Naira said. “Imagine the sort of trouble you’d get into without me.”

“You two are to look after each other,” Mr Corbin said as he waggled his finger at the two of them. “New Toeron is a big city and full of sin, full of places to tempt young minds down dark paths.” His tone made both girls straighten up and listen. He was looking out to sea, his steely eyes seeing something that made him frown. “I trained you both to be strong, and you will need each other’s strength in the years to come.”

“Yes, sir,” Naira and Adel said in unison.

Naira watched as the throng of people waiting to board the ferry began to thin. She nodded towards the crowd not really knowing how to respond to Mr Corbin's warning.

"We should probably go," she said as she forced herself to step forward so she was facing Mr Corbin. She wanted to make it through this without crying. "Sir," she started, forcing down a lump rising in her throat, "I want to thank you for everything you've done. You didn't have to help me, but your house was a sanctuary for me growing up. A place of safety when I needed it. I wouldn't have been able to get into the Academy without your help and support." That pesky lump was trying to force its way up, and Naira hastily wiped away a stray tear. "Thank you, Mr Corbin."

Her words seemed to crack Mr Corbin's rigid facade for a moment, and she was rewarded with the corners of his mouth turning up slightly. There was kindness in him, hidden behind the steel – you just needed to know how to look for it.

He surprised them both then as he put his arm around her and pulled her and Adel close to him. He hugged them both, and Naira could feel her breath quicken along with Adel's. Those rebellious tears were threatening to overtake her, and she saw Adel struggling to fight back the tears as well. She had never known Mr Corbin to display any public affection.

"Halom has guided you onto these paths, taking you far from here. I can only hope I, as his servant, have prepared you well enough for what lies ahead." His strong wiry arms squeezed them closer. The pressure felt good. "Trust in Him, and you shall be sheltered. When you are alone and in the dark, look for Halom, for He is in all things and His Song resonates within us. When hope is lost, know that He is there," Mr Corbin said, and released them.

"We will, father," Adel croaked beside her. "We will be strong. We will have faith."

Mr Corbin nodded, satisfied. "I know you will." He moved to Adel and grasped the long leather case she was holding. "Remember Fellow

Callahan; find him as soon as you can. He will know what to do."

"Last boarding call for the New Toeron ferry!" a strong voice bellowed from the behind them. "Last call!"

"That's us," Naira said, regaining some of her composure. She was buzzing with a mix of excitement and fear. She wouldn't miss Blossom Bay, or, sadly, even her own mother, but she would miss Mr Corbin and the farm. She found Adel's hand and gave it a comforting squeeze. "Time to go."

"Right." Adel nodded. Adel looked as if she wanted to say more to her father, but didn't. She nodded respectfully to him and they shared a quiet smile before parting.

Naira pulled her friend with her and ran down the pier. *Two village girls running to become Knights,* she thought to herself as she scampered onto the ferry's deck, *what a strange and wonderful world we live in.*

"Tickets?" A big blond bull of a man greeted them at the top of the gangplank and held out his hand.

"Henric," Naira said as she winked at the handsome young man, "always a pleasure."

"You working this trip, Naira?" Henric almost seemed hopeful.

When Naira wasn't working at the betting house, she had taken more than a few shifts aboard the *Shard Maiden*; an illustrious name for the less than illustrious ferry they now stood on. Henric had quite often attempted to flirt with her during those shifts, but she had never seen him as more than a friend. It was awkward at times, but Naira had dreams. Dreams which didn't leave time for men to slow her down.

"Not this or any other trip ever again, Henric," she said with a big sigh, "I'm going to be a Corsair. A Knight of Salucia."

"Wow!" Henric said. "Congratulations. You and Adel are both going then?"

"That's right," Naira said, putting an arm around Adel.

"Well," Henric said, "don't forget us little people when you're all famous."

"I don't think anyone would ever call you little, Henric," Naira said, which seemed to appease him.

"Do you think you'll get to sail on one of those new steam-and-sail hybrid ships they say they have at the Academy?" Henric's eyes lit up with excitement.

"Maybe," Naira said with a smile.

"I think I saw one of them on our last trip. Craziest thing I ever saw. It was either one of those new ships or it was burning. Smoke was chugging up out of a huge chimney right coming right out of ship. But I only saw it from a distance."

"If I do sail one of them, I'll make sure to brag about it when you're in port next," Naira winked at the big man and Henric chuckled before ushering

them on board with another friendly smile before taking the next person's ticket.

Naira pulled Adel with her towards the railing at the front of the ferry so they could look out to sea. This was it. It was really happening. Once they started out onto that great blue-green expanse she would never be back. She took a breath and savoured the moment.

A tall and very finely dressed man moved to make room for them as he too was staring out across the waves.

"Thank you," Naira said, smiling up at the tall stranger.

As she did, however, she found herself unable to look away. The stranger was darkly handsome in a way she had never seen before. He was beautiful. So much so that Naira found herself staring. He turned and his eyes met hers. They were of the deepest pale blue. Like the ice of a glacier. "I ... uh ..." She tried to speak but stood transfixed.

The tall, well-dressed man nodded in acknowledgement, and Naira felt her fingers tremble as he turned to speak to them. “Did I hear you mention you were headed to the Academy?”

Naira tried to speak but her tongue felt like it had suddenly gone numb, and a simple “Yes” was all she managed to stammer. *What’s wrong with me?* A man had never made her do this before. “Are you going to the Academy? My name is Naira by the way, and this is my friend Adel. And you are?”

She groaned inwardly at her impetuousness. *Stay calm! He’s only a man.* What had come over her? This was no time to be swooning! She felt betrayed by her own emotions. This was the sort of thing which happened to silly girls who thought a man was the answer to everything. *Like what happened to mother.*

The thought hit her like a brick in the head and sobered her enough to calm herself down enough to slow her initial shock from the beautiful stranger.

The man chuckled slightly at her awkwardness, which only made it worse. “Actually yes, I am also headed to the Academy, but not for the same reasons. No, I have other ...” he paused for a moment and winked at her “.,, interests in New Toeron, shall we say.” He bowed and took her hand in his, and then, gently but firmly, kissed the top of it. “A pleasure to make your acquaintance,” he said, and then repeated the same motions with Adel. “I am Thannis Euchre.”

Naira found her courage then. “Well, Thannis, we have a long trip ahead of us,” she said as the ship pushed away from the docks and the oars slid out below them, “Shall we find some seats together?”

“Yes,” Thannis loomed beside her and smiled playfully, “that sounds like an excellent idea.”

13 - Back Home

The Tiden Raika, that's what all of this is about. Somehow we had lost our way. We became untethered from that tremendous guiding force, and from within the chaos we had grown to become destructive to all things, parasitic and ... evil. It is my hope that the actions I take will lead us back to the true path, back into harmony with the flow of all things.

The only way to begin that was for a cleansing fire to wipe the world clean. The old diseased forest must burn away to let new saplings grow up into the light.

I was that fire. I wiped the world clean.

Now it is my job to help the saplings grow pure and healthy. So I will try to change those who inhabit this scorched world. Alter them so they can feel the very flow of the Tiden Raika. I will not live long enough to see this ability manifest, but I have faith in my skills and in those of the NREs.

We must succeed in this, or else all of this will have been for nought.

-Journal of Robert Mannford, Day 001 Year 00

Matoh

New Toeron, Bauffin

Matoh sat upon a giant stone, upon a cliff overlooking New Toeron's harbour, listening to the surf roll into the rocks below as the sun set. The Red Tower rose up above the city below on its crag across the sheltered harbour. It was beautiful up here, it always had been, and at that moment Matoh doubted he had ever been happier to be home.

"Gods, I love this city," he said with a smile. The sweat on his back was beginning to feel cold. He had just practiced the twelf sequence in his longsword forms. It had felt good to finally be able to move properly again. Well, almost properly: his leg still felt stiff and a bit weak, but it had held up to the demanding sequence.

The warmth of the giant stone beneath him felt good. Almost as if it seeped into him and warmed him to the very soul. The stones had always been warm, ever since he could remember. Not hot, never hot, just warm, but it was a warmth so comforting Matoh had found himself coming here more and more over the years. Although he didn't just come to the great circle of ancient stones upon the cliff for their warmth and the view.

This had been the last place he had seen his mother alive.

It was one of his earliest memories. It had been misty that morning, misty and somehow still bright. He remembered only the shadow of an almost completed Red Tower outlined against the light. She had been sitting right here on this very stone, holding him in her arms as she said goodbye. "I love you, Matoh. Be a good boy. Be strong."

"I will, mother," he said to the setting sun. He made himself stand, bracing himself against the stone before his memories could force a tear out of him. The setting sun meant he had to get back home. The gates between the districts would soon begin to close and he didn't want to have to convince the guards to let him through. Though he knew many of them by name now.

It would take him the better part of half an hour to get back, and with his tired leg it was best to set off early. He walked back down the hill, through a thicket of trees and out into the city he had spent nearly his whole life in. The city he called home. The city he would soon be responsible for protecting, and that thought made him smile.

As he walked Matoh greeted the people he knew along the way. He waved at Martha Glimmering, the leather merchant who had her shop at the bottom of the hill. He always liked the smell of the new leather as he passed by. She waved at him as he passed by.

He stopped to talk to Horace Thornsvale, who was packing away his stall of fresh fruit as he passed. He bought a small sack of apples, and Horace convinced him to try a strange purple-skinned fruit called a "treasure plum". They were supposed to grow on some of the rocky islands around Tawa. Matoh cracked a joke and Horace laughed as he boxed up the remnants of his wares.

As he walked further, he bit into the purple flesh and a burst of sweet juice dribbled down his chin. The flesh was golden and silky inside. It was wonderful. "This is really good!" he called over his shoulder, holding up the fruit for Horace to see.

"I know!" Horace called back. "Told you!"

Matoh grinned and happily ate the rest of the fruit, not caring about how sticky it made his fingers. It was just what he needed after his session of exercise.

He passed an Aluvikan style pub and saw Baraka Shem, a sailor who must have been enjoying some shore leave, who tried to get him to come in for a pint of ale. "They've tapped a keg of Ferret's Gold, Matoh!" Baraka called from the door.

"Tempting," Matoh yelled back. "But I have to get home. First day at the Academy tomorrow, you know!"

"Congratulations! You poor sod!" Baraka held up his mug in salute. "I'll drink one for you in commiseration."

"Better have two then," Matoh said with a wink raising his hand in farewell.

Yes, he loved this city, loved its people and the harmony they had found in the mixing-pot of culture that was New Toeron. How Wayran could think about leaving was beyond him. This city was everything Mother had been fighting for before she died. It was her dream, and they now lived in it.

A flash of guilt went through him then. Wayran hadn't known what to do with himself after their uncle's pronouncement. They were lucky to be alive, but Matoh knew Wayran didn't see it that way. Had all of that happened less than a month ago? His hand went to the shard of glass now polished and woven onto a chord hanging about his neck. It was the only thing he had brought back, but that shard had saved his life. It would be bad luck to throw it away.

He shook his head in a sort of baffled wonder at their adventure in the Wastes. Most of it seemed like a dream now, but the shard was proof that it had happened. Wayran said he had siphoned lightning, swore it. Matoh didn't know what to think about that. It couldn't be true. He would be dead, yet ... *something* had driven the Roc away.

These thoughts about Wayran were stifling his good mood. He would have to do something to try and help Wayran, but what that might be he had no idea. His brother was complex at the best of times and utterly incomprehensible the rest. It sometimes amazed him that they were related. Matoh spent the rest of his walk home trying to think of how to lift Wayran out of his gloom.

***

Matoh arrived home in better time than he thought. His leg had held up well despite the walk back feeling like it was all uphill.

He unlocked the door to the corridor beside the workshop and made his way to the stairs leading up. The familiar creaks of the wooden stairs comforted him. The warmth of the house made his cheeks glow as the vestiges of the cool autumn air of the night began to leave him. He idly let his finger touch the ornate wooden frame of the magnificent painting in the hallway.

He glanced up and knew he would see his mother's face looking back at him from that painting. Sadly, it was now how he remembered her features. He had been so young when she had left. Wayran said he could still remember how she had looked, but he couldn't. So he made himself smile back at the silver image of his mother. She was in full armour with her helmet tucked under her arm. She was depicted with her head held high, yet the artist had captured the hint of a smile on her lips as she stood proudly at attention.

Matoh's smile was genuine as he met his mother's painted eyes. She would be proud of him, her boy going to the Academy. He wasn't going to let her down, he would rise through the ranks and become a great leader like she had been, honouring both the Spierling and Koslov names.

He turned to leave and it was then he saw Wayran through the open door of his brother's room.

"What are you doing?" Matoh asked, shocked. Wayran was wearing his Academy blacks: the formal dress uniform all initiates wore on their first day. "Why would you do that?! Take that off!"

Matoh burst through the door but came up short as he saw his father standing in the room behind Wayran. His confusion only increased. This was all wrong. "Dad, what is going on? Why is Wayran in my uniform?"

His father held up a hand. "It's alright, Matoh. That's not yours. Yours is still in your wardrobe where you left it."

Matoh turned on his heel and barrelled down the hallway, jostling a small table and nearly dumping the array of collected oddities from its top. He cursed under his breath and shouldered open his bedroom door. He flung open his wardrobe and saw an identical black military uniform staring back at him. Relief flooded through him. He had been keeping the creases perfectly straight for weeks now. But what was going on?

"Why does Wayran have one?" he called loudly from his room as he looked at his pristine set of blacks.

"Come in here, Matoh," his father called back to him, "we'll explain."

He closed his wardrobe doors, careful not to jostle the uniform, and lumbered back to Wayran's room. "What's going on?" he asked again, more curtly than he had intended.

"Wayran is also going to train at the Academy. I got him a spot on this year's initiate list," his father said with a quiet firmness.

The look he received from his father said he had not appreciated his tone. Matoh shook his head and looked over to Wayran, who had just finished buttoning up the last golden lapel button on the far left side of his chest. Matoh thrust his chin at Wayran. "I thought you never liked the idea of going to the Academy."

He saw Wayran hesitate. His brother looked to be searching for the right words, and it made Matoh clench his jaw. They had fought about this very thing several times before. It was usually a topic they avoided.

"It's a smart choice for me at the moment," Wayran said slowly, deliberately.

His brother's words were pointedly not antagonistic, which of course antagonised him no end – and he had seen something else as Wayran spoke. There was anger in his brother's eyes, daring him to say something in retaliation.

And Matoh, of course, couldn't stop himself. Part of him was still stewing at seeing Wayran in a uniform his brother had never properly respected. "It's a smart choice any damn moment," Matoh hissed, "it's just not one you've ever recognised before. Why the change of heart, *brother*?"

"Stop it, the both of you," their father's voice snapped.

Yet Wayran ignored their father; his smouldering eyes were alight now. "Get down off your self-righteous horse, Matoh. You didn't exactly leave me with many workable options after you ruined my chances of being a Storm Chaser."

"So going to the Academy on a military scholarship, as that's what I assume Dad has got you, is something you will just have to settle for, is it?" Matoh said, almost wishing he could spit venom. "And what do you mean, 'ruining your chances of being a Storm Chaser'? You were right there in the thick of it with me."

"Only because you decided to take a joy-ride in someone else's glider and fly right into a giant gods damned sandstorm!" Wayran yelled back.

"You were right there behind me. Just as curious as I was," Matoh said stepping forward and poking Wayran in the chest.

"I was trying to get you to come back, you idiot!" Wayran yelled again.

"I said enough!" Their father's voice boomed through the small room, making both boys stop in mid retort.

He had a hand on both of their chests. Matoh hadn't realised he had dropped into a fighting stance and had squared up to Wayran. He now relaxed and stepped back, but didn't flinch away from Wayran's angry glare.

"You are both going to the Academy so you had better get used to it." Harold Spierling pushed both of them back firmly but not violently. "Now the both of you, keep your big mouths shut and listen to me." Their father waited, but Matoh and Wayran could both see the angry set to their father's jaw. He was in no mood for any further outbursts.

"Matoh, your dedication and drive to get to the Academy cannot be questioned, my son. However, you will not lord that over your brother. Each of us is different, and though we might come to the same place by different paths, it is how we move forward which matters. I love your passion, son, don't ever lose that, but you can't hold it against people if they do not have that same level." His father cupped his hand along Matoh's jaw and held his eyes for a moment. The look said he understood what Matoh felt.

"Wayran," his father said as he turned to look at his other son, "life almost never goes exactly to plan, in fact it rarely does. Do not blame others for happenstance. What would you have done? Let your brother fly off alone into danger? Let him die? No, you wouldn't, I would not have had you do one thing differently, even if that pirate of a brother-in-law of mine can't understand that. Brothers protect each other. Always."

He let his words linger in the air, making each of them meet his eyes. Then he turned back to Wayran. "You will have to make the most of whatever opportunities present themselves to you, even if they are not the ones you have tried to steer yourself towards." Their father held Wayran's gaze then, imbuing his words with weight. "Do not take this placement at the Academy lightly, for it was with your mother's reputation I acquired the spot, not mine. People at the Academy will judge not just you but also your mother's legacy by your actions. Which isn't fair on either of you, but it is the reality of things. Besides, Wayran, this could turn out to be a blessing in disguise." He tapped Wayran gently on the shoulder. "But you have to be willing to accept it."

Wayran bowed his head, showing a bit of shame, and appeared to take their father's words seriously

"Now, the both of you, head to your rooms, pack what you need, and get some sleep. Tomorrow will be a big day, you'll need your strength." It was more than just a suggestion, and Matoh turned away from Wayran without another word. He couldn't worry about Wayran, he had his own things to fret over. He had to make a good impression, and that wasn't going to happen if he was stewing over what Wayran might do.

Matoh had packed everything he needed in what seemed like no time at all. His mind still raced, not quite accepting the situation yet.

Wayran at the Academy? Matoh understood his father's arguments, but this had always been *his* thing. It was what Matoh had been striving for ever since he could lift a sword. It was all going to start happening for him tomorrow and now his sulking brother was tagging along as if it were some sort of punishment.

Matoh knew he was working himself back up, but he couldn't stop himself. His anger and frustration kept rising, drowning out his excitement, which only frustrated him more. He should be excited, and Wayran was ruining the moment for him.

"Aargh!" Matoh growled at himself. "Stop it."

It was then he heard a knock on the door. "Can I come in?" his father's voice said from the hallway.

"Yes, come in," Matoh said, forcing down his mounting frustration.

His father came in and gave him a wry smile. "You got everything?"

"I think so," Matoh said, slightly more clipped than he would have wanted.

His father sat down beside him on the bed and misinterpreted his short reply for nervousness. "You'll do great, Matoh. You've been training for this your whole life. Ever since you were little, this is all you ever wanted."

I know! Matoh thought, yet he kept his words civil. "And what if I mess it up?" He spoke his fear aloud. "What if –"

"What if a thousand possible things happen?" His father cut him off and put his arm around his shoulder.

What if Wayran messes things up for me? he had been about to say, but just then he let himself be hugged instead of continuing his argument.

There had been a time when Matoh had felt small in those arms, but now his father struggled to get his arm around his broad shoulders. "Well, some things might happen," his father said, "but you deal with them, head on, and you don't let them push you off track. The way you've always done, Matoh. When you set your mind on something, son, it gets done. You shouldn't worry so much, the Academy is just where you need to be and you are going to be great. Just remember to enjoy it alright?"

"I will, Dad." Matoh nodded.

"I mean it." Harold Spierling looked him in the eye. "You're too hard on yourself. Your mother would already be proud of you. You don't have to prove anything, understand?"

"I understand," he said. *But I do have to prove something*, he thought. *To myself. I am the son of the Silver Lady, and I will show them all what that means.*

His father hesitated, almost as if he were about to launch into another tirade. "Good. I hope you do, and, Matoh ... ?"

"Yeah?" Matoh raised an eyebrow.

"Don't give your brother a hard time about this alright? Your mother wanted you both to go to the Academy. Maybe she has a hand in all this, even if your brother can't see it."

Matoh grimaced inwardly. His father was probably right, but he just couldn't take that right now. His frustration and restlessness were still boiling within him, but he forced himself to say what his father wanted to hear, "Alright, Dad. I'll try my best."

"Good enough," his father said. "You going to turn in?"

Matoh knew he should, but he also knew he'd never find sleep in the state he was in. "I think I might step down the street to the Broken Clock, get a little help for sleep." It wasn't the healthiest choice, he knew, but right now he needed something to calm his nerves a bit. Ale, music and atmosphere were just what he needed to take his mind off Wayran and the Academy.

"Well, just don't get carried away. Lock up when you come in." His father gave Matoh a wry, knowing grin. "I'll walk you through the gates tomorrow. See you off before the shop opens."

"Alright, Dad." Matoh nodded and took a deep breath. "I'll see you in the morning."

His father smiled once more and then left him to his thoughts.

Matoh took one more glance at his packed belongings and then heard Wayran shifting things in the room down the hall. He rolled his eyes. Time to go get a drink and thump his feet to some music. He tromped back down the stairs and out onto the street, hoping to find a better mood and something to calm his nerves as he waited for the morning to come.

14 - The Fall of Dawn

Meskaiwa's journey started at the sea's edge.

Meskaiwa looked to the north and saw forests of pine, birch and bluewood. He looked to the south and saw plains of grass and winding rivers. Then he looked to the west and saw mountains, and knew these to be his destination. For the sea and the east was behind him, and his feet had led him back to the beginning, his feet had pulled him home to the west.

For twenty-five days and twenty-five nights, Meskaiwa stayed within the horseshoe cove into which the sea had delivered him. There he collected his strength and refined his mind for what he knew was to come.

And on the twenty-sixth day he set out towards the mountains, following the river up to its birth. He reached a summit on the twenty-ninth day, which was the last day Our Saviour walked this earth. For on the twenty-ninth day, Meskaiwa ascended to heaven and joined Halom in His vigil over this land.

- *Tenents of the Elohim*

Jonah

Dawn, Kenz

Dragonfly.

What a wonderful name. The giant insect alighting on Jonah's foot-bow somehow encapsulated all the magic that the name implied. It was sitting only a finger's width from Jonah's left foot, looking at him with its enormous multifaceted eyes. The dragonfly fanned iridescent wings in the sunlight, flashing the colours of a rainbow. Its head was so impossibly bulbous, with giant hairs sprouting from every angle, it was a wonder it could move at all, let alone fly. But fly it did, gliding over the long grasses Jonah now lay in, hunting for whatever smaller insects it surprised in its lazy flight.

Fin's friend, Oleg, the logistics officer, had asked a very nice farmer and his wife about the name of the giant hovering insects and then translated the name for him. Jonah had been watching them hovering above flowing grasses ever since. The vibrant reds, greens, and blues of their long, segmented bodies, the grace with which they glided through the warm summer air; they were magnificent.

"VOLLEY! AWAY!" The shout resonated above the grasses as a drum thumped near him.

Jonah reacted on instinct.

He released his two-handed grip on the thick width of string and surprised the poor dragonfly. The wicked, four-foot black arrow launched to join the thousands of others arcing towards cream coloured walls.

Jonah stared up as the sky darkened above him. The deadly cloud of arrows partially blocked the sunlight before it descended to deliver death beyond those walls.

Please surrender quickly, he said to himself. *The Empire does not lose, and the faster these people learn that, the better for everyone.*

He reached beside him to fit another of the huge arrows to his foot-bow. A gesture that was now as automatic as breathing. He wiggled his toes to keep the blood circulating in his feet and waited for the order to pull and release. Hurry up and wait, hurry up and wait. Pull and release, pull and release. This was Jonah's life in the imperial machine.

Tall green and yellow grass rose on all sides around him. And above, crystal clear blue skies. Not a day for war, not a day for death, but such things mattered not to their Prince, whom they had followed across the sea. They were here to enact the will of the almighty Empress, may she live forever, and she too cared not what type of day it might be.

Jonah could just see Branson's prone form lying on the ground through the tall grasses to his right. The outline of an identical black-lacquered foot-bow held against boots was the constant in the lazily waving world.

"Aim! Forty-two!" The order ripped across Jonah's serene world.

The tight, almost wood-like cords of his leg muscles pushed up hard. His back and arms strained against the pull of the thick bowstring in his gloved hands. The jagged arrowhead pointed up at the sky at the new angle Jonah knew by instinct. An angle copied by the thousands of other foot-bowmen lying on the grass around him.

"VOLLEY!"

Thousands of bowstrings snapped in unison, and Jonah's black missile arced skywards to join its peers. His legs dropped smoothly to the ground with the weight of the foot-bow hanging from the leather stirrups on his feet. Each time, the release of that tension was a godsend.

But that relief lasted for only the slightest of heartbeats, as the next arrow was notched, and Jonah gritted his teeth against the pain in his tired muscles, waiting to lift his legs skyward once again.

"How many more rounds do you think they will take?" Branson asked in the stillness which followed.

"I hope not many," Jonah said.

"Getting sore already?" Branson cackled. "Try being my age and doing this."

"Gnarled pieces of wood don't get tired," Jonah replied, and heard a satisfying chuckle from his old friend.

"Ain't that the truth," Branson sighed.

"You'll outlive us all, you know." Jonah didn't doubt his words. Branson had been old and tough back when he was a child.

"That'd be my luck," Branson grumbled.

"Ah, come now. It can't be all that –" Jonah was cut off.

"Shh!" Branson hissed. "I thought I heard something."

And then Jonah heard it too. Someone had screamed. The sound of metal on metal, followed by a whooshing sound.

"Bowmen, up! Fall back!" The unmistakable voice of Commander Naseen rang out above the grass.

Another scream. Another thump and whoosh.

This time, Jonah felt it in his chest.

"Get up! Get up!" Branson shouted down at him.

Jonah gathered his arrows and stood.

A nightmare greeted him.

Hundreds of the steel-clad knights were behind them. Bowmen were running in all directions; it was a rout.

"How did they get behind us!" Jonah yelled. It was then he noticed a group of other soldiers running with the knights, dozens of men and women in long yellow and blue tabards, holding deadly double-bladed spears. Their mouths opened in unison, and Jonah saw the grass ripple like a wave upon the ocean.

"SUUM!"

His breath left his chest.

He tried to suck in but found himself choking for air and was once more on his back within the long grass. His ears rang as if he had been next to a giant bell.

Air finally pulled into his lungs. "What happened?" he tried to say, but couldn't hear himself speak.

Suddenly, Branson was standing over him and pulling him to his feet. Branson's mouth moved, but Jonah couldn't hear the words.

He tried to understand what had happened. It felt like the time he had stood too close to a city gate during a siege back in Eura, and the sappers had set off some of their rock-splitters. But there were no fires or any indication of the sappers' chemics this time. What was going on?

Branson jerked him forward, and he found his feet moving.

They had to get back to the infantry, back behind the pikemen.

Jonah's ears finally stopped ringing, and the sounds of dying men and women rose to meet him. They were being annihilated.

“We're not going to make it to the lines,” he said aloud, but Branson kept pulling him forwards.

“Branson!” Jonah jerked his hand free and clapped his friend on the shoulder.

“What! Keep moving!” Branson shouted, apparently still not able to hear.

A group of three bowmen to their right suddenly stopped running and drew swords. An enormous knight charged into their midst and Branson and Jonah stopped in their tracks.

The knight's giant two-handed sword was on fire.

The first bowman was nearly cut in half; the next one screamed in agony as the flaming blade cut right through her leg. The last bowman staggered back to face the knight.

Jonah saw a woman in a blue and gold tabard standing behind the knight. She was singing! Her hand was outstretched and she was looking straight at the blade. Her voice rose and, incredibly, so did the flames circling the sword.

The singing was enhancing the demon magic of the knights.

"The people singing! Re-string!" Jonah yelled as he dropped to his back. He hauled Branson down with him. His hand found the loop of his second lighter bowstring, and his feet were already pushing against the tough wood of his bow to unstring it. His training took over, and the bow was re-strung just as he sprang up out of the grass, finding his target.

His hand closed around the soft feather fletching of the smaller arrows in the flat quiver on his back. "Shoot the ones in the blue and gold tabards!" he yelled. His arrow found a throat, and the ringing pitch in the air dropped slightly.

"Re-string! Blue and gold! Shoot blue and gold!" His voice found a familiar note of command. The fleeing archers all around him stopped immediately and dropped to re-string bows.

Two more of Jonah's arrows found their marks, and then the grass around him erupted as his fellow archers rose back up and let fly their arrows.

The singing mages began dropping like flies.

But that still left the knights and their demonic weapons carving through the archers' ranks.

A man not ten paces from Jonah's side screamed as he was skewered by a great sword, but the archer had dropped two of the singing mages before he died. Jonah avenged his fallen comrade as his next arrow found the gap in the knight's visor. His hand notched another arrow before the body hit the ground.

"Jonah!" Branson grabbed him by the arm. "We have to retreat, come on!"

Another boom knocked them to the ground. Obviously some of the singing mages were still standing.

Branson pulled Jonah to his feet and started dragging him back to the barricaded Euran lines. Jonah ran as fast as he could. If one of those metal-clad knights found them, they were finished. The grass whipped at his face and hands, and his heart pumped so hard he thought it might burst.

They reached a slight rise and could see the spiked barricade of the makeshift Euran fortifications. They'd be safe there. They could make it.

Branson pulled him forward, but then Jonah heard something that made his blood run cold.

Fin was yelling a challenge to one of the Syklans.

“No!” Branson yelled, but not for Fin. He was screaming at Jonah. “You can’t save him! Get back here!”

Jonah hadn't even known he had turned around when he found himself running.

The knight smashed his hammer forward, striking Fin in the gut and dropping him. Jonah's heart leapt into his throat as Fin fell.

“No, damn you! Not him!” Jonah grabbed his last arrow and fired at a full run.

The knight raised his wicked looking hammer above Fin’s head for the killing blow.

Jonah’s arrow struck the helmet, ricocheting.

The knight stopped, saw him running, and turned to face him. The giant hammer began to spark with energy and the strange spheres set into the pauldrons began to glow. The nightmarish figure paused to point at him, signalling that he was next.

Before Jonah knew it, he was too close to fire an arrow. The first hammer strike should have finished him, but he found himself twirling his bow as if it were a staff and deflecting the hammer to one side.

The knight recovered quickly and turned the swing into a backhanded attack as he pivoted on his feet. The hammer caught the bow, and its weight and momentum ripped it out of Jonah's hand.

Jonah didn’t think, but kicked forward as he rolled beneath the next hammer swing. His foot connected with the knight’s knee, making the armoured figure fight for balance.

Suddenly, a rock smashed down on the knight’s helmet. Fin sprang up behind the figure yelling like a madman as he slammed the rock down again and again into the helmet. The nightmarish knight fell to the ground.

“Keep your eyes on the prize!” Fin yelled as his arm pumped up again and again. The rock was covered in blood as Jonah grabbed him.

"Fin! Enough! We have to go!" he commanded, and again the note of someone used to issuing orders made Fin stop.

A concussive boom sounded beside them, and then a yell. Jonah and Fin both and saw one of the singing mages spear an archer.

"There's another one!" Fin stood and pointed, rage in his eyes. His hand went to his back and finding no arrows his eyes suddenly went to the dead knight at their feet. Before Jonah could stop him, he had picked up the hammer and started running at the mage.

"Fin!" Jonah felt helpless as he tried to catch him. There was something about this singing mage that looked different. His uniform was not like the others, and all too soon Jonah saw the singing mage spot Fin and then slowly smile.

The twin-bladed spear spun in a flurry over the mage's head, and something in Jonah recognised the move. This mage could not only kill with his voice but was a master of the spear as well. Fin would be dead in three moves.

Jonah's foot hit something, and he fell to find himself face to face with a dead woman who was wearing the blue and gold tabard. His hand found her double-bladed spear.

His hand touched the smooth wood, and it felt like an old friend. *Hang on, Fin!*

The training of long years took hold, and Jonah felt the power of his blood surge to life after years of dormancy. His feet found new speed, his pulse slowed, and within moments he found himself outpacing Fin.

There was a satisfying moment of surprise on the mage's face as Jonah reached the fight first. He countered the attack that would have skewered Fin, and spun into a slashing attack of his own at the mage's face. It forced the mage back.

Fin tried to push past him, so he turned on his heel and slapped his foot across Fin's face. Jonah flipped out of the kick and thrust his spear at the mage. "Stay back!" he commanded Fin. The very air snapped with the authority of his voice.

The spear moved like a viper in his hands, striking and snaking towards exposed holes in the mage's defence. He didn't have time to consider that those who saw him might discover his secret. All he had time for was counter, slash, parry and push the attack. He flowed like the wind over the grass as he overwhelmed the mage spear-master.

The wooden shafts cracked together, and the bladed spearhead shot down at Jonah, but his body flowed around the move. Too late he realised it was a decoy. This spear-master had another weapon.

The mage opened his mouth. "SUUM!"

Jonah felt the air leave his lungs and his back hit the ground, but he held on to his spear.

The mage's weapon slashed down at him. A strike sliced across his shoulder, and then his stomach; both had meant to kill, but his own spear had moved on instinct, saving his life both times.

Jonah spun, rolling onto his shoulders and propelling himself into the air as his legs spun like a tornado. His back foot connected with the mage's jaw. He landed, and his spear shot forward like a lightning bolt.

The mage opened his mouth, but this time no sound escaped, as Jonah's spear pierced right through its neck. Jonah watched the mage crumple. A look of shock and confusion was frozen on the dead man's face.

Jonah turned to find Fin staring at him.

"We have to get back to the lines," Jonah said. The old power he had used was gone, and it had left him drained.

"You kicked me in the face!" Fin looked positively horrified.

"You'll get another one if you don't start moving," Jonah said as he pushed Fin forward. Thankfully the big man didn't resist.

"When did you learn the spear?" Fin asked between breaths.

“I was just reacting,” was all Jonah could say.

“That doesn’t explain ...” Fin trailed off and cursed.

A metal-clad knight rose from the grass in front of them. A wicked two-handed sword sparked blue and the spheres on her shoulders were already glowing as the great knight turned.

"You still have that hammer, Fin?" Jonah asked, watching their death step towards them. Even with his spear and Fin’s hammer, he knew they wouldn’t beat this knight. A circle of over a dozen warriors lay dead at her feet in the grass around them.

"I lost it when you kicked me in the face," Fin said anxiously.

“Catch!” Branson’s voice yelled.

The knight's hand intercepted the lazily thrown projectile easily, but then Jonah saw what the knight had caught: a sphere which was hissing.

“Get down!” Jonah dived and knocked Fin down with his shoulder.

The air detonated above them, and Jonah looked back to see a smoking patch of grass where the knight had stood.

Branson walked through the smoke with murder in his eyes. "Now you two get your stupid, sorry asses back behind the barricade!"

They didn't argue and met no other resistance on their run back through the tall yellow grass.

"I thought you said it was stupid to carry sapper explosives," Fin huffed at Branson as they found themselves running beside many of the other retreating archers.

“I said it was stupid for *you* to carry them," Branson growled; the old archer's face looked like thunder. "For someone who knows about them though, they can come in handy."

They came to a rise and saw the Euran defences just in front of them. They ran down the small hill to safety.

Thousands upon thousands of Euran soldiers were marching up the hill. Pikemen, skirmishers, heavies, and even what must have been twenty units of the Eternal Hand, all marched like ants back towards the enemy.

“Prince El’Amin is obviously going to try and turn this rout around then,” Fin observed as he watched the Imperial horde move past them into the field.

"He's forced to make a statement now," Branson said with a slight sigh. "The enemy’s clever move has forced his hand, and them folks in Dawn are gonna wish their rulers hadn't been so smart." Branson pointed to nearly a dozen groups of sappers marching alongside trebuchet and catapult crews.

Jonah shook his head. “What do you think the Prince will target?”

Fin answered, "Intel says those lovely temples are the weak point of Dawn. Their people will be on their knees within hours once those grenados and the thumpers start blowing their holy temples to bits." Fin looked sad as he spoke. "Damn shame. I wanted to see those temples."

“Intel says that does it?” Branson asked as he looked at Fin suspiciously. “Or are you just repeating the rumours you dredge up?”

Jonah rolled his eyes at Branson and clapped Fin on the back. “Come on, you need to see a medic. That knight’s hammer caught you something fierce. I’m amazed you’re still breathing, let alone standing.”

Fin smiled, but a curious look crossed his face. "So you say you've never had training with the spear, Jonah?"

"Well ...” He was not quite sure how he was going to lie his way through this.

"Course you have," Branson cut in. "Remember? It was that tall scary fella who trained you. What was his name? Marrick, maybe?" Branson was wearing his “play-along” face.

Jonah remembered the old weapons-master who had trained him, a tall and intimidating man.

"I don’t know if I’d call those few lessons ‘training’, per se. It was more like getting my ass whipped." He tried to bend the truth, although the part about getting thoroughly beaten was all too true. Only a few lessons, however, was the lie, but it was a much smaller lie.

"True at that. You must have remembered something though. Obviously that week in Rakaisa was worth the money." Branson laughed. "Saved your skin it did."

"I'll say." Fin laughed, but then he looked at Jonah piercingly. "I just thought it odd how Jonah seems trained in the long-spear and can also shoot the eyes off a fly with a restrung foot-bow. It's almost as if he had the same training as the Royal Blood."

Branson missed a step, and Jonah saw a flash of panic in his old friend's eyes.

They looked at each other for a moment and then burst out laughing.

"Ha, ha. You've got me there, Fin!" Jonah bellowed loudly. "Yep, instead of lounging around all day in an imperial palace with servants at my every beck and call, I've decided to renounce my title, sail across the sea to what we all thought could be our doom, and then trudge mile after mile so I can break my back firing my damned foot-bow. My secret's out, Branson! Too bad, I'll have to go back to my life as a Royal."

"Well, obviously I know that isn't what happened. Empress save me, I was just saying it was weird is all," Fin retorted. The friendly joviality had come back into the big man's eyes, and he too was laughing at how ridiculous it sounded.

"About as weird as you caving in the skull of one of those monsters with nothing but a rock? Gods below!" Branson mocked. "Fin's pa must have been a giant and his mother a magical pixie. Pshaw, we all do crazy things in the heat of battle."

"Drop it, alright? I was just saying is all." Fin said looking slightly abashed.

"Can we just get back?" Jonah sighed. "I need to get another set of arrows, and I want some water and a bit of food before we have to march back out there."

"Finally, somebody with something sensible to say," Branson grumped, and stormed down the hill.

Fin shook his head and quirked his eyebrow at Jonah. "Humph. Old people, right?"

They started down the hill after their grumpy saviour, watching another set of sappers and trebuchets roll by.

"How many temples do you think they'll have to destroy?" Fin asked. The teasing spirit seemed to have been sucked right out of the big man as they watched even more sappers coming up the hill.

"Let's hope it only takes one, Fin," Jonah responded to try to reassure his friend. "Let's hope it only takes one."

* * *

It took three.

Three temples were obliterated and a large section of the outer wall blown wide open before the rulers and citizens of Dawn marched the remnants of the Salucian defenders out. The rulers of the city had wanted to surrender after the first temple, just as Jonah had guessed, but it had taken two more, and the loss of a defensible wall, before the enemy general finally capitulated.

Assurances of cooperation from the city's officials and Dawn's spiritual leader, the Hierophant, elicited a somewhat surprising promise from Prince El'Amin that the Eurans would rebuild the fallen temples.

It had taken less than two days for Dawn to fall, and with an entire campaign of only a few months, most of the country of Kenz was now in the hands of the Euran Empire.

Prince El'Amin sent his fastest ships back across the great sea to the north the day after Dawn was secured. On each ship there were a dozen messengers who would spread word of the new world and the chance of a glorious new beginning for any who would swear fealty to Clan Amin.

Also aboard these ships were messengers who carried a second command within a secret letter. The letters were specifically for the Prince's mother, Dinesa, Matron of Clan Amin. The encoded missives could only be read by the nobility of Clan Amin, and when received they would read very simply: *'Send all of our forces. Move the power of our entire Clan and everything we have across the sea. All of it. Now. Do this, and I promise you shall be the new Empress.'*

15 - The Gig that Changed Everything

I wonder how much of the junk we have mass-produced will make its way into the future, polluting their world just like it did ours?

Sadly, there was no way to get rid of it all. I apologise to the next generations in advance. Although, if the NREs suddenly came across a horde of preserved chocolate bars it would take all my willpower to tell them not to bring them back to base.

- Journal of Robert Mannford, Day 211 Year 002

Kai

New Toeron, Bauffin

Tonight was it.

If they didn't generate large enough tips and encores, Hanson was going to bump them for another act. Kai looked out from behind the curtain. A loud murmur permeated the smoky air of the small common room of the Broken Clock Inn. Kai spotted Hanson and caught his eye. *"What's the crowd like?"* Kai mouthed.

Hanson just shrugged his shoulders and gave him a hopeful look.

Not good. Hanson was trying to buoy his spirits. Not good at all.

The crowd could be up for it, Kai thought, looking at the happy faces, but his attention kept diverting to the plates of food dotted around the tables. His stomach growled at the wonderful aroma of cooked pork, roast vegetables and stewed apple gravy, all mixed with the sweet smell of wood smoke.

What Kai wouldn't give for a proper meal. Tonight was the last night of the harvest feasts and everyone was filling their bellies with the fruits of their hard labour. He saw someone had left a morsel of pork roast on their plate. Kai's mouth watered at the sight. He might get some of those leftovers tonight if Meriam, Hanson's wife and cook at the Broken Clock, didn't select it for a stew or something for tomorrow's meal.

No! Focus on the gig. Kai bit his lip painfully, making himself focus on something other than Meriam's excellent food.

It had to be tonight. It was tonight, or he'd have to tell Jachem they'd have to quit.

There were enough people. It might work.

But if it didn't, well, Kai didn't want to think about that. Jachem wouldn't handle the news well, but Sister Maria needed Kai to help pay the bills. She had never asked him to, and never took it for granted, but he knew there were all those mouths to feed at the orphanage, and he'd be damned if was going to let those little ones go hungry like he had.

It'll be alright. He felt for the purse of coins on his hip. He had already put in a double shift today at the docks. It should be enough.

"You better be careful, Kai, you're young and healthy now but one day that back of yours will start to feel the strain of all that extra lifting. And then where will you be?" Harbour Master O'Brian had spoken to him just this afternoon about all the extra shifts, but Kai had stopped listening when the harbour master placed a silver coin in the palm of his hand. Silver instead of copper.

"I'll have to worry about that when it happens," Kai had said, trying to sound respectful. They needed the money, and his back could take it. He was always sore, and stiff, but he could deal with that for now.

"Well, I don't want to burn out good workers either, Kai." The harbour master cocked his head. "Only one shift tomorrow alright?" O'Brian had said.

"But I can't. I need –" Kai had begun to protest.

"Lady take me!" O'Brian had cursed. "You're a good lad, but I'll be damned if I'm going to be the one to tell Sister Maria you broke your back at my dockyard."

O'Brian had put his hand on Kai's shoulder and looked him in the eye. "You work yourself too hard, son." Then he pushed a few more coppers into his hand. Extra coppers, above what he had earned. "*One* shift tomorrow. You got it?"

"Yes. Mr O'Brian. Morning or afternoon?" Kai had clenched his teeth against trying to argue further. He wasn't going to press his luck.

"Afternoon," O'Brian had said, satisfied. "Don't drink it all away now." The harbour master winked and waved him away.

Kai jingled the coins still in his coin pouch, thinking about the comment. *Not bloody likely*. He didn't have the luxury to spend his money on ale or spirits.

Bella, the serving girl, danced past him balancing a stack of at least ten plates. "So, Kai, are you guys going to play us anything *good* tonight?" She smirked playfully at him.

He could only return a weak smile. "I think so. I've managed to convince Jachem that some of his 'Jendar music' might be a bit too *advanced* for everyone."

Bella nodded, winking conspiratorially. "Oh, yes ... *advanced*. Not the word I'd use, but if it's done the trick."

"I think so, we've added a lot more traditional songs to our repertoire," Kai said. Bella was so lovely that he always felt in a bit of a daze around her. He found his eyes drooping to her deliberately low-cut top and exposed cleavage, but then jerked his gaze back up to her eyes, trying not to blush, as she must surely have noticed. "Uh, we'll be playing some local favourites, but with a bit of a twist. I think you'll like it."

Bella smiled. "Well if *you've* picked the songs this time, I'm sure they'll be good." She tapped the purple top hat on his head playfully. "Good luck tonight." She winked at him and was off, dancing her way through the crowd and managing to balance all the dishes with ease.

Kai sighed once more over the things he couldn't have. Pretty girls didn't go for destitute nobodies like him. Besides, he had responsibilities that tended to discourage any social life.

He closed the stage curtains and walked to the small dressing room. He knocked on the doorframe and ducked through. His tall frame meant he had to crouch even further than usual with the purple hat on his head to get into the tiny room. The hat was part of his costume consisting of a simple black vest which he wore over his bare chest, along with some equally garish purple trousers. But the hat had grown on him, and besides, it was what Jachem told him he had to wear. There was no arguing with his friend on things like this.

Jachem was sitting on the small chair in front of the mirror. He had the small black Jendar device he always carried with him. Light radiated from the device, illuminating the demonic make-up Jachem wore. Soft music floated from the face of the old relic and Kai stepped in behind Jachem to watch the incredible images dance on the surface of the strange black device.

"I still think it's pretty amazing that you figured out how to work that thing." Kai's voice startled Jachem out of his revelry.

"It wasn't that hard." Jachem's attention didn't wane in the slightest. Kai might as well have been invisible for all the attention Jachem gave him. "The first image was a code. There was a different symbol to press first, and then the rest of the sequence had a pattern to it as well. Most of the Jendar devices I've seen have the same symbols on the front of them, probably a security code or something."

Images of the kinds of performing people on whom Jachem and Kai had styled themselves moved across the glossy surface of the Jendar relic. "I still think you should take it to the Chroniclers," Kai said, "they might be able to tell you more about it."

"No. They'll steal it from me if I did." Jachem's tone was abrupt and his fingers moved in a series of delicate strokes over the surface. The images winked out and Jachem hid the device back inside his jacket.

I shouldn't have said that. Mention of the Chroniclers' interest in the device seemed to raise Jachem's anxiety levels, and Kai needed his friend to be as calm as possible tonight. Performing on a stage in front of people still seemed like a stretch for Jachem – seemed like asking a fish to climb a tree. Interacting with other people was something Jachem just wasn't good at, but he had become fixated on this idea of becoming a "superstar" just like the Jendar people on his relic.

It made Kai almost sick to think about how hard Jachem would take it if things went badly tonight. Almost on cue, Kai's stomach growled and he sighed inwardly. Tonight would be the last night of following this flight of fancy. They needed the money more. He would just have to deal with Jachem's gloom afterwards.

"Fame and glory, Kai. Fame and glory," Jachem said far too exuberantly, and punched him on the shoulder.

This again? Kai wondered where it was that Jachem was quoting those words from. Surely it wasn't something he had come up with on his own? It seemed too flamboyant and assertive, and Jachem was certainly anything but flamboyant, despite the odd clothes he now wore.

Jachem was smiling up at him, waiting for a response, apparently trying to cheer Kai up with his words.

Kai smiled back, eliciting a satisfied grunt from Jachem, and that did make Kai smile in earnest. Not many people understood Jachem as he did. Everyone always thought Jachem weird, or crazy, or unstable, or a hundred other socially unacceptable things. But Kai knew Jachem, and Jachem was just different.

"Okay!" He tried to reciprocate Jachem's energy, not wanting to show how much he doubted tonight's chances of success. "Fame and glory would be amazing, don't get me wrong, but let's try to focus on the moment for now, alright?"

"The moment! But our future beckons us with open arms! Fame and glory, my close-minded friend! Riches beyond our imagination!" Jachem was so excited he was dangerously close to having a fit.

Kai couldn't help but chuckle at how happy he looked just then, but he knew this level of excitement was not good for his eccentric friend. "Jachem," he said as he gently grabbed his short rotund friend by the shoulders and stared him in the eyes, "most of the people out there don't know about Jendar music, right? These 'superstars', as you call them, don't exist in our time, remember?"

Jachem's eyes searched his face blankly for a moment, but Kai saw him coming back down to reality. "Yes. I know that, of course," Jachem said as his eyes darted back and forth and he once again began piecing together where he was. "We'll just have to blow their minds with our originality, won't we?! Then *we'll* be the superstars! Kai! Us!"

"Sure," Kai sighed with a reassuring smile. "Now get out there, you crazy Jendar music monkey!" He gave Jachem a slap on the rump.

Jachem burst through the curtains of the dressing room onto the stage and yelled, "WOO!! ARE YOU READY?!"

Kai sighed to himself, *here we go.* He collected his drumsticks from the table, ducked through the curtain, and began whirling his sticks through his fingers as he tried to raise himself to some semblance of Jachem's enthusiasm. He greeted a room of shocked, wide-eyed patrons frozen in half fear and half amazement by Jachem's booming entrance. More than a few people had hands over their hearts, no doubt checking they still had a pulse after such a fright.

Jachem had his guitar in hand already and was gyrating his hips like he'd seen the Jendar musician do in the relic. Jachem, of course, was loving his entrance, but Kai could see a woman cringing and awkwardly trying to shuffle her chair back from the stage without drawing attention to herself.

Okay, got to save this quick. He rushed to his drums and gave the snare drum three quick smacks to get Jachem's attention back to the task at hand. Kai assumed his starting position, with his head hanging low and his shoulder-length hair falling forward to hide his face. It was the signal for Jachem to start playing.

"We are The Banditos!" Jachem proclaimed with a grand gesture, swinging his guitar around his body on its strap so that it did a full circle and landed back into playing position.

Kai and Jachem shared a moment of disbelief as that was the first time Jachem had ever successfully pulled that trick off.

Kai did a quick rimshot on the drums and symbol, and surprisingly it elicited a smattering of chuckles from the crowd, helping to warm them up.

Not a horrible start, he thought, cautiously optimistic.

Jachem's smile was beginning to look slightly demented, which did actually work with their look, so Kai snapped three sharp beats on his snare drum.

Jachem finally took the cue, and cried aloud, "And this song is called 'The Thief'!"

Kai slammed his drumsticks down onto the snare just as Jachem flung into furious action on his acoustic guitar. The beat of their first song was relentless and Kai quickly broke into a sweat, his black hair bouncing beneath the velvety purple hat in a mad frenzy.

Jachem's fingers danced across the fretboard of his guitar while he strummed rapidly. The notes sang out fast and furious.

Jachem launched into the first verse and spun the tale of a young down-and-out boy who had fallen hopelessly in love with a girl who had smiled at him to lift his spirits. The beat softened, the notes became delicate, trilling up softly up to match Jachem's high pitch. The girl of the song was whisked away by her tyrant father and scorned for having helped a beggar.

Kai switched to a staccato military beat as Jachem wildly gestured with his hands and sang of the conviction of the young boy. He would win the heart of the girl and save her from her evil father.

Kai looked up at the crowd for the first time. They were hard to judge. He knew their style of music was miles from the traditional fiddle, drum, flute and accordion bands usually seen in local tavern rooms.

There were more than a few perplexed faces among the crowd. *So not quite the raucous adulation we were hoping for,* he thought a bit anxiously. Yet most of the young Academy soldiers were grinning! *Right, we just need to get that group going, and the rest should join in!* Two Paleschurians were pumping their fists in the air, obviously enjoying things. One was a muscular, broad-shouldered young man, dressed in the local style, who sat with an older man who looked like he should be sitting on a Paleshurian warhorse in an old painting.

The two enthusiasts gave Kai hope. *Maybe this Jendar style of music could work after all*! He had doubted Jachem's conviction that the music would be a success. *Maybe he's not as crazy as he looks.* Then he saw Jachem out of the corner of his eye. His friend had his guitar behind his head and was sticking his tongue out at the crowd. *Nope, he's easily that crazy.*

Jachem's antics had a few of the young Academy initiates in stitches. They were attempting not to spill their drinks as they thumped the tables trying to suck in breaths between fits of laughter. *Well, at least they're having fun!* Kai thought as his sticks hammered out the beat.

The song ended as Jachem sang the last verse telling of the thief's triumph in securing the heart of the beautiful girl. Everyone had gone deathly quiet.

The seconds felt stretched into hours. Kai caught his breath, waiting for some response, anything to break the tortuous silence. *Did I misjudge the crowd? Somebody say something!*

“YEAH!!" The young muscular Paleschurian stood up with his older friend and pumped his fist in the air. Like thunder following a lightning strike, the rest of the room roared into life. People threw back their chairs, jumped to their feet and bellowed their approval.

“Yes!” Kai pointed at the young Paleschurian with his drumstick, giving him a quick salute. This was the excitement they wanted to inspire! *I owe that guy a drink!*

He laughed as he thought he saw a tear in Jachem's eye.

"Right! Well if you liked that one, here's a new take on an old favourite, ‘Pirates of the Old Sesquan’!" Jachem's caterpillar-like eyebrows worked overtime as he tried to pump up the crowd by playing the role of a madman. *Use what you know,* Kai thought, *and Jachem knows crazy like no one else.*

Kai stopped thinking and let himself get lost in the music, the beat of his drums filling him entirely, and soon everyone was thumping their tables in time with his beats.

The night began to blur into a riotous party.

Song after song, Kai and Jachem blared forth and the crowd rose to the challenge, drinking, dancing and becoming rowdier with each verse.

Most of their songs went over well. A few didn’t get quite the applause that their opening couple had, but everyone was happy and having a good time. Kai was immersed in his music. There was nothing that made him happier than thumping the taut skins of his drums and getting lost in the beat. The music touched his heart and then passed on to join a glorious chorus, so immense it was almost unfathomable. When he was laying down a beat with his drumsticks dancing in his fingers, it felt as if he could almost touch the great symphony of the world around him.

All too suddenly, Hanson gave them the cut-off signal, and with a sad smile on his face Kai put down his drumsticks. His corded muscles were shaking in his arms and only then did he realise he was exhausted, but still he wanted nothing more than to keep playing. *If only this night could last forever.* He held up his index finger to Hanson and mouthed, “One more?”

Hanson looked at the crowded room in front of him despite the late hour and shrugged his shoulders. “Alright one more,” he mouthed back.

"Alright, it’s getting late, we can only do one more song," Kai announced.

The crowd groaned.

"I know, I know, but even the wicked need some rest.” Kai winked at a beautiful girl who had been dancing quite expressively during their last song. "A request from the audience for our last?"

Several suggestions were shouted from the tables, with more than a few asking for very bawdy songs. *Definitely had enough liquid courage for one night,* Kai thought to himself, but he grinned at a few of the racier suggestions.

Then he saw her, and his heart skipped a beat. Long thin braids cascaded down onto her shoulders, framing broad, sparkling eyes. Her dark copper-brown skin glowed in the soft light of the tavern. She was the most beautiful woman Kai had ever seen – and then he recognised who she was ... yet he knew he must be wrong.

Princess Echinni, the High King’s daughter, was here in the crowd!

Every eye in the small room was drawn towards her as if they all suddenly realised an angel walked among them.

Kai gestured wildly to Jachem in the direction of Princess Echinni. Her hand was held delicately in the air. She had a request!

Jachem didn’t see her so Kai raised his voice to cut through the now fading din. "Your Highness!” He felt his throat go dry as he tried to continue. His voice seemed awkwardly loud and silenced the crowd almost instantly. “What song would please you?"

Jachem finally recognised who she was and did his best to make a flourishing bow. Unfortunately, his cummerbund popped a button and burst forth under the strain of his generous belly. A man in the front row rubbed his head from the impact of the wayward button, but Jachem didn’t notice.

To her credit, Echinni did her best not to laugh, but Kai saw the hint of a suppressed giggle and a sparkle in her luminous eyes. *I could die a happy man staring into those eyes,* he thought.

Princess Echinni smiled happily as she spoke. "Dispense with the honorific for now, it makes me feel old; besides, this is your show.” Her smile enhanced her exotic beauty and stole more than a few breaths from the patrons of the Broken Clock.

“As you wish.” Kai grinned, hoping his boldness wasn’t going to get him hanged. Nobles could be prickly sorts, but he wanted to keep that smile on her face.

The smile crinkled a bit impishly as she eyed him from the floor. “I would request ‘The Silent Passenger’ if it pleases the audience, but to the beat and melody of your third song.”

Jachem appeared somewhat hesitant to agree as that combination was new to both Kai and himself, but Kai jumped in before Jachem could say anything rude and pinched his friend hard on the arm. "No objections.” Kai smiled roguishly as he surveyed the crowd. “Right, Jachem, you heard the beautiful woman!”

Kai was about to start the beat when the princess held up her hand again, making his drumsticks pause in mid downstroke. “If you don't mind, kind sir ...” She paused almost shyly. “... could I be so audacious as to request the singing role?"

Kai was awestruck. The Princess Echinni wanted to sing with them, on stage! He was glad there were witnesses; no one was going to believe this otherwise.

Then, to his horror, Jachem looked as if he was about to say no! A well-aimed drumstick caught Jachem in the ear, who whirled towards him – but all objections died on his lips when he saw the fierce look Kai was giving him.

"Of course. We would be honoured!" Kai threw another spare drumstick at Jachem and hissed at him so only the two of them could hear, "Stop it! Just go with it!" *Now is not the time for your selfish antics, Jachem!*

Kai laid down a marching beat on his snare drum as Echinni made her way through the crowd. It was a bit too forward for propriety, but he thought he saw that hidden smile of hers again, as the crowd parted to let her through. *A princess who has a sense of humour? Who knows, maybe I've got a chance.*

As Echinni stepped onto the stage Kai pumped his arms to get the young crowd excited again. The crowd was in a sort of trance.

Well, here we go. He gave a silent prayer to Halom and laid down the beat from their third song; Jachem joined in after a few bars with the guitar.

Then Echinni, the young Singer prodigy, began to sing.

The purest, most pitch-perfect notes Kai had ever heard filled the room. The combination of her haunting voice and the different pace to the song mesmerised the crowd into enthralled silence.

Fingers grasped for armrests as people leant forward, unconsciously trying to get just a bit closer. Tears began to glisten and breaths quivered as the painfully beautiful notes kept coming.

Every note echoed through the heart. They could all actually feel the fear of the unseen shadow carried by the man in the song. The lights seemed to wane and the air cooled as hairs rose on arms held in trepidation.

Echinni, though, was oblivious to the effects of her song. She was lost in it just as much as the crowd was. Her body shook with anguish as she sung of the shadow's final attempts at the man's life.

The song came to a close and Echinni raised her clutched her hands gently to her breast. Her voice trilled down to a quiet bass note.

The room was silent; no one wanted to wake from their reverie. Mouths hung agape and eyes shone unabashedly with tears.

Echinni curtsied shyly to Jachem, to Kai, to Hanson and then lastly to the audience. She quietly walked through the parting crowd with a contented smile on her face. The swishing of her skirt seemed to be the only sound in the room as the beautiful young woman made her way towards the exit.

What Kai wanted to say was echoed on every face in the room: *Don't leave!* But he knew a request like that would be a step too far, no matter its reverent intent.

The most intimidating woman he had ever seen waited for Princess Echinni at the door. How he had not seen her before baffled him. She was at least head and shoulders taller than any man in the room. It was the one and only Yuna Swiftriver, another legend in her own right. Yuna Swiftriver had fought for the royal line of Mihane for years. She was rumoured to have quelled an uprising in the Blasted Isles single-handed, and was the wielder of the legendary sword *Hunsa*. Yuna was now the Princess's personal bodyguard and her mere presence was supposed to be enough to deter even the most ambitious assassin.

Looking at her now, Kai felt that the stories didn't do her justice. Intertwining black tattoos sat atop long thick muscles on her folded arms. Yuna scanned the crowd just as a mountain lion scans a flock of sheep. Her eyes waited for someone to detach themselves so she could sink her claws into them. Yuna carried the massive sword over one shoulder, a set of leather clips holding the scabbard in place. In a small space like this the giant blade would be difficult to draw and use. Which was most likely why her giant hands rested on the hilts of two of the daggers sheathed in a set of leather bracers strapped across her chest. Lethal proficiency radiated from the woman in waves.

Kai was suddenly extremely happy to be sitting on the other side of the inn from her.

Yuna waited for Echinni to make her way towards her, and no one dared move. Echinni must have sensed the tension. She turned in the doorway and again gave a shy curtsy. “Thank you very much for allowing me to sing. That was fun.” Then she smiled and walked out the door. Yuna’s massive form was not far behind.

It must have been nearly a minute before Kai finally spoke. “Hanson ...” The innkeeper’s face slowly swivelled towards him. Kai nodded dazedly. “I think we all need a drink after that.”

Hanson nodded and delivered the quietest round he’d ever poured.

***

Jachem was devastated. "*We* should have been the ones to have that effect on the crowd! What an exit! We were completely upstaged, Kai! How can you look happy!"

"That was Princess Echinni.” Kai shook his head again, still not quite believing what had just happened. “... and I’m glad because tonight is a night I will never forget. It’s a night none of us will forget, and all these people will remember that it was the two of us who played the music for Princess Echinni’s song." Kai shook his head again. “I still feel like I’m in some sort of dream.”

Jachem's eyes suddenly lit up and moved back and forth a little too fast, giving him that look he got when he had one of his crazy ideas. "Yes, she can sing, can't she Kai! She can SING!"

"I know. Actually, I believe everyone in the room came to that same conclusion some time ago." Kai's eyebrow had snaked up on one side, and he feigned a look of concern. “Have you finally gone all the way round the bend, Jachem? I’ll see if I can get an appointment with Doctor Mayez to get you confirmed. It’s best to have these sorts of things in writing.”

Jachem, of course, completely ignored his attempt at humour. "She can sing in the *band*, Kai! With your drums, my ideas, my flair, my style, my guitar playing, and her singing, we'll be as great as the bands of the Jendar! We'll be known across all of the Shards! Maybe even all of Salucia!"

Kai knew there was no stopping Jachem now, even though Echinni had not the slightest interest in joining their band. Telling Jachem this, however, while he was in one of his delusional fervours, would only end up with Kai having to walk away in frustration. He might as well go with it as he and would never dissuade Jachem from trying. He sighed and lifted his hand towards the door. "Fine, let's go ask her then."

Jachem jumped out of his seat. "YES! Fame and Glory will be ours yet, my friend! Our angel of song has graced us with her presence and we shall grovel at her feet, imploring her not to abandon us in our hour of need!" Jachem grasped the front of Kai's jacket in a death-grip and thrust his maniacal face a hand’s width from Kai’s own.

"Or we could just ask nicely,” Kai said calmly, trying not to laugh. “Maybe leave out some of the stuff about fame and glory?" He slowly broke the vice-like grip on his jacket, and moved Jachem in the direction of the door. "Come on, let’s go or we'll lose her." He knew he would get no peace until this particular itch of Jachem’s was scratched.

"This way, Kai!" Jachem sprung into action and whirled towards the door, rolling through the crowd like a mad bull. He careened into a young man at the bar and spilled all the ales which must have just been purchased. Kai groaned as he saw that it was the muscular young

Paleschurian who had cheered so enthusiastically for them at the start of the night. *Anybody but him.* Kai followed slowly in Jachem's turbulent wake and went over to the young man to smooth things over.

"My apologies, friend, my flamboyant compatriot gets far too excited. What's your name, I'll get you a round the next time we see each other," Kai said, hoping the stereotype about Paleshurians' quick anger would not prove true.

"No need to apologise, your music was exactly what I needed tonight, made me forget some of my troubles. We'll call the ale a sacrifice on Gideon's altar of chance. I would gladly sacrifice some ale for some more of your music. But if you feel that guilty, I won't turn down a free drink when it's offered, drummer man. My name's Matoh." The large Paleschurian smiled a crooked half-grin and held out his hand.

Kai clasped hands and then slapped the broad shoulder of this new-found supporter. "I'm Kai. The drink is yours, friend; spread the word about our music, we're called The Banditos! We could use some more avid enthusiasts like yourself!" Kai yelled as he tried to keep an eye on the fleeing Jachem. He saw Jachem clear the crowd and bolt out the door. Time to go. "But I have to run and catch up to my guitarist before he gets himself killed."

Matoh lifted what remained of his tankard in the air as a salute. Kai nodded his thanks and then rushed out of the door into the night to catch up with Jachem in his headlong flight towards destiny ... or possibly, and more probably ... death.

16 - Into the Street

It was the Raven who guided us out of our savagery.
Before Him and the Song, we were lost.

Stumbling in the darkness.
Hating those we called kin.

The Raven brought the light down to us,
So we might see.

The Raven opened the Song to us,
So we might hear.

And the Raven healed our hearts,
So we might love again.

- *Singer prayer to Meskaiwa, The Raven, Tenets of the Elohim*

Echinni

New Toeron, Bauffin

The cobblestones glistened with the mist-like rain ebbing down from the night sky. Slow-burning lanterns and charged santsi globes, unique to New Toeron's streets, gave the place a soft orange glow which was reflected off the wet stones underfoot.

The night was perfect.

"What fun!" Echinni said as she pulled her cloak tight and smiled up at the cool night rain. "No wonder people love going to pubs! We have to do that again." She grabbed Yuna's arm and pulled down hard. But as usual she couldn't even budge it. Instead, Yuna lifted Echinni off the ground and walked for a few steps with the Princess hanging like a tiny child off her arm, before putting her down. Echinni saw the giant woman roll her eyes at the silly game they had played for as long as she could remember.

"Oh, don't do that," she said as she grinned up at Yuna, who was as close to a sister as she ever had. "We never get to do anything fun. Every night is practice and study and etiquette, or balls and fake smiling. That was real! With real people." She spun in front of Yuna, dancing a few steps of the jig she had learned tonight. "And don't say you didn't enjoy it."

Yuna quirked an eyebrow. "Enjoy it? I spent the whole night watching a room full of people and cataloguing the most efficient ways to get you out of there with minimal casualties. If they had discovered who you were, how many enemies might have been in attendance? How many citizens of the Union would I have had to maim and kill so we could escape? You even let that one man touch you."

"He could have been my grandfather, Yuna!" Echinni danced a few more steps ahead on the glistening cobblestones, not caring at that moment how angry Yuna must be. "He wanted to teach me a jig! And I'm glad he did."

"Just because he was old and smiled doesn't mean he wasn't dangerous," Yuna growled. "The ones that smile are the worst of all." Yuna's look grew distant; the black tattoos around her eyes always made her glare incredibly frightening.

Echinni wondered what horrible person her bodyguard might be referring too. Yuna had been through a lot of war for someone so young. There had been years when Yuna had been gone, when Yuna had been so angry at Father and had to leave to find herself. But her giant sister had returned to them, so Echinni could, and always would, forgive her for her over-defensiveness and dark moods. The big woman didn't have much in her life to make her happy, and Echinni made it one of her missions to change that. Besides, Yuna was only trying to protect her, and that was her job.

Echinni reached for Yuna's hand, marvelling not for the first time at how her own still looked like an infant's in comparison. "I know you were there to protect me. But I have to live my life as well. I can't spend it trapped in the Red Tower all my life, and besides, didn't you think I sang well?"

Yuna's glare spoke volumes; it said, 'Don't try to charm me, little sister.'

Echinni gave Yuna's hand a squeeze and stepped into rhythm beside her. "Alright, it wasn't my best, but I was just so excited. And didn't you think that boy was cute? The one playing the drums? And I noticed some big men looking at you a few times, probably wondering what you have under all that tight leather of yours."

She danced away as Yuna swatted playfully at her.

"I'm serious. Some of them even had potential," Echinni teased.

Yuna rolled her eyes again and went back to watching the street. That was Yuna, always alert, always on guard, waiting for something to pop out of the shadows.

Echinni watched her stalking the street behind her for a moment. She didn't understand how Yuna seemed to have no interest in men. Yes, Yuna was taller and stronger than any man Echinni had ever seen, but she was still pretty, albeit in a savage sort of way. Yes, she scowled a lot, but her eyes were of the deepest green, and she moved like no one else could move, like a graceful mountain. "You know, Yuna, you just might like the touch of a good man, and there were plenty in that pub who would have offered. You just have to be nice to them."

Yuna pointedly ignored her comment, and Echinni knew she would get nothing more out of her bodyguard.

She thought back to the drummer of the band. His smile had made her stomach flutter and she had found herself appreciating his sculpted arms more than once. What would it feel like to have those arms around her? Echinni smiled. He hadn't been the only one to eye her up either. The attention had felt good. She had felt like a woman rather than a political pawn. Felt like a girl flirting with boys, rather than smiling at enemies and allies because it was her duty to do so.

Her life wasn't like the fairy tales; she had met real princes and kings. None of them looked at her with the same warmth as the drummer in the pub had. In her world, men saw her as the daughter of the High King, a means to an end. In that world, the glances of princes and kings were predatory, cold and calculating. They studied her as they would a chest of gold, or a treaty. She was a path to power for them.

But in that pub she had been a young woman, and it had felt like something she had been missing for a long time now.

Echinni knew she was supposed to be concerned with other things. Things like how to govern a union of strong nations, select economic principles, understand military strategy, debate religion, know how to manipulate people of power, how to play one nation off against another while gaining from both. All these things her father wanted her to know – but he didn't understand what *she* wanted to learn. There was so much more to life than responsibility and duty, and Echinni had experienced so little of it.

She found herself once again proclaiming to the Gods how it wasn't fair. Before her father was High King he had adventures, he had loved, and had fought for what he believed in. He had lived! And now *somehow* he had forgotten what it was like to be young, to be a person, not just a title. Now, her father was not just a man, he was the High King Ronaston, the ruthless warlord who had crushed the barbaric Navutians and forced peace on the warring nations of Salucia beneath the heel of his fearsome

Syklans. Her father wanted to keep Echinni insulated and wrapped in cotton wool until she became Queen and could cement his legacy.

But there was more to life, and she needed to experience it. At least, that's what Halom's Will was telling her to do, as best as she could interpret it. These strange feelings which were akin to a calling, an internal push, had continued to grow stronger within her over the last year, and had led them out tonight to that wonderful pub. Tonight was one more confirmation that this *feeling* was in fact what the Singers called Halom's Will.

If Echinni was honest with herself however, she wasn't as sure about this sensation as the Tenents of the Elohim described in its voluminous text. Could the Father God really be talking to her and directing her actions to fulfil some divine plan? It seemed too grand.

The Singers would say she was one of His chosen, that she was just like the Prophets, the Elohim, or even like Meskaiwa, the Raven, Halom's holiest servant.

All the signs were there, she had to admit. She had read the same scripture as they. The descriptions in the stories were similar and could not be ignored. She did feel the purity and goodness inside her when it came upon her, as if something divine were radiating through her.

And yet it didn't seem quite right. If it was Halom, why did he have to be so vague, so mysterious? Surely the god could find a better way than strange feelings to instruct his chosen. Most of the time, the feelings seemed to push her in a particular direction, like she had to be somewhere, or there was only one correct choice to be made from a dozen options.

"Why would Halom want me to go and sing in a pub?" Echinni questioned aloud.

Yuna sighed. "I honestly have no idea, but there have been too many miraculous coincidences for it to be random. There is something bigger at work. But if it leads you into harm, I will find the source and cleave it in two, god or no god."

Echinni could almost hear Yuna grinding her teeth in frustration. Yuna hated breaking rules, even if it made sense.

Well, it made sense to Echinni, and Yuna was right, it couldn't be random: tonight the feeling had been so clear and direct.

"I hope it takes us back to another pub," she said. "I like singing that way. There is something ..." Echinni bit her lip trying to think of the right word "... earthy, something alive about it."

Just then, the Will began to grow inside her once more. A faint buzz began in her stomach and grew stronger. Echinni closed her eyes to concentrate on the sensation.

Something was about to happen, here, in the street.

She felt Yuna grab her arm to pull her defensively behind her.

She watched as Yuna unbuckled Hunsa from her back, as the giant sword was too long to be unsheathed directly. The battlefield weapon would have room to operate in the street, and with the clasps and leather unbuckled, Yuna discarded the sheath and belts on the ground, then waited with the bare golden blade resting against her shoulder.

Echinni had only ever seen Yuna use the short knives before, and she didn't know if she wanted to see what was about to happen.

Her heart pounded as she tried to think of what might be after them. *Assassins?* That's what this felt like. Just like it had just over a year ago, when the feeling had suddenly spiked away inside her. It felt like something insatiable was hunting them down. Three masked warriors had attacked them from within a market crowd during a royal visit to Wadachi, in Xin Ya. One had touched her, but that been as far they got. Yuna had made an example of them, and none had tried since. Her father had not taken her on any more visits after that.

The buzzing inside grew yet more, and began to pound through her mind. There was no way to escape. Whatever was chasing them was going to catch them.

Yuna's body was poised like a viper ready to strike as she stared back down the street.

All was silence. A small breeze blew a wave of fine mist down the street, which glowed softly in the orange glow. A globe merchant's sign squealed on ungreased hinges in the wind.

Runes of blue fire sprang to life along the length of Yuna's giant golden blade, and the mist around her hand turned into tiny snowflakes as the big woman siphoned in a phenomenal amount of energy.

The very air began to crackle.

Then, footsteps.

A man-shaped shadow jumped onto the building across from them in the light of the street lamp.

He was just around the corner.

Yuna breathed in deeply and the santsi globes in her leather armour glowed white as they too filled to capacity. Small lines of static began rolling along the length of her golden blade.

Echinni felt as if the very world would explode.

A second shadow joined the first.

The sword dipped slightly, ready for the strike.

The man rounded the corner.

"Not the sword!" Echinni screamed as the Will surged within her, bringing blazing clarity about what was happening.

"Princess Echinni! Princess Ech –" The words turned into a gurgle as Yuna's free hand grabbed the man by the neck and lifted him off his feet and then slammed him down against the cobblestones. Lines of blue electricity exploded around her as Yuna touched the energy-charged sword to the ground beside the man.

Echinni gasped in horror.

Yuna stood and rounded on the second man.

"I did tell him not to run up on you like that," the second man said, and walked slowly as into the light with empty hands held high.

It was the drummer from the pub!

"Hello again, Your Highness. Bet you didn't think you'd see us again." He smiled nervously. "Surprise. Please don't kill us."

Echinni looked down at the stunned man on the cobblestones at her feet.

"I'm Kai Johnstone, and my friend there is Jachem Sanders. Once he can speak, he wants to ask you a question, Your Highness. That is, if he is able to speak, and if it's alright to do so. I'm a bit terrified right now, and seem to be blathering like an idiot." Kai stood with his hands up, and looked very concerned about whether his friend was still a young man or a new and permanent feature of the street.

"Help him up, Yuna," Echinni said, still having no idea what was happening, or why the Will still pounded within her. The one thing she was sure of was that these two were no threat.

"He is alive, isn't he? I didn't think he was going to run all the way here. I've never seen him do that before. I should have stopped him from getting so close. Oh, please tell me he's alright. I'm an idiot." Kai took a tentative step forward.

Yuna grabbed the lapel of Jachem's jacket and launched the man back into the air before setting him on his feet.

"Why?" Jachem's breath finally returned, though "ragged" only began to describe it. "Why did ... why did you do that?" Jachem looked at Yuna with such bewilderment it actually looked genuine. "That really hurt."

"People like us cannot just run up to a Princess, Jachem," Kai said patiently. "I'm sorry, Your Highness. I'm just glad he's not dead. I honestly thought I'd have no trouble catching up with him. He's much faster that he looks. We'll leave now, if it pleases you, sorry for the inconvenience." Kai began trying to pull Jachem away with him as he bowed his head again in deference.

Jachem found his breath and glared back at his friend. "No, Kai, let me go. Right, excuse me, Princess –" Jachem held up a finger to ask a question.

"No!" Kai insisted as he pulled at his friend. "Come along now, we're in enough trouble as it is." Kai was eyeing Yuna, noticing how she had taken a dangerous step towards Jachem again.

Echinni found herself struggling to hold back laughter, but didn't want to upset Jachem. He genuinely didn't seem to understand that what he was doing was very inappropriate. "No, it's alright." She smiled teasingly at Kai. "He can ask his question; he's already been through a trial of pain to ask it, hasn't he? A princess must reward such acts of bravery."

"I suppose so," Kai said, obviously unsure of the right response. "But, Your Highness, you really don't want to hear this."

"I'll hear it anyway, Kai Johnstone." Echinni used a hint of command in her words and it seemed to settle the matter.

Jachem was finally somewhat composed, and he bowed to her with an over-dramatic flourish. "Your Royal Highness, Majesty, Grace, Loveliness and Princess Echinni," he began.

Kai grimaced and closed his eyes in embarrassment.

"We, the glorious, innovative, nefariously and aptly named *Banditos*, whom you have just sung with, and, to be perfectly honest, whom you stole the show from, would like to invite you to join our band!" Jachem said, and spread his arms out like that of a posturing eagle.

He wore such a genuine smile on his face that it gave Echinni pause. He was being completely honest. This was not some sort of joke.

"Well, I ..." She quirked a questioning eyebrow at Kai.

"Yes, he is serious I'm afraid." Kai reached for Jachem, bowing his head apologetically to her. "I'm very sorry to have wasted your time like this. Thank you for singing with us. I do recognise that this is no way to repay you for that honour. Please accept our sincere apologies." Kai was pulling Jachem away with him once again, his face flushed red with embarrassment.

Echinni could not help but giggle slightly. "I'm flattered, truly." She put her hand to her chest forcing herself to give this strange little man a kind answer. He had apparently thought there to be a real chance. "And I had the most fabulous time tonight, however ..."

The Will rushed through her with incredible clarity, akin to diving into an ice-cold lake. The moment hung, waiting for her to take it, and Echinni knew exactly what it was guiding her towards; she just couldn't believe it. "Yes," she said.

All heads snapped to look at her. Even the tattoos on Yuna's face looked surprised. Echinni laughed at the sight, and her laughter echoed back at her from down the lantern-lit street.

"Did you just say ... *yes*?" Kai squinted at her with unbelieving eyes. He had stopped pulling at Jachem, frozen in his tracks.

"Yes ... I did ... and somehow ... I'm sure." Echinni couldn't believe it herself. It was right. The Will was without doubt in on this. This confluence of events had been what the entire night had been leading to. "How bizarre," she whispered to herself.

"Why do you look confused?" Kai was still squinting at her, trying to figure out what had just happened. "Did you say 'yes' but mean to say 'no'? I do that sometimes. That must be it. It's alright, I'll explain to Jachem later." He shook his head. "Come on, Jachem, let's leave these two lovely people to their evening."

"No," Echinni said, testing the feeling of the Will yet again – and the certainty remained. "No, I did mean to say 'yes'. Yes, I am joining your band." The words still felt incredibly bizarre to be saying aloud.

"Huh," Kai said as he dropped Jachem's hand, "that is not how I saw this playing out."

"Excellent," Jachem said. "We practice on Shirasday and Halomsday nights from roughly seven to nine. That's when Kai has his early shifts at the docks. Come to the door at the back of the Elohim Jonas's Church next Shirasday, it's the door beside the vegetable garden."

Kai's jaw dropped further. He looked mortified and asked Yuna, "Did he just tell the High Princess Echinni what to do?"

Yuna nodded, and Echinni had never quite seen such a look of utter bewilderment on the big woman's face before. If she hadn't been so shocked herself, she would have laughed.

The moment had passed, the Will was quiet again, but Echinni knew what she had to do, for despite her confusion she still trusted in the Will's guidance. "I'm afraid I won't be able to leave the Red Tower that often."

Kai nodded with a knowing look. "Ah, I understand." He bowed and gave a placid smile and reached for Jachem's hand to pull him away.

Echinni hurriedly continued, "Which means you'll both have to stay near the Oratorio. If I arrange some positions of work at the Academy for you both, we will be able to practice more often, as I spend much of my time training at the Oratorio anyways." She paused briefly at the once-again stunned look on Kai's face. "Is that suitable?"

"W-What," Kai stammered, "sort of position did you have in mind, Your Highness?"

"Well ..." Echinni started. Yuna was glaring at her with such anger it nearly made her gasp, but Yuna would not dare reprimand her in public. "Well, Jachem said you worked at the docks. I'm sure I could find you a similar position at the royal dockyard. Would that be suitable?"

"The *royal* dockyard?" Kai asked. "Yes," he laughed, "yes, more than suitable, Your Highness. It's just –"

"Let me arrange the details." She cut him off but gave him a reassuring smile, or as reassuring as she could muster. She couldn't quite believe all of this herself. "Don't worry, I'll arrange everything. I'll have a coach sent over to fetch your things." She paused. "Shall I send the coach to Elohim Jonas's Church?"

"The Broken Clock is better," Kai said. "We don't really have that many things, and Hanson keeps all our instruments safe there."

"It's settled," Echinni said. "Noon tomorrow, at the Broken Clock Inn."

The Will stopped buzzing within her and left her with an overall sense of satisfaction.

"Thank you, Your Highness," Kai said, bowing now and grabbing Jachem just as the shorter man was about to speak. "Thank you." He bowed again and made Jachem thank Echinni before they left, looking as if they had just stepped out of a dream.

"What was *that*?" Yuna demanded.

"I don't know." Echinni stared after her two new band members. "It was the *right* choice somehow. It spoke to me again. How am I to know the mind of a god?"

"How is this going to be kept secret?" Yuna growled.

"We'll find a way." Echinni smiled up at her. "Halom shall guide us."

Yuna sighed and rolled her eyes. "He better, otherwise I'll be guiding us to another country once your father finds out."

They slipped back into the Red Tower as silently as they had left, both pondering how on earth they were going to pull this off.

Halom was unhelpfully silent on the matter.

17 - Mother

The First Knights of Salucia stand to attention.
In Spring we open to the hope of the future,
In Summer we live, shelter, fight for growth and provide sanctuary
In Autumn we cry tears of pink upon green fields to remember those not here.
In Winter we cast shadows of duty, of honour, and of sacrifice.
We stand so you might remember today's peace is born of battles past.

- *On the plaques upon entering Sentinel's Woods*

Matoh

New Toeron, Bauffin

The enormous gates of the Academy were open and Matoh strode past them, not for the first time, and yet today there was a difference. Today he wore the black and silver uniform of a recruit, and was not visiting. Today he belonged within this hallowed institution rather than without.

Matoh joined the rows of new initiates flooding beneath the towering outer gate as they walked down the paved stone path between the trees. Fifty rows of towering red-spade beech trees stood on either side of them in Sentinel Wood, the main entrance to the Academy.

Matoh looked up to see giant red leaves and spiky green fruits upon silvery-grey limbs. The colours were so vibrant. *I love this time of year,* he thought as he sucked in the fresh morning air and took a sharp turn only a few rows of trees in.

The rest of the initiates streamed along the path behind him, gawking up at the rising golden towers of the Oratorio and the massive bulk of the

Red Tower, home to the Singers and the Syklan Order respectively. To anyone who had not set foot inside the Academy before, the sights would be overwhelming, and to this day Matoh still found it awe-inspiring; but he had a very special place to visit before he joined the others.

He ducked under a low-hanging branch and went deeper into the wood, passing row upon row of beech trees. He looked at the stones at the base of each tree and the names engraved upon them. He walked past another tree and saw again how each one was planted in perfect formation with the next. Straight rows of trees could be seen down each major and minor axis of the compass. They stretched off into the morning mist, and for a moment Matoh felt as if he were the only one in the subdued silence beneath the red canopy.

Some people said these particular trees had been picked because the red leaves represented the blood of the soldiers, or that every autumn the trees would cry for the fallen. Matoh liked to think both were true.

His slow, solemn trek came to an end beside a very familiar tree. It had the same smooth bark and bright red leaves as every other tree in Sentinel Wood, but this one was special. Matoh caressed the smooth bark and felt something wide and flat fall onto his shoulder. He looked at the leaf on his shoulder, feeling his throat tighten for a moment as he smiled and said, "Hi, Mum."

Natasha Spierling. Matoh looked at the name carved into the stone. A leaf obscured the '*Na*' of his mother's name, so he brushed the large, tear-shaped stray gently aside. He knelt down and put his hand on the curved trunk, and the contact felt good, reassuring.

"I wish you were here today," he said. "It's my first step to becoming a Syklan, like you were. I'll carry on the legacy. I'll make you proud."

A branch rustled to his left. He knew it was Wayran without turning, as he had felt, rather than heard, his brother's approach. *He couldn't let me have a moment. Lady take him.*

"I wasn't trying to earwig," Wayran said. "I wasn't trying to start anything. I just had a similar idea, I guess."

Matoh was trying not to care about what Wayran did or said today. He would not have his day spoiled, he had been waiting too long for this. But try as he might, he could feel his irritation rising, could feel himself getting wound tighter and tighter by his brother's mere presence. *That's probably why he's here right now, just to annoy me. To get under my skin.*

The malice between them was palpable. It seemed to buzz around them like some giant insect, incessantly drilling through their ability to ignore it. But Matoh *would* ignore it in this place. He tightened his jaw and forced himself to stand and acknowledge his brother. *Mum deserves to see our good side.*

He was fairly certain Wayran wouldn't start anything here either. When they were still very young, they had started fidgeting during one of their visits. A few poked-out tongues at each other had led to the all too recognisable play-hitting which could get under the skin of adults no end. Their usually unflappable father had snapped almost immediately and properly smacked the both of them. "Not here, damn you!" The immediacy of their father's anger had shocked them both. "You will show respect in this place, or so help me ..." The threat had not needed to be voiced, as the blaze in their father's eyes had never been so hot.

Remembering that day, Matoh forced himself to try and take the high road. Each word felt like a stone scraping its way out of his throat. "She would be happy with this, you know. Both her sons going to the Academy she had always dreamed of creating," he said as he stood up. He moved over and let Wayran kneel down to touch the name carved into the stone.

Matoh hoped the gentle reminder of their family's strong military tradition would knock some sense into Wayran and make him see how lucky he was to be here.

Wayran said nothing. Matoh watched as his brother crossed his hands in front of him and bowed his head towards the tree. *Perhaps he isn't here to annoy me.* He took a deep breath to calm himself, and then joined his brother in quiet contemplation.

Some people thought it odd that the Silver Lady's tree was not given a place of reverence, but Matoh knew that was how she would have wanted it. She had been a soldier through and through; fame and glory were merely a consequence of doing her duty: an addendum to her faithful service.

He touched the tree again. He wished she could see him, see them both. Two of her boys, selected to come to the Academy and hopefully rise to become full Syklan Magi Knights. It was a high honour to have one son or daughter selected, let alone two.

Matoh knew their mother's name gave them an advantage, so he had forced himself to be as good or better than others at all of the criteria needed for selection. He had trained harder than anyone else at the city schools. Many knew who he was, who his parents were, so he made sure no one could doubt his worth. No one would say his spot was given to him because of his mother. No, he had earned his place, and that was why what his father had done to get Wayran in was so galling.

"It's a high honour you know, Wayran. You should be proud," he said. He couldn't help the edge of anger in his voice. The self-imposed calm was being eaten away by the acidic feelings churning deep within him.

Wayran stood, and turned to face him.

Matoh set his jaw and shoulders, ready for the fight. *Do it,* he thought, *I bloody dare you.*

Wayran stared at him blankly, but Matoh could see the irritation behind his brother's eyes.

Orcanus's breath, he knows how to wind me up! He ground his teeth and clenched his fists. *Do it. I'll give you the first shot before I knock your damn head off.*

And then Wayran turned and just walked away.

Matoh's blood boiled and he took a step forward.

A wet red leaf somehow fell directly onto his face.

He jerked back in surprise and the small braid he kept behind his left ear fell out of place and softly slapped him in the face.

Matoh wiped the leaf off his face and turned back to the tree, chuckling to himself.

"Alright, I deserved that," he said to the silent, silvery form. He chuckled again as he tucked his braid back into place before sweeping his hand through the spiked stripe of hair atop his head. His hand found the smooth bark once more. "I suppose throttling my own brother on Initiation Day would be a bad way to start. Fair point." Then he looked up to the red canopy. "I love you, Mum. Wish me luck."

He kissed his hand and touched it to the tree before he turned to rejoin the tide of initiates heading towards the Academy and their future.

Two more tear-shaped leaves drifted down behind Matoh as he left, and settled on the exact spots where he and Wayran had knelt.

18 - Pressure

Ronaston Mihane bound the Nine Nations together much more thoroughly by choosing New Toeron as the new capital than he did through the might of his Syklans and military prowess.

New Toeron had always been an international city for as long as anyone could remember. New Toeron, the capital of Bauffin, neutral in most wars, renowned for its trade, its proximity to the Chronicler Archives, its natural harbour, and relative proximity to many of the other nations, was the obvious choice for his Military Academy of Salucia.

By building upon the ruins of Durand Castle and linking it to the famous Oratorio, the Academy became a hub of military, spiritual, and intellectual excellence. Singer Theologians, Chroniclers, warrior elites, the infamous Syklan order, intellectuals from all over Salucia, and artisans from every background imaginable, including those who craft the wondrous santsi globes, have all made the Academy a beacon of ingenuity and excellence within the new Salucian Union. It is meant to symbolize an era of peace and prosperity for all citizens of the nine nations.

- Chronicler Simon Rathelson in A Common History: 1851–2850 ATC, 45th Edition, 2850

Adel

New Toeron, Bauffin

Adel felt the rumble of the cobbled street through the seat of the small cart-for-hire, but she barely noticed. Her mouth seemed to be in a constant state of dropping open as she tried to take in the grandeur of the eternal city around her. There were smells and sounds, both amazing and disgusting, which she had never experienced before. People of all shapes, sizes and colours were pressed together so tight that she wondered how they could move, let alone flow around the cart in some sort of instinctive trek through the tight street.

It was madness.

The vibrant colours of clothing, the massive buildings closing in on all sides – nothing seemed less than a full three stories, walling her in. Some of the houses even leaned in over the street. It was just too much to take in, and she had been in a kind of daze for most of the ride now.

Finally, the cart stopped beside the biggest gateway Adel had ever seen. Her entire house could have fitted beneath this archway, with room to spare. She could see row upon row of towering red-leafed trees through the gates, and beyond that ... she gasped.

There it was.

"Naira," Adel whispered, and her hand shot out to find her friend's arm. "Look."

"I see it," Naira whispered back. "We're here. We're actually here."

The great Academy of Salucia stood at the end of the tree-lined path before them. Adel recognised it from the sketch Naira had bought off a sailor and kept in her bag. Dark stone, with slanted ceramic tiled roofs which wound along the stone cliffs like some great beast; and above it all was a soaring tower made from dozens of red layers, each with slanting roofs slashing into the sky above. *The Red Tower,* Adel thought with wonder, home to the Syklan order, and across from the magnificent tower shone the three golden domes of the Oratorio. The two buildings hovered above the Academy like proud parents.

Adel couldn't believe she was now going to call this home.

A lance of pain shot through her arm, and her revelry vanished.

No! she thought. *Not now!*

Adel ground her teeth and grabbed the iron rim of the cart's wheel, and let a burst of energy that she had siphoned flow into the iron. Her hand jumped away as the iron grew red hot for an instant. She had released the torrent of siphoned energy just in time, and no one else had seen.

The red glow in the iron faded, but Adel's panic grew.

The uncontrolled siphoning was getting worse with every passing hour. Her time on the ferry had been torturous. Her last attack had been last night, when she had awoken already siphoning. She had leapt out of bed and grabbed her father's black sword. Sparks had shot off the dark blade, almost as if it were happy. She had started to cry and she hated herself for the weakness. The sword felt cold, and somehow deep, in her hands. Yet, horribly, while she was holding it in that moment, she had felt as if she were not alone. What would her father think, a trained warrior of Halom whimpering in the darkness? It was shameful. Yet despite her shame Adel had stayed up for the rest of the night until the early rays of sun rose to show them the coastline of Bauffin Island, and there was no one else in her room.

Ghosts in the sword? she had chastised herself. What would she think of next? Singing trees, or chatty stones? She was losing control of the situation, and Adel was a person whose entire world centred on control.

The sword at best would only ever be a type of crutch in re-establishing control over her siphoning. Yet for now it was the best she had.

Adel made sure no one watched her get down from the cart, as her legs were wobbly from the episode. Lack of sleep and another attack now had left her drained and exhausted.

Her hand dug through the packs on the cart and found the hilt of the black sword. Touching it reassured her, but she knew she had to move quickly, or else the next attack might just finish her.

“Come on, we need to get going,” she said, grabbing her rucksack from the back of the cart.

Naira and Thannis ignored her.

Great, Adel thought. Naira had suddenly become infatuated with this man. Adel understood the reasons of course, this Thannis was tall, handsome, refined, witty, and polite. He wasn’t the sort of man you would find in Blossom Bay, but she had thought Naira above such things after all the experiences she had had with men.

But Adel had no time to concern herself with the possibility that Naira might enjoy this man’s company, as she began to feel the all too familiar tingle as she unwillingly began to siphon in the energy around her once more.

No! Her mind screamed and she began to panic. A second bout had never happened so quickly after the last, but already she could feel how fast she was pulling in energy. Something was different about this time.

She was out of time.

Her skin began to feel as if hot thorns were scratching her. She picked up Naira’s rucksack and tossed it at her. “Catch!”

Naira jerked back from the sailing rucksack, yet caught it just the same. She gave Adel a glare which could have melted glass.

“We need to go,” Adel said firmly.

“You’ll have to excuse my rude friend. Manners were obviously not stressed on the farm.” Naira put her rucksack on and gave Adel a pointed look.

“The gates are already open. Initiation has started,” Adel said bluntly. Her hands were beginning to throb now.

“Ah, the military and their schedules. They do love to keep everyone on their toes.” Thannis looked down his nose at Adel. “Well, if there is nothing else, I shall take my leave. Good luck, I’ve heard the first day is rather difficult.”

Thannis stepped in close to Naira, and Adel grimaced as she saw a spot of colour rising in Naira's cheeks. Her took her hand in his and kissed the top of it. "A pleasure, Naira O'Bannon." His hand lingered on Naira's which, at any other time, would have made Adel cringe.

"I do hope I can find such delicious company elsewhere in this city," Thannis said with a final suggestive smile at Naira. Then he stepped towards Adel.

She jumped back into a fighting stance without even thinking, pulling her hands back so as not to allow him to take them, partly on instinct, but also because she would have pulled energy in from his hands. Unconsciously, she felt for the pommel of the black sword underneath its leather wrapping.

Thannis's eyes flashed, but his grin widened. He had recognised the fighting stance. "Now, now." He shook his finger slightly. "Naughty girl. Someone should teach you how to play properly." He bent down slowly and whispered in her ear. "You seem so eager to dance, my dear sweet, Adel Corbin." Silent as a snake, his hand wrapped around hers. He had a grip as hard as iron. Adel couldn't draw the sword even if she'd wanted to. Thannis's eyes widened slightly – he must have felt the icy tingle in his hand, telling him she was siphoning.

"Remove your hand," Adel said. Every bone in her body wanted to twist and throw this man to the ground, yet somehow she found some restraint. He was a noble, and her father had warned her against their kind.

"You are a strange one." Thannis squinted slightly and Adel had the strange sensation he was sizing her up, like a farmer would a piece of livestock.

"If you two are finished flirting the driver needs to be off," Naira said with a wry smile.

"I ... it's not me. He ..." Adel spluttered, but Thannis stepped away so smoothly it looked as if he had done nothing at all.

"Just a slight jest at young Adel's expense," Thannis grinned. "Childish of me, apologies."

Adel clutched the length of the black blade in its leather case and found she was shaking.

"I won't take up any more of your time. Good morning to you both." Thannis winked at Naira, who was again grinning back at him.

Naira rolled her eyes and laughed. "Always the gentlemen?"

"Not always," Thannis answered with a coy smile as he turned on his heel and walked away.

Thank Halom, Adel sighed. Almost on cue, she felt her skin grow warmer with the effort to contain the siphoning. They had to move.

Sweat burst out on her forehead as she looked around. The guards still stood at the gates. *Of course - why would they leave?* Adel couldn't brandish the sword. They would think her some sort of lunatic. Too late: the guards were already looking at her suspiciously. She forced herself to sling the leather cord of the wrapped sword across her back and chest.

The energy began flooding into her.

Naira was saying something as she watched the departing Thannis, but it didn't register to Adel. She kept putting her feet in front of her and pulled Naira forcefully up to the gates to present her papers to the guard.

"Adel what are you doing!? Get a hold of yourself." Naira pulled her hand free and looked back, but Thannis was already gone. Naira glared at her angrily and gave her own papers to the guard. "Thanks a lot, my so-called *friend* – he's gone."

Adel ignored her; her attention was focused on the officer studying her papers. She bit down on her lip, attempting to make herself concentrate, but her skin felt as if it was on fire.

The guard ticked off something on his list and held out her and Naira's papers. He was looking at her strangely. "Everything looks in order. Proceed to the ... Sorry – Adel, is it? Are you alright?"

"Fine. Thank you, sir." She snatched the papers from his hand and ran through the gates, dragging Naira with her.

"Hey, stop right there!" The guard had his halberd in his hand now and began to give chase. He waved to his partner to alert the inner gates.

"Enough!" Naira slapped her hand away. "Adel Corbin, you are embarrassing the both of us. What is going on?!"

Adel spun to look at her friend and felt tears rolling down her cheek. There was a group of guards gathering now, staring at them, but the pain inside her rose again. She wasn't going to find Fellow Calahan in time.

"Adel?" Naira said, finally understanding that she was panicking, "what is it?"

But Adel couldn't talk, she couldn't think. All she knew was if she pulled out the sword, the guards might attack. She had to get away from all the people.

Her body felt as if it were on fire, the energy pulsing in her now, a pressure building. The tears streamed down her face and she cried out as she saw steam curling up from her cheeks.

She was going to die, right here at the Academy gates.

The trees.

She pushed Naira away and ran into the trees. The massive trunks sped by, but she could take no more. Hopefully this was far enough.

Adel flung the leather case off and drew the sword. She screamed, and white-hot fire coursed through her into the blade. Blue sparks leapt through the air, showering down on her. Something in the sword seemed to glow and she slammed the tip into the ground.

Grass burst into flames and the air crackled all around her.

But the energy was gone.

The pulsing inside her subsided and Adel dropped to her knees and let her tears flow. Red leaves floated down from the trees all around her.

"What is happening to me?" she whimpered, and dipped her head. She had just sealed her fate.

"Step away from the sword," a stern voice said from behind her. The guard had caught up with her. He wasn't alone. Adel turned to see five other guards, all holding halberds pointed at her. Naira stood behind them, watching, terrified.

"I'm sorry." Adel held her hands up. "There is something wrong with me, I –"

"It's alright, Vince," a different voice said. This one came from a broad-shouldered young man in a black Academy uniform who had stepped out from the trees. He must have seen the whole thing.

"She pulled a weapon, Spierling," the guard named Vince said.

"I think you might be lucky that she decided to use it on the grass instead of anything else," the young man replied casually, nodding to the burnt circle around Adel. He knelt down and met her eyes. "Are you alright?"

The look on his face clearly showed that he doubted she was: it was a mixture of concern and surprise. Strangely her mind fixated on how good-looking this young man was. It would have been nice to touch a man that handsome at least once before she died. She came back to the present. He had asked a question. "No." Adel said as she began to shake, hating herself for this display of weakness, but she wasn't alright. She needed help. "I need to find Fellow Callahan." *Well, they aren't going to let me in now. I've just thrown away my spot as an initiate.*

"It's fine, I can take it from here, Vince," the young man said to the guards. "Is it alright if I sheath that sword of yours?" He smiled. It was a pleasant smile, genuine and warm. Adel thought it was possibly the best smile she had ever seen. Not like Thannis at all.

"I'll do it," Adel said, a bit defensively. She pulled the weapon out of the ground and retrieved the sheath beside her. The five halberds twitched at the move, but she put the sword back in its case and slung it over her shoulder. "It was my father's. I'm the only one who should touch it."

"Fair enough." The young man waved the guards away. "Really, Vince, it's alright. I know where to find Fellow Callahan, and I'm pretty sure the Head of Siphoning will want to know about what we just saw." He stepped to Adel and offered his hand to help her up.

Adel took his hand and stood. The young man had feathers tied into a broad stripe of hair. On the shaved side of his head was a long thin braid tucked over his ear. *He looks like an old Paleshurian warrior out of the history books. Who is he?* "Thank you, Sir Spierling." That name, was he related to the Silver Lady somehow?

"I'm not a sir just yet. I'm an initiate, like you," he said. "Come on, let's go find Fellow Callahan."

"Are you going to report me?" Adel wiped the tears from her cheeks in annoyance. *Knights don't cry.*

"For what?" He tapped the grass with his feet. "I think it looks better this way."

Adel laughed and then noticed she was still holding his hand, and pulled it away. "Sorry." She cringed up at him. He had the loveliest brown eyes.

"Adel," Naira said, coming to stand beside her now. The guards were returning to the gatehouse. Whoever this young man was, he had some pull with them. *Spierling*, Adel thought again – could it be?

"Uh ... this is ..." Adel looked up apologetically at him.

"Matoh." His eyes locked onto Naira. "Matoh Spierling."

"And you can command five guardsmen to leave, Matoh Spierling?" Naira questioned.

"I've known Vince my whole life," Matoh said. "We both live only a few blocks away. Though I suppose I live here now, same as you." He seemed to find that odd.

Adel tried to compose herself. "This is Naira, and I'm Adel."

"A pleasure," Matoh smiled.

Adel couldn't help trusting this young man entirely.

"You'll have to teach me that trick," Matoh said to her.

"I ..." Adel began, but stopped. The tingling sensation had started to creep back into her as she once again began to siphon.

"What is wrong, Adel!? Talk to me," Naira said.

"Fellow Callahan," Adel said between ground teeth. "I need him to help."

"Follow me," Matoh said, sensing her urgency. "Fellow Callahan's quarters are this way. Hang on."

Adel hoped she could.

19 - A Bit of Sport

It would appear the global thermohaline cycle has changed as I predicted; however, some of the consequences have been truly spectacular.

One being the self-perpetuating storm cell rolling along across the North Ocean. The extremely warm currents coming up from the sea and the heat charged air coming off the now extensive deserts on the continents have created a storm system which may last possibly thousands of years.

Nature's fury is awesome to behold.

- Journal of Robert Mannford, 096 Year 045

Thannis

New Toeron, Bauffin

That was tedious, Thannis thought, rolling his eyes and walking away from Naira and Adel. He had categorised them both as potential targets, but as they were going to be at the Academy, he would either need opportunistic settings or much more elaborate plans to misdirect the constabulary.

Thannis had siphoned off enough of their energy to know Adel was also a gifted siphoner, while Naira's talents seemed more unique. Both would be extremely satisfying, and delicious in their own ways, but they were not the experiences he needed just now.

He had been cooped up on that shoddy boat for far too long. The girls were pretty, but not particularly stimulating conversationalists. He had spent most of the time they conversed pondering over how to properly hide deaths on a ferry that small. It had provided some quiet mental fun, but in the end he decided that the challenge and reward was not worth the effort required. Too many things could go wrong and far too many scenarios ended up with him having to kill everyone.

So he had waited; but now it was time to sink his claws into this city.

As he moved down the busy street and away from the Academy he lingered on the irksome fact that he had used his real first name; yet he concluded it could not have been helped. His cousin Dennis, who worked at the Academy and was an excellent resource to help maintain an alias, of course knew him as Thannis. Dennis, while having an excellent scientific mind, was anything but competent at subterfuge, and there was a possibility that he would need Dennis to corroborate some part of his story. There was just no way around it, there was far less chance of error that way. Besides, the family name he had given was false, so no one other than Dennis would know that he was *the* Thannis, Prince and heir to the Nothavran throne.

Enough wasted thoughts; he had come to this city for its abundance of diverse and fascinating people to experience. Thannis had a whole city full of prey, and so he began to hunt.

A lewdly dressed woman stepped out in front of him and winked at him in her garish make-up. “Hello, handsome, fancy a bit of fun?” She smiled, showing several gaps in her yellow teeth.

Thannis’s lip wanted to curl back in disgust, but he made himself respond appropriately. “Not today, love. Too early for me I’m afraid.” He winked and spun smoothly around her, not even breaking his stride. Hopefully he was already forgotten by the wretched street urchin. He thought about how the polite smile he wore hid his murderous urge to slash open her neck just to see the surprise on her face.

Moving away from the woman, Thannis quickly merged with the flow of the crowd. His eyes started seeing opportunities in the crush of people. He could kill easily enough. A hidden dagger thrust here, a feigned stumble and stab there. He judged he could silently cull maybe a dozen people before anyone noticed the danger. Yet so far there were no opportunities for the privacy he craved to truly experience them. So he walked another ten blocks, observing the people and getting a feel for the rhythms and sounds of the city, before he disappeared into an alley and began the hunt in earnest.

Three steps, a barrel, and he was on the roof surveying the maze of buildings and streets. Thannis could still see the massive domed roof of the Oratorio, with the three golden towers soaring to the sky around it. Beneath that giant golden dome were enough Singers to placate him for a very long time. The thought of it made his muscles twitch with excitement, and he smiled; but he needed to satiate his urges on something a bit less rich, else he would spoil the experience. *Something a bit more common to cleanse the pallet,* he thought.

He slipped across the rooftops towards the bazaar in front of him. He perched just back from the edge of the building, watching as a falcon would. It always amazed him how few people looked up.

Just then he saw a shadow move from the corner of his eye. A flash, nothing more, but it had been there, and he knew to trust his instincts.

Someone was watching him.

It shouldn't be possible; how had they found him so quickly?

Thannis pretended he hadn't noticed and waited for whoever it was to give themselves away.

There. He whipped around and threw.

His hunting knife sank deep into the brown mortar of the wall behind him.

There was no one to be seen.

Odd, he thought to himself. *I could have sworn ...*

He heard footsteps from behind the door to his left, and his hand went to his other knife and he tensed, ready to strike.

A woman in a yellow and orange dress opened her back door and stepped out with a basket full of laundry. She jumped when she saw him, but her surprise turned to anger. “What you doing on my roof?”

Not what I was expecting, yet opportunity knocks but once, he thought.

He sighed as he spoke: “The fault is mine, madam. I appear to be jumping at shadows.” He stepped closer and held his hands out innocently.

“That don’t explain you bein’ on my roof. Get away, you.”

“Of course.” Thannis bowed and thrust forward.

Her anger turned back to surprise as his knife stabbed straight up through her lower jaw and into the brain.

Thannis let the body sink to the ground, watching it twitch. He thought it funny how he could see the flat of his knife through the gap in her teeth.

He waited for a good long while, listening for any hint of detection, or movement from any others in the house below him.

But there was nothing.

The common din of the bazaar was uninterrupted by screams of outrage or shock.

He wanted to siphon, wanted to taste whatever energy was seeping out of this laundry woman as she died, but she had not been the one watching him. He could still feel the tickle on the back of his neck of unseen eyes.

Frustrated, he jerked his knife free and wiped the blood off on the dead woman’s dress. He had to either shake off or dispatch his pursuer before he could truly enjoy himself.

Thannis closed his eyes and let all the years of training in the woods with his forestry master take over. He let his ears become accustomed to the sound, let himself be silent and still. He listened for what was out of place.

And then he heard it.

A footstep, scraping on the roof to his right.

He uncoiled like a viper and shot towards the sound.

Thannis opened his eyes as his knife flashed out and he saw an old woman's face with a painted skull on it. Surprise and panic filled her eyes as he was now only one pace from slicing her wide open. Thannis had the odd feeling her recognised her.

He did! This was ...

She flung her hand out at him and touched the crown of her head with her other.

His mind went blank and the woman in front of him disappeared from sight.

***

Thannis blinked and then had to squint against the bright sunlight and the pain it was causing his head. He rubbed at his eyes, as if waking from a dream.

He was standing on the roof once more, looking over the bazaar, yet now he had no desire to hunt here.

The docks. It was so obvious. Those arrogant dock workers had sneered at him earlier when he had disembarked the ferry. *Yes, they were perfect.* He grew excited at the prospect of the burly men trying to take him down; their energies would be full of rage and anger. Yes, that would do perfectly, it would purge the pent-up frustration.

He felt his pulse quicken, but then hesitated. *No,* he thought, taken aback, *they have seen me already, what if not all of them are still there?* That would leave witnesses. The dock workers were horrible targets. Why ever would he think he should go after them?

He shook his head, trying to clear it, then studied the bazaar below and saw a beautiful Tawan sailor swaggering down through the markets.

He will do nicely, Thannis thought, and stepped towards the edge. There was a spot just out of sight he could slip down to.

Pain shot between his eyes and his vision blurred. He stopped in his tracks.

No, he told himself, *the docks. I should go to the docks. I* must *go to the docks.* He would make one of those warehouses his killing field. It would be glorious; each kill would sweeten the next one. Any other target would pale in comparison.

All doubt was swept away with the pain in his head, and once he began moving towards the docks the pain began to dissipate.

Thannis raced away across the rooftops, placing careful feet upon the domed ceramic tiles as easily as the stealthiest thief, yet this time he did not notice the shadowy figure creeping along behind him.

Esmerak made sure to keep her distance. The blade Thannis had thrown had nearly pinned her skull to the wall.

20 - An Old Man

Today Kali recommended introducing some of the mutagenic inducing proteins into the crops of some of the established settlements on the north end of the continent.

I don't know if I really believe the expected results, some of them are truly incredible, but this could be a major step in bringing our species back into harmony with the world.

I have to maintain hope.

- *Journal of Robert Mannford, Day 312 Year 015*

Adel

New Toeron, Bauffin

Sinuous vines covered the dark stone walls framing the borders of the serene garden that Adel now sat in. The leaves of dark red and green popping up from those vines somehow instilled peace in the beautiful space.

It's a good place to die, Adel thought. Her body was exhausted, and all she could do now was try to hold back the fire coursing through her for as long as possible. Hold it at bay, for she knew that if her concentration slipped it would all be over.

Keep the energy moving. It burned like white-hot ants crawling beneath her skin, but she kept that molten flow coursing into the black sword. She had lost track of how long she had sat here, but it didn't matter any longer. Her mind could not think of the progression of time. All she had left in her world was the pain of the fire within her. But the pain meant she was still alive.

Her muscles burned and she could feel the sweat dripping from her brow. A steady rhythm of blue sparks dropped from the shining black blade onto the grass.

Matoh had led them to this garden, but Fellow Callahan had not been around. The nice young man had gone to get help. Naira had offered to stay with her, but Adel knew her chances would be better if there were two of them out there searching.

Naira could do nothing for her except watch her die, and Adel didn't want that. She didn't want to burden her friend with her horrible end.

So she had sent her only two friends in the world away, and that had seemed a lifetime ago.

The end was close. Adel knew her body well, and she knew the limits of her endurance had already been far surpassed. Part of her wanted to let go. Surely the pain would be blinding if she did ... but then there would be an end to it.

She lifted her head in agony and made herself look around, forcing herself to see the beauty around her. She had heard it was best to die thinking of something beautiful, of something that made you happy.

Strange dark blue statues stood amongst the vibrant autumnal colours. Almost as if silent watchers of her end. Some looked like ancient warriors; others were draped in flowing stone robes, holding books and branches aloft. What they were meant to represent she could not tell, but she could feel their eyes staring at her, like they understood her somehow.

She listened to the quiet roll of water on stone behind her as the water from a central fountain spilled down the pyramid shaped rock at its heart. Water lilies floated on the slightly disturbed surface of the pond around the fountain.

Water! The thought pushed through the pain in Adel's head. She was an idiot!

She took one hand from the sword and plunged it into the pond. The water felt as cool as ice, and for a blissful moment some of the fire within her quieted.

She drew in a shuddering breath and then panted as she savoured the blessed coolness of the water, but then her dread began to rise once more as she felt the relief from the water begin to bleed away. The water's temperature was also rising, and in the back of her mind she marvelled at the torrent of energy which must be flowing through her to effect the change so quickly.

A tear fell down her cheek and she put her hand back on the sword. Her body shook. *Not long now,* she thought. The sword had initially felt like a bottomless reservoir, but now she began to feel resistance to more energy being pushed into it. The sword would not be enough. The flow was too strong. Her body was going numb; already she was losing the feeling in her hands. Soon she wouldn't know if she held the sword or not. *And then I'll burn.*

Adel closed her eyes and took her hand out of the water, placing it back onto the sword. The black blade's point dug into the rock at her feet and sparks began to pulse from the black metal, falling in waves upon the fountain stone. *I'm sorry, Father, I've failed, I've let you down.* She was going to die for her failure, for her sin. She wished she was home, wished she could have died in a place she knew.

The numbness was spreading into her legs and face, and that was dangerous indeed. Pain she could at least feel, but the nothingness in her hands meant she was losing the fight. She opened her eyes and saw her breath in the air, smoke arising from the sword's pommel, and blood running between her fingers. Her hands must be blistering.

It was beginning.

This is why it is forbidden to use your body as a conduit. Halom was punishing her for her arrogance; she had committed blasphemy and no song or hymn, no measure of repentance could save her now. She felt blisters begin to swell on her back. *They almost feel cold.*

As if in a dream, she fell forward and one hand let go of the sword to fall back into the water with a splash and slip beneath the surface. Adel watched numbly as a golden carp swam from beneath a lily pad and found her fingers. She felt the pressure of its mouth as it probed inquisitively.

She laughed through the numbness and her tears. *Thank you, silly fish.* Its scales glistened in the sunlight. *Beautiful,* she thought vaguely; *hold on to the image.* She felt her body spasm and felt she could take no more.

The dam inside her broke.

Adel felt an ocean of power rushing towards her, blasting forth to consume her.

But then . . . she didn't die. Something had touched her wrist, right at the last moment.

The dreaded onslaught never came. Instead the burning torrent began to ebb away, like water seeping into the soil after a hard rain.

And then it was gone. It was all gone.

She opened her eyes to find a strange bracelet on her wrist.

"You're fine now," a man's soft, deep voice said calmly.

Adel blinked and tried to focus on the face beside her. It was an older face, tanned, kind and strong.

Gentle fingers turned over her bloody hand and something damp was pressed onto the popped blisters. The relief from the throbbing pain was heaven.

The kind face smiled at her. "My apologies for being late. I'm Fellow Callahan, you're safe now."

Adel tried to speak, but her mouth didn't seem to work.

"Don't try to talk." His hand left hers and Adel saw that the cold feeling was coming from a compress of what looked like ground leaves and mud. She noticed he was humming, deep yet soft, and overwhelmingly soothing.

She tried to wipe the tears from her face, but his strong hands held hers down gently.

"Now, where else are the sores?" He rolled up her sleeves and sucked on his lip. "Oh my, you poor thing." Blisters ran all along her arm. She watched as he took a mixture from one of his pouches, dipped it in the fountain's water and placed it upon her burns. It felt wonderful, like all the hurt was being somehow leeched away.

She watched as he moved from one blister to another, until he came to her wrist. She suddenly remembered the strange bracelet. It was made of the same strange blue-black stone as the statues. It was heavy and gloriously cool against her skin. "I don't understand," she croaked – but then saw her hand was empty. *I'm not holding the sword!*

Adel twisted frantically. "Where is it!?" There was anger in her voice. "I need the sword!"

"Enough of that." Fellow Callahan's large hands held her shoulders. "Calm down, it's just over there." He nodded to his right, and Adel saw it resting on the grass.

"I need it," she said. The urge to grab the sword was impossible to ignore, she must hold it again.

"Best not to." Fellow Callahan's strong hands turned her face to look at him. "You're fine now, Adel. Let go, relax." His green eyes studied her methodically.

Something in his voice made her trust him, and only then did she feel how tense her entire body was. "Alright." She made herself breathe slowly, but her heart still pounded.

"That's better." He studied her a moment more, then looked towards her sword. "How did you come by that sword?"

"My father gave it to me," Adel said as she fought her way through the fog in her mind. It seemed a strange question.

"Did he now?" Fellow Callahan's eyes narrowed slightly as they probed for truthfulness. "And does he still ..." He paused for a moment. "Does he still live?"

"What?" Adel didn't understand. "Yes, he still lives. He said the sword would help, and that I had to find you."

Fellow Callahan thought for a moment. "He *gave* it to you. Interesting."

"What do you mean? My father was helping me." Adel was taken aback by this strange man's judgement of her father. *He held me, he loves me.* "The sword saved me from burning. Who are you to –!" She was surprised by the heat in her voice.

"Calm down." His disarming grin reappeared. "An old man shouldn't ramble. It's a bad habit of mine." He went back to studying her. "Now," he said as he stood and offered her his hand, "you'll need to come with me if you still want to make the opening ceremonies."

"But ..." She pointed down at the sword. It was all so confusing. "What ...?"

Fellow Callahan chuckled. It was the most musical chuckle Adel had ever heard. "You'll be fine, old Callahan will have you fixed up and ready to go." His eyes nearly disappeared into his tanned face as he smiled. It was impossible not to like him.

"Alright." She took his offered hand and stood groggily to her feet; she had to lean against him for support. It felt like leaning against a small oak tree. "Thank you, sir ... I don't know how to thank you."

"Quiet now, child. There will be time for that later." He smiled at her and patted her hand. Only then did Adel notice Naira and Matoh watching. There were tears in Naira's eyes.

"Are you okay?" Naira's voice quivered. Adel had never seen her this upset.

"I think so," she said.

"Come, the both of you." Fellow Callahan motioned for them to come over. "Help me get her to the house."

"Don't ever do that again." Naira ducked her head under Adel's other arm. "Why didn't you tell me about any of this!"

"I didn't want to ruin today for you." Adel bowed her head. "You've been looking forward to this for so long and I just thought –"

"How can someone as smart as you be so dumb?" Naira shook her head and hugged her close. "You tell me from now on, alright?!"

"Yes, Mother." Adel had to laugh. She saw Matoh grinning behind Naira's back.

"I might as well be. Goodness me." Naira wiped her eyes and took a deep shuddering breath. "Right, so is she okay now?" Naira looked to Fellow Callahan.

"We will find out very soon. This way." Fellow Callahan held out his hand for them all to follow. "Matoh, would you be a gentlemen and take over from me?"

Matoh took her hand from Fellow Callahan and put his arm around her waist. It felt a bit like having a bull under your arm. "I'm glad you're alright," he whispered.

"Me too," she said and tried to smile. "Thank you."

They walked towards a small cottage near the back wall, almost hidden amongst small trees and plants. It looked as if it had grown right out of the ground.

"What a nice house," Adel said. Her head was feeling fuzzy. She looked over to Matoh. "And you're a nice man." She laughed. "Everything is nice, and I think I feel a bit funny."

Fellow Callahan smiled. "Ah good. The salve is starting to work. Are you feeling a bit 'floaty'?"

"Yes, actually." Adel giggled. "That's exactly what it feels like!

Floating. But I can see my feet moving. How am I floating?"

Matoh and Naira smiled for some reason.

"You have a nice smile," Adel said to Matoh. "Doesn't he have a nice smile, Naira?"

"Yes, he does." Naira laughed, and for some reason that only made Matoh's smile broaden.

"And you've got lots of muscles. I can even feel them through your uniform." His shoulders were so wide she could barely get her elbow round to the other side of his neck. It was then she noticed something odd about the stone bracelet on her wrist.

It had begun to glow orange.

She froze as the familiar tingle began to warm within her once more. She was siphoning.

"What's wrong?" Matoh asked. He had stopped with her.

"No, not again," Adel whimpered.

"Well, that was fast." Fellow Callahan shook his head and walked over to them nonchalantly.

"Let me see that, maybe a slight ..." He trailed off as he took her wrist and placed his hand on the bracelet. He began to croon softly, and all of a sudden she could feel the bracelet vibrating, as if it was singing back to him.

"How are you doing that?" Adel watched in amazement as the orange pulsing within the bracelet stopped and seemed to settle into a thin and almost imperceptible line within the stone bracelet. The tingling stopped as the bracelet quietly hummed.

He took it from me. Somehow Fellow Callahan had controlled her siphoning.

"How?" Adel said. The faint line of orange running along the inside of the stone was like a line of fire beneath black ice.

"So many questions. Just like your father." Fellow Callahan chortled to himself. “There will be time for answers, but first we need some more bandages – and a spot of tea, I think.”

They reached Fellow Callahan’s strange little cottage and stepped inside.

“Are these still alive?” Matoh asked as he ran a hand along one of the wall beams. Green leaves poked out from the beam near the window.

“Yes, that is Merryweather Elm, a very cooperative tree. You can get them to do all sorts of tricks if you have the patience,” Fellow Callahan answered, as if it was the most normal thing in the world. “Sit down, sit down. Get comfortable and I’ll brew us a pot of Bo-Ling tea.”

“Bo-Ling tea?” Matoh asked.

“It’s a blend of raspberry leaf, nettle, and a special black tea I grow,” Callahan answered

“Sounds horrible.” Matoh grimaced and gave Adel a funny look.

She smiled at his attempt at humour, but she was too exhausted for any sort of real levity.

“Does the body good though.” Fellow Callahan’s eyes twinkled and gave his chest a solid thump.

Adel’s head felt as if she had lost a sparring match. She sat down and looked out of the window. “Hey, those stones are glowing, just like the bracelet.” Each of the great blue-black stones which stood outside had a soft orange glow within its core.

Fellow Callahan nodded. “They are linked. I’ll explain more later.”

Naira looked outside and then back to Adel. “What happened to her?” she asked Fellow Callahan. “She’s sat down now, we’re having tea. It’s time for you to supply some answers.”

Fellow Callahan smiled at Naira’s tone and shrugged. “Adel has opened a sort of conduit within herself. She doesn’t yet know how to control it.”

“Inside herself?” Naira asked.

"Yes, very few people survive it anymore. It's what you call 'burning out'," Fellow Callahan said as he bustled around the small fireplace, picking leaves from different jars and placing them in the little iron pot hanging above the fire.

"Will it happen again?" Adel heard herself ask. Her body felt as if were made of glass, like she might break if she moved too fast.

"Yes." Fellow Callahan nodded. "But in time you should learn to control it."

Adel felt as if a weight had been lifted from her. So there was hope. "Thank you." She could feel the tears of relief in her eyes.

"Enough of that now." Fellow Callahan handed out cups and poured everyone tea. He paused before giving Adel her cup and sprinkled a few different leaves into it, then stirred it quickly with a small spoon. "Here, drink this."

The tea tasted strong and bitter, but with only a few sips Adel felt her body begin to relax.

"Your father should have sent you to me earlier," Fellow Callahan said sternly. "Leonard should know better." He trailed off, mumbling angrily to himself.

"I only told him just before I left. His church?" Adel asked. What did the Singers have to do with any of this? Her mouth felt as if it were full of cotton. "What did you put in my tea?"

"You need rest." Fellow Callahan smiled gently at her.

Adel struggled to stand, "No I need to go ..." but she trailed off as Fellow Callahan put a comforting hand on hers.

"What you need is rest. I'll have you as fixed as I can get you and ready in time. You'll make the initiation ceremony. You might as well catch a few hours' sleep while I work. Besides, they won't begin the ceremonies without me. We have time." Callahan smiled at her and Adel knew she could trust him. "And if you need something to mull over in your dreams, young Corbin, lesson number one is stop being so hard on yourself. It was a lesson your father could never learn, but one I'm going to make sure you do."

"I'm not sleepy." Adel yawned.

"I beg to differ." Fellow Callahan winked at her. "Matoh, there is spare bedroom just back around the corner. Help Adel to it please."

"Sir." Matoh nodded. He trotted over to her and picked her up as easily as if she were a child.

"I'm not sleepy," she protested again. *I need to get ready for the initiation ceremony.*

She felt a soft mattress beneath her as Matoh set her down. It felt so wonderful, the tea was so warm, and everything was cosy and lovely. She was safe, the siphoning was under control, and the tension in her body let go for the first time in a long, long while.

She was asleep before her head hit the pillow.

* * *

Fellow Callahan looked at the two young recruits watching him as he administered the salve to Adel's back, and shook his head sadly. *How she held on for so long is a miracle. She should be dead.*

He could almost sense the connection between these three. How their paths were connected was unclear, but he could sense the intertwining nature of what lay ahead of them.

He touched the blue stone bracelet on Adel's wrist once more, making sure it felt in tune with the flow coursing beneath her smooth skin. *Just a little more.* He found the note he knew the stone would resonate with, and hummed in such a melodious tone it could have been on an organ. He pushed the note out of himself and coaxed it towards the bracelet, caressing the stone with the soft music. The inner ring of orange began to glow again within the stone. "There, that's better. It should keep you safe until we learn to control it." Fellow Callahan knew Adel slept deeply, but he also knew that part of her mind was still listening.

He smiled down at the young woman, glad that he had given her some peace, for he knew that the daughter of Leonard Corbin would not have experienced much peace in her short lifetime. Then he sighed, for he knew she was unlikely to have it in her future either.

"Rest now," he said softly. "Rest now, young Arbiter."

21 - Royal Repercussions

Amongst the Old Gods, Halom, The Singer of the Great Song, Creator and Lover, saw the plight of humanity and was moved. Long had His people forgotten Him, yet now was a time of new birth.

The Jendar paid for their sins with their lives. Lady Death and her Black Whale, Orcanus, harvested the souls of the unbelievers as they fell to the wrath of the Old Gods upon land and sea.

Decades of destruction wiped the unholy Jendar scourge from the earth, leaving it clean to begin anew.

- *Tenets of the Elohim*

Echinni

New Toeron, Bauffin

"**A**re you out of your bloody mind?!" Ronastan Mihane's voice boomed through Echinni's room like thunder.

"No, I was out of *the palace* actually," Echinni replied. She knew her tone would only infuriate her father further, but the shock of just how quickly her secret sojourn had been discovered was making her especially irritated.

"Do not twist my words." Her father spun around and fixed her with a threatening stare. He was a man so powerful with muscle that the violence of the move made Echinni take an involuntary step back.

Her father, High King Ronastan Mihane, was a true son of Asgur. He had muscles like fat snakes cording around his arms, and hands so big he could grab a person's head as if he were holding a small melon. Scars and tattoos marked his dark arms. He wore his gold pendant of Fenris, the Wolf of Asgur, on a gold chain hanging between his massive chest muscles, which showed above his deerhide waistcoat. He was brutal, ruthless, passionate and powerful, all of which was on full display now. Violent rage shone behind her father's hazel eyes, a rage which had brought nine nations to their knees.

Yet Echinni made herself stand tall, and she tilted her chin up, daring him to strike her. Her voice was cold. "Yet that is what you have trained me to do. To twist words, to use them as weapons. Who better to practice on than a tyrant?"

As soon as she said these words, Echinni knew she had gone too far. Ronaston Mihane loomed over his daughter so much like the Iron Bear he was named after. Nearly as tall as Yuna, he towered over Echinni and could have snuffed her out in a heartbeat if he had decided to. He huffed bestially and clenched his hands until Echinni heard his knuckles pop from the pressure. He had killed many with those same bare hands.

"Bah!" The High King spun and smashed his fist through the door of her cabinet as easily as if it had been paper. The cabinet remained on his arm. Instead of removing it, he just twisted and hurled the entire thing against the far wall, shattering it.

Echinni had stood in the eye of this storm before. Where others would shrink and cower, Echinni knew how to survive this. He would not strike her; it was a line she knew deep down he wouldn't cross. She knew he was fearful of his own power around her. Yuna had told her about how he had dared not touch her as a baby for the longest time because he was scared he would crush her delicate bones.

He had never hit her, and he wouldn't now.

"You put everything we've fought for in danger! Don't you see!? We have enemies all around us," he pleaded. The fragments of wood sticking out of his knuckles were so insignificant to him they might as well have been flower petals alighting there. "You must stay where I can protect you."

He looked at Yuna pointedly and the big woman hung her head in shame.

"You can't keep me locked up like this forever. I am a person, not your prisoner ... or am I?" Echinni could feel her voice shaking, and her eyes began to moisten. "How am I meant to learn to survive in this blood-soaked world you are bequeathing unto me if I stay locked away from it? How am I meant to understand my people if I never meet any of them?"

Her father paused at this. His breathing slowed and he picked some of the splinters from his knuckles. "And frequenting rowdy taverns is meant to toughen you up? Educate you on how best to *serve* the people?" His voice dripped like acid. "Or is it our reputation you want to drag through the mud as some sort of childish rebellion? Is that what you were going for? Royal tramp? Queen of loose morals? Echinni the Unchaste?" He growled, "Your mother would have been ashamed."

Echinni's retort died on her lips. The comment had been a slap worse than any his giant hands could have delivered. "It wasn't like that ... I ..." She suddenly realised he had said nothing of inviting Kai and Jachem to stay at the Oratorio, and that surely if he had known, he would have brought it up. Apparently the spies had missed something, so she decided to keep quiet.

"Well, I'll be sure to correct all the whispers in court then." Her father had finished picking the wood from his fist and turned to face Yuna.

"And you!" He stepped towards Yuna, and this time he did not hold his hand. The slap would have fell a horse, yet Yuna stood with her eyes downcast, taking the punishment without a hint of retaliation. Echinni had never seen him hit Yuna. It shocked her.

"What in Halom's name were you thinking? You stupid ox! Letting her run around the city like that!" Her father was the only person who could make Yuna shrink, despite the fact that she was still half a head taller than him. "You think you are so capable? That you are the only protection she needs against an entire city? That damn sword on your back has made you too confident. But now it's not just your own life you gamble with. It's my daughter's as well." He stepped towards Yuna again. "Is that how you repay me? Taking chances with the little girl I know you love?"

It made Echinni hurt inside to see Yuna wilt like this. "Don't touch her," she hissed, and grabbed his arm. "Stop it!"

The High King shook his head and glared at Yuna. "Won't do any good anyways. I try to raise you to be respectable, honourable. I give you responsibility. Yet you can't get away from the wildness within you." Yuna didn't move and kept her eyes down. Already Echinni could see the red mark showing beneath Yuna's face tattoos.

Despite being possibly the greatest member of the Syklan order, a hero of the Merikas Skirmishes, a woman so feared that an entire battalion had turned and fled rather than face her, Yuna Swiftriver – the bearer of the mythical sword *Hunsa* – was still a tragic little orphan girl when she stood in front of her King. For he was the man who had given her a home when no one else would, and the man who had spared her life.

"Leave her alone!" Echinni didn't know what had come over her. "Stop it. Enough. Can't you see it's enough." She slapped the back of her father's head and scratched his arm with her nails before she knew what was happening.

Her father stopped and looked down at her. "Here is something new." His voice had gone quiet, and somehow that was more frightening than his rage. He lifted the arm with Echinni on it as a tree might lift a squirrel to get a look at it.

"You don't *ever* get to hurt her!" Echinni could feel the tears running down her cheeks, knowing she must look ridiculous hanging from her father's arm, although she didn't care. "You don't get to judge her. Not after what you did to them."

Her words scored a hit, as she saw some of the fire leave her father's eyes. Sadness filled the void left behind by the rage.

"Fair enough," he said sadly, looking at his daughter almost in a new light. "Let go," he sighed, and lowered her gently to the floor.

Echinni let her arms drop and her father turned away.

"So it's true then." Echinni's mind reeled. She had heard a strange version of the Battle of Istol, the battle which had defeated the Navutians once and for all, and yet she had not believed it. Not until now. "All of them? Even the children?" Echinni couldn't believe it, but her father did not respond. "You're ... a monster."

His shoulders slumped, almost as if she had stabbed him. Then he turned to look at her with sad eyes. "Yes," he said, "I am. A monster who changed it all, because sometimes it takes a monster to do something momentous." He made her meet his gaze and the anger returned. "But then I think of your dead mother, or your dead baby brother, and I am glad I am a monster, because I know that no more mothers or children will die under the axes of Navutian raiders again. So yes, I killed them all, bar the one standing in that corner." He pointed at Yuna without breaking his stare at Echinni. "Yet I will let Halom, Fenrir and the Lady judge me for what I have done, not a naïve little girl."

His eyes were ablaze once again, but Echinni could see the hint of tears in them. She had never heard her father speak so openly before.

"Yes, I was reckless, and I've done stupid things. But I won, Halom be praised, I won somehow, and, Lady take me, I've tried to make things better." Her father was forcing himself to talk through his emotions, and his voice cracked because of it. "Yet ... I can feel it all slipping away."

"What?" Echinni asked as she clutched her hands together. "What do you mean?"

"I am surrounded by sharks, Echinni. In that council room when I sit upon my throne I can feel them, nibbling away at the foundations of what I've created. Yet I don't know how to fight back. I do not have the weapons for this battle. You can't hack at law until it submits, or smash mutually beneficial trade agreements, or chop up the right amount of taxation." His voice was not much more than a whisper. He had turned to look out of the window now. He stared up at the soaring heights of the Red Tower, and then shook his head and turned, stepping towards her. Echinni shrank back.

"Don't cower. Look at me," her father said as he stood before her. "Maybe I should have tried to explain all this earlier. But you are still so young to have such burdens." He placed a hand on her shoulder, and this time it was gentle. "Some part of me wanted to keep you young, to try and let you enjoy your youth, like your mother would have wanted, but I have failed in that too." He shook his head.

Her father's unfettered, unabashed sorrow was something Echinni had never experienced before, and she could not bear it.

He now flung up his hands. "It is time to end this charade. It is not working. So be it." He looked at her and appeared to steel himself for what he was about to say. "The other kings and queens, the rulers of the nine nations, they plot and they scheme and they will eventually take the power I have gained. They dance rings around me with political skill I am no match for. I have the threat of my army, I have promised violence on my side, but fear will not hold them forever, and already there are plans to overthrow us."

"But ..." Echinni was trying to catch up. She hadn't realised it was this bad. "But what you said is true. All nine nations are safer and overall wealth has increased in these last fifteen years. All of my economics instructors say the same: we are experiencing an unprecedented period of prosperity. The other kings and queens must see and hear the same."

"Yes." He smiled at her. "They do. But who is prospering? I have won the hearts of the common people. Many of them have grown rich under my new rules. Merchant classes have grown powerful and there is new upward mobility through the classes. Hard work, cunning, ingenuity and entrepreneurship are rewarded with profit, and those profits benefit us all because the wealth is then distributed to others. Yet in this new system, it is those who do not adapt who suffer. The nobility were always staunch supporters of keeping the status quo. All this change has upset the old order of things. I should have seen it. I too was naïve about how the world works, and the consequences of my actions are catching up with us."

Echinni thought about this, and it did make sense. The fake smiles were covering thoughts of revenge and plots to return things to how they had been before, with the nobility at the top and all others beneath them. Before the Union Wars, the Mihanes were minor landowners in Asgur, but the might of her father had landed them at the top, and everyone else they had passed on route was now trying to find ways to pull them back down.

"Yes." He nodded, smiling at her. "You recognise already what I had to learn the hard way. You are smarter than I ever was. Their power is being eroded, and this new prosperity is threatening their positions and legitimacy. They are going to strike back soon, I just can't see how." Her father sighed, "And on top of it all there are rumours of rebellion and war in Kenz once more. Someone has raised an army and it is headed to Dawn. So, now you must understand why you cannot go gallivanting off to a local tavern simply because you want to experience what young women are meant to experience. There are those who would hurt you, or hurt you to hurt me. You have enemies because I have enemies, and because you will be Queen. Our role is not to be good or evil, but only to retain the power I have taken. We must use that power to keep our people safe, to keep order, and hold the horrors of the world at bay so the men, women and children we protect can go to sleep at night knowing their world will not be torn apart by the morning."

The truth behind his words was like heavy stones being placed on her shoulders. Echinni wanted to say that she had never asked for any of this, that it wasn't fair that she had this burden to carry, that she didn't want to be a queen. She wanted to scream that it wasn't fair that she couldn't experience life, to know joy, and love, and all the good things the wars had been fought to achieve. She only had one life – why wasn't she allowed to live it her way?

"I know," he said tenderly, and his eyes showed just how tired he was of it all. He had been fighting his entire life. Fighting the world, and now he was overmatched, and struggling to hold it all together.

"My life for the stability and safety of millions," Echinni said as the reason behind all of it clicked into place. "That's what being a true ruler is about, isn't it?"

Her father nodded, and in that moment she could almost see the burden he carried. The burden she was meant to inherit.

"You see it," he said, "and I am sorry for I did not see what this would mean for you until recently. If only I had your mind, my beautiful girl. You do not have the luxury of a normal childhood." The High King moved to the door and looked back over his wide shoulder. "Think about all this the next time you want to play truant, and what the consequences might be if it went wrong."

The High King closedbbb the door behind him. His boots echoed down the marble floors as he went.

Echinni hugged her knees to her chest. The world felt cold and ugly now, when only last night it had seemed wondrous. She rocked back and forth and let her tears stain her silk dress.

It was then she felt the warmth of long arms wrapping around her. She hadn't heard Yuna come over, but the giant woman now held her as a mother would a babe.

Echinni felt empty and had no more tears to cry. She thought of the hurt her family had done to Yuna, and how that horrible action had brought nearly a generation of peace and stability; but it was all too much: too and real and too brutal.

"It's all so terrible. Is nothing simply honest and good in the world?" she sobbed. *Yes,* she answered herself, *the Will is. Whatever it is that I feel and hear, that is good and true.*

"Shhh. Quiet now," Yuna crooned, and held her, rocking back and forth with her.

"Did he hurt you?" Echinni asked.

"No. He could never hurt me." Yuna swept a huge finger across her tight braids.

She found Yuna's arm and cradled it against her cheek. "How can you stand it, Yuna? How can you love us?"

The warrior didn't answer right away. Echinni could feel the scars on Yuna's arm against her cheek. *She has so much pain inside.* Echinni wanted to take that pain from her but knew she wasn't strong enough.

"I love you because you are my sister, and you love me back," Yuna said simply. "And I love him because he is my King, because he spared me and took me in when everyone else in the world wanted me dead. He raised me as his own even though every time your father looks at me he sees the people who murdered his wife and child. I love him because he recognises the monster in me, has allowed me to grow strong, and yet still allows me to love the only person he has left in this world."

"You're not a monster, Yuna." Echinni held the big arm against her face, trying to comfort the huge woman.

It was then she heard the bells within the Oratorio sing out against the noon sky.

"Help me out of this dress, we need to send someone to fetch Kai and Jachem," she said. "No, forget that. We need to go right now. You are going to use your rank and put together a very hasty but dangerous and trustworthy honour guard. Every guard you see along the way to the gates will do. We can get a carriage along the route. That way we are taking precautions, and no one has expressly forbidden us from entering the city as of yet. So technically we are not doing anything wrong. We will be as official and protected as anyone could hope. You might need to put the fear of Halom into some people, but I'm sure you can manage," Echinni finished, pleased with her plan.

Yuna just chuckled, and Echinni saw her shake her tattooed head in mild disbelief. "We are still going through with this? Did you listen to your father at all?"

"Yes, I did listen." Echinni huffed a bit at that. "He may be High King," she said as she headed to the boudoir to find something official and regal, "and he may know about horrible things, and may have made some excellent points, but I am the one who can hear and feel the Will, and it is telling me Kai and Jachem are important. They need to be here."

Yuna sighed. "Alright, but we're swinging by the armoury. I don't want guards with ceremonial weapons. And if there is a hint of trouble, we are turning around and coming right back. We should take the servants' corridors as well to try and get out of the tower before any further orders can be implemented."

Echinni smiled and opened the hidden servants' door leading down to the kitchens. "We'll try not to get caught this time. Don't worry, we can't get in trouble for this."

Yuna rolled her eyes and looked at the small service door. "Sometimes I wish I was a *smaller* monster." She unbuckled Hunsa from its over-the-shoulder strap so it wouldn't scrape the low ceiling, and then had to turn sideways to get through the door.

Echinni smiled at Yuna's comment, and she grabbed her adopted sister's hand and made her look at her. "Yuna, you are not a monster."

The corners of Yuna's mouth turned up slightly. "Yes, I am, little one. But it's fine. I'm *your* monster." She gently squeezed Echinni's hand. "Come on, let's go shock those two crazy boys."

22 - Catching a Break

For a society which could make marvellous wonders, gadgets and artefacts which may last for many more thousands of years, the Jendar sure made a lot of useless junk, or maybe I am just missing the significance of why I would need a 'floating tissue box'. I fear I may never understand their weird and wonderful civilization.

- Chronicler Talbot in Observations Log: Device Determination – "floating tissue box", Item Tag: RC-4567LM.

Kai

New Toeron, Bauffin

Today was the day.

"I still don't know if I believe it," Kai said to Hanson.

"Don't you go ruining this, Kai Johnstone. Gideon's blessed you with some luck, Halom knows why, but he has." Hanson rubbed clean a wooden tankard and set it down with a thump. "And another thing, you probably haven't thought of it, but don't give anyone any ideas that you might be trying to win the princess's affections. The High King would skin you alive in front of the whole city if there is any hint of romance between the two of you."

"I never thought of that!" Kai quailed as a shiver ran down his spine. He had only seen the High King once, during a parade, and even from that distance the giant man looked absolutely terrifying. "What if he thinks I'm trying to seduce her? Or taking advantage?"

Hanson dried another mug and considered for a moment. "Well ... I imagine he'd kill you." He put the mug down and scratched his chin. "Not have you killed neither. No, a man like that would do it himself. Probably with those huge hands of his. Rip your head off, or something equally dramatic."

"How in the nine hells is that supposed to make me feel better?" Kai waved his hand in frustration.

Hanson laughed. "Oh, I don't think there's any point trying to make you feel better. From where I'm standing you're proper screwed. A beautiful woman like the Princess, and a roguish devil like yourself? What else would her father think?"

"I thought bartenders were supposed to give sage advice and all that sort of nonsense," Kai said. "Not describe in detail how you're doomed. Gods, Hanson, you're terrible at this, how have you stayed in business so long?"

"By steering clear of princesses mostly." Hanson grinned.

"Oh, shut up," Kai huffed.

The sound of hoofs on cobblestones stopped just outside the entrance to the pub. Kai went to open the door, but what he saw made him go pale and dive back inside.

"Holy Halom!" he shouted.

"What is it?" Hanson asked.

"There must be a dozen guards outside!" Kai scanned the room, looking for an exit.

The driver of the carriage called out in a loud voice, "Kai Johnston and Jacehm Sanders, we are here to escort you."

Hanson went to the door and poked his head out. "They're in here. I'll send them right away."

"What are you doing! They're probably here to arrest us or something!" Kai threw his hands up at Hanson.

"If they are, you think I'd hide you in here and risk losing the pub?" Hanson quirked a nonchalant eyebrow at him. "Hold on, I'll ask." He turned to the open door and bellowed, “Are you kind people here to arrest the two aforementioned gentlemen?”

“No, good innkeeper, we are here as an escort only. Can you please tell them to hurry, we need to load their belongings and then be on our way,” the driver of the carriage said.

“I don’t trust them,” Kai said, “those guards don’t look happy.”

“When have you ever seen happy on-duty guards?” Hanson asked. “Now get your things. Either they are here to arrest you or to take you off to the Oratorio like the Princess said. Either way you’re doomed, best just get on with it.”

“You are the absolute worst.” Kai shook his fist, but got up from hiding behind the table.

“If they were here to arrest you, they wouldn’t be waiting outside, you daft boy.” Hanson chuckled at Kai’s expense. “Now get your gear and your partner, and get on with your adventure.”

“Jachem! They’re here.” No sooner had Kai said the words than Jachem appeared, bundling past him packed and ready. By the time Kai had grabbed his own bag, Jachem was already giving the driver detailed instructions on how to pack their instruments.

“Be careful with that, if you jostle it too much it will take much longer to tune when we arrive,” Jachem advised, holding his head. “No! No, no, no. I’ve changed my mind. No, put it back!” He grabbed his guitar case from the driver. There was panic in his eyes.

Kai should have thought of this. This was a monumental change, and he had been so caught up in it all he hadn’t thought how Jachem was going to react. Blast it. “Sorry, sir!” Kai held up an apologetic hand to the driver. “Just ... give us a minute.”

“No, Kai. No, it’s too much. I want to go back to the church. They’ll break our things. I don’t know where I’ll put my guitar. Where is it going to go? Where do we sleep? Where will I put my things?” Jachem was visibly sweating now.

"Look at me, look at me." Kai gently put his hands up to Jachem's head, using his palms to block out some of Jachem's peripheral vision so Jachem had to focus on his face. "You know my face. I'm right here. I'll be with you the whole time. Remember what we talked about last night?"

"Yes," Jachem said through quick breaths.

Kai had his attention. He could fix this. He just had to go slow. He smiled reassuringly at his friend. "Repeat to me what we said."

"You said there would be a spot just as good for my guitar, and that we will practice the same songs, and that I can put my clothes in drawers, and that I can move the bed to the right side of the room. I asked about when I would need to get up, and you said it would depend on work but we could try to get your hours to be the same. You said that you would go over the new routines with me ..." Jachem summarised the exact order of the conversation. It was an improvement over his old habit of repeating everything verbatim.

Kai smiled. "That's right."

Just then the carriage door opened and Princess Echinni stepped down.

Kai was amazed she had actually come herself. He thought for a moment she was angry that they were delaying, but then he saw the concern on her face as she looked at Jachem.

"I will have someone put your room any way you like. You can tell them just how you want it. A perfect place for everything you have," Echinni said softly to Jachem.

"You see," Kai said, trying not to tear his gaze from his panicking friend to gawk at the stunningly beautiful princess on his right. "It will all be fine." He could hear Jachem's breathing slow slightly. "Now we are going to let this nice man put our things up on the carriage. He knows how to pack things as that is part of his job and this is his carriage. Our things will be safe. What you need to do is get up into the carriage and sit across from Yuna. Alright? You can do that, can't you?"

"Yes, I can do that. She's not going to hurt me again, is she?" Jachem said, eying Yuna as if she might pick him up by the neck once more.

"Well, that depends on whether you are going to run up behind her like a madman," Kai smirked.

"No. I'm just going to get into the carriage," Jachem replied, once again not understanding Kai's sarcasm.

"Well, I'm sure Yuna won't hurt you then," Kai said, hoping the great warrior was in a cooperative mood.

"She won't. Come on, can you give me a hand up?" Echinni asked, smiling at Jachem.

"Yes," he replied, and finally he was settled into the carriage along with Echinni.

"Thank you, Your Highness," Kai whispered up to her. "You've had experience with this sort of thing before?"

"There is a young girl studying at the Oratorio who can recite back any text she has ever read. She has some of the same anxieties Jachem does," Echinni said. "You're very good with him. He trusts you completely."

Kai shrugged. "Jachem is like a brother to me. I understand him in a way other people don't. Jachem has a similar type of memory, except his is more for reading music or figuring out Jendar relics."

"Relics?" Echinni asked.

"Oh yeah, Jachem has been invited to help out at the Artificium a few times. He's even cracked a few of those puzzles the Jendar have on those glass tablet things," Kai said with pride.

"Really?" Echinni said. "I'm surprised the Chroniclers haven't tried to enlist him."

"Oh, they've tried. They even gave him his own relic as a thank you for his help, but when I explain to him what the work would involve, he doesn't seem that interested. That's where all this started." Kai waved at their musical instruments. "There was some sort of moving picture the relic showed, in which Jendar musicians were performing. Ever since, Jachem has been obsessed with music. That was about four years ago."

"Hmm." Echinni looked distant for a moment. "Well, it would seem the pair of you have quite an interesting history. Let's get on our way and you can fill me in on the details as we ride."

Kai got the distinct impression that the Princess Echinni was nervous for some reason. Her eyes kept darting around as if she was expecting someone to pop out from around the next corner.

"Are you alright, Princess?" he asked.

"Fine," she replied with a quick glance behind the carriage, and then back at him, seeming to realise that she must look a bit suspicious. "We just have a lot to do today," she said smiling.

"Alright," Kai said as he jumped up into the carriage. He couldn't quite believe it as he watched Echinni sit down across from him. This was actually going to happen.

As she sat, he got a whiff of her heady perfume, which made him smile. A smile which immediately dissolved, once he opened his eyes and saw Yuna glaring at him. She was so big she had to hunch over while she sat. Her shoulders were nearly at the roof, which made her look like some sort of predatory bird.

Kai coughed nervously and looked at Jachem, who already had his relic out and was walking his fingers across the surface. The image of a man singing on stage played across the relic's flat face.

"We are going to be just like these people," Jachem told the group, and Kai recognised the comment as his friend's acceptance of Echinni and Yuna.

Echinni and Yuna watched spellbound as Jachem shared the magic of the Jendar relic with everyone in the carriage. The dark interior came alive with dancing images which Jachem directed with intricate moves of his fingers. They all watched the performance from thousands of years ago which had inspired Jachem to become a musician.

Kai was about to tell them Jachem had never shown anyone his ability with the relic other than himself and Chronicler Talbot, but then decided he didn't want to break the spell his friend had woven over all of them. He watched the show absently, as he thought about just how much his life had changed in the last day – all thanks to the beautiful, young, kind-hearted woman who sat across from him. She was a woman who loved music, who commanded attention and adoration, who had a voice purer than an angel's, and who accepted his strange adopted brother as if it was nothing, when so many would dismiss Jachem as strange and annoying.

Kai continued to steal glances at the Princess while she and Yuna watched in wonder what Jachem could do with the Jendar relic. With each passing moment Kai felt a warm glow growing inside him, and it was then he decided that Hanson had been right.

He was doomed.

23 - Onlookers

Multiple organised religions have taken root within two generations of those who survived Kali's first sweep.

The variety of beliefs is incredible, and, as always, there are those who forcibly espouse their version of the truth above all others.

I'm not certain how I feel about this.

On the one hand, there will most likely be fanatics who rise to power and will commit egregious acts of horror in the name of their faith, which can lead to very skewed worldviews. On the other hand, reverence is much of what was missing from the world when I decided to act. Reverence of some sort will be absolutely vital for this to work, and institutionalised reverence might be a control measure that is needed.

Time will tell.

Yet ... they cannot take too much time.

Kali is watching.

- Journal of Robert Mannford, Day 233 Year 54

Jonah

Dawn, Kenz

Jonah felt the golden spring sunlight beat down upon his face and it made him smile as he and Branson walked down the market street. Sandstone cobbles rolled along underfoot as the pair passed below ropes decorated with multicoloured flags strung between the stalls on either side of them. Men and women holding parasols or wearing wide hats bobbed through the crowd, creating a rainbow of constant motion.

Branson grunted angrily beside him. Someone had jostled the

grizzled veteran and was now getting a glare from hard eyes.

The culprit, a young boy, wilted under his gaze as the boy's eyes registered the insignia on Branson's tunic. The boy said in their common dialect: "Sorry, sir. My apologies, won't happen ag –"

"Bah, on your way, pup! Get!" Branson growled in Euran Imperial as he spat on the ground in the boy's wake; his white beard had narrowly escaped his own spittle.

"Ease up, old-timer," Jonah said. Jonah had recognised some of the boy's words. His lessons had begun to pay off. "He was trying to apologise. I'm sure even you must have had a childhood, terrorising your house mothers all the while no doubt."

"Me? Nah, I was born with whiskers and a knife in hand. Fight-ready as soon as I popped out: kicked the midwife, and was on my way." Branson's face showed no hint of a lie. Possibly a reason the old buzzard was so good at card games.

"Must have been a tough birth for your Lady Mother," Jonah said as he watched the elaborate parasol twist in the young woman's hand in front of them.

"Ha! You said it, Jonah. All of us from Clan Delagoth are the same: ornery as they come and just as soon spit in your eye as knuckle a forehead. You should see when our Lady Mother calls a reunion. It all kicks off then." Branson's dark face lit up with the memories.

"I can only imagine," Jonah replied, not hiding his grimace.

Shops selling everything imaginable were huddled together, almost on top of each other. Food of the sort and smell he had never experienced before, right beside religious relics and trinkets whose use Jonah could not even guess at.

Some had even begun selling Dawn-inspired tokens aimed at the Imperial Army. "Send some home to loved ones," they cried from their stalls. *Who had ever heard of such things*?

Overtopping all the markets, between the gaps in the hanging shades soared the spires of churches. Everywhere you looked was a spire or domed roof rising towards the heavens. Many had different religious symbols announcing the faith within at their zeniths, showing a certain tolerance of religious worship which Jonah was glad to see, despite the Singer faith clearly being in the majority here in the city

The churches amazed him. The skill and labour which had gone into each and every building was nothing short of miraculous. It was easy to feel the holiness of Dawn, and easy to understand why this Hierophant accepted occupation so easily. War machines would destroy in a few days what must have taken centuries to build.

"Crazy bunch, ain't they?" Branson said to him as they passed a vendor trying to sell some sort of melon. "If I buy a melon, I damn well want it to taste of something other than water. That is if the name of it holds true. What's the point in that?"

"It does look nice though. That lovely pink flesh inside looks like it would be delicious on a day like today." Jonah observed several young children crowding around the vendor's red and green fruit. The poor woman behind the stall seemed to have her hands full trying to keep all the little urchins from scampering off with pilfered pieces.

Then it occurred to him that Branson had actually understood the vendor. "I didn't know you were actually trying to learn the language."

"Languages come in handy, Jonah. Besides," Branson tapped himself on the chest, "this old goat has more tricks up his sleeve than meets the eye."

Jonah didn't doubt that. "Have they fixed the wall yet?" He knew Branson had been out to the exterior wall this morning; while also being too good at cards, Branson was a dab hand at masonry and had decided to use some of his off time to help out repairing the wall.

"Oh, we've done better than repair it, sonny. Made it better, stronger." Branson's chin lifted slightly with pride. "I'd say that section is probably twice the strength it was before our engineers taught the local masons their special mix of reinforced mortar."

"Great news. This city is special. They knew it already and we felt it as soon as we arrived. This city could be the jewel of the Empire on this new continent." Jonah said, and then pointed. "The cathedral is going up fast." Layers of soaring scaffolding were crawling with both Euran engineers and Dawnish citizens.

"Lots of things happen quickly when the Prince personally funds the project and puts his best engineers on the job. He's smart, that Prince of ours. It's said that their Hierophant had been wanting a cathedral greater than all the others, taller than all the others, ever since he was proclaimed holy leader nearly forty years ago. The Prince had his architects draw up plans right away, and the Hierophant looked like he would have a heart attack when the Prince told him he could make any modifications he wanted and could have it made within a few years."

"That'll get the religious leaders over to the Prince's side pretty quick I'd imagine," Jonah said.

"Lining people's pockets and stroking their ambitions usually makes you some pretty quick friends," Branson nodded.

Jonah sighed. It was good to stop marching for a time. Dawn was exactly what everyone had needed. A respite from killing, and a chance for them to focus on the true work of the empire: building, growing and enriching. Everyone in the army had a secondary skill to their martial one, allowing the Imperial army to remain extremely effective and productive at times of peace.

Jonah and Branson reached the bottom of the street, which opened up into a plaza. One of the more prolific styles of church dominated the end of the street and served as its focal point. A crowd had gathered around the central feature of the plaza, a raised bed filled with enormous plants.

A big man with blond hair stood near the back of the crowd and waved for them to join him. It was Fin of course.

Jonah heard a sigh beside him as Branson commented, “Well, I had a few moments where I was actually enjoying myself there. We better go see what this is about or he’s sure to cause some sort of trouble.”

Secretly Jonah knew that Branson actually was quite fond of Fin. They joined their comrade-in-arms at the edge of the crowd.

“So what’s all this then?” Branson demanded of Fin.

“Don’t know yet, but people look excited,” Fin said easily as he watched over nearly every head in the crowd.

“Hungry, are we?” Jonah asked with a smile, pointing to the sack of chewed green melon rinds at his feet.

Fin grinned at the remnants. “The melons are delicious, but I didn’t eat all these. I’ve made more than a few friends.” Fin pointed at the horde of children running around the crowd with slightly pink dyed lips.

“You spawn quickly don’t you,” Branson said, rubbing his chin. “You part frog or something?” A little toddler pushed through Branson’s legs squealing as a larger boy chased him, but was cut off by the back of Branson’s thighs. “Get off!” Branson grunted, but Jonah saw the hint of a smile the veteran was trying to hide.

“So you’ve got all these little runts hyper on melon juice have you?” Branson growled. “Their minders will love you when you send them back all wound up like that.” He nodded at the sack at Fin’s feet. “Why are you saving the rinds anyways?”

“Good for compost of course.” Fin shook his head as if everyone should know that. “You can have my last few pieces if you want, but you’ll have to be quick!” Fin roared playfully at a little child who had attempted to snatch one of the wedges off his plate.

The dirty-looking child laughed as she bounced away waving her hands, only to come right back to Fin. The big man handed down one of the wedges happily once she had stopped and asked politely for a piece. "That's better, little one. You need to ask politely now don't you?" he instructed in what seemed to Jonah like fluent Salucian.

"Where did all these kids come from? Where's their Clan Parent, or whatever the equivalent is over here, and why are they filthy?" Jonah asked curiously as his eyes followed another of the seemingly unattended children. There had to be nearly two dozen of them milling about the square.

"They don't have anyone looking after them." Fin's voice took on a sad tone, before he looked up to see the shock on Jonah's face. "I know! Crazy isn't it. Apparently they have so many children over here they are allowed to run free. Like this little guy! Come here, you!" Fin switched back into Salucian as he bellowed and then chased after a small boy who had stolen his last piece of melon. Jonah couldn't tell who had the bigger smile, Fin or the boy. He shook his head in admiration.

If the Empire had a thousand more like Fin, there would be no need for a war. They could simply let the army of Fins loose and the whole continent would be charmed into submission.

Branson nudged Jonah in the ribs as he watched Fin play with his new group of happy adopted children. "How is it that that big oaf can already speak the local language like he was born to it?"

"I'm surprised you don't know," Jonah said. "Fin was training to become a logistics officer before he joined the army. You know what they're like. Logistics officers need to speak just about every clan's language, the way they travel about like they do."

Jonah watched with a smile as the children seemed to have Fin pinned beneath him and were attempting to tickle him to death, before Fin roared theatrically and slowly stood up with eyes wide, pretending to be some sort of monster. Dozens of children scattered, shrieking in mock terror. The eruption of noise drew more than few angry looks from those at the front of the crowd.

"Apparently Fin was a natural. Gifted when it came to languages." Jonah stood on his tiptoes to try and see over the heads in front of him. "What is everyone waiting for? What kind of plants are these that they can draw a crowd?" he continued.

Branson ignored his questions. "So what happened? Logistics officers get paid a lot more than a lowly archer. Fin's clan would have crucified him for losing them that much money." Branson looked confused as he stood on the balls of his feet to try and see over the crowd.

"Fin explains his fall from grace as a 'disagreement' he had with a House Parent during one of his monthly checks." Jonah smirked, remembering Fin's version of the story. "It was in one of those remote villages in the south – I guess the House Parent had been abusing the children in his care," Jonah recounted with a sad grimace.

"What?!" Branson yelled, scaring the two bystanders beside him. He cursed under his breath a string of such nasty words that they could have scoured stone. Jonah was glad the people of Dawn didn't speak Euran.

"So what'd Fin do?" Branson looked over at Fin, still chasing children around the square.

Jonah shrugged. "Well, Fin being Fin, he kind of lost it. Brained the fellow with his bare hands. I think we all would have felt it was justified, but there are laws. Can't go around smashing people's heads in, and apparently this particular person was closer to the Empress's Holy Lines than most: the Clan Parent had been banished from Eura City, but still, we all know the Royal Lines are damn near untouchable. Fin was stripped of his rank and tossed out by one of the Blood. An agreement was made between the heads of the two clans involved and Fin had no options left but to join the army," Jonah finished with a sigh.

Branson ran a hand through his curly white hair and looked at Fin in a different way than he usually did. Then he stopped short, looking as if he had just realised something horrible. "So Fin has the touch then? He can tell if people are fertile?" Branson said, his eyes wide with terror.

"Yeah, I suppose he does," Jonah said, and laughed. "Why? Are you worried Fin might find out whether you or I can father children?"

Branson didn't say anything back and seemed lost in troubled thought.

Jonah thought it odd, but now was more intrigued with the energy in the crowd around him. He leaned towards the person standing to the other side of him, and tried to use some of his newly learned language to ask, "Pardon me, sir. Could you explain what's going on?"

"Gladly, friend," The stranger answered. Jonah saw the stranger point through a gap in the crowd. "See those flowers? Those are *diffuses uliginosus,* or, as they are locally known, 'Sunbursts'. They are plants from an age long ago, and once they used to grow on almost every continent. Now there are but a few left. Their flowers open for one day a year and the church's gardener has said that it will happen at any moment now."

Jonah noticed that the stranger dressed a bit differently that the rest of the Dawnish locals. He wore a curious conical hat and, despite the heat, was draped in a long grey cloak, which caught the light in an odd way.

Jonah only wondered momentarily at how well he could understand the stranger's speech, as his attention was diverted to the thick green stocks holding aloft buds larger than a man's head. The outer petals of the flower heads began to slowly curl back.

"Life, in all its myriad forms, never fails to amaze. Life is what your empire fights to sustain does it not? Life above all else," the stranger said quietly to Jonah. His accent sounded odd, like rough stone scraping over smooth steel. "Maybe Wunjo was not so wrong after all." The last words seemed to have been private, but Jonah heard them just the same.

The stranger put his hand on Jonah's shoulder then, and Jonah heard him whisper, "I'm sorry for what this will do to you, but know that it is necessary."

"What do you –" Jonah tried to say, alarmed, but stopped as he began to recognise the strange flower. Memories began to stir from somewhere deep within him, somewhere that had been buried.

One after the other, each flower head burst open in an explosion of colour. Vibrant red, yellow and orange ringed petals as long as a man's arm sprang forth like a fire roaring into life. The stamen of each rose out of the petals and pods burst open. Pollen shot high into the air and began to drift over the crowd like rain. The sun illuminated the tiny umbrella-like spores, making them look like tiny drops of sunlight floating down to the ground.

With that pollen, a thick and spicy-sweet aroma filled the plaza while the crowd gasped in awe and wonder.

And it was the smell which unlocked his memory.

They had had these flowers in Eura. In the Imperial palace, where he and Ilene had lived. But they had called them Fire Blossoms. And they had bloomed on that night.

The night he had killed Ilene.

"NOOOOO!!!!" Jonah screamed.

Suddenly he was back there. He saw it all again.

Ilene had been trying to give him children for years – so many years, and so many stillbirths. It had driven her mad, but they had shared something forbidden within the Blood, something which had pushed Jonah into a state of madness himself. They had been in love.

His position had granted him certain courtesies that others within the Blood were not allowed, and so his infatuation with Ilene Herimachi had been tolerated by his Matron for longer than was considered proper.

Yet when, miraculously, he and Ilene had conceived, she did not believe it. Even when she had their child, Amber, Ilene had thought she was crazy. Ilene had become more and more distrusting of reality. Even went so far as to call their darling little girl a demon, an abomination.

Jonah had brought in physicians to help her, and for a time she had seemed to be getting better.

Then the Fire Bloom festival had arrived. And Ilene had been left in her room with a headache and Amber had gone down early for the night.

When Jonah had returned to their wing of the Palace, covered in the scent and pollen of the Fire Blooms, he had ducked his head in to check on his sleeping daughter.

Instead he saw Ilene holding a bloody knife above their daughter's crib, and smiling as if she had just done something righteous.

When he went over to the crib and saw those lifeless eyes he lost part of himself forever.

He remembered Ilene trying to justify what she had done. In her crazed mind it had been right.

Jonah couldn't remember how many times he had stabbed her. He just remembered how red his hands had been.

"ILENE! WHY!" he had screamed, and had dropped to his knees.

The memories took over his mind and he relived that moment again and again as the Sunbursts' pollen fell around him.

"I am sorry," the stranger said as he left, his swirling red eyes trying to offer what little compassion their synthetic glow could.

"Damn it, no!" Branson yelled, looking at the flowers for the first time. "Fin! Get over here! Help me with him!"

The crowd had turned to stare at Jonah, who was writhing on the ground screaming and crying as if he had just had his heart ripped out.

"What in the Empress's name is going on?!" Fin yelled as he ran up and lifted Jonah onto his shoulders.

"Just get him to the inn!" Branson yelled back, "I've got a tonic that will knock him out. Hurry, before any of our officers see him!"

* * *

"Are you going to explain what the heck that was?" Fin asked as he took a drink of his ale.

Branson had his head in his hands after an hour of holding his friend down on the bed while the tonic took effect. "I suppose I'll have to."

"Who is Ilene? And Amber?" Fin asked. His face was white as a ghost.

Branson took a deep breath and scanned the room for what must have been the hundredth time, but he couldn't see anyone who wasn't in his employ. No eyes or ears around, other than those he was paying.

"Ilene was Jonah's consort. Amber was his daughter," Branson said simply. He had no idea how to start. He had kept this secret for over a year now, but Fin had heard too much and had saved Jonah's life.

Fin grimaced as if confirming a theory.

Of course, Fin would already have known that Jonah was fertile. Fin couldn't help but have touched Jonah on dozens of occasions during their time as soldiers. Yet he had kept it quiet. The truth, though ... it seemed too much.

"He's one of the Blood, isn't he?" Fin stated more than asked.

Well, sometimes it is just best to dive in. Branson ground his teeth and said, "Yes."

"What the hell is he doing pretending to be a regular archer then?" Fin asked, holding his cup as if somehow seeing the answers in his dark ale.

"He's supposed to be dead," Branson said softly, checking around him once again for anyone listening who shouldn't be.

"What? What are you talking about?" Fin said, and then finally noticed he had a drink. He finished his ale in one long pull and held up a finger for another.

How much to tell? Branson asked himself. Fin seemed trustworthy, but could he trust him completely with something this big? Branson shook his head: they were going to need all the help they could get. Someone would have seen that display at the flowers, someone would start rumours flowing, and one of those rumours might reach the ears of Prince El'Amin.

"Fin," he said seriously, and waited for the big man to meet his eyes, "what I am about to tell you is a secret which will threaten your life. Do you understand?"

Fin took his meaning and nodded slowly. "Yes, Branson, I understand. This is a Blood secret; I know what that means."

Branson gritted his teeth before speaking. "Jonah's loss was tragic and it drove him over the edge. I don't quite understand the psychology of what's happened to him. Something about his mind cocooning itself against the tragedy he experienced. What he remembers, well, most of it, it seems, steers away from any memories of his Blood connections, the Imperial Palace, and his life there. I guess all of it is just too painful. His mind seems to have fabricated a rather simple existence which Jonah can operate within from day to day. But have you ever tried to ask him about his past? About what he did before he joined the army?"

"Well ... no. Not really," Fin said. "It's considered rude on the whole."

"A point I was counting on. I've tried to elaborate on the things he remembers and fill his head with stories about his life before the incident. It's worked up till now, but that damn flower – it seems to have unlocked something in him. Fin, if any of the Blood who travelled with us find out who Jonah is, they'll kill him, and anyone who knows of him."

"Alright." Fin took another drink. "But why, Branson? Why is he supposed to be dead? Who *is* Jonah?"

Branson took another drink to wet a throat which had suddenly gone dry. "Jonah is the Empress's son, Ja'Al Ona Hashi, Grand Duke and

General of the Empress's Glorious Imperial Army – and presumed dead by everyone in Eura."

Fin's jaw dropped, "Holy sh –"

"Yes," Branson agreed as he put a hand over Fin's mouth so the big man could recover from his shock, "and he would outrank Prince El'Amin and every other member of the Amin Clan which has been landing in Dawn these past few months."

Fin nodded. "So what do we do?"

Branson shook his head. "We let him sleep." He looked up to the ceiling above which his friend the Grand Duke slept sedated in a locked room. "And we see who wakes up."

24 - An Old Book

NRE 5 surprised me today. It and the others wanted new names. Why I hadn't expected them to want their own identity, I don't know, but the question was unexpected all the same.

My second surprise came when NRE 5 named itself Raidho. The others followed suit by all taking the names of ancient runes. They even went so far as to etch the old symbols into their foreheads, like some sort of branding or tattooing ceremony of a new tribe.

Michael and I designed them, yet I will never know the poetry that sings within a mechanical soul. I doubt I will ever truly understand my synthetic companions, though they are now the closest thing I have to family ... I'd best learn.

- Journal of Robert Mannford, Day 004 Year 05

Wayran

New Toeron, Bauffin

Well, here he was, at the Academy. Wayran had never felt so out of place in his life.

He wandered somewhat aimlessly, zigzagging his way through the middle sections of what was called the Grid. Tall arched doorways stood open at each compass point of the interconnected garden courtyards.

As he walked, Wayran saw other initiates nervously scampering behind Fellows upon the balconied terraces above him. The black uniforms and youth of the initiates clashed with the loose red flowing suits and, more often than not, the white hair of the Fellows. Wayran felt an eagerness to please and a general excitement all around him. It made him want to retch.

He felt like such a traitor. Sure, it all made sense. Financially it was his best option, and the military training he would receive would open a lot of doors for him; but he was an imposter here. Matoh had spoken the truth of it. He hadn't earned it. Of course, that wasn't what father would say. No, he would say his sons earned their places the moment their mother left on that ship heading towards Navutia, towards Istol.

And Wayran understood that too, yet he just couldn't shake the feeling that he needed to hide from all the other bright, eager students. For many of them, like Matoh, this was their dream, and Wayran didn't want to sully that for anyone, and yet he felt his mere presence was doing just that.

His toe caught on the edge of a cobblestone. He stumbled forward and nearly dropped the book in his hands. *The* book, the one he took from that strange building buried beneath the sands. His only trophy from the life he had wanted.

Wayran gripped the book tight. He needed to get his mind off his predicament. He had registered early, and the registrar had stamped his papers and assigned him a bunk. He was supposed to go straight to the male barracks and claim his allotted piece of space, but there were still a few hours until the initiation ceremony, which he had to attend. He didn't want to spend those hours being forced to get to know the other initiates. Gods, what was he doing here?

Instead, he had decided to try to avoid formally joining the military for as long as he could. Despite his somewhat aimless wandering, he found himself outside the building he wanted.

In tempori prait est cognitusem magnutia. The words were carved into the archway above him. It was ancient Jendar, and a phrase he knew well. *In the past, there is great knowledge.* It was the motto of the

Chroniclers, and Wayran pushed open the doors to the Artificium in the hope that someone else at the Academy would also be interested in the book he held.

Stepping through the doors, he immediately felt a sense of relief. The walls were lined with the innumerable square black Jendar devices, which lit up when touched. Wayran let his finger trail along the surfaces of the polished black artefacts and grinned as light followed his fingers' touch. The same swirling image popped up on each surface. The Chroniclers had found no better use for these than decoration. He knew Chronicler Mortigo had found these particular relics in what must have been a Jendar warehouse. However, most Chroniclers agreed that these Jendar devices were useless until someone could solve the strange security riddle which popped up when a person touched them.

Wayran had seen the rows of crates holding hundreds more of the thin black devices in the bowels of the Artificium, so he knew the Chroniclers could afford to wow visitors by putting this particular collection on display at the entrance.

He had asked Chronicler Talbot once about what the devices were used for. "We don't know yet," the portly Chronicler had said. "They all appear to be locked or encoded, not at all like those other devices old Uther Sanders brought us all those years ago. Such a shame: almost all of them have lost their power now."

Wayran remembered when he had watched Chronicler Talbot demonstrate what the relics could do, on one of the old, unlocked devices. It had been like watching magic, as the Chronicler's fingers were somehow able to control hovering images of light.

Why didn't I take one of those black tablets? he scolded himself. There had been thousands of them; surely one of them would have been unlocked? Yet he and Matoh had checked hundreds of them and nearly all were similar to the ones on display near the entrance here. The same swirling pattern lit the surface when touched, which, as far as anyone could tell, might be all the devices ever did. *But there had been other treasures,* Wayran told himself for the hundredth time. *Countless Jendar riches and technological wonders – and I brought back an ugly old book. I'm such an idiot.*

"Is Chronicler Talbot in?" he asked the woman who sat behind an enormous desk. She had what looked like a Jendar tablet on the desk in front of her, yet it was in pieces. The sight of it shocked him. "Lady take me!" he gasped. "Is that what they look like on the inside? Incredible."

Tiny lines of metal ran in neatly crafted geometric patterns along what looked like a thin sheet of somewhat opaque blue glass. Wayran recognised two halves of one of the strange black devices lying in pieces around the desk. "How did you get it open?" he asked, still somewhat awestruck.

The woman smiled rather wickedly and pointed to the large hammer on the corner of her desk. "I persuaded it to open," she said. "Though it took quite a *bit* of persuasion; and yes, Chronicler Talbot is in."

"I'm Wayran Spierling, ma'am, the Chronicler will want to see what I've found."

"Ah, yuck," The woman said cringing. "I am definitely not a ma'am. I'm maybe a year your senior, and I know who you are." She cocked an eyebrow at him. "You don't remember me, huh? Sad, you've been gone a few years and already forgotten your betters. I'll have you know I'm one of Chronicler Rutherford's apprentices now."

Her look of disdain and amusement jolted the memory awake within Wayran. "Bree Olmson? Is that you?"

"Course it is! Gods, you had me worried the sand had replaced whatever it was you had between you ears. Good to see you back in civilisation, though the Wastes seem to have done you some good." Bree winked at him as she appraised his tall and lean physique.

Wayran felt his cheeks colour. Bree had also changed dramatically from an attractive girl into a stunning and trendy young woman.

"What you got there?" Bree asked. "Looks important."

"Ah....I don't know," Wayran said as he only half-registered her question. He was still getting over how she had seemed to be impressed by his physique. He had been sure his crush on her had been only one-way.

Wayran then realised she was still looking at the book in his hand. "Oh, it's a book, but you have lots of books. Where I found it is probably more important."

"But look here," Bree said while pointing as she went to take the book from him. Wayran instinctively held on to it. "Easy now," Bree said, "I'm not going to bite, and I'll give it back." She held out her hand. "Can I please see your book?" She rolled her eyes at him.

Wayran handed it over, somewhat embarrassed but also slightly excited by how close she was standing. He steeled himself against the butterflies in his stomach and tried to reassert some cold logic into himself. He wasn't just going to give the book away, no matter how worthless it might be, or how pretty the person asking. It was a link to what he could have been.

"See here?" Bree pointed to something in the corner. "That's the crest of Mannford."

"Mannford?"

"Robert Mannford," Bree said and scoffed. "You know, the guy who was supposed to be some sort of all-powerful wizard or something? The legendary Jendar inventor who disappeared?"

"Right, yeah, I think I've heard the name," Wayran lied. He didn't want to look stupid.

Bree looked at him sceptically, then pointed to the walls of the entrance behind him. "Well, you see all those glowing surfaces you just touched?"

Wayran nodded.

"They all have the same mark." Bree put the book down and started sorting through the shards of the black casing on the desk. "Here, look." She picked up a triangular piece and held it up to the light of the lamp for him to see. "Just there."

"Ah, yes. I see it." It was the same symbol that was on the corner of his book. "What does this mean then?"

"Probably that Mannford's group made the book as well, or it was the property of his servants, or something like that. Talbot will want to see it. He loves anything Mannford-related. He's in the library, probably at one of the reading desks near the big window."

Wayran assured Bree that he knew how to get there. He had visited Chronicler Talbot in exactly the same spot dozens of times. He set off down the hall to the library.

Chronicler Talbot sat at his usual table with a quill and inkwell at his side, a series of Jendar surfaces laid carefully around him, and a notebook directly in front of him. Talbot tapped on one of the surfaces in a certain sequence, nodded and made a note.

"How many is that today, sir?" Wayran said softly beside the large Chronicler.

"Seventy-three," Chronicler Talbot sighed without looking up at Wayran. "I'm off my pace today. No one else calls me sir and actually means it like you do, Wayran."

Chronicler Talbot carefully put the quill down and turned to face him with a smile. "You're back from the Wastes already? How was it?" He eyed Wayran's uniform with a cocked eyebrow.

"Eventful," Wayran groaned. "A bit too eventful unfortunately."

"Explain?" Chronicler Talbot prompted.

"Well, the short of it is my glider was destroyed along with enough santsi globes to keep me penniless for life; then my brother and I stumbled into an incredible Jendar building. We were nearly killed, a few times, and once by a giant white Roc. Which is how I got this beautiful scar on my head." Wayran pointed to the now bright white line of hair on his head. "Then I was kicked out of the Stormchasers. But on the bright side, I brought back this ratty old book."

"Well, that does sound eventful," Chronicler Talbot said. "And you're in luck: ratty old books are one of my specialties. Let's see it then." The Chronicler nodded towards the book Wayran held.

"It must have been important for you to take this above the other treasures," Chronicler Talbot said as he took the book reverently. "What made you choose this?"

"Well ..." Wayran thought back to the ghostly blue figure which had spoken to him. "It was next to a dead man. He looked like some sort of king, I thought." He struggled to explain. It had all been so surreal. "When I came close to to the dead man, his ghost stood up and spoke to me."

"Incredible." Chronicler Talbot was entranced, hanging on his every word. "What did he look like – no, even better: what did he *say*? Could you make out any of it?"

"He was tall, regal-looking. He seemed like a man who was used to getting his own way. And no, I couldn't understand what he was saying to me. Trying to read Jendar is one thing, but hearing it spoken is entirely different. I attempted to copy some of it down though. Phonetically, that is. Here is what I heard as best as I could interpret it." Wayran handed Chronicler Talbot a piece of paper which had the words he had copied from his arm on it. "Also, Bree thought you might be interested in the crest on the back cover. She says it's Mannford's crest?" Wayran pointed at the corner of the book.

"What's this?" Chronicler Talbot flipped the book over in his hands and his eyes widened. The Chronicler looked back at his papers slowly, and then quickly flipped open the book and started to try and read the first page. Then Talbot stood up, covering his mouth with a shaking hand.

"What is it?" Wayran asked.

"Wayran, my boy," Chronicler Talbot said, almost breathless. His eyes were wide with shock. "This – this is the personal journal of Robert Mannford."

"What? Really? How can you tell?" Wayran asked excitedly.

"Because –" The Chronicler put his finger to the words on the first entry and read aloud: "'My name is Robert Mannford, and I saved the world by killing it. Now, I sit here, watching the world die around me, knowing I had to do it, knowing I am the monster who caused this ...'" Chronicler Talbot paused to take a moment to shudder.

They stared at each other for a long moment.

"Wayran," Chronicler Talbot held up the book as if it were the holiest of artefacts, "you've just found what could be the most important book ever written."

Wayran opened his mouth to respond, but his heart skipped and his mouth went dry.

A metal-faced man with red swirling eyes was staring at them through the window.

Wayran shouted as he pointed, yet as soon as he had moved, the strange man disappeared from sight. Wayran sprang to the window, his hands hit the glass and he pressed his face up against it to try and see where the man had gone.

A cloak flapped from around the corner of the building.

"He's not getting away this time," he growled to himself. "Stay here, Chronicler!" he shouted, "Protect the book. I think something's followed me back from the Wastes!"

Chronicler Talbot's face drained of colour as Wayran ran from the room. This mysterious red-eyed man was linked to what happened to him in the Wastes, Wayran was sure of it, and he was going to find out just what in the nine hells was going on.

25 - Brothers at Arms

Another year has passed – another year of dwindling hope.

And as ever, my silent companions, with their damnable red eyes, watch me. Swirling and swirling.

I don't think they trust me anymore.

- Journal of Robert Mannford, Day 001 Year 50

Wayran

New Toeron, Bauffin

Wayran burst from the front of the Chroniclers' Artificium at a full run, chasing the flap of a cloak as it whipped around the corner.

Not this time. Whoever it was stalking him, he wasn't about to let him get away again. *Not this time.*

Wayran ducked through the small stone archway into an open garden. Dry leaves whipped around him, and he caught sight of a fleeing figure just as it disappeared through an identical archway on the other side of the garden.

This person was bloody fast, whoever it was.

"This way," a voice said as Wayran ran through the archway. It sent shivers down his spine.

He saw the man standing at the end of the colonnaded arcade branching off to his left. *How in the ...* this person was almost *too* fast. Impossibly fast.

But he'd be damned if he was going to give up now. Wayran sprinted after the figure, who paused to watch him approach, those strange swirling red eyes boring into him as he ran.

Just before Wayran got to him, the man turned and disappeared through the doorway.

He followed, and then a wall of noise hit him as he ran straight into a person's back.

Wayran grabbed hold and whipped the figure around.

"Hey!" a young man yelled, and stared angrily back at him. His eyes were brown, not red.

"What are you doing?" The young man twisted so Wayran lost his grip.

"Sorry," Wayran said, confused. He looked around and saw thousands of people cheering, and all eyes were pointed towards a central ring. "I thought you were someone else. Sorry." Wayran held up a hand to show he meant no harm. "Did you see someone run past?"

"No." The young man eyed him. "That'd be quite a trick, mate."

"What?" Wayran asked, still trying to get his bearings. He was at the initiation ceremony. That must be what this was. The central ring was the sparring ground.

"Running past. That'd be quite something with this many people crammed in here," the young man said. "You know what this is all about anyways? Someone told me to show up to the parade grounds at four bells. So here I am; but now what?" The young man was slightly shorter than Wayran and had cropped brown hair. He looked lanky, athletic, and had a somewhat roguish quality to the way he bounced around. "Name's Kevin by the way," he said, extending a hand in greeting.

"Wayran Spierling." He grasped Kevin's hand and gave a quick smile. Kevin's '*t*'s sounded more like '*d*'s, and there was a bouncing musical quality to his words. Tawan, probably, if Wayran got the accent right. "I'm pretty sure this is the initiation ceremony," Wayran responded to his question.

Where had the red-eyed man got to? Surely a person like that couldn't hide in this. No, he wasn't hiding, Wayran realised. Somehow, he had given Wayran the slip, again.

The clock tower boomed out four long ringing notes.

Tong, Tong, Tong, Tong.

Wayran saw the great black hands on the polished brass and marble face of the clock and saw the dark clouds begin to roll in above the elaborate wrought-iron spire atop the clock tower.

He felt something strange in the air, and knew he had felt it before, but couldn't place where.

The crowd began to hush as their anticipation grew. Wayran turned to go; he had lost the red-eyed man, but Chronicler Talbot still had Mannford's journal; he needed to get back to the Artificium.

"Hey, where you going?" Kevin asked. "Off to find another group of mates?"

"No, no. I ..." Wayran hesitated. He wanted to know what was in that journal, even though that was a part of the life he had been banished from. But he needed to stay and get this ceremony over and done with. He sighed inwardly; Chronicler Talbot would definitely keep the book safe, so he didn't have to get back right away. Besides, it would take time for the Chronicler to translate a lot of the journal. "I don't really have any other mates here; I was just distracted."

"Speirling, huh?" Kevin asked as he quirked an eyebrow at him, apparently accepting Wayran's weak explanation. "Any relation to Natasha Speirling?"

"You could say that. She was my mother," Wayran said as he remembered the hurtful words of Matoh at their mother's tree.

"Well, we know how you got in then, eh, mate," Kevin elbowed him in the arm and winked.

Wayran felt his cheeks warm in embarrassment; this was the first of many who would think that. He tried to come up with a response. "Well –

it's not like – well, maybe, but – my qualifications are more than adequate."

"I'm just ribbin' you! More than adequate, ha ha," Kevin laughed, "My pa was in the military. Jason Bertoni, maybe you heard of him? Died at Istol, same as your ma?"

Wayran hesitated, as he had never heard of a famous Bertoni, but he didn't want to offend.

Kevin didn't wait for his answer. His very eyes seemed to laugh as he continued, "Ease up, brother. Loads of people here have family in the military. Everyone has to have decent qualifications and we all's got to pass basic training anyways before we get any sort of rank. If you're here, I'm sure you deserve it just like the rest of us." Kevin clapped him on the back of the shoulders, "Lighten up, mate! This is gonna be great!"

"You know we're supposed to fight at this, right?" Wayran asked.

Kevin's smile could not have been filled with more mischief. "Oh, I know. That's why I'm looking forward to it. I plan on making my tussle quite memorable."

"Don't you think it a bit barbaric on the first day?" Wayran said.

"What?" Kevin looked over at him almost offended. "Are you kidding? This is a great way to meet people and make friends."

"By punching them in the face?"

"Of course!" Kevin threw his hands up with excitement. "Haven't you ever been in a bar fight? Two big louts start jawing, they introduce their knuckles to each other and at the end of the night they're buying each other drinks and singing side by side with matching split lips."

"No," Wayran shook his head. "I can honestly say that's never happened to me."

"Well, you are in for a treat, mate! Probably gonna meet your best friend in that ring there." Kevin nodded to the square of sand, already rolling his shoulders and jumping up and down occasionally.

This – somewhat disturbed – Tawan was certainly up for it. Wayran couldn't help but be drawn into his enthusiasm, and found himself cracking a smile.

"That's the spirit mate," Kevin said, practically buzzing.

The crowd went silent.

The captain had finished his inspection of the centre square and stood waiting for the murmurs to dissipate.

"I am a Fellow here at the Academy, but out in the field I have the rank of Captain. So you grubs will call me Captain Miller. I am your drill sergeant from this moment on and I have the honour of opening this year's initiation ceremony. It is your first step to becoming a Knight of Salucia!"

A cheer went up from the crowd and the hairs on the back of Wayran's neck rose.

"You will be seeing a lot of me shortly; which you may learn to dread!" A malicious grin crept onto the captain's square clean-shaven jaw. "You've all been selected on your previous accomplishments, and they must have been exceptional for you to be here now." The captain's deep, gravelly voice boomed through the parade grounds while he slowly paced from one side of the square to the other. "But as of today, that means nothing. Your past has got you this far, but your future belongs to me." His grin was almost evil. "Tonight is your first opportunity to impress me and to show your nation why you were allowed through those gates."

Nervous and eager faces looked at each other, at the new people they had just met; more than a few had grins on their faces, just like Kevin did, but no one dared speak.

Wayran looked up and saw that the upper terraces were filling rapidly with people. Officers of all ranks, the sandy-brown uniforms of general academy staff, red Corsair uniforms, the aprons of kitchen staff, the long flowing blue robes of Singers with their golden embroidery; there were even a few long white coats emblazoned with the red santsi, shield, and sword of the Syklan Order up there. In moments, all four storeys surrounding the central square above them were filled with people.

As if as one, they all began to stomp their feet. *Thump, thump. Thump, thump.* Louder and louder.

Wayran could feel his breath quicken, his heart pounding to the rhythm.

Captain Miller picked up two staves and the crowd roared. He walked to the edge of the square and slammed one into the fine white sand, standing it upright. Then the captain slowly strode to the other end of the plaza and repeated the gesture. He raised his arms in the air. Silence followed.

"You want to be knights, do you? Well, knights like to fight!" Captain Miller yelled. Thousands of voices roared as one and Wayran felt his stomach lurch.

"The staff is your first weapon, and today is lesson one." He paused as the officers on the terraces all gave a unified "HOO-RAH!" to punctuate his statement. The young recruits jumped at the boom of voices.

"The rules are simple! Start when I say 'fight', stop when I say 'stop'." He grinned menacingly. "And win. It's important to win." Another roar swept through the crowded terraces. The eyes of young faces on the ground level were now filled with a mix of excitement and nerves. The very stones under Wayran's feet seemed to shake from the noise.

"Everyone gets a turn; I want to hear cheers when I call out names!" Captain Miller motioned another officer to him. She held out a sack and the captain put his hand in and drew out a piece of paper. "First up: Jerome Dangstrom!" He paused after the eruption of noise. A confident-looking young man stepped onto the fine white sand. He was tall, lean and had very long arms.

"And your opponent: Kevin Bertoni!" Another cheer echoed through the square.

"WOO!" Kevin gave a holler. "They obviously want to start this party off with the main event, eh?" He winked at Wayran and smacked himself in the face. "Yeah!" Kevin yelled, and began jumping through the crowd towards the square.

Well, he's excited. Wayran watched Kevin jostle and chest-bump people out of his way, grinning the entire time like a madman. He wished he felt excited like that. *Maybe they won't call my name; I was a late entry after all.* But Wayran knew he was being silly. He was more than capable in a fight, but the crowd and its energy scared him.

"Save it for the fight, son!" Captain Miller's voice boomed over the crowd. He was smiling at Kevin. The captain took up position in the centre of the square with both the young recruits standing at the staves stuck in the sand at either side. Jerome's tall and lanky frame looked taut, like a ship's rigging taking a strong wind.

"Pick up your staves!" The captain pointed to each of the combatants.

Both pulled their weapons out of the sand, shaking their limbs loose as they stared at each other. Jerome Dangstrom looked focused, calm, and determined. Kevin, by contrast, looked about to pop, barely able to contain his excitement and wearing a wild grin to match the wildness in his eyes.

"Fight!" Captain Miller's command snapped like a whip, and the voice of the crowd thundered in response.

Wayran watched as the two circled each other for a few moments before the first crack of wood on wood smacked through the square, eliciting a collective "Ay!" from the crowd. Wayran felt the wild energy buzzing through the crowd all around him, and despite his earlier misgivings, he was finding it exhilarating. *What a rush!* This was like the big tournaments he and Matoh used to enter, except on an entirely different level. The noise was making his heart pound.

The wooden staves smacked against each other for nigh on three minutes before a unified "OOH!" resounded throughout the grounds as Kevin took a strike across the face. Jerome Dangstrom moved with the grace of a panther, flowing from one move into the next. But as gracefully as he moved around on the sand, he was having difficulty pinning his opponent down. Where Jerome was controlled and smooth, Kevin was unpredictable and explosive. Kevin had a huge welt already showing on his jaw but he also wore the biggest grin Wayran had ever seen.

Kevin grabbed Jerome's staff as he moved in to strike. The two struggled for control of the weapon, then Jerome shifted like a viper with an astonishing twist and sent Kevin flying over his shoulder. Kevin actually laughed as he slammed into the sand, and then was forced to stop as he struggled for a breath.

Jerome moved forward in a surge, but Kevin kicked his foot into the air just as Jerome bent to punch. Kevin's heel slammed into the bridge of Jerome's nose and made him stagger back.

Kevin swung his legs up into the air and sprung up and forward off his shoulders. He landed on his feet and used his momentum to head butt the sprawling Jerome.

Kevin wobbled from the impact, but Jerome fell on his back. The tall young man tried to get back to his feet but fell back in a daze, holding his head.

"STOP!" Captain Miller jumped between them and lifted Kevin's hand, saving Jerome from an overhead strike from the staff Kevin had reclaimed. "Winner!" The captain held up Kevin's hand and the square erupted in cheers.

"That's bloody right!" Kevin pointed at Jerome, his words slurred slightly. Captain Miller let go of Kevin's hand, and the crowd gasped as Kevin fell face first to the ground; unconscious.

Jerome Dangstrom had recovered and was the first one over to the unconscious form of his former opponent. He carefully moved Kevin into the recovery position, and the crowd cheered in relief as Kevin's eye's blinked open.

"He's alright!" Jerome called out in a rural Aluvikan accent. "Crazy Tawan."

Once he had lifted Kevin to his feet, they raised each other's hands and both smiled as the crowd cheered them again for a fantastic fight.

The two were directed to the medic at the side of the square. They walked off laughing with each other as Kevin showed his bloody teeth to Jerome.

Insane, Wayran thought as he watched, but Kevin had called it: they now seemed to be fast friends, and all they had had to do was beat each other senseless.

Two more names were called and the crowd once again roared in applause.

Kevin was still laughing when he made his way back to Wayran with Jerome tucked under his arm. "Hey mate! Good tussle wasn't it?! This jerk damn near knocked my teeth out!"

"I was watching, and I would guess you've probably broken his nose in return," Wayran said. Jerome laughed, but Wayran didn't understand why it was funny: Jerome's nose was most definitely broken.

"Jerome, this here's Wayran, he's a bit stiff but seems an alright fella." Kevin nodded towards him.

Jerome shook his hand in greeting while holding a cloth to his nose and trying to keep his head tilted back. "Pleased to meet ya."

Wayran smiled and shook hands with the tall young man.

"Ya see, mate, it's all in good fun, everyone in here enjoys a good fight on some level. Otherwise, they wouldn't be here, would they?" Kevin's grim smile emphasized his point. "Besides, there's nothin' like spillin' a bit o' blood to make friends." The sandy-haired youth gave Jerome a slap on the shoulder.

Jerome smiled faintly and shook his head. "Tawans and their luck."

"Pah. Like you had a chance." Kevin shook off the challenge. "And there's no need to get all nationalistic, son. I mean, I wouldn't want to bring up how Aluvikans let their horses eat at the table, or anything like that." He winked at Wayran.

Jerome suddenly had a face like thunder, and his back went rigid. He stepped up to Kevin and poked his chest angrily. "I'll have you know horses are excellent conversationalists. Patchy and I shared many a good chat over a plate of hay." The violence in his voice was lethal.

Kevin's eyes went wide and Wayran tensed as Jerome reached behind his back and pulled out ... nothing.

"Gideon's balls! I thought you were serious there for a second." Kevin slapped Jerome on the shoulder happily. "Watch out for this one – meant for the stage he is!"

Jerome smiled and Wayran couldn't help liking the pair. They seemed so carefree and their energy was infectious.

Captain Miller's voice reverberated off the walls of the terraced garden and they all turned to see who had won the fight. A tall, lanky lad, who would almost definitely wake up tomorrow with a black eye, had his hands up in victory. Again the two combatants shook hands afterwards, reliving their moment of glory.

The crowd fell silent, waiting for the next set of names.

"Adel Corbin!" The now familiar cheer rang out and the initiates on the ground level parted to let the new fighters enter the centre square.

Wayran forgot about everything else as he watched a beautiful woman take one side of the plaza. She was short, lean, but strong-looking. Her golden hair was tied back in a ponytail and her skin seemed to glow in the filtered light of the cloudy sky. Everything about her spoke of intensity, and Wayran felt inescapably drawn to her, as if there was a physical force linking them together. He took an involuntary step forwards and felt his heart beating like a drum.

Flash.

Suddenly he was remembering part of his recurring dream. The part where he was standing at the door, unable to use the key. As he stared at this Adel Corbin, he could almost feel the sandstorm of his nightmares closing in around him. Something grabbed his arm and he spun, looking for the shapeshifting black monster closing in on him. He heard its voice: "GIVE ME THE KEY!"

But when he turned, the monster was not there.

It was just Kevin.

"Woah, you've got it bad, son. That girl made you fly off to love-land. You were in a world of your own." Kevin laughed as he gripped Wayran's arm, but there was a note of concern there as well. Jerome laughed beside him and gave a low whistle.

"Yes ... I ... well, she is pretty." Wayran shook himself. He'd never had that happen before. The nightmares had never affected him during the day – but there was something about this girl. She was linked somehow, and he almost felt like he knew her.

He watched as she strode out onto the white sand. He could see that her hands were wrapped in bandages and there was an odd bracelet on her arm. His mind kept focusing on the image of a dark blade. What did that have to do with this?

Something hit him in the ribs.

"Ha! The man's gobsmacked Jerome! Look he's standin' with his mouth open and everythin'." Kevin was grinning up at him knowingly.

"I'm not," Wayran tried to say, but then realised his mouth actually had been open. "I was just assessing her chances; did you notice that her hands are bandaged?"

"Sure, sure, mate. You got it bad." Kevin clapped his hands together. "Right then, let's get closer to the action so our boy here can have a proper gander at this little beauty." He grabbed Wayran's wrist and pulled him forward through the crowd.

"... Bastion Thurson!" The announcement of the second name brought a cheer from the crowd and a massive shape pushed its way through the wild horde of recruits.

"A little girl!?" A deep guttural voice rang out as the huge shape stepped past the last line of onlookers. Bastion was a beast. Wayran had never seen anyone so big in his life. He looked like he could fling a horse over his shoulder without missing a step, and his hands looked as big as Wayran's head.

"Ooh, that's a big one," Kevin whistled.

Flash! ... Wayran's mind strayed. He saw a giant warrior standing atop a dune, waiting to kill him, with a storm closing in around them. "Give me the key!" the warrior yelled, and the heavens erupted.

No, wait. That's not what Bastion had said. Wayran blinked in confusion and tried to listen. It had happened again.

"Give me another opponent, sir! I want a challenge." Bastion sneered down at Adel.

"You fight who I tell you to, initiate," the captain snapped at the big man, and Wayran noticed something odd then. Captain Miller appeared to be hiding a smile.

"Oh, that's not a fair match, is it? Must be Asgurdian, that one. Those brutes are ruthless." Jerome shook his head as he sized up the match. "Not much better than the Navutians were."

"The High King is from Asgurd," Wayran said.

"Exactly," Jerome said. Kevin shook his head sadly.

Wayran took another look at Captain Miller and turned to his two new friends. "Five marks at two-to-one that Adel wins."

They looked at him as if he were mad.

"Well? Quick, it's about to start," Wayran said, holding out his hand. "Any takers?"

"I'll take your money," Jerome said.

Kevin laughed, but then shook his hand in agreement. "You're on."

"FIGHT!" The captain's voice split the buzz of murmurs from the crowd and the square went silent.

"Sorry, little girl, I'll try not to hurt you too bad." Bastion lifted his staff out of the sand; the weapon looked tiny in his massive hands.

Adel said nothing and raised her own staff, and everyone got a good look at the bandages on her hands.

She made her way slowly to the middle of the square and waited. Bastion chuckled and made a show of an exaggerated step forwards.

Then he charged, much faster than a man that size should have been able to move.

Bastion's staff blurred through the air. The match was going to be over in a flash: Adel couldn't hope to block that much power.

So, she didn't.

Sand sprayed up as the powerful swing missed and hit the ground. Bastion's grin faded. Adel had gently sidestepped the blow at the last second, barely appearing to move.

The crowd gasped collectively.

She must have felt the air as it went by, Wayran thought. His head twitched backwards as he thought he heard the rumble of thunder in the distance. He was beginning to feel uneasy about this whole situation.

Bastion swung upwards and three more vicious attacks followed. Adel hardly seemed affected. She moved with such efficiency it looked effortless, as if they had choreographed the entire thing.

A deep growl, like that of a bear, rumbled from Bastion's massive chest, and then his staff whistled into a backhand strike towards Adel's head.

Adel bent at the hips and let the staff glide past. Her own staff speared forward, slamming into Bastion's sternum. The big man's body convulsed and everyone heard the gasp of pain and shock. Adel slammed two more strikes to the inside of Bastion's upper thighs. The big man's legs buckled. As his knees hit the sand, Adel landed a spinning heel kick to the Asgudian's thick jaw just below the ear.

She stood over him and watched him hit ground, unconscious. Then she calmly put her staff back into the sand and walked over to slumped figure. She put two fingers on his neck to check his pulse before nodding with approval.

Captain Miller pointed to Adel with a grin on his face. "Winner. Medic, just double check he's alright."

"Holy Halom," Jerome said in shock. The rest of the crowd seemed similarly affected.

"That was something else," Kevin whispered. "How did you know?"

Wayran smiled absent-mindedly as he found Adel being congratulated by a group of initiates. She didn't seem interested in accolades and almost looked embarrassed by all the attention. A dark-haired woman came to shoo away the group which had formed around Adel, and with her was ... Matoh.

Wayran had forgotten about his brother. What was he doing with them? Oh, it didn't matter. Matoh seemed to know just about everyone in whole darn city, and made friends as easily as getting wet in the rain.

The medic was attending to the still unconscious Bastion. She held something up under the big man's nose, and his eyes shot open. He sat up with a start. They helped him get back to his feet, and moved him back into the crowd once he finally realised the match was over.

"I want a rematch, little girl," he called out over the din of the crowd. The wicked smile on his face chilled Wayran to the bone. "I will break you next time."

There were a few nervous chuckles from the crowd, though none from around the giant man being escorted to the medic's booth.

Wayran relaxed his hands, pointedly ignoring his companion's grinning faces.

"Bit tense there, were ya?" Kevin winked at him.

"Oh, shut it. I believe you each owe me some marks," Wayran said as he held out his hand.

"Ah, the Bauffish." Kevin pulled out a money purse. "Never miss an opportunity to fleece the rest of us out of our hard-earned cash."

"Well, I believe," Jerome said, taking Kevin's money purse and snatching the coins out of Wayran's hand, "you should probably use *your own* coin." Jerome tapped the shoulder of another initiate, who stood beside Kevin, and handed him the money pouch. "Excuse me, you dropped this."

The young man looked startled and felt inside his jacket. He took the money pouch back and looked at Jerome suspiciously.

"No harm done, friend," Jerome said somewhat intensely and waited for the young man to take his coin purse and walk away, no doubt deciding it would be better to find another spot from which to watch the fights.

"*Hard-earned,* was it?" Jerome said, glaring at Kevin. "It was *that* fellow who earned the money. You stole it."

"He was barely holding on to it," Kevin protested unashamedly. "I just taught that poor sucker a valuable life lesson. Can you imagine if he went out to the streets flaunting his money like that? Did him a favour really."

Wayran found himself laughing.

"Don't encourage him," Jerome said, stern-faced, still with that unsettling smile. There was a hint of command in his voice, as if he was used to being listened to. "There will be no more of that. A Knight of Salucia does not steal."

"I didn't," Kevin grinned, "I borrowed it, and you gave it back."

Jerome's smile faded and was replaced with a look similar to that which a mountain lion might have before it pounced.

Kevin rolled his eyes. "Alright, fine. No more stealing." He placed some marks into Wayran's hand, from a pouch retrieved from inside his own coat this time. Jerome followed suit, watching Kevin the whole time.

"Those coins were yours?" Jerome asked.

"Yes, they were mine, Mr. Goody-Goody. What are you, some browncoat or something?" Kevin laughed.

"I used to be," Jerome said, puffing his chest out. "I got my badge last year as a junior officer in the Aluvikan Constabulary. One time during an arrest I found out I could siphon. Now, I'm here." Jerome looked Kevin up and down. "What's your story, Mr. Quick-Fingers?"

Kevin grinned. "Let's just say his Highness, the High Lord Ronaston, has need of people with all sorts of different skill sets."

"So you actually *were* a thief?" Wayran asked. "And you're Tawan?" Wayran grimaced. "You're really not helping with that particular stereotype."

"It was only on the side," Kevin said, as if that made it all better. "I had other jobs. Sometimes."

"Like?" Jerome asked.

"I sold things." Kevin grinned. "And delivered things."

"Things you stole?" Jerome asked.

"Well, that can neither be confirmed nor denied." Kevin shrugged. "It's history now, and the Academy people know all about my past. It's not a big deal, Jerome. We came from different worlds and now we're here."

"He's got a point there." Wayran said, but his friends had stopped listening as a name had been called out just as he had spoken.

The crowd hushed as they waited for the next name.

"Wayran Spierling!" Captain Miller's voice rang out.

"Well, get movin' then, friend." Kevin gave him a friendly push towards the centre. "You're fighting! Get movin', soldier!"

Butterflies jumped into Wayran's stomach as his boots hit the sand. Thousands of eyes watched him. *All these people.* And then he noticed that many who watched him had a look of mild confusion on their faces.

Why are they ...? And then Wayran saw why.

Matoh was standing across from him on the sand. Thunder boomed in the distance, and this time everyone heard it. Wayran could feel the approaching storm's strange energy all around him.

Images flashed into his mind, and he felt the wind pick up. Sand began to hiss as it rolled across his boots.

Flash.

"GIVE ME THE KEY!!" A voice screamed in his head, and suddenly he was standing on that dune again. The black-armoured warrior stood in front of him with a giant sword ready to kill him. Red glowing eyes shone from within its dark metal helmet. "You're going to destroy everything," the armoured monster said. "You've been chasing a lie."

The sandstorm was closing in, and Wayran could just make out the door atop the other dune. He had to get to the door.

"Wayran, don't do it." The monster held out its hand.

Flash.

"Wayran!" This time it was Matoh shouting his name. He was back in the square, with everyone watching him.

"What is this? No. I won't. I don't want to fight my brother," Wayran said. He blinked away the confusing images as his head began to throb in pain. Something was wrong. "Pick another name, I'll go next."

The crowd inhaled as one.

"You will address me as *sir*, initiate," Captain Miller's voice snapped.

Wayran tried to make sense of what was going on, tried to push through the murk in his mind. *I've just been insubordinate*, he realised, and then looked up to the teeming balconies around him. *Insubordinate in front of the entire bloody Academy.* He turned back to Captian Miller and tried to cobble together a proper salute. "I'm sorry, sir. It's just I –"

"A cruel twist of fate to be sure," Captain Miller said, looking sternly at him, "but the name came out of the hat just like it did for everyone else. And, son, you don't get to choose who you face on the battlefield. This will be a lesson."

Wayran knew that look on Captain Miller's face: he was to be made an example of now. He understood it, and he kicked himself for being an idiot.

"Just pick up the gods-damned staff!" Matoh shouted. "You've embarrassed her enough already."

"I ..." Wayran said, clenching his jaw. He hadn't thought of that, of how this would reflect on their mother's legacy. Matoh would have been all too aware of it however. Damn it.

"Pick it up," Matoh hissed.

Fine, Wayran thought. If his brother wanted a fight, he was going to bloody well get one.

He bent down and snapped up his staff. He twirled it through the air, let the polished wood drop onto his neck, where he spun it once, flicked it into his hand and dropped into a low stance. Sure, he preferred his books over training, but he had always been just as quick in the study of martial forms as he was with academic ones.

The crowd roared at the display.

Captain Miller raised his hand, and suddenly Wayran found his attention oddly fixated on a group of four standing on the second level. The image of the four was incredibly clear. A tall man with a purple hat was tapping his finger against the railing in time to a tune Wayran had started to hear. A short slightly pudgy young man stood next to him, with wild-looking eyes and an absurd haircut. The third and fourth members were just as unique: the Princess Echinni and the legendary Yuna Swiftriver. They all seemed to be humming. Humming the same tune.

A tune he had never heard, and yet somehow knew.

"FIGHT!" Captain Miller's voice boomed.

Staves whirled, meeting with a thwack a split second before Matoh's fist cracked across Wayran's jaw.

* * *

On the second-floor balcony, in that odd group of four, Jachem's voice piped up. "Why are your tapping your finger, Kai? And why are you humming, Echinni?"

"The music, Jachem," Echinni said. "Can't you hear it? It's soft now but it's building to a crescendo."

Kai's finger was tapping a beat to the song Echinni was humming, and Jachem thought that odd, because he too could hear music now, above what Echinni and Kai were doing. Something was radiating from within the square.

"Hey, I know that guy, the big tough one with the stripe of hair with feathers in it," Kai said, oddly distant and dreamy. "Matoh ... yeah, that was his name. I owe him a drink."

"Why do you sound like that?" Jachem got no response; it was as if Kai hadn't heard him.

Jachem felt as if he should recognise the tune, but at the same time he also knew he had never heard it before. He could remember every song he had ever listened to. Just like he could remember everything he had ever read, so he knew absolutely that he had never heard this song before. And yet somehow it was familiar.

"Excuse me," he said, tugging on a cloak worn by the stranger standing beside him. "Do you hear that music? What is it?"

"I hear it, friend," the stranger said. "Odd that you can as well." The stranger paused to watch the wiry-framed brother with the shock of white hair spin and strike his brother in the stomach with the butt end of his staff. "It is returning," the stranger said, almost to himself. "Stronger this time, and somehow different."

The music grew louder, and Jachem turned to tell the stranger, but then stopped as he saw the stranger's swirling red eyes and metal face. Jachem saw a symbol etched or burnt into the forehead of the metal face.

"That's a Jendar symbol, isn't it? It means fire, or wisdom, or something like that, doesn't it?" Jachem pointed at the symbol etched into the metal mask on the man's face.

He heard what could have been a chuckle from the stranger with red eyes, but then a silver hand reached out from beneath the cloak and touched his shoulder, making him jump.

"Interesting," the stranger said. "And yes, it is Kenaz, the symbol for the fire of knowledge and wisdom. But do not concern yourself with me, friend. Listen to the music, something is about to change."

As the stranger disappeared back into the crowd, Jachem leant over the railing and watched the fight unfold upon the sandy courtyard floor, letting his fingers play invisible strings to a tune he felt he should remember.

* * *

Matoh charged, and Wayran saw the staff in his brother's hands blur as it swooped down at his head. He raised his own staff high on instinct and blocked easily. He shifted his weight and sprang to the side, dodging the second attack, which he knew had been aimed straight at the midriff.

One of Matoh's favourite combinations.

Wayran countered with a flurry of quick, spearing attacks at Matoh's feet, driving his brother back, though he scored no hit.

Back and forth they went. The years of training together ensured a long fight, and Wayran understood that it would be the mistakes they made which would determine the victor, not some explosive offensive combo, as the they knew each other like they knew themselves.

Sand flew from missed strikes and shifting feet. Staff snapped against staff in quick staccato rhythms followed by silence as they broke apart for brief respites.

The crowd had grown silent, almost as if it held its collective breath. Glory within the Academy hung on the outcome of this battle, yet none knew who would rise to the top.

Matoh sprang forward and the power of his attacks were thunderous, yet Wayran shifted into wind stance, countering each attack and deflecting his brother's staff to avoid the brunt of his overwhelming power.

They moved so quickly it was hard to follow; fluid and efficient, intricate yet smooth. Their violence flowed back and forth with greater and greater intensity.

Then something began to change. Like a fledgling finding how to fly, the atmosphere within the square evolved and grew into something new, as if it were charged.

Each smack of wood reverberated in the chest of the onlookers, forcing a rhythm into their very souls.

Smack, crack, crack, THWACK! Pause.

Soon the entire courtyard and everyone in it felt a resonance with the battle between Wayran and Matoh. They could feel it as the brothers did, while experiencing the entire symphony springing forth in front of them. They were the brothers then; they knew what they knew, felt as they felt.

Thunder boomed above the crowd and no one noticed how odd it was for the sky to cloud over so quickly. The deep bass rumbles from above blended seamlessly with the beat of the brothers' staves.

Thousands of people gazed, mesmerized by the whirling staves as one brother would attack furiously while his mirror knew every move and countered, as if they were two sides of a spinning coin. Attack into defence; defence into attack. Back and forth they went across the sand, and the thunder grew louder and louder.

Wayran pressed his advantage. He saw Matoh's staff droop slightly as his brother tried to recover his defensive stance. Wayran's hands blurred as he twirled his staff in a wide arc and then spun to strike high then low, an uppercut to ribs, right, then left, step in and pivot into an elbow strike. A hit! Wayran spun low and kicked out his leg, catching the back of Matoh's foot as he stepped back.

Matoh fell, and the crowd gasped in unison.

Wayran stepped forward to strike, but halted.

Flash.

Another vision. He was standing on the dune once more. He held a white knife in his hand. As he looked over at Matoh, he saw pain on his brother's face, Matoh held his stomach against the tide of blood gushing forth. "Why?" The vision of Matoh screamed at him, "Why?!"

Flash.

Lightning arced overhead and Wayran shook himself. He was back in the square, holding a staff not a knife.

Matoh had rolled backwards and landed in a crouch.

He could have sworn sparks of electrical discharge were jumping away from Matoh's hands. But it couldn't be: the staves were wood, insulators. No amount of siphoning would do that. Could it?

Thunder boomed and then it was Wayran's turn to retreat. Matoh's first strike made the wood in Wayran's hands vibrate, deadening his grip on the weapon.

Matoh grabbed the staff and slammed an open palm onto Wayran's chest, sending him staggering back. He had never felt such power from Matoh.

He tried to suck in a breath and hold on to the weapon but could only watch as Matoh ripped the staff from his hand, planted it in the ground and kicked right through the wood, snapping it in two.

Matoh threw the piece that was still in his hand at him before charging.

Lightning flashed again. The very air felt as if it was crackling. Wayran caught the piece of the staff right out of the air and stepped forward, ducking under Matoh's next crushing strike.

Using all his strength, he slammed the short stick into Matoh's ribs. It staggered him, so Wayran snapped the short stick up to slap the back of his brother's head. He spun and drove an elbow into the side of Matoh's head.

The rhythm of the fight faltered, as if a violin string had just snapped.

The trance of the crowd wavered.

Flash.

A vision.

Wayran was in a large room, at its centre an enormous machine of some sort. It looked Jendar in nature, with slick surfaces, glowing panels, and a level of intricacy he could never have imagined. He took a step forward, and noticed he was not the only one in the room.

A man with a metal face and swirling red eyes stood beside the machine.

Waiting for him.

He took another step forward.

Flash.

Matoh's fist drove into his gut with such force that it knocked him off his feet.

"Whatever is happening is becoming very inconvenient," he gasped as he tried to get back up to his feet.

He rolled onto one knee and saw Matoh waiting for him, which shouldn't have been possible. His elbow strike had been perfect, right on the button. Matoh should need smelling salts right now, but instead his brother was glaring at him with white-hot rage.

They stood facing one another, the rhythm resumed, and Wayran felt the hairs on his arms begin to rise. He knew what would happen next: he had felt it before, in the Wastes.

Matoh stepped forward, and lightning shot down all around them.

Yet this time Wayran felt its energy as well – felt charged by it.

Like a wave created from a stone thrown into a pond, force barrelled out from the two brothers towards the crowd of spectators, blasting them over and lifting people off their feet like small toys.

Rain began to fall, cold as ice, and it felt good. Wayran had the vague impression of the crowd trying to get to their feet, then saw Matoh attempting to sit up.

This wasn't over yet. But he was going to bloody well win.

The two met in the middle of the square like two giant rams slamming horns.

They had given up on weapons. Now, it was a blur of hands, feet, elbows, knees, grabbing and pulling.

Again and again the force slammed into the onlookers, and everyone but the brothers could hear a sound like the world ripping open.

Suddenly Wayran slammed his forehead down onto Matoh's face, staggering them both.

Wayran recovered first and speared his shoulder into his brother's stomach, forcing him to the ground. He raised his fist to finish it.

The energy around him stopped pulsing and surged into him.

Flash.

His mind barely registered what he saw this time. Flashes of light in the distance, so bright he had to turn away. Then silence, as the very air felt as if it were trying to escape. Fire and light engulfed him.

Flash.

He stood watching cities burn. Watched as tornadoes, dark as night with lightning coursing within them, ripped trees and buildings from the ground as if they were nothing but bits of ash.

Flash.

Matoh tried to knee him in the back, Wayran countered by throwing his weight back against the knee before it finished the strike. The impact almost knocked the wind from him, but he was still on top. He cuffed Matoh in the ear with an open palm strike, making his brother's eyes swim for a second.

Flash.

Wayran strode through cities of the dead. People coughing and falling to the street to lie still and unmoving. City after city filled with corpses.

Flash.

He stood at the cliff where he had said goodbye to his mother for the last time, and watched as a wave the size of a mountain rose to blot out the sky above New Toeron.

"She has chosen," a voice said from beside him.

Wayran turned and started as he saw Red-eyes watching him.

The man's metal face turned back towards the giant wave and he bowed his head. "And she has found you lacking."

The wave crashed down on them and Wayran heard the screams of everyone in the city as they died.

Flash.

Wayran gasped. The square was silent, and the pulses of lightning had stopped. The entire world seemed to be waiting for him to do something. He realised he still sat on his brother's chest, with his fist raised. "Do you yield?" his voice croaked. "Do you yield?!"

Matoh blinked in dazed surprise, as if he too had just come out of a trance. His brother's eyes tried to focus on him. "I ..." Matoh started, but then jerked his head to the side as something drew his attention.

Wayran turned as well. Just in time to see Captain Miller diving through the air.

Well, that's not fair, The thought hit Wayran a fraction before Captain Miller's shoulder did, and for the second time within a few heartbeats he was lying face up on the sand with the wind knocked out of him, feeling cold rain splat against his sweaty forehead.

The captain pinned his arms down as if he were some sort of animal.

"Stay down! The both of you." Captain Miller's voice bellowed. "Whatever that stunt was, we've had enough of it. You hear?!"

Wayran didn't know what to say. The captain's fury was completely unexpected.

It was then he heard Matoh laughing. His slow, mirthful chuckles were the only sound reverberating around the parade grounds.

"The look on your face," Matoh said between laughs. "Ha! Your face!" Matoh was holding his stomach, trying to breathe between laughing and coughing fits. "Bam!" Matoh smacked his fist into his own hand, mimicking the hit Captain Miller had delivered on Wayran. "Right in the gut," Matoh snorted, and broke into another fit of laughter.

The rain continued to fall. *How ridiculous,* Wayran thought to himself as his brother's laughter began to infect him. *About to claim victory only to be blindsided by the referee!* He couldn't stop himself from smiling as he started to chuckle up at Captain Miller.

"You think this is bloody funny?" Captain Miller stared down at him, then glared at Matoh, still chuckling and sprawled out on the sand.

"No, sir, well, yes, sir," Wayran tried to say. "It's not often you have to worry about the referee as well as your opponent – if you don't mind me saying, sir."

"Well, you better laugh now, son. That bloody stunt of yours is going to strip the funny right out of your damn bones. We'll see how much you laugh after a night in the cells."

Wayran stopped laughing, and as he did, he tried to make sense of what had just happened.

This time he hadn't been dreaming. This was more like a vision, and it had been so clear, so vivid and real. The echo of a name had been present in all visions: Kali. The keys were linked to this name somehow.

"Kali," he said aloud. "Why does Kali need the keys?" And what had all the scenes of destruction meant?

He let his head hit the sand and sighed inwardly. This was the second time he was lying on the sand utterly and completely clueless about what was happening to him, knowing that his world had just changed, but having no idea what to do about it.

He was beginning to hate sand.

* * *

"That was amazing! Did you see that!" Jachem was buzzing.

"A good match. Strange ending." Kai realised he was still tapping his finger against the railing, and stopped. Oddly, he felt a bit dazed. *What was the tune I was tapping to? "Gideon's Wild Night"? No ...* Kai shook his head. Now that he had stopped tapping, the tune seemed to fade.

"A good match!? Strange ending? Of course it was strange! That energy or whatever it was knocked everyone over like some sort of tidal wave!" Jachem was irate.

"What?" Kai looked over to Echinni, who shrugged at him in confusion. "Did you see?"

"No." Echinni shook her head. She seemed as dazed as Kai felt.

"What was that song?" Kai tried to remember. Echinni had been singing.

"I was …" Echinni shook her head and trailed off before laughing in confusion. "I don't remember. How strange."

"There was a song," Jachem said as his fingers tried to move across invisible guitar strings. "But I can't … remember."

Kai huffed at that. "Well if *you* can't remember, Jachem, then it must not have been a song we've played before. But …" Kai's eyes grew distant. "… I feel as if I did know it."

"You two didn't see anything?" Jachem said.

"No, I'm afraid I don't recall seeing this energy you speak of, I …" Echinni started as she turned to leave.

Yuna had drawn her sword and was staring down at the two brothers being escorted out of the courtyard. "Yuna?"

The big woman didn't respond. She had a death grip on the pommel of Hunsa as she continued staring blankly ahead. Her muscles bulged along her arms as she gazed down into the square. Her breath came in rasps and there was sweat on her shaved head.

"Yuna?" Echinni touched her bodyguard's arm, and the giant woman shook with a gasp. She looked rattled as she looked around and sheathed the great golden sword so quickly that it might as well have never been drawn. Then she squinted, closing her eyes as if against a migraine.

"Yuna?" Echinni said again.

"I'm fine," Yuna growled.

"I think we all need some food." Kai looked at Yuna strangely.

All four left the courtyard feeling slightly dazed, and as if they should remember something, yet none could quite place what it was.

* * *

A solitary figure remained unnoticed atop the clock tower overlooking the courtyard grounds. Its oddly shaped hat protected it from the rain, its black scarf and grey cloak remained strangely still in the wind, and its red eyes swirled as it processed the meaning of the events which had unfolded below.

Something has changed. It knew that to be true. It was as close to a feeling as it would ever know. The flow had shifted, eddies were forming, and within those eddies ... *opportunity.*

It had been navigating these currents for countless years and seen thousands upon thousands of permutations; but this ... this was different.

Its eyes slowed in their constant cycling and it let itself report what it had seen.

Yes. It responded to the silent question which had been asked after it had reported.

And as simply as that, a new path had been chosen.

Maybe this time.

This had felt different, but its mind remembered one of its kin saying those exact words once before.

No. This time, it *would* be different. They had learned from their past mistakes. The lessons had been hard, but they had learned.

This time, it would be different.

It had to be.

For this would be the *last* time.

26 - Blood and Clues

Thurizas has been studying several large bird species colonizing many of the cliffs along the coast of what was once Farajun. It has reported an accelerated mutation factor in most, and they appear to have several thriving nest colonies. I am amazed by how well they are doing. I questioned Feyhu on what I thought were anomalies but it assures me the data is correct. Life is ever more inspiring.

We have agreed to call this new species "Rocs", like the giant birds in the old fairy tales.

\- *Journal of Robert Mannford, Day 307 Year 23*

John Stonebridge

New Toeron, Bauffin

There were times when John hated being right. The perpetrator was here, in New Toeron, and his killing of Princess Elise Syun had made him fearless.

The bodies had been found between rows of stacked wooden crates inside the warehouse John now stood within. They had missed him by a few hours at most.

The victims had been dockworkers; their colleagues stood at the entrance to the portside warehouse, shaken and horrified by what they had seen when they opened the doors.

John could still feel the wrongness in the air, as if the small piece of reality within the warehouse had been altered – as, in a sense, it had been. The memory of finding the grotesquely drained shells was imprinted on the minds of everyone who worked here. Their relationship with this space would never be the same.

He stroked his thick horseshoe moustache in contemplation while he catalogued everything in front of him. Emotion only clouded the facts; there would be time for that later. Right now he was an observer, detached yet focused.

As John surveyed, he wrote. Never looking down, letting his practiced hand glide across the pages of his journal. He tried to describe in painstaking detail every bit of minutia he could see. It was tedious, but this method of his had caught more vermin than anyone else in the Constabulary and was what had got him promoted to Senior Prefect.

A young man of about nineteen years of age lay in a large pool of blood with his throat slashed open so far that John could see vertebrae. A swathe of sprayed blood was on the crate to John's left, and the footprints indicated that the victim had been running. John saw the scene play out in his mind. The killer had known his escape route and had reached the choke point before the young man, then surprised him with enough force to nearly sever the head and arrest any forward momentum.

Their killer had used these crates like a maze, and yet the murders couldn't have been premeditated. Everything else pointed to a crime of opportunity and the killer had managed to quickly study the surroundings to use them to his advantage. The same killer could carefully plan out a precise assassination, and immediately adapt to a new environment. The combination spoke of high intelligence – but that was something John already knew.

John saw the same brutal efficiency displayed by the bodies of the next four victims. The fifth dead man had been hamstrung before having his spinal cord cut in just such a way to paralyse him from the neck down. The fifth lay huddled against a crate, positioned to watch what happened next.

The final dead man was of large build, thick with muscle from years of physical labour. There were hard scarred knuckles on his big hands;

the man had been a brawler. Probably part of one of the bare-knuckle boxing circuits which were so popular here in the Docks District. Yet this practiced fighter had been systematically taken apart. Shallow, measured, and precise cuts lined the big man's body. The accuracy of these cuts spoke of how the killer must have studied anatomy. Expertly placed and meant to enrage, while also to incapacitate. *Our killer doesn't like tough guys. He saved this one until last.* There was a message here, a definitive expression of being able to dominate those who believed themselves strong. *Does this monster have Daddy issues?*

John let his pen stop and carefully closed his notebook, replacing it in his breast pocket next to the specially made pen holster. While he filled journals by the dozen and was careful with them, his pen was another matter entirely. It was handmade and a work of art in its own right. A special cartridge held the ink, and when he wrote with it, there was never an errant splotch. The nib was perfect and never wore out. He had refused the pen at first, as it was a gift, but the artisan had insisted on it as repayment for saving his little girl.

John loved this pen because it represented someone he had actually saved, and he always told himself it didn't matter that the artisan and his daughter were Xinnish. But he knew that was a lie. Deep down, it mattered.

Whenever he went through Wadashi, he made sure to stop by that little pen shop, made sure to bring that little girl a piece of Asgur rock candy, and always spent a small fortune on the beautifully engraved steel ink refill cartridges. It was money well spent, even if John knew he was actually trying to buy forgiveness.

Ink refills and hours listening to the sermons and songs of the Singer faith. None of it was going to erase the scars of his past, but he had to keep trying, and catching this killer might nudge him a bit further away from damnation.

John stood and took one last look at the scene. *Messier than usual. Odd.* Yet all six had *the eyes.* Those cold screaming eyes, trying to tell him of the horror of their last moments. It was as if the peace of absolution, the slow fade into the afterlife as the body shut down, had been horribly interrupted.

And all six had been Xinnish. Halom was truly testing him now, challenging him to become better through placing paths to redemption at his feet. Yet try as he might, they had been too late to save these men. The killer was still out there, and he would kill again.

It was then John saw some odd-shaped blood marks. His journal and pen were in his hands without thinking.

"He kneels over them ... at the end, I mean?" Miranda asked, grimacing. "Creepy."

He kneels over them. It took John a moment to register why Miranda would say that, and then he saw it: the blood had coagulated around the exact spaces where two knees and two booted toes would have been. John could almost see the killer kneeling, close to sitting on his heels, watching the life ebb out of his victim. This moment at the end – this is why he does it. John was sure, it was almost ritualistic. And he would have missed it, if not for his junior partner.

He turned now to look at Miranda. He should praise her, tell her she had talent for this. But then she absently twiddled the bone ring in her brow and John's stomach lurched. "'Creepy' is a word which will colour your interpretation of the observable facts. Keep your own damned moral compass out of it." He carefully replaced his journal and pen in their allocated pockets and straightened, gritting his teeth against his hypocrisy.

"Well?" he sighed, waiting for the inevitable retort.

"What? You've probably got a point, with the moral compass thing. Though that sounds more like theory and ideology than practical realism." Miranda quirked her eyebrow at him and played with the jagged bone ring through her brow, grinning at him as she did.

"Stop that," John growled, but it turned into a laugh. "Gods, you're such a brat. How did you ever get into the Constabulary in the first place?"

"Talent. And the fact your superiors knew I would drive you crazy ... but mostly talent." Miranda pointed at the blood-free spots on the floor, "I'm right, aren't I? He does kneel over them. The question is why? Oh, have you seen the big words written in blood at the back?"

John sighed; she was just so ... *Xinnish*. Old grudges and blood feuds had no place in this new world he was trying to help create. *Change with it or get left behind*. The words of his long-dead father echoed through his head. *True enough, Pa, true enough* – but he didn't have to like it.

"What bloody words?" he snapped.

"You had better see for yourself." Miranda pointed him to the back of the warehouse. When they reached the back wall, she retrieved a torch and held it aloft to illuminate the wall.

"'*This is but a taste. Death to the Xinnish dogs*,'" John read aloud. "Now, this is different. It's not quite right, is it?"

"Politics doesn't seem to fit," Miranda said. "I mean, I would guess this guy as a psychopath rather than a sociopath. Although there have been a lot of Xinnish corpses recently. Must take you back to the wars, eh, old-timer?" Miranda chuckled.

John saw red, and the anger surged through him.

"That's not funny!" He could feel his heart thumping. "Do you know what I've done to stupid kids like you?! With that same too-smart-for-my-own-good smile? Do you!? How many I've left rotting in the gods-damned ground! So don't twist that damned bone ring at me and think it's funny. Don't think it means nothing! You don't talk about the war! You don't know a gods-damned thing."

He spun threw his sai with such force that it exploded right through the side of a wooden shipping crate. Grain spilled out of the hole punched in its side. John watched it fall into the blood on the floor as he tried to gain control of his breathing.

"Exactly," Miranda said as she walked over and stuck her hand into the grain to retrieve his sai. "Who in the nine hells would try to start that war again? Certainly not anyone who lived through it. There are deep scars on both sides, John, scars that no one will talk about. Both the Xinnish and the Kenzians have buried that hurt so far down it takes ridiculous provocation to even get one of us to talk about it. Which then makes you think, if it's not Kenz or Xin Ya, who would benefit from a renewed Border War?"

John panted, trying to make sense of her words, and as the cloud of rage cleared he could see the truth she was pointing him towards. She was right, the youth of Kenz and Xin Ya had made almost miraculous reparations between the two countries. They had made astounding moves towards peace within the new Salucian Union. It was only old codgers like himself who held on to their hatred. The killer wasn't Kenzian or Xinnish. They had enough eye-witness accounts of the killer to know that he was from one of the southern islands.

Miranda handed the sai back to him almost delicately. "My father was on the other side from you once, John, when he was just a kid. He was at Huron's Point."

John cringed inwardly at the mention of that horrible battle.

"He survived, and won't talk about it either. He hates himself for what he did, same as you." Miranda gave him a sympathetic smile and patted him on the shoulder. "No one who had anything to do with those wars would want them brought back."

John felt his throat tighten and he coughed a few times to try and clear it. *Damn girl,* she had seen right through him. Cut right down to his soul with a few words. She was bloody good.

The wheels in his head turned freely again, having cleared the mud of his emotion. He looked back to the blood-scrawled words on the wall. “How many people would you guess saw this, saw the bodies and the words before we got here, before we barred entry?” Something was starting to make sense.

“Must have been twenty to thirty people,” Miranda said, “death always draws a crowd.” She nodded as she silently packed a small lump of tobacco into her pipe.

“Princess Elise Syun had a reputation for philanthropy, she was well loved by her people,” John said, the pieces clicking into place now.

“Yeah,” Miranda said as she lit a stick in a lantern. “That’s what I was afraid of.”

Riots. He should have seen it. Lady take him, he was better than that. *Stupid old fart.* He should apologise, should praise this brilliant young woman who had been partnered up with him. She had seen it straightaway.

“Don’t.” Miranda shook her head as John opened his mouth. “You’ll probably have a heart attack or something, and then I’ll have to explain how I guilted you to death.” She smiled.

“Do you think it’s the witch?” Miranda finished her smoke and tapped her pipe against the heel of her boot. “That’s changed him, I mean?”

John nodded. He didn’t like where this was going. Not at all. “We need to move fast.”

Miranda put her pipe back into one of her pockets almost mechanically. “Six already, and this is only the first day. Halom help us.”

They had a job to do. His guilty conscience could wait. “Find that ferry. With any luck it’ll still be in port. Talk to the captain, get a list of names and physical descriptions of everyone on board.”

Miranda nodded; it seemed she had already anticipated what he had been about to say. "Meet you up in the Academy Registrar's office?"

Yes, she had known. "Yes – hopefully we get lucky when we cross-check the names."

Miranda sprang into the saddle of her horse in one fluid motion, then rode into the night towards the Academy port where the ferry had put in. John watched her go for a moment before he joined the group of constables waiting for instructions near the large wooden doorway of the warehouse.

She had to be Xinnish. He shook his head at himself. *And, the Lady take me, she had to be bloody excellent.* Well, he couldn't let himself get attached, they were going to need *excellent* to stop what was coming, because every instinct he had was screaming out the same message.

Someone was trying to start a war, one that was going to rip this city apart.

27 - New Possibilities

The invention of santsi globes has allowed the art of siphoning to surge forwards in leaps and bounds. The santsi allows the practitioner to draw in what was once barely controllable and store it safely in a temporary repository. This temporarily banked energy then allows the practitioner to control the level and type of flow back from the santsi globe, increasing both available power and level of precision for the siphoner.

The sand used in making the santsi globes is absolutely crucial to their efficacy. So far as we know, only the aptly named Santsi Sands of the Great Wastes have yielded sufficient conductivity when making the specialised glass of these globes. Further research into the sand used should be considered of paramount importance.

- Professor Attridge during a lecture in Introductory Santsi Creation, 2854 A.T.C.

Thannis

New Toeron, Bauffin

Thannis made it back through the main gate of the Academy just before the enormous wrought iron gates closed. He might have still been able to get in after hours with the letter from his cousin on him, but he didn't want to chance it on his first night. Better to stay unnoticed and off the sentries' radar. Continual lateness would be noticed, since these guards held themselves at attention and everything indicated that they took their duties seriously. Thannis made sure to kowtow appropriately, hoping to show just the right amount of humility for his lateness.

The guard sighed at him, but that was all. Thannis doubted this was enough to register in the guard's memory, but he would make sure to avoid this particular gate for a few days if he could.

Within, the Academy was still abuzz with activity, and Thannis set himself to melting into the crowds to make his way towards the Research Wing. He had memorised the layout of the Academy grounds while aboard the ferry. As he flowed through the crowd, he caught snippets of conversation. Apparently an accident of some sort had cancelled the initiation ceremony. That was odd: these military types weren't ones to let an accident stop something as important as *tradition*. Thannis listened for more information but most of what he heard was wild speculation and rumour, and while he wanted to know more, now was not the time.

As he navigated the maze of interconnecting outer gardens, squares and side streets, a thought began to trouble him. At the warehouse there had been moments he now couldn't remember very well. It was like half the time he had been in a daze or dream state. And the whole attack, while satisfying, had been sloppy.

That bothered him ... he was never sloppy.

He tried to think back to his kills at the warehouse, but just then his head began to pound as if a hammer was trying to break its way out. Thannis had to stop and brace himself against the wall of a small shop. He closed his eyes and forced his mind to take control of the pain, to own it, to dive into it and make it powerless, make it just another sensation.

In a few moments the pain had dulled to the equivalent of background noise in his mind. As he opened his eyes, he thought he saw a horrible face staring at him from across the street. A cowled woman with a tattooed white skull upon her face. *Esmerak? What is she doing here?*

Her eyes bored into his and the pain he had tried to suppress exploded back into his mind like a knife.

"Gods!" he cursed, and nearly lost his balance as the wave of vertigo hit him. Nausea enveloped him and it was all he could do to stay upright and keep from vomiting.

Then, as suddenly as it had hit him, it was gone.

Thannis opened his eyes and stared at the wall he was leaning against. Why had he stopped? He couldn't quite remember. He shook his head, trying to clear the fog from his mind. He needed to get moving; people would notice some idiot huddled against a wall.

As subtly as he could, Thannis faked a cough and cleared his throat, pretending he had swallowed a bug. Performance done, he moved on and merged once again with the flow of the crowd moving down the street.

Soon he was at the doors of the Academy's Research Wing, his episode on the street forgotten.

"Can you inform Denis Beau'Chant that his cousin has arrived?" Thannis said to the young clerk sitting behind the guard's desk.

"Lord Beau'Chant did not make me aware that he was expecting visitors today," the young clerk interjected.

"I'm sure he did not, as this is a rather unexpected visit. But I assure you, Cousin Dennis will be very excited to see me." Thannis smiled.

"And, sir, who may I say is here to see him?" The clerk had a rather sceptical eyebrow raised. Dennis was rather infamous for his reclusive ways. Visitors would be a rarity.

"Tell him his cousin, Thannis Euchre, is here to see him," he replied. It was an easy lie, for they really did have a cousin named Thannis Euchre. A distant relative of enough importance that it would force Dennis to tear himself away from whatever book or experiment he was currently engaged in. Ignoring a family member at a respected establishment like the Academy would be too much of a slight even for Dennis.

The clerk nodded appropriately, but Thannis knew the young man must still be sceptical. Before long, however, the clerk came back, and the look on Dennis's face was absolutely priceless.

"Thannis ..." Dennis stuttered.

"Euchre," Thannis interposed before Dennis could ruin everything. "Yes, I know my visit is unexpected, but the family has heard such good things about your research. I just had to come and see what you do for myself."

"They have? You did?" Dennis was staring at him as if he were an Onai demon which had just invited itself in for tea.

"Of course, cousin. You set a tremendous example. For one of the royal line to commit himself so selflessly to the pursuit of science, well, it is truly commendable." Thannis was laying it on thick for the clerk's benefit, who, having heard his sycophantic tirade, had promptly begun to ignore them and had returned to reading the book he had been engrossed in before his arrival.

"Well, yes, I suppose it is commendable." Dennis had recovered from his shock and was trying to play along. "You must have travelled a long way, cousin. Let me show you to a guest room. Frederique! A key to one of the guest rooms. Second floor to your liking, cousin?"

The clerk nearly fell out of his chair at Dennis's tone, but retrieved the key promptly enough.

"That will do perfectly." Thannis smiled. He liked Dennis: reliable, intelligent, and eager to please. Hopefully, he wouldn't have to kill him. It was such a shame when family had to be dealt with.

Dennis led him up to his room to deposit his suitcase, and waited by the door, obviously not sure whether to interrogate his surprise visitor, or run.

"Step inside and close the door," Thannis said.

Dennis complied, but he watched him with suspicion. Dennis was a Beau'Chant after all, and only five steps removed from the throne. "May I ask to what I owe the pleasure of your company, cousin?"

"So very polite, Dennis. Now, now. I know I've surprised you, but you needn't be so formal. We grew up together, didn't we?" Thannis grinned, watching Dennis for his reaction.

"Yes ..." Dennis hesitated. "That we did. Which is part of why it never crossed my mind as even a possibility that you would ever want to come and see me."

"Was it so bad, cousin?" Thannis mocked with a pouting face. "Growing up in one of the wealthiest estates in all of Salucia must have been absolute torture."

Dennis sneered as much as he dared. "You and I have very different views of our time together I think."

"Ah," Thannis said, "it seems you've grown more of a backbone away from home."

Dennis sighed and shook his head. "What do you want?"

Thannis dropped his mocking tone. "Believe it or not, Dennis, I actually do think your work here is commendable. When we were growing up, you were completely oblivious to how to gain allies at court, or how to navigate even the simplest social environments. I had to, of course, ridicule you with the others and distance myself from you, quite often taking the lead in such matters. You were essentially poison within our social circles and, at the time, you had next to nothing to offer me. Secretly, however, I too have a love of science, though I knew, given our families' connections and alliances, that I could not brazenly display this lack of respect for the Singer order or divest myself from family interests. Not publicly, that is. So, while you were blind to the advantages your station offered, I do think your pursuit of science is commendable."

Dennis's face had shown a reflection of confusion, pain, then shame, anger, and finally disbelief. "You really came here to ask me about my research?"

"Partly." Thannis smiled. "But you haven't been completely listening.

I have given a false last name, so I am not here in an official capacity. No one, and I mean no one, is to know that the Prince of Nothavre is here." He fixed Dennis with a stare. "And you will keep that secret as if your life depended on it. Understood?"

"Yes, Thannis," Dennis said.

The slight annoyance Dennis had showed towards Thannis was gone now, and he was satisfied that his cousin was properly cowed.

"Good." Thannis smiled and clapped Dennis on the shoulder, making him flinch. "Now, why don't you show me this research that you've thrown your title away for?"

"Really?" Dennis shook his head.

"Well, if I'm going to be working with you, I'll need you to fill me in on the details, won't I?" He guided Dennis out of the door.

"Working with – ?" Dennis started, but then thought better of it before continuing, "The Professor won't like this."

"I suppose it'll be our job to make him like it then, won't it?" Thannis grinned. "Lead the way."

"Right." Dennis sighed and shook his head. "Follow me."

Before long they had navigated a labyrinth of hallways and were somewhere below ground level when Dennis finally stopped in front of a large set of wooden doors.

"Professor Attridge is known to be blunt and quite miserable to most people, so be prepared for poor manners. He is, however, one of the greatest minds in Salucia."

"I know who he is," Thannis said, "and I am pleasantly surprised at your choice of mentor. I have read several of his papers on santsi capacitance, and his theories on the dynamics of siphoning."

Dennis looked at him in wonder. "All that time growing up. How could you have faked your disinterest all that time?"

"People see what I mean them to see," Thannis replied, forcibly ending that line of questioning. "Now, let us find the Professor so you can introduce me."

As they entered the cavernous room beyond the wooden doors, Thannis had to let himself smile. A multitude of oil lamps lined the great ceiling and lit the room with a steady yellow light. The soft glow illuminated row upon row of shelves containing the most complete set of scientific equipment he had ever seen. Glassware of every description, metal clockworks, copper vats, jars filled with everything from catalogued minerals to animal parts, and dozens upon dozens of contraptions whose use he could not even guess.

Yes, this is where science truly came to life. He had come to the right place and could feel it right to his core. It was almost like stepping out of a dream and finding yourself where you always should have been.

"Your father was an idiot if he could not see the potential in what you were pursuing. In fact, too many in Nothavre have become infatuated with their own entitlement and lack of progress." Thannis snarled, "They would be content to stagnate and become obsolete as long as the status quo was upheld. Sickening."

Dennis smiled at that, as Thannis knew he would. Thannis wanted his cousin's loyalty, as it would make his charade much easier to maintain. Letting his cousin think he had a hidden ally all those years as kids was a good start. Though Dennis would no doubt need his ego stroked several more times before subservience was assured.

Thannis did actually believe a bit of what he had said this time. He did see how petty and delusional the aristocracy had become. Their complacency and blindness to the real world had been a major reason why that barbarian, and now High King, Ronaston had ridden roughshod over them and forced Nothavre into joining his Salucian Union.

Dennis led them to the back of the laboratory, where recent experiments still sat in their apparatus upon benches. Within one such contraption was the most perfect santsi globe Thannis had ever seen.

Golden wire, thin as a spider's thread, hung down from a series of clockworks and entered the globe, which was pulsing with light. Professor Attridge was bent over the high bench, absorbed in what looked like delicate work.

"Dennis. Where have you been? I needed an extra set of hands half an hour ago. Gods take you, get over here," the Professor ordered.

Thannis put his hand on Dennis's chest and winked at his cousin. "Allow me," he said with a smile. He walked to stand beside the old man and dutifully took the shining dark blue mineral that was offered to him.

"Put this in the discharge bracket." Professor Attridge didn't look up as he wound a thin golden filament around one of the many copper pegs in front of him.

Thannis smiled and took a closer look at the apparatus. A bracket directly opposite the santsi globe had a spot in which the strange mineral in his hand would fit. He went to the other side of the bench and looked at the instruments available.

"This is covellite," he said, somewhat shocked. Covellite had incredible conductive abilities but was extremely hard to find. The size of the chunk in his hand would be worth a small kingdom in the right circles.

"Of course it is," Professor Attridge scoffed, still not looking up. Thannis could see that the Professor had a series of magnifying lenses on one side of his glasses, which partially explained why he had not been noticed yet. "Stop gawking at the size of it. Came in just this morning and I want to see if it increases the accuracy of our readings from this new globe. It should tell us the truth about whether we have finally made a santsi which can hold charge indefinitely."

That sparked Thannis's interest. He placed the covellite into the bracket and turned the golden receptor screws until they held the mineral in place.

Professor Attridge glanced up quickly at Thannis's work, having finished whatever it was he had been working on. "Good, now go and get the charged santsi so we can transfer the charge to this new one."

"No need, Professor," Thannis said, his eyes now drawn to the central santsi globe, "I can be of assistance." He looked to the large fire burning in the hearth, just a few metres away, and then placed his fingers gently upon the santsi within the apparatus. He took a breath, closed his eyes and began to siphon, feeling the chaotic energy billowing forth from the fire begin to coalesce around his hand, to then be pulled inside him. The familiar tingle and numbness surged through him and Thannis pushed it through himself and into the santsi.

His eyes shot open as he felt the energy leave and enter the santsi almost effortlessly. The size of the void within this globe was so much greater than anything he had ever felt before.

Thannis regained his focus and increased the flow from the fire, watching the flames begin to lick towards his hand. The flow within him increased and was pushed into the globe with no more resistance than before. "Incredible," he said, "how much can ... ?" He trailed off and decided to see for himself; and as he did, an idea began to take shape in his mind.

Without thinking about the consequences, he opened himself up fully to his siphoning, allowing as much to pour into him as possible. The fire billowed outwards from the hearth and was sucked straight into his outstretched fingers. Pain blossomed as the energy started to burn within him, but Thannis just smiled, because the globe was taking all of it.

He tried to pull harder, sensing the latent energy within the room around him, within the air, the bricks, down into the vast but sluggish store within the earth beneath him. He pulled it all to him, everything he could find. He felt the fire wink out and the water in the air begin to crystallise as it turned to snow around his hand. And still the globe took it, drinking in everything he could push through him. The light within the santsi pulsed with a brilliant blue-white glow, like a tiny sun had come into existence within the small lab.

Thannis's arms shook and then went numb; he couldn't pull any more. The energy was too far away, there was too much resistance. He finally had to stop, clenching his teeth against the pain. But pain was just a feeling – and Thannis pushed it away and forced himself to move. He put his hand against the frost coating the wall of the chimney flue, and sighed as the icy coldness touched his fingers.

"Incredible," Professor Attridge whispered as he watched the dial on a small capacitance meter. "You've pushed more energy into the santsi than the combined effort of the four other siphoners we employ. What is your name, young man?"

Thannis needed a moment before he could speak, trying to absorb as much of the cold that he had conjured into his tingling fingertips. "Thannis. I'm a distant cousin of Dennis's, and I was hoping to follow in his footsteps in the pursuit of scientific discovery."

Professor Attridge was scribbling in his notebook, only half paying attention to Thannis's words. "Dennis, check the decay rate readout. We should be getting a reading with that much energy in the globe."

Dennis had been staring at Thannis for a long moment, in awe of his cousin's display of siphoning, but the Professor's voice made him jump to his task. "You're going to want to see this, sir," Dennis said with a slightly dumbstruck look.

Professor Attridge snatched up his notebook from the bench and shuffled over to look at the meter Dennis was attending to. "Check the connections. We've seen faulty wires or loose connections give false positives before. Go over everything."

Dennis embarked on a frantic but what looked like practiced series of checks on the apparatus. The professor tapped the meter gently with his quill before once again noticing Thannis.

"A distant cousin, you say, coming here to help Dennis? I thought the Beau'Chants and their ilk detested all this science and dark magic business we do. They essentially disowned Dennis for following his passion. Why the sudden interest?" Professor Attridge stared sceptically at him.

"To be honest, sir, I'm here under false pretences." Thannis gave a placating gentle smile. "I am meant to be visiting the Oratorio, for spiritual fulfilment and education. At least, that's what the paperwork I had sent to my family expresses." He watched the Professor swallow his lie. "After what they did to Dennis, I have to be cautious, lest I be equally besmirched."

"I see." The Professor narrowed his eyes.

"I can't find anything, Professor," Dennis said, having completed his circuit of checks, "but I can check each of the wires if you need me to."

"No, that's alright, Dennis. I checked them all this morning, they should be fine." The Professor put his quill down and tapped the meter one more time. "Zero decay. We'll need to try some more tests, but we may have just created a santsi which can hold a massive charge indefinitely."

Dennis was practically buzzing. "This will change the world, sir!"

"Yes, Dennis, I think it will." Professor Attridge let a small smile slip through his critical features, and then looked Thannis up and down. "You want a job, huh? I can't pay you much."

"I'll work for room and board, sir." Thannis nodded as he focused on playing the role of eager student, but in truth he did not have to try very hard to maintain his enthusiasm. He was genuinely excited. A santsi globe which held the amount of energy he had pushed into it indefinitely? That was truly remarkable. His mind was already racing. Dennis was right, this would be a giant technological shift forward. It would change the world, yet Thannis had some very unique applications in mind. "And I would be willing to use whatever assets I can acquire to help fund this research."

Dennis's eyebrows shot up at that.

"Is that so?" The Professor eyed him again. "Seems suspect, but I'll not argue that you've got a talent we could sorely use. And any ties to Beau'Chant money would certainly go a long way."

"I have but one humble request." Thannis was practically salivating at the prospect.

Professor Attridge huffed, "I see, put your money on the table and suddenly there are conditions. Go on then, what is this request?"

"That a large proportion of my assets be put into the production of more santsi like this one." Thannis pointed to the glowing sphere on the bench.

"Not to worry," Professor Attridge chuckled, "I was thinking the same thing. Now, tell me what you've studied."

For the next few hours he was grilled on his scientific background, what he had read, what sort of experience he had and the like. Most of what he said was true, apart from where he had been trained, of course, and Dennis corroborated his entire story.

By the end of the day he was set to work, draining the energy from the new experimental santsi globe and then refilling it to double check readouts and test for any energy decay. He happily set to the work, and despite being exhausted once it was all over, his mind was ablaze with what this meant for his own brand of research. He knew he needed to get his hands on one of these santsi globes as soon as he could, because, if he was right, these santsi would hold the energy he fed on during a kill. He would be able to keep that delicious cocktail of ecstasy indefinitely.

The possibilities and delight of it nearly drove him mad, and Thannis smiled.

The Beau'Chants were about to heavily invest in the santsi business.

28 - Visions

Kali, my daughter and goddess, who I have bequeathed to the world. Her arms wrap around the globe, protecting it from the ones on whom she sits in judgement.

She is the new goddess of time and of judgement, and is the one who brings things to life or to an end. Kali will watch over the world once I am gone, and the fate of us all will be in her hands.

She will stand guard against another rise of demons, and shall meet them with a wrath and fury powerful enough to scour the world of their pestilence.

Note on this entry: Perhaps a bit much, yet still accurate enough as to what Kali can, and was born, to do. I felt the need for some reverence today.

- Journal of Robert Mannford, Day 142 Year 34

Wayran

New Toeron, Bauffin

Wayran stood atop the sand dune staring at the hulking warrior across from him. Yet something was different.

He looked down into his hand, and saw a book. The book he had brought back from the Wastes. The wind picked up and he felt sand rasp against his cheek. He turned his head slightly to shade his eyes, then started.

The man with the metal face and glowing red eyes stood beside him, and yet, as Wayran recovered from his shock, he noticed that the strange man was not looking at him, but rather at the dark warrior. The red-eyed man's wide conical hat and cloak were somehow unaffected by the blowing sand.

"We have little time left, Wayran Spierling." The strange man's words came into his head, though Wayran had not seen his mouth form the sounds.

"We?" Wayran questioned. The dream was odd this time: he wasn't as scared, and he felt almost like he was a spectator rather than participant.

"Give me the key!" the warrior yelled at them.

"Hurry, get to the door. He will follow." The red-eyed man sprinted down the dune.

"I can never open it!" Wayran yelled as he followed.

The hulking warrior transformed into a giant black snake. Glowing orbs, like santsi, pulsed along its back as if it were diseased, and the great serpent opened its mouth to show golden, sword-like teeth.

Wayran's panic began to rise. This snake was faster than the others had been. He wasn't going to make it to the door.

"Quickly!" the red-eyed man's voice screeched in Wayran's mind.

"*You* open the door! You must know how," Wayran yelled back.

"The answer is in the book. In the book!" The red-eyed man turned away as Wayran slid down the dune. Sand was ripping at his skin on the wind, but he didn't care, as the dune behind him was collapsing from the weight of the giant snake.

Something black streaked past him. The red-eyed man put up a hand, but the snake's body smashed into him, and the red-eyed man shattered into a thousand pieces.

The snake turned and found Wayran; it morphed into the tall handsome man who held twin hunting knives dripping with blood.

Flash.

They were no longer outside, but within the Jendar complex. They stood in a room dominated by a console beneath a wide glassy surface stretching across the top of the wall and ceiling.

The tall man was still with him, but kept shifting forms between the dark, metal-clad warrior and the tall man. “Enough! I will not allow you to let that thing decide all our fates.” The tall man pointed to the console at the front of a great machine.

“But we have the keys, we can end this,” Wayran heard himself say.

Three vertical slots dominated the face of the console, each designed to fit the appropriate key. Above the three oddly shaped slots was a large word written in Jendar.

A word Wayran recognised.

“Kali,” he read aloud. “She can stop everything ...”

The words died on his lips as the tall man’s knife slashed across his neck.

Flash.

Wayran shot upright with a scream.

He was in a dark room, and his back was killing him. In fact, he felt like he had been in a fight. *Oh, that’s right,* he thought. He *had* been in a fight – with Matoh. The memories came flooding back as he realised he was no longer in the nightmare.

“Ah, good, you’re up.” said a rough-looking man, giving the bars a whack with his cudgel. The sound made Wayran wince against the headache now throbbing in his skull. The rough man didn’t look happy, and had the uncanny resemblance of a prison guard.

Ah, yes. He had been taken to the lock-up after what had happened during the fight.

Wayran shook his head. What had actually happened? There had been pulses of energy, yet at the time he hadn’t thought that strange. He had felt the need to keep fighting, to allow the energy to take its course. He remembered the feeling of being thrust into something much bigger than a grudge match with his brother.

"What was it?" he wondered aloud.

"You and your brother's stunt ruined the initiation ceremony, that's what. Could've killed people, stupid bloody idiots," the guard growled at him. "Now get up, you've got a visitor."

"Kill people? No, there was something else going on. I –"

"Save your excuses for someone who cares, kid." The guard cut him off and rapped his cudgel on the bars again. "Like I said, you got a visitor. Save your words for him."

Wayran stood up and went to the bars to look out into the gloomy light of the hallway beyond his cell, and saw Chronicler Talbot.

"We're locking up soon, you've got ten minutes, Chronicler," the guard huffed, and walked to the end of the hall to wait where he could still see them both.

"Wayran, my boy," Chronicler Talbot said, almost breathless. "Are you hurt? I heard you and your brother were involved in some sort of malicious stunt at the ceremony? I was worried after you ran out and didn't return. Who were you chasing?"

"I'm fine. Just sore is all. I didn't catch him." Wayran looked sheepishly at the Chronicler, not knowing if he should share about the red-eyed man. Yet circumstances couldn't get much worse. "I thought I saw something or someone who was at the Jendar complex. I thought they somehow followed me back to New Toeron."

"Really?" Chronicler Talbot looked amazed. "A stowaway? But how could they have got onto your uncle's ship without being noticed? It flies, for goodness sake."

"I don't know, Chronicler," Wayran sighed, "it doesn't make much sense to me either. I don't even know if I'm just seeing phantoms and imagining the whole thing."

"I wouldn't discount the possibility this being is real just yet." Chronicler Talbot leaned in and pulled the book Wayran had found in the complex from beneath his long coat. "This journal talks about so many things I don't understand, but it would seem that Robert Mannford was not completely alone at the end. He talks about these beings called NREs more than once, and from the context it seems these beings were not human. Are you sure there was no one else in that complex?"

A shiver ran down Wayran's spine. Part of him had wanted to believe that the man with glowing red eyes was just a hallucination, and now to have someone else voice the possibility of his being real terrified him.

"Did you happen to find a woman's body? He keeps referring to a woman named Kali in what I've translated so far." Chronicler Talbot's finger was tracing some words in the book. "He talks about her living longer than he did, but she must be thousands of years dead as well."

The memories and visions flashed through Wayran's mind in a blur. The word "Kali" resonated like a thunderclap in his mind. "Kali's not a person, it's a machine. A machine that has great power."

"How do you know that?" Chronicler Talbot asked.

"Because I've seen it." Wayran remembered it now. He and Matoh had poked their heads into that room, but as there was nothing in there but a console which hadn't responded to their touch, they had left it without another thought.

"Chronicler, could you write this name Kali, as it would look in Jendar?" Wayran asked.

Chronicler Talbot narrowed his eyes in thought, but indulged Wayran and wrote the symbols for Kali in Jendar in the dust on the floor.

"I've seen those symbols." Wayran said. He now remembered the console flashing through his visions during his fight with Matoh. He should have thought of it earlier. "They were on the console of a giant machine within the complex."

"Was it still running?" Chronicler Talbot's voice had taken on a tense edge.

“Well ... it didn’t turn on when we touched the console, but most of the complex still seemed to be working.” Wayran thought of his visions. “Though I can’t be sure. Matoh and I might have wrecked a few things on our way out.” He grimaced.

The Chronicler’s face went white.

“What is it?” Wayran had never seen the Chronicler look so uncomfortable before.

“Mannford talks about Kali waiting in judgement ...” Talbot’s hands flipped the book open and found the page he was looking for. He began to read: “... She will wait for the thousands of years which I cannot, and she will judge whether mankind has changed. She will decide if they have reconnected with Tiden Raika and the great planet they reside upon. If found lacking, she will scour the planet clean and tear down the destructive and pestilent civilisations that once again mar the face of our home.” He stopped reading. “Can it be true? Surely these are just the ravings of a madman.” Chronicler Talbot seemed to be imploring Wayran to confirm his conviction.

The vision at the end of his fight with Matoh came back to him. The wave crashing down onto New Toeron, the cities full of death, and destruction on an unimaginable scale.

“I don’t think so, Chronicler.” His heart began to pound. “I think those old myths about the Ciwix, about the catastrophes at the end of the Jendar civilisation, may be true.”

Chronicler Talbot’s legs wobbled and the big man thumped down to the floor. “But ... what do we do? What *can* we do? Where do we even begin?”

Clarity came to Wayran as if he had been dropped in a vat of ice. His dreams were more than just dreams. They were visions. Just like when Matoh was about to crash and he had seen how he could save him. This was the same, yet on a massive scale. He was seeing possibilities, and he knew what needed to happen.

"There is a door, a door with three keys. The console! The console is the door." He looked at Talbot, who was staring at him bewildered.

The answer is in the book, the red-eyed man had said in his dream. "We need to translate that book. Everything – because I think this Kali is still working, and our time is running out."

"Jailor!" Chronicler Talbot shouted, "I need you to release this young man immediately!"

"Stuff that, old man." The guard spat on the stone floor. "I don't know what nonsense you two are going on about, but that kid stays where he is. You don't like it, take it up with the Doyenne; she runs the Academy and I'm answerable to her, not you."

"It's alright, Chronicler," Wayran said. "I need to think, to make sense of some things I should have paid more attention to. Just get everyone you can working on translating that journal."

"Come on, time's up." The guard moved towards them and looked to be in no mood for discussion.

"Alright, I'll be back soon though." Chronicler Talbot dusted himself off, regaining his composure. "I have more questions, a lot of them."

Wayran nodded, and watched the Chronicler leave.

So the red-eyed man, his visions, all of it, might just be real. His mind was still reeling at what that meant as he sat back down on his bunk, but as the shock wore off, purpose began to grow within him. He felt a sense of urgency, the pull of something greater than himself, just like he had during the fight with Matoh, just like he had in the Wastes.

He knew what he had to do.

Find the three keys, or else Mannford's invention was going to destroy the world, just as it had done over three thousand years ago.

It was insane, but Wayran knew he was finally seeing the truth of it all.

He had to get back to that complex, and he had to find the keys.

He might be stuck in a cell this night, but his soul had never felt so free, his vision had never been so clear.

End of Book 1 of the Syklan Saga.

List of Characters

Wayran and Matoh

Wayran Spierling - brother of Matoh. **Place of Origin:** New Toeron, Bauffin
Matoh Spierling –brother of Wayran. **Place of Origin:** New Toeron, Bauffin
Sandra Koslov – Aunt of Wayran and Matoh, cook for the stormchaser's and wife to Aaron Koslov.

Aaron Koslov – Captain of the Storm Chasers. Wayran and Matoh's uncle, brother of Natasha Spierling. **Place of Origin:** Palisgrad, Paleschuria

Natasha Spierling – X - (maiden name **Kozlova**) -The Silver Lady. Mother of Wayran and Matoh, wife of Harold. **Place of Origin:** Palisgrad, Paleschuria

Ariel Laurent – Healer, Storm Chaser. **Place of Origin:** Saint Miro, Nothavre

Marcus Hanz – Lead Storm Chaser. **Place of Origin:** Aspen Hills, Aluvik

Harold Spierling - Father of Wayran and Matoh. **Place of Origin:** New Toeron, Bauffin

Chronicler Talbot – Chronicler at New Toeron Artificium, specialises in codebreaking, mathematics and decrypting. **Place of Origin:** Narrows, Aluvik

Bree Olmson – Works at the Artificium. Apprentice to Chronicler Rutherford. **Place of Origin**: Sudgard, Asgur

Chronicler Rutherford – Chronicler at the New Toeron Artificium, specialises in Physics and Chemistry. **Place of Origin:** Dawn, Kenz

Kevin Bertoni – Initiate in the Academy, **Place of Origin:** Tawa City, Tawa

Jerome Dangstrom – Former constable, Initiate in the Academy. **Place of Origin:** Narrows, Aluvik

Bastion Thurson– Initiate in the Academy, **Place of Origin:** Blainheim (village near Vestgard), Asgur

Captain Miller – Fellow of Military Tactics and Basic Training at the Academy. Holds the rank of Captain in the Syklan Order. **Place of Origin:** Freeport, Bauffin

Jonah

Jonah Shi – Foot bowmen in Imperial Army. **Place of Origin:**

Fin Gunderson – Foot bowmen in Imperial Army. **Place of Origin:**

Branson Delagoth – Foot bowmen in Imperial Army. **Place of Origin:**

Commander Diya Naseen – Commander of the Black Rain, Foot bowmen battalion of Euran landing force.

Prince Samar El'Amin – First son of Matron Dinesa of Clan Amin, leader of the holy pilgrimage across the Barrier Sea.

Note: *In Eura, if you are directly related to the Empress you are part of "the Blood" or "the Fecund Blood." Currently only select members of Clan Hashi. Matron Dinesa is the Empress's sister, so cannot be Matron of Clan Hashi, therefore she is bestowed leadership over her husband's clan, Amin.

Thannis

Thannis Beau'Chant – Prince of Nothavre. **Place of Origin:** Orlane, Nothavre

Michael de La Quan – Alias of Thannis. Looks very similar to Thannis. **Place of Origin**: Orlane, Nothavre

Elise Syun – X - Princess of Xin Ya. **Place of Origin:** Wadashi, Xin Ya

Ole Sigurn – X - Bodyguard to Princess Syun, Syklan Knight. **Place of Origin:** Vestgard, Asgur

Henriette Gelding – X – Bodyguard of Princess Syun, Hafaza Guard. **Place of Origin:** Dawn, Kenz.

Esmerak – Powerful priestess of the Vinda Sisterhood. **Place of Origin:** Vinda, The Blasted Isles

Dennis Beau'Chant – Royal in Nothavre. Cousin to Thannis. **Place of Origin:** Orlane, Nothavre

Professor Attridge – Researcher and Lecturer in the Research Wing of the Academy. Santsi specialist. Mentor of Dennis Beau'Chant. **Place of Origin:** Dawn, Kenz

John Stonebridge

John Stonebridge – Prefect in the Constabulary. **Place of Origin:** Alansworth, Kenz

Miranda Holvstad – Junior Prefect in the Constabulary. **Place of Origin:** Qi Gong (Border City to Kenz), Xin Ya

Gary Hornwright – Chief of Narrows Constabulary. **Place of Origin:** Narrows, Aluvik

Adel and Naira

Adel Corbin – daughter of Leonard Corbin. **Place of Origin:** Blossom Bay, Bauffin

Leonard Corbin – Adel's father. **Place of Origin:** Unknown

Naira O'Bannon – Adel's best friend **Place of Origin:** Blossom Bay, Bauffin

Fellow Callahan – Fellow at the Academy, syphoning expert. **Place of Origin:** Unknown

Echinni and Kai

Kai Johnstone – Orphan, Jachem's friend. **Place of Origin:** New Toeron, Bauffin

Jachem Sanders – Orphan, Kai's friend. **Place of Origin:** New Toeron, Bauffin

Hanson Rivers– Innkeeper of Broken Clock Inn, husband of Meriam. **Place of Origin:** New Toeron, Bauffin

Meriam Rivers – Innkeeper of Broken Clock Inn, wife of Hanson. **Place of Origin:** New Toeron, Bauffin

Bella – serving girl at the Broken Clock Inn.

Harbour Master O'Brian – Kai's boss at the docks.

Echinni Mihane – High Princess, daughter of High King Ronaston. **Place of Origin:** Born in Sudgard, Asgur. Spent most of her life in New Toeron, Bauffin.

Yuna Swiftriver – Syklan and bodyguard of Echinni Mihane. **Place of Origin:** Istol, Navutia

Ronaston Mihane – High King of the Nine Nations of Salucia. Defender of the Singer Faith. First of the Syklan Order. Father of Echinni. **Place of Origin:** Sudgard, Asgur

Sister Maria – Sister who runs the orphanage which Kai and Jachem grew up in. **Place of Origin:** Two Ports, Labran

Maestra Lascotti – Maestra of the Singer Faith and Echinni's Singing trainer. **Place of Origin:** Dawn, Kenz

Made in the USA
Columbia, SC
07 January 2019